Praise for *THE ELYSIUM COMMISSION*

"*The Elysium Commission* is a complex science-fiction detective tale starring a fascinating individual. The story line is action-packed. . . . A fun futuristic mystery."
—*Midwest Book Review*

"Modesitt delivers a more action oriented and less philosophically based novel than some of his other works. Readers can enjoy *The Elysium Commission* on many levels."
—*SFRevu*

"A far-future tale of intrigue and mystery featuring a tough but admirable sleuth."
—*Library Journal*

"With a well-realized world, an original plot twist, and a cliff-hanger ending—space opera by a first-class librettist."
—*Booklist*

Praise for *THE ETERNITY ARTIFACT*

A *LOCUS* YEAR'S BEST 2005 NOVEL

"This is hard science and *really* hardball politics described by somebody who knows them from the inside out. A powerful novel on a sweeping, mysterious stage."
—David Drake, author of *The Way to Glory*

"Captivating far-future tale of life in space, from the author of *Flash* . . . Modesitt's prose is lively, and there's enough sense of wonder here to satisfy even the most jaded. . . . A must-read for Modesitt fans, as well as those of Jack McDevitt and Arthur C. Clarke."

—*Kirkus Reviews* (starred review)

"An intriguing vehicle for exploring interstellar fundamentalism." —*Entertainment Weekly*

"A glorious space opera set in a distant future when humans spread to the stars and splintered into a number of subsidiary civilizations. . . . Very enjoyable, lots of sense of wonder, and I even liked the characters."

—*Science Fiction Chronicle*

"This stand-alone novel addresses relevant political and economic issues within the framework of rip-roaring space adventure. . . . A must-read for fans of interstellar fiction." —*Romantic Times BOOKreviews*

"Superior science-fiction adventure writing."

—*Science Fiction Weekly*

"L. E. Modesitt is one of those special authors who brings a great deal to his work: a love of words, an understanding of people and cultures, and an interest in great stories and ideas. It shows in every line of his tale. I read *The Eternity Artifact* with pleasure, and felt well rewarded even beyond the last page." —David Farland

Praise for *FLASH*

A KIRKUS SELECTION FOR BEST SCI-FI OF 2004

A *VOYA* SELECTION FOR BEST SF/FANTASY & HORROR OF 2004

"*Flash* is a classic thriller. . . . Modesitt makes deVrai's daily routines interesting through his meticulous narrative, and when deVrai steps out of his routine there is plenty of action."
—*The Denver Post*

"Good solid speculation over how the future might undergo tectonic paradigm shifts. Modesitt supports his vision with deep political, economic, and cultural knowledge and speculation, producing a world that actually makes its own kind of sense. . . . His people are genuine inhabitants of this world, not transplanted twentieth-century souls. . . . In short, he performs the core task of the kind of pure science fiction that often seems in danger of disappearing from the shelves. . . . You'll find yourself propelled into a robust adventure."
—*Science Fiction Weekly*

"Another political yarn set in the future world of Modesitt's superior *Archform: Beauty* (2002). Modesitt's abundant novelistic virtues—great characters and plotting, impressive attention to detail—aside: this is smart, aware, provocative, and engrossing on several political, economic, and professional levels."
—*Kirkus Reviews* (starred review)

THE
Elysium
COMMISSION

TOR BOOKS BY L. E. MODESITT, JR.

THE COREAN CHRONICLES

Legacies	*Alector's Choice*
Darknesses	*Cadmian's Choice*
Scepters	*Soarer's Choice*

THE SAGA OF RECLUCE

The Magic of Recluce	*The Chaos Balance*
The Towers of the Sunset	*The White Order*
The Magic Engineer	*Colors of Chaos*
The Order War	*Magi'i of Cyador*
The Death of Chaos	*Wellspring of Chaos*
Scion of Cyador	*Ordermaster*
Fall of Angels	*Natural Ordermage*

Mage-Guard of Hamor*

THE SPELLSONG CYCLE

The Soprano Sorceress	*Darksong Rising*
The Spellsong War	*The Shadow Sorceress*

Shadowsinger

THE ECOLITAN MATTER

Empire & Ecolitan
(comprising *The Ecolitan Operation* and *The Ecologic Secession*)

Ecolitan Prime
(comprising *The Ecologic Envoy* and *The Ecolitan Enigma*)

The Forever Hero
(comprising *Dawn for a Distant Earth*, *The Silent Warrior*,
and *In Endless Twilight*)

Timegods' World
(comprising *The Timegod* and *Timediver's Dawn*)

THE GHOST BOOKS

Of Tangible Ghosts
Ghost of the White Nights
The Ghost of the Revelator
Ghost of the Colombia
(comprising *Of Tangible Ghosts* and *The Ghost of the Revelator*)

The Hammer of Darkness	*The Octagonal Raven*
The Green Progression	*Archform: Beauty*
The Parafaith War	*The Ethos Effect*
Adiamante	*Flash*
Gravity Dreams	*The Eternity Artifact*
The Elysium Commission	*Viewpoints Critical**

*Forthcoming

THE
Elysium
COMMISSION

L. E. Modesitt, Jr.

A TOM DOHERTY ASSOCIATES BOOK • NEW YORK

THE ELYSIUM COMMISSION

Copyright © 2007 by L. E. Modesitt, Jr.

A Tor Book
Published by Tom Doherty Associates, LLC
175 Fifth Avenue
New York, NY 10010

www.tor.com

Tor® is a registered trademark of Tom Doherty Associates, LLC.

ISBN-13: 978-0-7653-5654-3
ISBN-10: 0-7653-5654-6

First Edition: February 2007
First Mass Market Edition: March 2008

Printed in the United States of America

0 9 8 7 6 5 4 3 2 1

In Memoriam
Walter S. Rosenberry III

THE
Elysium
COMMISSION

1

All cities have their shadows, as do all souls.

Under the stars of the Arm, murmurs drifted up from the promenade overlooking the Nouvelle Seine. The red tinge of the full second moon—Bergerac—lent a smokiness to the night. Voltaire had already set. The gray stone walk that bordered Les Jardins des Sorores was a favorite for poor lovers, those young and not so young. The sweet scent of honey lilies filled the late-evening air. It gave the South Bank a grace it lacked in the light of day.

At night, in my grays, I often stroll the streets of Thurene in the shadows. Call it a habit. Call it repentance. Call it penance. Call it what you will. Being who I am, I find it necessary.

Some might call it slumming, but the South Bank isn't that low, not unless you're Princesse Odilia. Or one of the Sorores. Or an aristo of commerce.

I didn't lurk in the shadows of the hedges and topiary. That wasn't necessary. In my grays, few could see me unless they concentrated, and those enjoying the promenade were not inclined to look beyond their companions. They felt they did not need to look elsewhere. The Garda's hidden monitors made certain that no malefactor escaped. That did not deter all malefaction, not where the perfume of hearts and jealousy mingled.

Beneath a yew trimmed into a fleur-de-coueur—not that most would notice—two lovers embraced. They clung so tightly that even I could not tell sex or attributes.

With a smile, I stepped through the stone gates that marked

the east end of the gardens and followed Oisin Lane. Ahead were the bistros and the patisseries that remained open into the early morning.

The first bistro was Kemala's. The scent of true garlic enshrouded it. I passed by. My business lay not in the bistros, but beyond. Two women stood outside Memnos. They held hands and studied the posted bill of fare. They appeared young. All women in Thurene—even the poorest—were young in body. The healthy ones, that is.

The Lane was safe enough. Memnos might not be. It is on the South Bank, and the Garda only monitors the public areas of Thurene. All the South Bank bistros serve nanite-adjusted wine. The process makes decent plonk, but plonk without character.

Voices, more than murmurs, issued from the side lane ahead and to my left. They were not the sounds of lovers. I edged into the darker area against the closer wall. There I paused in the shadows, listening.

". . . I can't, Jacred . . . I just can't." In the cool breeze of early autumn, the woman shivered. It was not because of the chill.

"He doesn't care for you the way I do." The man put his hands on her shoulders. They were squared-off, nondescript hands. They belonged neither to a crafter nor an aristo.

"He doesn't excite me, but he cares deeply . . . and . . ."

"I do care!"

I could sense the explosiveness within him. Civility was a breaker unequal to matching his green rage.

So I coughed and stepped forward. I was still in the shadows.

He turned. His eyes darted from side to side, trying to focus. They widened, and he lunged at me. I slipped aside and let him stumble into the solidity of the brick wall in the comparative darkness. Comparative only. The streets of Thurene are never fully dark, and the scanners of the Garda are everywhere.

"You!" He turned and lifted a poignard. "Shadows cannot save you." He charged me.

I disarmed him and cut his feet from under him with a side kick. While he struggled to rise, I snapped the blade of his dagger with my bootheel. "Despite legend, poignards carry no special virtue."

When I stepped away, the woman had vanished.

I slipped down the lane toward Benedict's, leaving him cursing. I heard a Garda flitter humming toward him. They might find me. They might not, but I had not permanently harmed him, and that wasn't worth their trouble.

Not this time.

2

The Aurelian Way was crowded, as always, in late evening on Sabaten, crowded being a relative term, because, on any of the Worlds of the Assembly, unlike Elysium, the scattered handfuls of individuals strolling down the stone paths flanking the Fountains of Fascination would scarcely have been considered a crowd, but more likely a relief. Yet all of them were happy to be on Elysium. How could it have been otherwise?

Lifting the crystal goblet that caught the illumination from the sparkle-lights floating around the balcony, I smiled across the pale green linen of the balcony table at Magdalena, conveying effortlessly an interest intellectual, but not without some sensuality.

She met my gaze with eyes as black and deep as night. "Brains or beauty this evening, Judeon?"

"Anything of depth requires both, and it's been a shallow week."

"You dislike shallowness, and you always have. That is delightfully predictable about you." Her words caressed the soft air, and her smile was both beguiling and gentle, as it should have been, for we were in Elysium. Like those below us on the Aurelian Way, she was far better off than she could have been on Devanta, and for that she was grateful, and that also was how it had to be, for was not Elysium the city of light and beauty?

She sipped from her goblet.

Below us, the couples strolled the Aurelian Way, enjoying the perfumed air of yet another Sabaten evening in the city that I, from the intricate image in my mind, had forged in man's materials, in white stone and without death birds on enamel.

In time, I stood and took her hand, gloved, as always, in black velvet, as she rose from the table like that ancient pagan goddess had from the shell upon the foam, when men had but dreamed of Elysium, unable to create such a city, unable to ensure that those who inhabited it appreciated it and worshipped it.

3

All choice is based on illusion.

Incoming from Seldara Tozzi. Max alerted me to the vidlink.

I was mind deep in the datastacks, trying to integrate Western Ocean anchovy patterns, Antarctic currents, solar fluctuations, and a dozen other variables. My hope was to find a predictive regression pattern that would allow me to anticipate probable seasonal arbitrage variances employed by the energy brokers at places like Cartiff and Selemez Sisters. It wouldn't be highly profitable, but it would add to my credit balance. That would be useful, because matters had been slow in my normal line of work. More than slow.

It would also be personally satisfying. Satisfying is always good.

It was also a distraction from the hangover of the nightmares.

Seignior Donne . . . Max reminded me.

I straightened in the chair behind the table desk and smiled politely. *Accept.*

The holo image appeared in front of the table desk. The very fair-skinned Seldara Tozzi had the excessively fine features of an older woman. Modern medicine kept complexion and skin and body healthy, but a certain fineness still appeared with age. She wore a jacket and trousers of a slivery gray with brownish tones, and a cream blouse. Her hair was jet-black, as were her eyebrows.

Max, quick profile on Seldara Tozzi.

"Seignior Donne? Real or simulacrum?"

"Real, and real-time." I pulsed a vid-ID.

"Thank you. I have a modest commission for you."

At the moment, any commission would be better than modest. Over the years, I'd found that business was either nonexistent or everyone wanted something immediately. But you have to take clients when they arrive because that's when they need you. They don't pay when you need the credits, but when they need the work. Those times seldom coincide. "I'm available. I'll need some details to determine whether it's something I can do."

"It's very simple. It's also rather embarrassing and disgusting. Not for me. For the family."

I nodded. I wasn't about to comment on what other people thought embarrassing or disgusting. I was also skimming through the profile Max had pulled and displayed on the recessed screen on the table desk.

Seldara Tozzi was one of the grande dames of Thurene. One of those whose names never appeared, except as a patron of all the arts. Her wealth was estimated at well over a billion credits, and she had three homes. She was a widow, with three children and four grandchildren and eight great-grandchildren. She lived in a palacio almost as grand as Principessa Odilia's—virtually next door to Odilia, as such matters went.

"I have a great-granddaughter," began the seigniora. "I have several, but one of them is considering marrying a most unsuitable man. He is exceedingly handsome, well educated, well-bred, and intelligent. He is also without a definable moral code and represents himself as normal—what I believe is called straight-straight—when I have been led to believe he is keeping another man. I have no problems with his personal habits or sexual orientation. I have great difficulties with his misrepresentation of his orientation to my granddaughter."

"I assume you wish ironclad documentary evidence of his character and deception, preferably in his own words."

"I would wish his complete vanishment, but that would

be most unsuitable and would certainly reflect negatively upon us both in these times. Your suggested alternative will have to suffice, unless you can persuade him to depart Devanta and reject my granddaughter in a fashion that will illustrate his true lack of character."

I laughed, sympathetically. "I can't promise anything without details and looking into the matter first."

"I would not expect otherwise. Despite your . . . shall we say shadowy . . . reputation, you are known as honest and trustworthy. I propose an initial retainer of two thousand credits for your assessment. That is yours, even if you believe you cannot assist me, but I would like a written report explaining why not. If you agree to proceed after the assessment, I will provide another five thousand credits as an initial fee. Beyond the first ten stans, you will document your time, and I will pay you at the rate of five hundred credits a stan. If you are successful in a graceful resolution, I will provide a significant sum in gratitude."

I inclined my head. "Those terms are most acceptable, with one addition. If I cannot resolve the matter in less than a hundred billable stans, I will not charge more than the initial retainer plus twenty stans."

"You're that confident, Seignior Donne."

"No, Principessa Tozzi, I'm that proud."

She laughed. "The credits and the information are on the way. So is a contact code. Good day, Seignior Donne."

"Good day."

Max, check incoming and credit transfers.

Data is ready for you. Incoming has accepted seven thousand credits. Max the scheduler and villa intelligence served as my alter ego. To me, Max's full name is Maximus Tempus, but officially, he's Time/Events/Systems Maximizer, Mod VIII, version two. With a number of custom adjustments unknown to the Civitas Sorores. Quite a number.

Interrogative seven thousand? From Seigniora Tozzi?

Seven thousand from the Tozzi palacio account.

I laughed. The principessa clearly didn't want me to refuse the commission.

I called up the data and began to read.

The great-granddaughter was Marie Annette Tozzi. Unsurprisingly, according to the images that accompanied the data, she was a dark-haired beauty, but of the severe type. Whether that beauty had been inherited naturally, genetically enhanced, or medically improved—or all three—wasn't a matter for conjecture. With the Tozzi wealth, only the relative contributions of each component were in doubt. She was young, in her late twenties, and pursuing a medical doctorate at L'Institut Multitechnique. She lived in a villa with her mother on the grounds of her grandmother's palacio.

The unsuitable man was Guillaume Richard Dyorr. He was a doctor at L'Institut Multitechnique with a specialization in consciousness plasticity. He had a town house in the Heights and a retreat at Lac de Nord in the Nordmonts . . .

Seignior Donne, your hour-ten appointment is approaching. Max had reserved ten hour on Marten morning for a Seigniora Elisabetta Reynarda. She had refused to state her business, only that she needed to meet with me personally. With no clients at that time, high expenses, and a dwindling free credit balance, I had accepted.

"Yes, Max, I know." I saved the data on the Tozzi commission and stood. Then I stretched.

My office/study/library is on the north side of the villa's entry foyer. My dwelling doesn't really qualify for villa status. That's another issue. The city sisters let me keep the status in return for earlier service. They're more than the city sisters, but the term dated back to the first colonists. Devantans are traditionalists. That might be why Devanta never had to suffer an Assembly reformulation.

The system fed me the image of the woman crossing the entry foyer to the door of my office and study, guided by the holo versions of me animated by Max. I moved from behind the table desk and waited.

Seigniora Reynarda stepped into the study. She was neither tall nor short, a touch less than 180 centimeters. Her hair was a natural stormy blond, and her skin was the pale gold of mixed ancestry. Her eyes were large and black and dominated a face with a straight neat nose, a wide mouth, and lips too thin to be called rosebud. She wore a single-suit of deep gray, with a short black jacket and black boots. The attire suited her.

"Seignior Donne." She stopped less than a yard from where I stood.

"Seigniora Reynarda, I believe." There was something about her—or not about her.

"That will do." The seigniora surveyed the study. Her deep black eyes moved from point to point, as if my office were an artifact to be cataloged. She did not attempt flash-code communication. Since she did not, I was not about to. Besides, the study was secure, even against vibrosonic taps and coherency analysis.

The north and east walls are mainly glass—intelligent glass—set between the square golden stone columns. There are two sets of French doors on the north wall. They open onto the columned north verandah. It's anything but large, a mere ten meters by five. Except for the double cherry doors from the entry foyer, the inside south wall is all book-shelves. So is the west inside wall. I like the feel of books. I've actually read many of them—as books. Some aristos read them through the datastacks and display the bound originals as trophies. Me, what I peruse and study through the netsystems is for work. What I read off the shelves is for pleasure.

The furnishings are simple. All the links and perceptual-electronics are behind the bookcases. What's left are a circular conference table for four, with stylized captain's chairs, a broad table desk, with my chair behind it, and one comfortable green reading chair in the northwest corner.

"I'd heard you were tastefully . . . modest, Seignior Donne. It appears as though the reports were accurate." The black eyes focused on me. They reminded me of the feral cats that frequented the darker fringes of the Parc du Roi.

I was percepto-linked to my system, trying to run traces and comparisons, but they all came up blank. Who she was remained a mystery, as did much on Devanta . . . and on most of the Worlds of the Assembly. "I've always believed in modesty, both personally and financially. What can I do for you?"

"You have an impeccable reputation."

That statement meant trouble. I waited.

"I have a commission for you."

I gestured toward the conference table.

"No thank you. I won't be here that long. Are you interested in a commission?"

"Is it the kind I'd wish to take?"

She smiled. The expression was pleasant and meant to hold a hint of sensuality. It didn't. Again, I didn't understand why not. She had all the equipment, and she didn't come across as a samer.

"I understand you prefer a challenge and ample remuneration," she said after a long pause. "I'm prepared to offer both."

"I don't take commissions that involve breaking the Codex." Not since I'd been regened and retired from the Assembly's IS SpecOps.

"Unless you are far less resourceful than your reputation suggests, you will not need to worry about trivialities such as the Codex."

"You know I must ask your name and identity."

She flashed a coded ID bloc, but no words with the bloc. The systems verified that it was a "real" identity.

Theoretically, if I did something against the Codex, her ID could be revealed if a justicer determined that she had been in fact instrumental in aiding or abetting an offense. That is, if the coded bloc happened to be accurate and not merely well enough designed to deceive my systems. My systems are better than any but those of IS or internal Garda security.

"Are you satisfied?"

"Enough."

"I would like you to discover and ascertain in evidentiary terms the exact relationship between Eloi Enterprises, Judeon Maraniss, and Elysium."

The first name was dangerous, the second puzzling. The third? I'd never heard of Elysium—except in classes in antiquity years before when I'd been at the Institute. That wasn't what the lady meant—assuming she was either a lady or female in other than bodily form.

"The remuneration?"

"A flat retainer of five thousand credits for this appointment and the first ten stans of work. After that, we meet again and see if further investigation is necessary, possible, or required."

"How do I reach you?"

"You don't. I'll contact Max."

I'd never used that name outside the villa. I smiled. "You are very persuasive. I will accept—for the first ten stans."

"I thought you would." Another coded link flashed from her to the systems.

The backlink verified I had five thousand credits I hadn't had a few moments before. My accounts were far healthier than they had been two stans earlier.

"I look forward to your first report." She gave a polite but perfunctory nod, then turned and walked out of the study.

I watched her closely until the door closed. The systems tracked her until she left the courtyard in a gray groundcar. It was an unmarked and armored limousine.

Who was Seigniora Elisabetta Reynarda? The mind behind the body was either very wealthy or very powerful. Probably both. Whether she were even a woman was another question. On Devanta, as on most worlds, the protocol, the appearance, and the legalities of identity didn't always match. Appearance often matched neither protocol nor legality. She was an advocate, or someone familiar with terms of law, and she was playing for high stakes. Anyone who referred to the Codex as a triviality and meant it had to be. Yet she had not used verbal flashcode, and that suggested that the body was not hers. Or that the code usage might reveal more of her origin and background.

And there was something else . . .

I almost laughed. No pheromones. Even samer women,

who had little interest in men, often used pheromones beyond the natural to provide an edge. Practicing samers had different pheromones, but they were there. Seigniora Reynarda had not had any. Yet the body had been physically real. The most likely explanation was a recently decanted clone with a cydroid shunt. That raised other questions, principally urgency.

I dropped back into the datastacks. My first scan search was for quick specifics on Eloi Enterprises. The name was familiar to anyone around the entertainment sector of Devanta. Legaar Eloi was "Seignior Entertainment." He'd also been informally linked to more than fifteen erasures or vanishments, not that there was any proof.

The datastacks had little more on him personally. That included the public stacks and the privates to which I'd wrangled access over the years. Eloi Enterprises specialized in explicit entertainment and gratification provided through every possible format and medium developed over the prehistorical, historical, and posthistorical span of humanity. Seigniora Reynarda could have easily been one of those mediums. She was striking enough. Formally, Eloi Enterprises was wholly owned by Legaar and Simeon Eloi, with worth and assets unknown, but estimated in excess of a billion creds. I skipped over the details of exactly how they provided for their clientele. I might need to investigate that in greater depth. I hoped not.

Judeon Maraniss was next. I'd heard the name but hadn't been able to place it. He was a specialist in population dynamics and had his own consulting operation somewhere in Thurene, physical location confidential.

The numbers of references to Elysium were staggering. I had no idea how many hotels, resorts, consulting firms, and unrelated operations had decided that the ancient classical name was their codebloc to success. On the other hand, there were no links between Elysium and either Maraniss or Eloi Enterprises. I hadn't expected there would be, but it's better to eliminate the obvious when you can.

There was no Elisabetta Reynarda. That didn't surprise

me. In fact, I would have been surprised if she had been listed anywhere. There were no current Reynardas anywhere in Thurene or anywhere else on Devanta. The name wasn't proscribed, but it had been abandoned after Marshal Reynardo's execution two centuries earlier. Even the escapades of the Fox a century later had not revived the surname except as a whispered epithet, when no other hero would light a lamp.

I still had to wonder on whom the Seigniora Reynarda body and persona had been modeled. There was *something* there. That had been intended. The fun of attempting to beat Cartiff and the ladies Selemez at their own profession would have to wait. I needed to set up a more targeted data approach and then talk to some people. In person.

I also needed to finish reading the material on Marie Annette Tozzi and Dr. Guillaume Richard Dyorr and set up the initial scan searches on them.

4

*The degree of emptiness in life is proportional
to the density of the observer.*

As with all those who possessed wealth, there was little information on Marie Annette Tozzi. The initial search did come up with a bit more on Guillaume Richard Dyorr. He'd been born in Bretcote, to a fishing family. He'd excelled in racquets and parlayed that expertise into an admission to L'École de Mérite. From there he'd gained a full scholarship to L'Université de Vannes and then another to the Medical College at Vergennes, on the far east coast. He'd graduated second in his class. The honors, research, fellowships piled up. From what I could tell, he'd had no female liaisons of a lasting nature. All of his mentors had been male. Suggestive, but for from conclusive. If anyone would know, it would be Myndanori, when I could reach her.

The Reynarda commission would take even more work, and I'd need to talk to Odilia. Technically, I could have virtied her. I didn't. Virtual visits were not de rigueur in her circle. So, immediately after the seigniora left, I arranged an appointment with Odilia for Miercen. Then I called the groundcar service and ordered the small special limousine. Anything less, and I wouldn't have gotten through the gates of the Palacio Ottewyn.

I decided to let matters stew in my subconscious for a bit.

News scan. I prioritized the items, starting with non-Assembly news, then began to run through the items.

"Technarcheologists representing the University of
Muriami reported the discovery of the remnants of an
alien spacecraft . . . in an undisclosed location in the Drift
region . . . the craft is estimated to be a billion years old.
Because of extensive damage that presumably immobilized the vehicle and the debris that accreted around it, the
technology used to propel it is unknown, but the design of
the craft is similar to that of existing human jumpships . . .
and contains fossilized remains . . . no other data have yet
been released . . ."

Every decade or so, someone found some technological
artifact that they claimed was of alien origin and represented high science. So far none had. Most were common
devices with common purposes from peoples who had
come and gone.

"Ahrham Khan, Shiite League legate to the Assembly,
informed Premier Ferraro that the League would take
whatever steps might be necessary to restrain Frankan ex-
pansionism in the Sack area of the Trailing Arm. He repeated that statement in a public statement delivered
before the Califya Stellar Traders . . ."

I snorted. Everyone anywhere close to the Frankan Con-
federation declared that they would take such steps. So far
as I knew, only SpecOps had ever done anything. Most of
that had been hushed up, and kept hushed up.

"The art exchange between the Columbian Federation
and Chung Kuo has been canceled. No reasons have been
given . . ."

Skip. I didn't need to know about art exchanges.

"The Republic of Zion has launched another colony ship
that will incorporate both jump-generators and suspend
systems with the most advanced AI guidance systems.

With a target of the 'meadows' section of the Greater Magellanic Cloud, the LDSS *John Lee* will undertake the longest missionary flight ever attempted . . ."

Skip to Devanta news. Saint missionary efforts were worse than art exchanges.

"The Gallian Sector Four Fleet continued deep-space maneuvers last week, and encountered armed scouts of an unidentified force. One of the scout ships was destroyed. The other escaped . . . Sources close to the sector command of the Assembly Defense Ministry reported that the scouts' profiles matched those of either Frankan or Argenti vessels."

I would have thought that deep-space military scouts were more likely to be Argenti, since the Frankans had backed off after the lower Trailing Arm disaster. Both had targeted the Gallian sisterhood in past centuries. They had felt it was the weakest subsector of the Assembly of Worlds. They'd been repulsed, defeated, and annihilated in successive campaigns. I'd had something to do with the last. Those outcomes had not changed their opinion. Not for long. Sweet reason insisted that worlds ruled by women were better targets.

"Soror Prima Juliana signed an amendment to the Gallian systems charter yesterday that would require mandatory licensing of defense-related technologies to the system or planetary authorities. Full royalties would be paid, but the owner of such technologies would not have the right to prohibit their use. In addition, the government would have the right to prohibit sales of such technology to governments deemed hostile . . ."

That worried me far more than fleets prowling around the Gallian systems. Any time a government had to compel commonsense measures of those who provided weapons systems, it suggested that short-term greed had won over long-term survival. But then, history was filled with societies that had collapsed because of excessive greed in its various manifestations.

Because of my musings over technology-leasing, I hadn't been paying that much attention to the other news and missed the lead of the next report.

"... outbreaks of spontaneous crime and violence continued to drop in Thurene and other urbanized areas ... population dynamicists note that the decline in such offenses merely mirrors the decrease in the numbers of those members of society most likely to commit such crimes ... no explanation for such a population decline. Sister Quinta refused to comment on the report that disappearances are at an all-time high in lower-income quadrants, particularly in Thurene and in Vannes ...

"The Sorores Civitas are little more than a feminist tyranny." That was the latest pronouncement of Josiah Brigham at the annual meeting of the Masculist Forum in Testaverde yesterday. Members of the Forum pledged support to develop a political alternative to the current Devantan government, one more aligned with the best in human tradition ..."

I snorted. The Masculists and their female counterpart— the True Traditional Women—wanted to roll back political, economic, medical, and social developments thousands of years in the name of tradition. They didn't like equality for the sexes or a medical technology that could transform women into men in every aspect or men into women, even to removing the differences in the Adam's apple, and they certainly didn't like women running the planetary government.

Krij will be here shortly, Max reminded me. *With her partner.*

Thank you. I cut off the news feeds.

I could feel myself tightening inside. When my sister

visited, I still felt that way. Was it that she was a decade older and had always exhibited superiority, regardless of how matters had changed since we had been children? Had it been the sudden and untimely death of our parents while I'd been in the service that had forced her into that role? Or was it me? I'd tossed those questions over in my mind for years, never satisfied with the results. As always, I pushed them back into the shadows of my mind.

Siendra wasn't Krij's partner in the samer sense. They were business partners. Krij had been married to an advocate—once—and I had a niece I saw occasionally. Krij and Siendra were regulatory compliance auditors—not for the Assembly of Worlds or for the planetary government of Devanta, but for wealthy individuals and small corpentities. Those were the people who had the most to lose from failure to comply with the myriad of energy, environmental, accounting, taxation, and employment regulations.

Should I start on the Reynarda commission? Or the Tozzi one?

I decided against either. Krij was always punctual. She was due at the villa in less than ten minutes. Instead, I checked on messages. There weren't many. There never were.

Antonio diVeau's smooth face projected into the air before the desk. "Blaine . . . are you interested in a cataract river ride in Novem? I've got space for two . . ."

I'd turn that down. Tony was the type that professed profound love and devotion to his wife and daughters, then left them for every exotic adventure he could find. He tried to use those adventures to gain clients for his bank—I presumed. We'd never been close, but I didn't like to alienate anyone for no reason. Not when they might someday need my services. If I'd been his wife—or her brother—I'd have vanished him long ago. But I wasn't, and he'd married wealth and the kind of woman who'd vanish herself rather than disappoint him. Besides, I wasn't looking for more excitement. I had enough professionally. Paying for it in my personal life was insane.

Next in the message queue was Lemel Jerome. He was an

inventor who fancied that his ideas were always being stolen by others—usually by others who claimed precedents established centuries before.

"My idea for quark-electron regression holo recording and display. I registered that ten years ago, and now the Classic group is looking into that approach. They won't answer any of my inquiries. I'd like you to look into that . . ."

Lemmy always wanted me to look into things. He paid, but slow, stingily, and late. I wouldn't have time to talk to him at the moment. I'd return the vid later. I still could use more credits. I started to call up Myndanori's message when Max interrupted me.

Krij and Siendra are here.

I stood, then watched as they stepped into the study. Krij turned and shut the door. Siendra stepped to one side to let Krij continue to take the lead.

"Good morning, Blaine." Krij smiled brightly. She was striking in an understated way—with wide-set green eyes, a patrician nose, shoulder-length jet-black hair, and flawless pale skin that had just enough color to let her eyes and features dominate her countenance. She was slender in a muscular way, but obviously well curved. When she was being professional, as she was at the moment, she suppressed her pheromones to a simple restrained declaration of femininity. So did Siendra, but whether that was because of her inclination or Krij's direction I didn't know. I wasn't about to ask.

I'd never gone in for pheromone manipulation, and I hadn't had to. Mine were in the acceptable range, and the readings said they made me mildly attractive to women.

In a sense, Siendra was Krij's opposite. Nothing stood out. Her brown hair was smooth and cut into a bob. Her eyes were somewhere between light brown and hazel. Her nose was neither pug, nor small, nor large, not crooked, but not markedly noticeable. She had a feminine figure that was neither angular nor outrageously curved. Her voice was pleasant.

"Good morning." I nodded to them both, then gestured to the conference table.

"This won't take long," Krij replied, although she settled herself into one of the chairs. "It's good to get off my feet."

I hadn't seen Siendra sit down, but she had taken the chair to Krij's left and my right.

"We finished the audit, Blaine."

"And? Am I out of compliance in something else? Besides the supplementary schedules for independent subcontractors?"

"We fixed that. More a technicality than actual noncompliance. But they would have fined you. As for the others . . . Out of compliance, no. Likely to encourage a sisterly formal audit by the Civitas Sorores, possibly."

Much as I might joke about the sisters and audits, that was the last thing I wanted. Not when they administered all Devanta, even though they styled themselves merely the Civitas Sorores of Thurene. "With what?"

"Your equipment expenditures. You spend more on equipment than do some corpentities ten times your size."

Siendra nodded, barely perceptibly. "Your equipment descriptions are on the general side."

I had the feeling that Siendra had studied me when I wasn't looking at her. "They have to be. First, most of it's custom. Second, I'd rather not give a full description."

"Don't." Siendra laughed. It was a warm expression, the first thing about her that had stood out in the five years she'd worked with Krij. "Just give it an official-sounding label. If you have Moore-Jobi build you a special nanite diffuser, call it the MJ Diffuser, Model BD-1 or 2 or 3, whatever number it happens to be. The bureaucrats will accept that more happily than a detailed description."

"Others build diffusers, and they don't cost nearly so much," I pointed out.

"Then add that it has a Special Adapter, Mode 3."

That would probably work. I wished I'd thought of it, but that was why I'd asked Krij to audit my reports—and why I'd pay her the going rate—or almost. Since she was my sister, she'd give me a thirty percent discount. "Anything else?"

"Get married."

"What?"

"Men who are married have half the audit rates of those who aren't." Krij grinned. "They also live longer." As usual, she'd given her opinion in her own inimitable way.

"I wouldn't have to worry about being audited at all. To stay married, I'd have to give up most of what makes credits for me. I wouldn't be able to afford the villa, or your services, elder sister."

"I have to give you some advice you won't take, Blaine. Otherwise, you think I've wasted your time and credits."

She was right about that. She was usually right. I'd learned that years before. Back then, it had irritated me, particularly when she'd told me that I'd be accepted for Special Operations, but rejected for IS pilot training. I still remembered what she'd said.

"The best pilots are at home with boredom. They don't want excitement. They'll train and prepare for years to avoid excitement. You can't live without it."

I'd protested and taken the tests and exams. When I got the responses, SpecOps had accepted me, and the space service had rejected me. But it wasn't that I couldn't live without it. It was more that I wanted to tame it and couldn't live without that effort. Krij would have called that my own power trip. She would have been right there, too. But I had gotten into piloting through the back door of Special Operations. Small spacecraft and flitters only.

"You won't waste my credits. That wouldn't fit your professional self-interest, elder sister."

That got smiles from both Krij and Siendra.

Then Krij stood. "I'd better not waste your time, either." She tilted her head in the quizzical expression that was hers alone. "Brunch on Senen? Eleven hour?"

"At your place?"

"Where else?"

"I'll be there."

I didn't see Siendra stand, but she had.

I accompanied them all the way out of the study and through the entry foyer and down the steps to their limousine—small standard gray corpentity transport. Solar-electrofuel-cell, like most models.

Before Siendra turned to follow Krij into the limousine, she smiled politely. Her eyes met mine, but I had the feeling that there was some sort of barrier there. It wasn't dislike, and it wasn't fear, but more like the feeling of distance. Maybe it was because she and Krij minimized danger, while I wanted to master it.

I watched the limousine glide out through the gates and the gates close. Then I walked back up the stone steps and across the foyer to the study. When the door closed behind me, the villa felt emptier after they left than before they had arrived. I knew why, but explaining to myself would only have made it worse.

Besides, I had the rest of Marten to dig further into the Reynarda and Tozzi jobs—and to make the changes in the descriptions of my equipment, as well as a cryptic reminder to myself about using model and make numbers for what I purchased.

Then, too, I needed to go through the rest of the messages.

My boredom threshold has always been low. The more mysterious work was always more appealing. That looked to be the Reynarda commission. I set Max to work on two mathematical analyses of possible civic registry keys. The first was based on all the numbers and phrases likely to be common to the Eloi brothers. The second was an improbability analysis, designed to develop uncommon keys, or rather, keys the Elois would think were uncommon. I had Max's backup cull all public video that could be found of either Eloi and of Judeon Maraniss.

Then I had him do the same for the Tozzi heiress and the doctoral fortune seeker.

After that, I went down below, where I went through a full real-body physical workout. Two solid stans. After that, I cooled down, cleaned up, then returned to the villa's lower levels, where I put myself through the armed deep-space scout refresher—version three. That was using an actual cockpit interior, with enough virtie assist to make it more real.

After a quiet and very late luncheon or early dinner by myself on the verandah, I girded myself up to study all the vid-shots of my targets and see what associations I could draw from them and the backgrounds. That's never as simple as it sounds. That and catching up on various odds and ends took the rest of the early evening.

5

The ancient peoples believed in deities that could be evil and uncertain; few modern societies do. The ancients, for all their lack of technological knowledge, were far wiser. Assuming there are deities, exactly why should they be benevolent?

The shadows are deeper around and within Deo Patre. I couldn't say why, only that they always are. Just as it seems that the light of Voltaire never falls directly on the front entrance, although that of Bergerac does, contrary as that may seem. Not many people visit the old cathedral anymore, even to look at the exhibits in the day. Never at night. Especially not on a Marten eve, not after the exploits of the Fox—Reynard de la Nuit. That had been a century ago. But in our Post-Deist Age, superstitions die hard. There's no god to remove them.

Why was I standing in the shadows inside Deo Patre?

When I'm not involved personally, I have a good sense for trouble. When I am, I don't. Rather, that sense is less accurate. Tonight, someone was going to need me. If not, it was a quiet night for a stroll and a visit to the past. At times, my visits to the past are untroubled. Those are few, though.

I heard footsteps on the permastone of the walkway that led up to the main doors on the west end of the cathedral. The doors opened, and three figures stepped inside—two taller ones and a slighter figure.

"Just take a look. You won't believe it. It's a real cathedral."

"It's the only one in all Thurene, maybe in all Devanta."

I watched from the shadows behind a column that was the last of the line of those separating the nave from the north aisle.

"I don't like this." The slight figure was a girl—a real girl, not a nymph.

The two muscular youths turned and grabbed her simultaneously. One slapped a gag across her mouth, while the other used a restrainer. She sagged, but still attempted to struggle. Between the restrainer field and the strength of the young men, she could do nothing. After a moment, there was a dull thump as the antique entrance bar dropped into place, locking the main doors.

"You're sure about the scanners?"

"I'm the maintenance tech. They aren't linked to the Garda net anyway."

The slightly less muscular youth carried the squirming woman down the nave. I paralleled them, carrying my own darkness from column to column of the north aisle.

"On the altar. It's no good if you don't do it on the altar."

I didn't see or sense weapons—such as sacrificial daggers. That suggested either straight rape for thrills or a twisted ceremonial deflowering. But you can never tell. I slipped from the end of the aisle up through the side entrance to the transept. The less-massive youth looked around, then bent down and ripped off the girl's trousers and undergarments.

That was intent enough. I stepped out into the chancel, coming from the left side of the altar, facing it, that is. I've always favored the left, in this case, the left hand of darkness.

"Look! The shadows!" The one stripping the restrained girl looked up.

I stepped forward, holding my darkness.

"Not that impressive. It must be some sort of projection." The heavier youth stepped toward me. His face was a near replica of the statue of Ares in the Palatinium in Zeopolis. I sensed the plastiflesh.

It was almost a shame to immobilize him with two blows he never saw coming. Almost.

The would-be rapist bolted to his feet. He got no farther before I took him down.

Then I took the commlink from the girl's belt. Her eyes widened, in even greater fear. But I just pressed the Garda distress stud and set it beside her. Then I released the restrainer field and reset it to cover both the would-be assailants. Then I turned, gathering darkness around me.

Behind me, she half screamed, but she'd recover. I could sense her grabbing for her garments.

I went out through the chapter house exit because the shadows were heavier there.

The two had obviously planned their escapade for some time. Plastiflesh faces and synth DNA and pheromones, and no obvious clues to their identification once they used the girl. They'd meant to dose her with mem-ex or something similar. Without any memory from the girl and no traces to them, they might have gotten away with it. They might not have, but the damage would have been done to her. The eons-old problem with law has always been that it cannot prevent what might happen without destroying all freedom. I'd had to wait long enough for their intent to be clear. That had been cruel, but necessary.

Once out in the shadows, I walked past the open gate to the graveyard and glanced sideways at the statue of the sorrowing angel. Beyond the angel stretched the headstones. Not quite midnight in the garden of good and evil. That had been before the bodies beneath the stones had been removed. The stones and their inscriptions had been left for illustrative purposes. Meaningless illustrative purposes for an age in which death was infrequent and treated as if it were an avoidable accident that had been the deceased's personal fault. Death was often no longer the greatest of calamities. Life was.

From the grounds of Deo Patre, I walked through the shadows of the past and the present toward an unknown destination.

6

While there is doubtless great relief in surrendering one's destiny to a deity, it's the coward's way out.

A purplish gray line of amorphousness oozed over my fingers and across the back of my knuckles. I tried to yank my left arm away. It would not move. Somehow I was restrained. My other hand and arm would not move, either. Neither would my toes nor feet. Overhead was a greenish white mist. It could have been centimeters or meters away from me. I couldn't tell. I was neither hot nor cold.

"Just relax. You'll be all right." The voice reverberated in my ears and jolted my skull. The voice was meant to be reassuring.

It wasn't.

The purplish gray mass engulfed my hand and wrist. White-hot needles burned all the way up my arm. Every muscle in my body convulsed, yet nothing moved. My mouth opened, but no sound came out.

"Just take it easy. You'll be all right."

It didn't feel that way. What was happening? Where was I?

I tried to remember. How had I gotten here, wherever "here" was?

I'd been scouting a possible Frankan installation on Pournelle II, a hot near-airless planet that was mostly nickel iron. It might have been the core of a gas giant once. Whatever else had been above the core had been stripped away when the star it circled had gone nova. Now all that was left was a dwarf star with a few clinkers orbiting it.

But the Pournelle system was less than two light-years

from the fringe of the Gallian subsector and made a good advance base. At least, Assembly IS had thought there might be Frankans there. So SpecOps had sent me and Brooke in with stealth needleships. He'd always protested that he was a great lover, and fighting came second. If fighting came second, I'd never have wanted to be in love with any woman he'd desired.

For all that, his ship-shields had failed, and I'd gone after him. After some considerable difficulties, we'd finally been headed out-system. Clear of the Frankans, I'd thought.

After that . . . I couldn't remember.

More of the purple-gray oozed over my right hand and up the arm. As it did, another set of blazing needles seared me.

An involuntary moan started in my throat. It never got any farther.

"You'll be all right . . ."

How could I be all right when I was unable to move and being swallowed alive by some sort of nanetic gray goo?

I kept trying to twist free, to break away from whatever held me. I could feel sweat popping out all over me, but my body wouldn't move. I had to get free. I just had to.

Abruptly, I was free.

I was also sitting up in my own bed—alone. I'd ripped a section of the high-count sateen sheet apart and clutched it in my left hand. My sleeping shorts were soaked, and so were the remnants of the sheets.

Interrogative time?

Zero four thirteen, sir.

Thank you. Not that Max needed thanks. I just needed to thank him.

Slowly, I swung my feet out of the bed and onto the floor. The thick Arasian wool carpet felt good to my feet. I stood and walked to the window. From there, I looked into the garden courtyard. The view didn't help. The hazaleans looked gray-ghostly under the silvery light. Voltaire was only half-full, and the stonework was morgue white.

I turned and took in the bed, the night table, and the long and low chest that held clothes. They were all clean-lined gray ironwood. Shadow furniture to match . . . what? A shadow knight? Except I'd never called myself that. Others had. They didn't really know me.

I was Blaine Donne, wasn't I? That was my name. Or it had been.

But was I still? If not, who was I?

There was no point in going back over that.

I took a deep breath and walked slowly back to the chest to take out a dry pair of sleeping shorts. I'd have to change the sheets as well. Unlike many, I still preferred natural cotton. That said something about who I was. Didn't it?

7

Although I'd gone to bed late and had another nightmare, I still woke up early, right after dawn. I took my time getting to breakfast, then managed my morning workout. When I'd cooled down and cleaned up, I went back to work on setting up more investigative searches on my targets.

I'd tried to reach Myndanori and a few other sources, but all I'd gotten were talking heads. All that took the rest of the morning on Miercen.

Just past one, I checked my gear and shields, then stepped out of the villa and down the wide and gray granite steps to the limousine. The blue-green sky was clear. Mostly. There were clouds to the north of Thurene, over the Malmonts. That was true of most days. That rain was what fed the Nouvelle Seine.

The car looked like every other small limousine. The driver was a woman. Autovirtie drivers were also verboten for all hired vehicles. Drivers for the special limousine required additional qualifications. I flashed the ID and code, and got the confirmation back. The rear door opened. I eased into the seat.

"Seignior Donne, to the Palacio Ottewyn?"

"The same. You're to wait."

"Confirmed on full alert."

I nodded. The service organizations were among the few one could trust. Rigorous impartiality was a necessity for them to remain in business. Expensive as they were, they were far cheaper than betrayal. Especially in Devanta, where one of the unspoken rules was that the habit of secrecy was both politic and moral.

The driver eased out through my plain iron gates, simple vertical bars, nanite-reinforced, and down Cuarta Calle to Le Boulevard. She drove the left-hand side of the Parc du Roi, then took Maiden Lane through the Boutique, rather than Vallum through La Banque. In Thurene, at times more credits passed through the fashion lanes than through the financial center.

At the far end of Maiden Lane, she entered the traffic circle and came out on Boudicca, less than a half klick from our destination. The limousine stopped at the gatehouse to Odilia's palacio. The gatehouse was half the size of my villa. It was also twice as ugly. I'd never voiced that to Odilia. The limousine went through the full surveillance array—tags, snoops, and sweeps. There were some I could sense, but not identify. That was one problem with going civvie. I'd kept up as well as I could, but the best personal technology was still IS and, to a lesser extent, Garda.

"Blaine Donne for Princesse Ottewyn."

"You are expected." The virtie guard nodded, her dark eyes never leaving the driver.

Unlike some in positions of power, Odilia did not make her guests climb a flight of stone steps from the portico to the main entrance. My guests had to, but that hadn't been my choice, and I wasn't about to rebuild my villa. Odilia's rotunda was covered and less than ten meters from the arched and columned entrance to the palacio.

That entrance was a facade. Behind it was a long, marble-paved walkway, also flanked by golden stone columns. Beyond the columns on either side was an interior courtyard garden, a jungle representation of fallen temples from ancient Earth. Someplace called Angkor. Beyond the courtyard garden was the receiving hall. The floor was polished pale blue marble. This year. The last time I had been in the palacio the marble had been rose. Black granite columns— shot with golden streaks—formed two semicircles, split by the entry archway through which I had entered and by the grand staircase. The staircase was also of the gold-shot black granite. The columns soared ten meters to the base of the dome, whose surface displayed a changing iridescence created by the millions of nano-tubes that picked up the sun and shifted the light according to some pattern I'd never been able to analyze. The hall was a good thirty meters across and empty of all furnishings. There were no hangings between the columns or the pale white marble walls behind them. Not a single work of art was visible anywhere. The intent was to diminish anyone who called, although I knew that fountains, furnishings, and art could appear within minutes.

I waited a good quarter stan in that starkness before Odilia made her way down the grand staircase. Then I bowed.

"With such a poor excuse for respect, I should have made you wait longer." Odilia curtsied. Despite the full antiquarian skirt, she made it look graceful. This year, she was petite, black-haired, with a heart-shaped face and an impossibly slim waist. Last year, she'd been blond, better endowed curvaceously, and with a wholesome and slightly oval face. "You always look the same, Blaine, year after year. Depressingly unchanged. The same black hair that looks almost dark gray. The same military gray trousers, the black jacket, and silver blouse . . . accouterments of the shadows."

"Shirt. I don't wear blouses." I did bow more deeply. "You've decreed that this year the fashion must be Imperial?"

"It has been a while, and Imperiale is formal upon the surface and decadent beneath." She raised her right eyebrow not quite imperceptibly. *And are we not most decadent here in Thurene?* That came by flashcode, virtually impossible to intercept as close as we stood, unlike sound waves.

"Surfaces are most important. They conceal or reveal what is desired." *And you conceal most revealingly and charmingly.*

"And what is it that you desire, Seignior?" *Since you never come to see me unless you want information.* With the words came the slightest hint of very feminine pheromones, but ones I'd have called virginal lust, not that Odilia was anything close to virginal.

"You, most certainly. Why else would I throw myself at your feet?" *You'd never want to see me if I didn't, dear Odilia. It makes you feel valued and important—which you are—or I wouldn't be here.*

"That is the most eloquent you have been in years. Do you know that the ancient Tarot is the new fashion?"

"I had not heard. I'm not one for changing fashion, as you have pointed out." *Judeon Maraniss—what have you heard?*

"Do you think more highly of the Fisher King or the Hanged Man?" *He's rather dull. The only thing interesting about him is the rumor that he's connected with Legaar Eloi.*

"I doubt that any would wish to suffer the real death, Principessa." *In what fashion?*

"Imperiale suggests 'Princesse,' Seignior Donne." *Some disgusting commercial venture . . . Judeon needed financing for a project, but he refused to provide proprietary information to La Banque de Thurene . . . or the First Commerce Bank, so I was told. So he went to Legaar.*

I ignored the fact that Odilia's considerable fortune was based on sordid commercial dealings by her late mother. Eleyna Ottewyn had maintained that she'd never lifted a finger to deal in commerce. She hadn't. It had all been done in flashcode. Sometimes on her back, it had been rumored. However she had accomplished it, Eleyna had made certain that her daughter was powerful and well-off.

"I apologize, Princesse." I bowed again. *What kind of project?*

"I will consider accepting your apology." She lifted the left eyebrow. "If you are suitably contrite." *Something that mixed civic planning and entertainment, probably taking the worst from each.*

"How could my most sincere contrition be other than suitable?" *How many creds? Do you know what Legaar Eloi asked in return?*

"Your contrition is always so heartfelt, Blaine, even when

you don't mean it. That's what makes you so charming." *Several score million, I understand, and a minority interest close to a majority.*

"I'm only charming to you, Seigniora. You're the only one who deserves it." *What sort of project would a specialist like Maraniss have that cost that much?*

"You also lie charmingly, Blaine." *I don't know. No one I know does either.*

"What else can I do? The truth would not be gracious enough, and grace itself not truthful." *I'm also looking into a Dr. Guillaume Richard Dyorr. He's attempting to wed one Marie Annette Tozzi. I understand she's the granddaughter of one of your neighbors.*

"There is more than one meaning to grace, as you well know." *Seldara was a contemporary of my mother's. She's the only one who cares about the great-grandchildren. Everyone else just waits for her to die. They'll wait decades. Marie Annette is the only one of the lot worth worrying about. I haven't heard anything.*

"All meanings of grace apply to you. How could they not?" *Can you tell me anything else?*

"With such eloquence, you simply must accompany me to the opening of *Hyperion* this coming Vieren." *Perhaps then I'll know more.*

I bowed. An invitation to appear in public with Odilia was not to be missed. Not in my line of work, but not for the reasons most people thought. I also might learn more. "I would be honored." *Thank you.*

The faintest smile appeared on that beautiful heart-shaped face. "I will see you here at even-six of Vieren. Good afternoon, Seignior." *Don't spend too much time as the knight of shadows.*

"Your wish is my command." *If not me, then who?* Old lines, contrasted, but perfectly acceptable. I bowed again before making my departure.

The sun had dimmed close to thirteen percent by the time I returned to the limousine. The solar screens beyond the atmosphere had adjusted to the solar variability. The variability had not been that obvious more than a millennium before when the planoforming of Devanta had been completed and colonization begun.

Once outside, before stepping into the limousine, I tried a system-link back to Max. The first reason was to have him schedule the engagement with Odilia. The second was suspicion.

Personal security caught the linktrace in nanoseconds, before I even flashlinked. I made the link anyway. *Max, reserve the evening this Vieren, from five-even on.*

Yes, Seignior.

Max . . . detect alpha one.

He didn't respond to me. That was the confirmation.

Odilia's gates were cupridium thorn-olives that shimmered even in low light and radiated enough in normal light to make it hard to look at them without retinal adjustment. They were strong enough to remain intact under any energy flow short of a nova. The driver eased out through them and went the other way onto Vallum. Halfway into La Banque area, she turned right and took Swift Alley into Dauphine Drive. The hazalean trees were still flowering, cascading blossoms onto the blue-green turf of the Parc. Each one released a flash of purple as it touched the grass. It wouldn't be that long before the long autumn turned to winter.

In minutes, we were headed back up Cuarta Calle, and I went to passive mode, listening. I did pulse the gates, and they opened. The driver eased the limousine to a stop at the foot of the stone steps.

From out of what most would have received as white energy, the implant pulled Max's transmission. *Simulacrum at your 330. Range Amorphous energy concentration at your 217.*

Before exiting the limousine, I calculated the angles, then eased to the door behind the driver. "I'll be getting out this side."

"Yes, Seignior." The driver stiffened.

I could sense all the limousine's defense screens and shields. That was fine with me—exactly what I wanted.

I put my own nanoshield on full, stepped out, turned, and . . . dropped to one knee.

Energy coruscated off the limousine and its shields.

The driver reacted, and a fine-line particle beam took out the "amorphous" energy source. It also left a large hole in Soror Celestina's outer vallum. She'd complain to the Sorores Civitas, but since the transport company had been fired on and responded, there was little recourse against me. Much neater that way. Also much less on my dossier with the Garda. There was already too much there as it was.

"Thank you," I told the driver.

She smiled. "It comes with the service, Seignior Donne. There will be a surcharge."

"Of course."

I maintained my nanoshield only so long as it took to climb the steps and enter the villa. I was sweating and overheated anyway. A shield strong enough to divert even moderate energy will cook the user in five minutes—sometimes less. That's why they're usually pulsed. Pulsing doesn't work against high continuous energy discharges, and those are what anyone serious uses. Except on my forays in the shadows on my own, I usually only encountered serious users. With all its limitations, a nanoshield still had its uses.

When the doors of the entry foyer closed behind me, I direct-linked with Max. The patterns the system had observed and recorded didn't reveal much more than I'd calculated in the backseat of the special limousine.

Now the question was who was after me. I doubted seriously whether a fortune hunter like the good doctor would have known I was tracing him—or how to put together a team that could bring that much energy to bear in a matter of a day or so.

Had Seigniora Reynarda commissioned me merely to get rid of me, or to get me irritated enough to take on Legaar Eloi and Judeon Maraniss? Or to see if I were able to do so? Or to get me vanished later on so that an official investigation by the Garda under the instigation of the Civitas Sorores would reveal whatever connection she wished raised? That certainly would be cheaper than paying me what it would cost. It also had downsides, because there was always the possibility that it might reveal who or what was behind the mysterious seigniora.

I spent the rest of Miercen afternoon finishing up my formal report to Lewiston Aslan, II. I'd finished his dark materials investigation two weeks earlier, and I'd briefed him at the time. That was one where I'd had solid inklings of what lay beneath it all from the first, unlike whatever it was that Seigniora Reynarda wanted. Aslan had still wanted formal documentation. Behind that bluff leonine facade, he was more than a little parochial. I hated formal reports, but I wouldn't get the last ten percent of my fee without the report. My dislike of leaving creds on the table was far greater than my distaste of perfunctory documentation of what I'd done and found. So I gathered everything together, added the summary of my activities and findings, and sent it off. One encrypted version through the net, and a hard copy conveyed by Thurene Secure Couriers. At least the dark materials investigation hadn't been as bad as the Kung Chuo lost station problem. When someone inverted power nodes into spinspace, it got messy. After that one, it had taken the best reconstructive surgeons on Devanta to restore me. Krij had been less than pleased about that. It still hadn't been as bad as the complete regen that had required my medical retirement from SpecOps.

Then, after a light supper on Mercien evening, I accessed the complete system archives—the ones for which I paid an exorbitant sum every time I used them—rather than just the planetary archives, to see what else I could discover about Maraniss and Eloi. Elysium was a total loss. The word itself meant so many different things to so many people—and had for so many millennia—that even with maximum sort, full analysis, and minimalist definitions, the processing time on the amount of information would have taken months—and the cost would have been far in excess of what Seigniora Reynarda would have paid.

The complete archives didn't produce much more in the

way of usable information on either man. About all I learned new was that Judeon Maraniss had first taken a doctorate in some obscure branch of physics. He'd gotten into a disagreement with senior academics at L'Institut Multitechnique before turning his skills to obtaining additional degrees in more humanistic areas. Those records were sealed. That was an indication of system security, and that didn't happen often on the access level I was employing. Maraniss had been a professor at the Father Roger College at the University of Cluny until a decade earlier, when he'd established himself as an independent academic. He had multiple degrees and certifications in almost every branch of population studies and societal and sociological analytics. His studies were netsys-accessed enough that he probably made a decent living off those alone, and that didn't count whatever he might be providing in studies for governmental organizations, institutes, foundations, or corpentities.

The detailed record on Legaar Eloi was broader, shallower, and even more shadowed. He'd been trained as an advocate and actually practiced as a public advocate for a time, a good ten years. Then he'd dropped out of public view for several years. There wasn't any mention of him in any records. The next reference to him was as one of the partners in something called Classic Images. I'd tracked that down as well. Classic Images provided private escorts—men and women—based on classical images. Did the Directeur of Dorchan Delite wish to spend an evening with Helen of Troy or Dian duBlandeis? Did Madame Directeur prefer an evening with Don Juan or Genji le Shinto? Contact Classic Images.

From there, Eloi's tastes declined as his fortune mounted. The one question that came to my mind, right from the beginning, was where he'd gotten the credits to launch Classic Images. He'd needed a few millions for the biosculpting and psyche sets for his living images. And if he'd used clones, he'd have needed far more—either to buy the legal variances from the Civitas Sorores or to pay off the Garda. Or both. The record didn't even have any hints in that direction, and that suggested even more millions from unknown backers to encourage reticence on the part of the Swift Street media types.

Besides a too-sketchy background, I also got sets of pictures, dating farther back in time than the recent vid-clips I'd already studied. They didn't add much.

The scattered images of Maraniss all looked the same over the past fifteen years—black-haired, broad-shouldered, square-chinned with deep blue eyes, and clean-shaven. An image-boy for academics. Funny thing was that he'd looked that way all along.

In his first images, Legaar had started out as a tall and lanky figure, with dark red hair cut short and a narrow face under a broad forehead. His eyes were brown. Over the years, he'd let his hair grow a shade longer, and had a bit of work done on his ears so that they didn't protrude as much, and he'd added just enough weight to shift his image from one of lankiness to one that was imposing.

Those current images were subject to change, based on whim and credits. I didn't think either was the changing type. Not when neither had shifted appearance in years. Physical bodies indicate more about people than they think. If they're unchanged, then they're based on their genetic background. Those who don't alter their bodies significantly, either genetically or cosmetically, when they have the resources to do so, exhibit various kinds of pride and arrogance. Makes them harder to deal with. Both Maraniss and Legaar Eloi looked to be that kind.

I fell somewhere in the middle. I'd opted for casual handsomeness close to my genetic appearance, along with high muscle mass, but optimized for my bone structure, so that I appeared solid, but not overmuscled, with a lot of fast twitch muscles. Black hair, a shade that was really deep dark gray, call it shadow gray, and light green eyes. Totally unremarkable. It fit my persona. I knew I didn't wish to be remembered for being physically striking, one way or the other. If I were remembered, it would be for what I'd done. That was vanity as well, but I knew it. No one is remembered for long after they've vanished. Especially those who work the shadows. Even the greatest leaders and artists are remembered as images molded by culture to depict psychic and political necessities.

There were more than a few background similarities between Legaar Eloi and Maraniss. Both were somatically and base-genetically male. No sex or sex preference changes for either. Each had held to the same self-body-image for years. Both tended to dominate their immediate environment to the degree that there was no mention of partners, spouses, liaisons, or offspring. That also suggested another possibility—that what they did created enemies, and they preferred to minimize collateral damage.

All that didn't preclude the most likely possibility that they used virties for most appearances and shape/face screens in public areas. But I hadn't been hired to find them, just the connections between them and something called Elysium.

The system archives didn't provide much more on Dr. Dyorr, either. I'd definitely need to talk to Myndanori.

8

*Beauteous and sycophantic baud, worthy yet
of all praise and laud.*

A gentle breeze blew past my face as I stood on the balcony outside my office, gazing down on the white granite ramparts of the grand canal that led out to the harbor and encircled the city proper. The bright blue banners of Fall Festival waved in the wind that left ripples on the deep green water. Although I stood in the shadow of the late-afternoon sun, the soft white of the stone facing of the tower provided just the right amount of illumination from the servant sun, the rite of light.

Beside me, Legaar cleared his throat, then spoke. "Did you hear what I said? Zuse has vanished."

"I heard you. Zuse has vanished. Scores vanish every day throughout Devanta. We are the source of that, and some of them survive to prosper here. We are better off, and Thurene is far better off. For all that, such disappearances happen here in Elysium. They come, and, despite our best efforts, matters are not as they wish. The Hedonics Patrol must deal with them."

"They wouldn't deal with Zuse. He was on Devanta."

"True, but he could have fled anywhere. A few have."

"That might be true of many, Judeon, but not of Zuse."

I didn't have Legaar's faith in the Kempelen Zuse's stability. Emotional master patterners saw, sensed, and integrated all aspects of economic and social behavior on both the micro and macro level. Anyone who felt and manipulated all that well was always on the brink of instability, and Zuse was certainly one of the most accomplished of master patterners. He had done well in setting up the parameters and population dynamics of Elysium. But no subordinate was indispensable. "That may be, but his staff is capable."

Legaar raised his thin mahogany eyebrows but said nothing.

"You're afraid that Marcel Maelzel cannot continue the plans for the next phase?"

"Compared to Zuse, Maelzel is no more than a touring buffoon."

"He may be a bit of a buffoon, but he's learned a great deal from Zuse." Still, Legaar had a point, if not the one he thought he had. "Do you think Zuse was vanished?"

"It's early to conclude that, but there are rumors that the Fox is about—in Devanta."

"The Fox died decades ago."

"That's true enough, but that doesn't mean there wasn't a personality imprint, and with high intelligence and the imprint . . ."

"But . . . who? L'Ombre de la Nuit?"

"The shadow knight is not involved. To pay for his lifestyle, he must prevent untoward marriages and chase down incompetent thieves with societal connections. Then he must pay for that in the shadows of Thurene. His illusion is that aiding individuals makes a difference."

Legaar never could have made that analysis. I wondered from whom he'd commissioned it or for what favor he'd obtained it.

"This is something different. Very different." Legaar cleared his throat in the self-important manner that was his alone. "I thought that you might be able to come up with an analysis of the attack vectors from Devanta, those centering in Thurene."

"You're worried about someone interfering with the energy setup? I thought we already had arrangements for the system that would make the separation permanent."

"That will come. The arrangements are . . . en route, shall we say."

"The Frankan Alliance?"

"Now . . . Judeon, I don't intrude too deeply in your specialties, do I?" Legaar's voice lowered into that warm confidentiality that was more threatening than a snarl.

The breeze intensified, with the hint of a chill, coming off the sea beyond the harbor with the tang of salt. The wind cracked the banners for a moment before it dropped back to a gentler and caressing breeze. "Curiosity isn't intruding. If you feel I shouldn't know something, just inform me."

"I just did."

"And I respected it." I watched as a large yacht swept beneath the balcony, white-green foam curling away from her bow, heading out for a night of pleasure on the deep green sea. I would have liked to be aboard with Magdalena for a week, but such extended pleasures would have to wait.

"And I don't like meeting here."

"Elysium is the best and most secure place to meet." I couldn't help but smile. "You were the one who pointed that out. Your experts designed the security and screen systems, and they're the best in the Assembly worlds."

"It's not the security here; it's the transit."

Legaar had a point there, but that problem would be resolved shortly. He'd indicated that himself. He just didn't know how much I'd really discovered, and it was better that way.

"You'll take care of analyzing the possibilities and letting me know?"

For all that Legaar had phrased his words as a question, they weren't. "It could take some time, Legaar."

"I know. That's why I'm here." He stepped back from the cupridium railing, turning toward the open door back into my office. "I'll expect periodic reports until you have results." He didn't look back when he left.

I watched the grand canal as the shadows lengthened. I wasn't about to forgo my evening with Magdalena, short as it would be, but, for all that I'd protested, it appeared that I'd have to return to Devanta, whether I wanted to or not.

Even if the sisters had Zuse, no one would believe him. That was just one of the beauties of Elysium.

9

Matter is not the universe, but rather only a single-dimensioned manifestation perceived by human beings.

I didn't sleep all that well and was up before dawn on Jueven. That was unheard of in Thurene. Rather, to admit waking that early was unheard of. Instead of lying there looking at the ceiling or turning on the slumbereze, I got up. The slumbereze was for emergencies. It always gave me a headache the morning after I used it. The villa medcenter said it was mental. It was wrong. I knew that aspect of my physiology far better than it did.

My study was even quieter before dawn, and work was more restful than trying to sleep. I decided to work on the Reynarda commission. That made sense since it was most likely someone involved there was trying to kill me—or warn me off.

The best places to find information about people are in their bedrooms and from their lovers, their real financial accounts, and the tax and regulatory records of the government. Discovering the first source would have meant days, if not weeks, of digging to determine who their lovers were and where those bedrooms were located—and the next steps would have been both illegal and dangerous. Attempting to find their real financial records, especially those involved with Eloi, would have been more dangerous and also illegal. That meant the easiest source of information would be the records of the Civitas Sorores itself, and breaking into those records was far less dangerous and comparatively less illegal. Not that I intended to get caught, but no good thief ever does. Besides, I could claim it was only research. I might even get away with a research claim since I'd never been caught before.

I settled into my chair. Comfortable as it was, it had other functions. Most important were the full-physiological links that allowed complete virtie access to the netsys, along with full-band back access to Max and the analyses he'd run earlier.

Civitas Publica.

With that command, I stood in a soaring foyer. The walls were golden brass and the floor a shimmering black marble. Black stone and gold must be embedded in the human psyche. There were no windows, just four high archways. Set in onyx letters above each brass arch was a sector name—REVENUE, FINANCIAL REGULATIONS, RECORDS, TAXATION/TARIFFS, HEALTH, ENVIRONMENTAL MANAGEMENT, PUBLIC SAFETY. There were archways for all of those departments, and more, yet there were only four archways. That's what you can do in a virtual setting. I tried not to think too hard about the implications and walked toward the Records archway.

An androgynous golden-haired clerk sat on a stool behind a raised podium of the golden brass. He/she smiled politely and warmly. "Your inquiry?"

"Corpentity records. Public registrations, entertainment."

"Through that door." A solid golden oak door and doorway appeared in the solid brass wall to the clerk's right. On the door was the legend PUBLIC REGISTRATIONS, ENTERTAINMENT.

"Thank you." Politeness never hurt, even to system virties. Especially since the sisters recorded and kept records of virtie access. Most people didn't really understand. Those records could be used in both civil and criminal justicing.

I walked to the door and opened it, then stepped inside, into another foyer. From it radiated another set of archways. Each held an illuminated set of letters stamped into the brass in the area that would have held the keystone, if the

arch had been stone. I took the "Pleasure-Related" archway.
Beyond it were illuminated displays, each almost like a museum case. Each case was fronted in antique glass, under
lights, and the framed space displayed large text on creamy
parchment. The corpentity's name was at the top, followed
by the registry number, local virtual address, local physical
address, and key officials. Beneath that was a description of
the business activities.

Eloi Enterprises was fairly far along the virtual corridor.
The local virtual address was Gibson Gates. The physical
address listed the Eloi Complex, Pier One, Left Bank, Nouvelle Seine, Thurene. I copied those to my own files—
through Max and his security system.

Registry numbers all had keys, encrypted keys.

My system was simple enough—try all the combinations
that Max had worked out and get around the three-times
rule through a little program to bypass and reset the clock
back several hundred nanoseconds after each try, thereby
erasing the record of each previous attempt. It wouldn't
have worked unless someone had the kind of resources I
had, and most who did wouldn't have needed to do what I
was doing.

That's always the best position to be in—where the defenses are designed against someone else.

Even so, it took almost ten standard minutes. That's a
long time for that kind of virtie operation. Then the front of
the display case swung open, becoming a glass door. I went
into the small chamber. The door didn't close behind me. It
re-formed closed, behind me. Slipshod programming. What
else could you expect from bureaucratic virtie program-
mers?

A thick black book sat on a reading stand. I opened the
cover.

The first page was more description. There wasn't much
there. Eloi Enterprises was wholly owned by the brothers
Eloi—surprise. It had six subsidiaries: Classic Escort Services, Classic Entertainment, Classic Properties, Classic
Media and Publications, Classic Investment, and Classic

Research. I read the following pages, a page for each subsidiary. Each of the first five was exactly as anyone would have expected from its name. The description of Classic Research started out with the usual combination of verbal pabulum and boilerplate and kept going until near the end. I reread the one paragraph closely.

> ... Classic Research is engaged in determining optimal receptivity to its services, and to those of other subsidiaries of Eloi Enterprises, primarily on reality-based perceptual levels ... research is also ongoing on other integrated perceptual levels, both reality-based as well as including traditional virtual settings, in order to establish services better adapted to clientele on an individual basis ...

All that sounded perfectly logical, but there was something about the phrasing, especially the term "reality-based." It could have been badly written, but I didn't think so. The way I read it was that Classic Research was up to something, and they had to at least use broad weasel words so that when it came out they could claim it was in their registration, since ongoing registrations were also considered as updates and modifications to the original charter granted by the city sisters. And the city sisters didn't care so much what the corpentities did, but they cared a great deal about businesses misrepresenting what they did.

I turned the pages to the financials.

Abruptly, the figure of a woman appeared from the page, less than a yard high, yet somehow towering over me, in that fashion possible only in virtual settings. She was one of the Virgines Vestales. Although she was empty-handed, blue-green rays radiated from the extended fingers of her right hand. "Access here is restricted." Initially, her fingers were too bright to look at directly, even on the sysnet.

I clicked in vision control. That compromise was unsatisfactory. Toning down the glare left everything else too dark to discern. That suggested the glare had another purpose. I tried programming in polarization. Some freqs made the glare worse, but one combination almost eliminated it.

There was a keyhole in the middle of the locket on her right wrist.

Before I did more, I rummaged back through all the old city codes, then asked Max for a pattern—how lock codes tied to entity names. He came up with three.

The second one worked.

Like that, I had the financials up before me. I copied them almost without scanning them. It wouldn't be long before something negative happened. Fast as my systems were, they weren't finished with the copying before a line of fire slammed through the back of my brain. My virtual brain.

SYSTEM ALERT! A siren screeched. It wasn't a Civitas alarm, but mine.

Home. Full defense!

I didn't leave the chair, not with all the links. I scanned all my systems and defenses.

The villa was isolated. The attackers had boosted energy inputs on all the civic power lines and commlinks. Max, as programmed, had severed the links. For most villas, that would have dropped them into a standby status—or at most onto stored power, solar inputs, or fuel cells. But most didn't have solar panels and fuel cells adequate for full functioning. The taxes on "excessive" independent power were designed to keep all but the very wealthiest from building self-sufficient strongholds—or those of us who had sacrificed luxury for independence. Then, too, I'd found creative ways around the law—such as two inefficient, but powerful Varian generators that weren't listed as an independent power system in the Tax Code. I also had two separate fortified underground entrances/exits not on the plans filed with the Civitas Sorores, a definite violation of the Codex.

Interrogative power status? I pulsed Max.

Alternative power sufficient to maintain all defenses.

Interrogative attacks?

Null this time. Energy concentrations built on Civitas power feed. Bypass of restrictors on main system in place.

That meant someone had played with the external power feeds. Once my system "thought" the crisis was past and attempted to resume normal operation, the energy surge that followed was designed to overwhelm my secondaries, and that would allow dataworms, viruses, and general mayhem into all my systems. My secondaries were stronger than that, but the surge could cause more unnecessary damage. *Interrogative mobile repair module?*

Sensors have detected probable clone operatives with high-explosive delivery systems.

Clones or cydroids with grenade launchers—all three illegal in Thurene or anywhere on Devanta. That almost certainly pointed to Eloi Enterprises. Could I drag in someone else? It was worth the effort.

Call for a special limousine. Promise maximum emergency fees.

Landlines have been severed and an electroshield projected around the villa walls, replied Max.

Are the operatives inside the shield?

Affirmative.

The operatives were disposable. Illegal clones. That meant Legaar—or their creator—wanted to push me into doing my own dirty work. Or Max. Anything I did would all be recorded and documented, with a civil and possible criminal complaint to follow. There wouldn't be any direct evidence of the electroshield, either.

I ran through the analyses of the attack. It was all AI response.

Did Eloi or Maraniss have sublinks and portals into all of Civitas Sorores? Even if Eloi had trap warnings and AI response just on the official records for Eloi Enterprises, that was a violation of Civic Codex. The only problem was that to reveal that, I'd have to confess to having violated the Codex as well. Legaar and his corpentity advocates had certainly thought that through.

*Project mobile repair module image toward initial sever-
ance point.*

I watched in my mental screens as an image of the mobile repair unit moved out of the utility space.

It was barely clear of the villa when the first grenade
came flying across the dead outer defenses of the wall. It
exploded satisfactorily, and Max projected external damage
to the module—twisted metal over the forward treads and a
rear skirt on the same side ripped clear. The holo projection
kept moving, if more slowly.

Two more grenades followed. One came from the northwest corner, behind the cherry orchard, my very small orchard, that was homage of sorts to one branch of my family,
a reminder that selling orchards led to little good, except
perhaps literature or drama. The other grenade came from
the northeast, more from the space between my wall and
Soror Celestina's. Many villas shared walls, but the previous occupant hadn't cared for the sister, nor she for him.
But then, I hadn't cared for him, either.

Both landed close enough to the projection that Max
turned the image into little more than scrap metal with treads.

Send another projection. Use evasive tactics.

The attack was AI-directed and clearly a response to my
snooping into the registry. I doubted the AI knew what exactly was inside the villa. I wanted the clones occupied
while I tried some of my new toys.

One was a nanite-burst englober, with an energy tracker.

I sent one toward the clone operative hidden between my
wall and that of Soror Celestina.

He/she/it never knew what happened. The englober projected a high-energy shield around the energy source of the
target, then disassembled a very small amount of ultra-ex.
Since the field held the energy within the shield—for less
than half a second—before the shield and miniature generator failed, everything englobed was reduced to very small
fragments. Unfortunately, as I discovered, looking at the
large gap in my wall and the section of the sister's behind,
the explosion created larger fragments beyond. It also

destroyed the electroshield, most probably carried by the operative.

Max took out the other operative, who suddenly stood exposed on the wall beyond the cherry trees. Nothing exotic. Just an instabile bullet fired from an old-fashioned slug thrower. No sense in using the new toys where Civitas surveillance could record them. The electroshield had covered the englober, but once the shield failed, the slug thrower was better.

Leave the mess for the Garda to observe.

Affirmative.

With broadband open again, I fired a report and complaint to the Garda.

They wouldn't be happy. They never were.

They didn't even bother with a virtie response. Instead, a patrol flitter dropped into my front courtyard in less than three minutes. That was most revealing—and disturbing.

The scans revealed a real patroller, if in nanite armorcloth, with shifting bodyshields. That was very bad.

I decided to walk out and meet him. It was better than allowing him or her inside.

The morning sky was a silvered blue-green. By even midmorning and especially by afternoon any place without climate control would be hot and muggy. I couldn't recall an autumn day as unreasonably hot. Maybe the sun's radiation had peaked, and the atmospheric service was having trouble with the orbital solar screens. I was sweating slightly by the time I walked down the stone steps to where he waited by the one-person flitter. His namestrip read JAVERR.

He didn't look at me. Not at first. He pretended casually to survey the damage—another gap in the upper section of the wall overlooking Soror Celestina's garden and a crater in Cuarta Calle outside my gates. I hadn't noticed that before. He pointedly overlooked the three areas of shattered paving tiles outside the utility entrance.

"You arrived quite quickly," I said pleasantly. "Thank you."

"I'm surprised that you filed a report, Seignior Donne.

Unauthorized use of ultra-ex within Thurene carries a heavy penalty. I trust you realize that."

"I'm quite aware of that, Patroller Javerr. However . . . I wasn't the one who employed the explosives. You might test the outer surfaces and the pavement outside my walls. I think you will find that the attack was directed at me."

"That is quite possible, but if you are found responsible, even as a target, for inciting the attack, there is the charge of complementary accomplicement."

The young patroller had clearly been briefed—and paid off—most likely by Legaar—in some fashion impossible to track. He'd also been told to use the letter of the law—or the Codex. So I'd been threatened in two fashions, one after the other, and all because I'd wanted to see the financial registry figures on Eloi Enterprises. The ones I'd copied only bore a passing resemblance to the actual figures. Of that, I was certain even before studying them. But that resemblance might be enough to give me a better idea of what Legaar was hiding.

Maybe it didn't have anything at all to do with Maraniss and Elysium, whatever and wherever Elysium might be. Maybe it was just a programmed response as well, warning anyone who got curious to leave Eloi Enterprises alone.

"I'm certain that whoever is behind the attack would enjoy that, but if you check the past records of the satellite surveillance monitors, they should show the slightest haziness that accompanies the use of an inward-directed electroshield."

"The feeds were disrupted, but we will check the original records, Seignior Donne. We always do, especially in your case. You've been known to follow the shadows, and that is where vanishments occur. The sisters are not pleased at unexplained disappearances."

"I've had nothing to do with anything like that."

"Not that has been proved. That is true. For now."

Another warning. Two, actually.

"I do appreciate your directness. Thank you." I smiled. I kept smiling until he was in his flitter and well on his way back to his Garda station.

THE ELYSIUM COMMISSION   55

Then I walked back into the villa. Unexplained disappearances? I'd never vanished anyone. Caused a death or two, yes. Were there so many disappearances that the Garda was looking for someone to pin them on? Why me?

Max, commission an independent lab to take samples from all the outer walls. Promise anything, but get them to authenticate the results and send a copy to the Garda. Three copies. One for our records. One to Officer Javerr, and one to Captain Shannon.

Yes, sir. Max was programmed for SpecOps salutations, to me, and to those who respected them, and to the customs of others, insofar as the system could determine them.

An analysis of the figures I'd copied was next. I couldn't exactly claim I'd stolen them. The "originals" were still in the registry, and were the city advocates or the Garda to charge me, I'd claim that I had nothing. I wouldn't by then. They'd look silly trying to claim that I'd breached their systems. Besides, if I'd wanted to have paid an advocate three times my fee, I could have gotten most of what I'd lifted under the Open Records Act. The problem was that it would have taken close to a year, and the process would have alerted Legaar Eloi and given him a year to target me before I could even find anything.

Less than a stan later, I had an answer . . . of sorts.

I'd had to compare Eloi's financials to the major pubs and the overall trade and commerce stats, but it was clear enough that Legaar was funding some sort of major research effort. Compared to pure tech operations, Classic Research had a similar level of expenditures, but why did Eloi need a pure research budget at all? For an entertainment corpentity?

Of course, no other source anywhere in the public domain had any information whatsoever on Classic Research. I was going to have to get very creative. And I'd have to survive while I was being creative.

10

*To believe without knowledge is to live
without thought.*

The problem was that, creative as I needed to be, I was having trouble thinking of exactly who had information and who might be willing to tell me anything about Legaar Eloi. Those who were willing didn't know what I needed to discover. Those who knew weren't about to talk if they valued their own survival, except for Odilia, and I would be seeing her—and the opera—on Vieren.

While I was wrestling with that, Max alerted me.

Incoming from Myndanori Morgan.

Accept.

"For a straight-straight who operates out of his own villa, you're a most difficult man to reach." She smiled generously, with wide and full lips. "She" was a nominal term, since Myndanori was somatically and physically female and genetically male. I wouldn't have known that, except she'd been a client where I'd had to know such things. She wore a jacket and trousers, navy blue, with a cream blouse, severely cut. That didn't disguise a figure that was the best that credits could engineer and purchase. Her carrot red hair was bobbed.

"I was originally trying to return your link," I pointed out. "You're the difficult one to pin down."

"Oh? Have you ever tried?"

I winced. Straight-straight, and a straight man to boot. "I'm returning your vid, returning mine, returning yours."

"You remain particularly well-mannered." The friendly

smile returned. "I'm having a few friends over next Sabaten evening. Not this one, but next week. I was hoping you'd join us. Either by yourself or with a friend."

"Most likely by myself."

"You're no longer . . ." Even that was pressing, but Myndanori usually did.

"Rokujo?" I laughed. "I refused to give up the villa for a more splendid palace with four interconnected villas. It wouldn't have been mine, and it was outside Thurene."

"You always have done things your way, Blaine."

"What can I say? A week from Sabaten? What hour?"

"Eight. I'm opposed to early."

That I knew.

"I also had a question for you."

She raised her perfect eyebrows.

"A Dr. Guillaume Richard Dyorr. You're in the medical field. What do you know about him?"

Myndanori frowned. Her eyes glazed slightly, with the expression that came to some people when they linked to their systems.

I waited.

"His list of pubs and studies is amazing for a doctor that young. He's head of consciousness studies and therapy at the Institute. You've got to be good even to get on staff there. He's obviously better than good."

"Do you know him?"

"I'm in gender ID and reinforcement. We've probably never been in the same room. I'm a psych theoretician, not a practicing medical doctor."

"I just wondered."

"You never wonder. What's the problem?"

"I've got word that he's a hidden samer who's proposed to a young woman—straight-straight. Family thinks he's not after her but her inheritance."

Myndanori winced. "Nasty business."

I understood what she meant. If it weren't true, it didn't help the doctor. If it were, it didn't help Marie Annette—or the Medical College of the Institute.

"You think it's true?" she asked.

"That's what I have to find out. And I need to find out without ruining people. Unless they deserve it."

"You'd better keep the knightly ideals in the shadows, dear man. They don't even cover expenses."

"Who would you suggest I talk to?"

"You could try Jaelysana Hurrtedo. Here's her code. She's an admin clerk for the Devantan Medservice Review Board. She knows the grime hidden in the deepest corners."

"What about the stuff that's hidden in brilliant light?" I laughed. "Will she talk to me?"

"You're charming enough that even a samer hardfem would talk. She might laugh, but she'd talk."

"I love you, too."

"Talk like that could get you in trouble, Blaine."

She was right about that as well.

"I'll link and tell her to expect you."

"Thanks. And I will be at your place next Sabaten."

"With all I've done for you, dear man, I would certainly hope so." Her smile held both good humor and restrained lechery. Sometimes, I wondered if I was hopelessly straight-straight, or just hopeless.

I decided not to tackle more on the Elysium commission until I talked to Odilia.

Over the next half stan, I read what looked to be the simplest of Dr. Dyorr's many short publications. If I understood it—and that was open to question—he was suggesting that human consciousness was the result of what I would have called sympathetic biological resonance with the quantum effects of the sub-brane interactions between dark energy and solid matter. At least, I thought that was the point. The study didn't go anywhere near that far. It just noted the resonance correspondence.

After I shook my head, I tried a vidlink to Jaelysana.

She took it, but with no background. That meant it was her personal link, but she was at work. She was a broad-shouldered woman, with a wide forehead, and large blue eyes that looked innocent under butch-cut blond hair.

"Seignior Donne. Myndanori said you'd link. You want to take me to café in a stan and a quarter?"

"I'd be delighted. If you can tell me where you are."

"Here's the map."

It flared onto my recessed screen, and I saved it.

"I'll meet you at Michaela's," she added.

In the end, I took my own groundcar. The Medical Service Board was located off Bizet to the northwest of the Boutique. The area was a mixture of small restaurants and shops at street level, with various unnamed commercial establishments above them. In practice, most of the upper-level space was consumed by systems, with a few handfuls of techs and infocessors, along with the directors and subdirectors who still had to meet and direct people. Some aspects of civilization still didn't virtie well. They probably never would.

The carpark was a long block from Michaela's. I still made it with ten minutes to spare.

The decor of Michaela's was meant to replicate an ancient old Earth cigarette factory, and there were bullfighting posters on the walls. Jaelysana already had a small table by the wall.

"You're no Don José," were Jaelysana's first words to me.

"I'd hope not. Like a lot of people, I'm trying to do a job." I used the pop-up holo menu to order an earlgrey. Jaelysana was already sipping a tall dark café that blended cinnamon and chocolate and who knew what else.

"Myndanori said you have some questions."

"They're the delicate kind. I'm trying to find out whether there's reason for rumors about a well-known doctor. I don't want to spread rumors by asking, but if the rumors are true, someone else could be hurt."

Jaelysana shook her head. "About half the docs in Thurene have rumors about them. Most aren't true."

"These are more personal. What have you heard about a Dr. Guillaume Richard Dyorr?"

"He's a fashion plate. In a restrained professional sense. Everyone respects him. He's never had a claim brought forward against him. He gets better results than anyone in function restoration."

A serving girl slipped my earlgrey onto the small circular table. The tannish crockery mug had two handles. I didn't want to speculate on what they might put in it that required both hands.

"He's very proper, then. Formal and slightly cool?"

She shook her head. "Formal, but friendly. Not an arthropod at all."

"Does he have many friends?" I sipped the tea. It was strong, black, and more bitter than I preferred.

"From what I've heard . . . I haven't heard that much, you know . . . he's friendly to everyone but not particularly close to anyone, except his fiancée."

"That's Marie . . ." I let the name drop.

"Dr. Tozzi. She's a surgical resident."

That was interesting. Great-grandmother Tozzi hadn't mentioned that Marie Annette was already a doctor. As a resident, she was also a student of sorts, but most people would have noted she was a doctor. Noted with pride.

"Is she good? As a surgeon?"

"She can't be bad. They only take the best."

"But it's hard to tell from outside when they're still residents exactly how good?"

She nodded.

"Are there people who are jealous of Dr. Dyorr's success?"

That brought a laugh. "When you've got academics and doctors in the same place, there's always jealousy. There's less with him. Some of the other doctors are jealous of Dr. Tozzi."

"Women?"

"No. The women don't seem to mind. It's some of the junior docs."

"Any names?"

She smiled. "That's not something I'd feel comfortable saying."

"I understand."

"The two most junior docs are in trauma surgery and endocrinology."

Jaelysana didn't care for either. That was clear.

"Is there anything else I should know?"

"I need to get back to work." She eased herself and the backless chair away from the table. "Just tell Myndanori she owes me."

"So do I. Thank you."

She stood. "I'll keep that in mind, Seignior Donne. Sometimes we all need a friend."

I rose as well, nodded, and let her leave. Then I paid for both café and tea and headed back to the carpark.

I needed to find a time and place where both doctors would be present . . . and where I could observe them. I also needed to find out more about two junior docs.

11

In whose darkless streets light blazes,
incandescent words drown phrases.

Beyond the high windows, the muted lights of the Left Bank outlined the river, yet the tower sitting room was cramped, or so it seemed, after the airy lightness of Elysium and the open expansiveness of Gaiea beyond my white city of the golden light. Coming back to Thurene, or anywhere on Devanta, was always hard, for there were too many narrow-minded aristos whose idea of greatness was anticipating the next fashion trend and sculpting themselves into it.

Even the brilliant ones like Eleyna had succumbed in the end, and her daughter, who could have done so much, had become a mere doyenne of display, a manipulator of men, and a sycophant of the Sorores. The Institute had become ever more rigid and doctrinaire, so much so that even its brightest graduates were little more than semi-independent cydroids, good for little more than suggesting minor improvements and writing enormous studies with involuted equations proving the ultimate anthropic principle—that we all lived in the best of all possible universes. Even as they toiled over such trash, they believed that they were being candid and not just providing a gloss upon the forbidden fruit of knowledge, which they had plated so heavily with words and studies that it was neither edible nor understandable.

I could offer back the garden, and yet no one could see beyond the Writ of Wrightsen, the almost-but-not-quite perfect Theory of Everything. No one wanted to admit that the

Sage of Sangloria had stubbed his toe on the hidden branes of the multiverse.

The single sheet lay on the side table. I didn't need to read the hard-copy lines again. Those who needed such repetition were mentally and morally deficient, not to mention intellectually indolent.

> The Fox has been reincarnated. The Shadow Knight has been engaged. Remain on Devanta and use your abilities. You're welcome at Time's End, and that would put you closer to matters.

Closer to matters? More like under Legaar's ever-constant scrutiny. Yet the offer was tempting, if only for the privacy and the greater ease of departing for Gaiea once what the Elois thought was a crisis had passed. What mattered if a broken and regened special operative might be investigating? There was nothing to find, not anywhere that he could penetrate. That was just one of the beauties of it all. Even Legaar didn't understand, and he wouldn't, not until it was far, far, too late, and then the Frankans and the Assembly bureaucrats could blame each other. It might even be interesting to see whether hostilities got to the point where the Alliance and the Assembly discharged their energies in more than verbal virtuosity and insidious intrigue. Or if the Assembly forced a reformulation upon the Civitas Sorores.

Time's End—at least the view would be better, and my position would be best there, especially since Legaar would suspect less, having made the suggestion himself.

To purchase the temporal space I needed might require a slight bending of the mirror of Chronos to locate and neutralize the so-called shadow, not that he would cast such for long. That would not be difficult, and would be far easier from Time's End, since I could draw on the estate's power grid.

More than two "woulds" diverged from the path I traveled, and the one that I'd not taken could not but make the difference, and the shadow would not know. How could he?

12

I finished up the emendations to my personal civic business registration early on Vieren and sent it off to the Civitas Sorores registry, along with the requisite fee. After my obligatory workout, of course. And after a thorough physical and virtie check to assure myself that Max and all systems were back in full operating order. I also checked my emergency bolt-holes. Then I made the round of returning messages. I always started with those from individuals with whom I did not particularly desire to talk. That way, I missed talking to some of them personally, and I dispensed early with the unpleasantness of those who did take my vids.

I started with Antonio diVeau. He wasn't personally available.

His talking head was. "Hello, there, Blaine." Following the words came a warm smile, the kind I associated with sales types and persuaders. "I hope you got my message about a cataract ride in Pays du Sud in Novem . . ."

"I certainly did, Tony, and I appreciate your thinking of me, but I'm deep in several commissions that may last until the first of the year . . ."

Next came a reply to Garda Officer Javerr. Unfortunately, he was in.

"Oh, Seignior Donne. I was hoping you'd get back to me." His smile was as warm as the ice that fed the cataracts that Tony wanted to ride. "We never could reclaim the images from the satellite feeds the other day." He paused. "We did get the results from Independent Forensics. They're not the preferred form of evidence, Seignior Donne."

I nodded politely, waiting.

"In the absence of other evidence, however, Captain Shannon has decided that they will suffice to prove that you did not use ultra-ex and acted in self-defense."

Javerr had made it clear. Shannon had overruled him, but Javerr was still after me on any legality he could find. He wanted me to know that. "Thank you very much for letting me know, Officer Javerr. I appreciate it."

"We do our very best to let people know where they stand, Seignior Donne."

"That I appreciate. After all, at times, it's best to let the tiger turn tail."

"Only in the name of the Empress of Time, Seignior."

We nodded to each other, and he broke the link. He was definitely not a better man than I, water boy for the Elois that he was.

Next came a return of a message to Selenthat Schweitzer, who had shamelessly wanted to sell me a series of antique bound books by various unknown authors, such as Jordan Roberts and Hart Davidwell. I'd never heard of either, although Schweitzer assured me that they were both amusing, if dated. I would have bought a D. D. Fratz, if only for personal pleasure in seeing the illogic and lack of understanding of social and technical interaction as influenced by technology. He didn't have one, and I demurred on buying anything else.

I'd just finished regretting my inability to attend the Ars Lyrica Musica benefit for musically dyslexic children when Max pulsed me.

Captain Shannon, incoming.

The projected image that hung in the air across the table desk from me was unembellished. Piercing blue eyes fixed on me. They dominated a square face with thick black eyebrows and a strong, jutting jaw.

"Colonel . . ."

"What are you up to, now, Donne?" Shannon had been SpecOps, except he'd stayed in long enough for a stipend and left as a colonel. He saw the Garda as a far less dangerous way of keeping his hand in, even with the nominally lower rank.

"I wish I knew, Colonel. I took a simple contract for some research, and I've taken one virtie and two physical assaults in three days."

He snorted. "Word is that you're poking around where you shouldn't. It's not a good time for that. Vanishments and disappearances are up."

I'd heard that on the news. The numbers were not that large and of the type of individuals society did not usually miss. The sisters didn't like even those types vanishing without a trace. That was the sort of thing that the Assembly of Worlds frowned upon. If there were too many, reformulation often followed. No one in their right mind wanted that. Restructuring planetary governments was messy. "There's always someone who's not doing what they should and doesn't want it known."

His expression softened—from adamantine to merely sandstone. "That's true enough, but it doesn't matter if you don't live to get the word out."

In short, I translated, you're mostly on your own. Shannon would try to keep the Garda impartial, but his success in even that would be questionable. "I'm just looking, Colonel."

He shook his head. "Wasn't that what you were doing when the Frankans nailed you on Pournelle II?"

He was right, but who would have thought that they'd have mounted a full particle beam array on a planet that was mostly a chunk of hot, hard rock? Or that they'd use it on a needleship when it revealed their position and resulted in their destruction? It verged on technological pornography— mounting and applying that much technology because they had it and could, not because it was appropriate—or even tactically necessary. That had been a lesson in human and military nature. I'd been bushwhacked and paid dearly for assuming the fundamentalist Frankans were rational in their use of force.

"I see your point, Colonel."

He nodded brusquely. "Have to go, Donne."

The projected image vanished, and I was looking across the study at the east windows. They were tinted at the moment to block the still-low morning sun.

I needed to follow up with the junior doctors. I also had get back to Lemel Jerome about the Classic group's possible infringing on his patent, although I couldn't imagine what any subsidiary of Eloi Enterprises would need with something like quark regression, whatever that exactly entailed. Maybe Lemmy knew something about Legaar Eloi.

I triggered the vid codes and waited.

A talking head appeared. It wasn't a version of Lemmy, but that of a mature and attractive woman. "Might I announce you and the reason for your inquiry?"

"Blaine Donne for Lemel Jerome. I'm returning his vid."

The woman's image faded. It was slowly replaced by that of a thin-faced man, with lank black hair half-falling across a slightly bulging domed forehead. His eyes were brown and intense.

"You took your time, Blaine."

"You take yours when it comes to paying for services, Lemmy."

"Let's not argue, Blaine."

Who was arguing? He stated a fact. It was true. I stated a fact. It was also true. "What do you want me to do? I'm not a patent infringement advocate."

"I know that. You know I know that. I need proof that they're infringing before I can act, but I don't need an advocate. Besides being an inventor, I'm also an advocate, you might recall."

How could I have forgotten? I waited.

"I need proof," Lemel repeated. "I'll pay your exorbitant rates to get it."

"What kind of proof? Which Classic subsidiary do you think is infringing on your patent?"

"Classic Research, of course."

"The whole Eloi Enterprise group is into entertainment, Lemmy. Your patent deals with hard science and technology. What does entertainment have to do with that?"

"I don't know. What I do know is that they've ordered all the components to duplicate my patent. They aren't paying royalties or seeking a license, either."

"Was this quark-electron regression holo recording and display business?"

"No. They agreed to that. I just misplaced the information on that. No . . . this is something different, and I have better indications on it."

How he discovered things like that I'd never known, but he'd always been right before. If after a few false starts. "All right. What does your device do?"

"What I designed it to do."

I was the one to sigh. "I'm a consultant in finding and discovering and resolving things. It helps to know what they do."

"There's no simple answer. It's an oversimplification, but it measures the deformation of space in certain circumstances which allows greater precision for jumpship transit choices."

"Is that all it does?"

Lemmy shrugged. "It might do more, and there might be other applications, but that was what L'Etoile Transport needed. It reduced energy costs by almost twenty percent. I don't invent what's not commercial. But that's not the point. Even if they're using it for something else, they still need to pay for it. It's still infringement."

Great. He had a device used on jumpships that was possibly being used for something else by Classic Research, and I was supposed to come up with some sort of proof.

"Blaine?"

"I was just thinking. How exactly can I even determine something like this?"

"If you'll take the assignment, I'll send you a small detector. If they're actually using my system, it will record and authenticate the use."

"You don't need me, then."

"There are reasons I do. First, how impartial am I? Second, you're better at running down locations than I am. Third, I can't invent if I'm spending all my time tracking down infringements."

"And fourth," I pointed out, "you make more credits inventing than chasing those infringements. Or this one, anyway."

"Precisely. Don't go over ten hours without reporting to me."

"I won't. Now . . . what do you know about Legaar Eloi?"

Lemmy frowned. "I don't know anything. I've never even met him."

His response rang true . . . unfortunately. "You don't know anyone in the Classic group?"

He shook his head.

"I just wondered."

"I need to go."

After he broke the link, I leaned back, but I didn't have much time to think about the implications.

Incoming from Civitas, Max informed me. *Undercode unknown.*

Full defenses. I couldn't afford not to answer a valid Civitas inquiry or communication, but after all the inquiries and research, an unknown undercode suggested yet another branch of Civitas or an attacker using a Civitas cover. Neither possibility was good.

I triggered the acceptance.

The first image was that of Soror Prima, serene-faced, her gray eyes seemingly fixed on me. Then the image swirled into a spray of color.

I closed my eyes—but a moment too late. I could see nothing, and knives of fire lanced through my skull. I could sense energy flaring everywhere before Max and the secondaries shut down everything.

Max, interrogative status?

Full power on backups. No penetration, and all systems are clean. Forty-three percent of the cutouts will need to be replaced. External channels limited.

Not only was I close to retinal burns, with hypersonic shock, but more of my equipment was shot. Someone was making it very costly for me, and all I'd done was accept two recon jobs dealing with Eloi Enterprises and sneak a peak at the corpentity's pseudofinancials. Before long, I was going to get more than a little redded-off.

Interrogative physical security? Even that inquiry gave me a headache.

Physical security has been maintained, sir.

Keep it that way.

Max would, in any case. The headache, the watering eyes, and the high-pitched whining in my ears had frayed my normally good disposition.

In less than ten minutes, Max had some comm back up. He was good. He should have been. He'd cost me a lot.

Eight minutes later, Myndanori was in-linking.

"Blaine . . . how did your visit with Jaelysana go?"

My eyesight was intermittently blurry, but I could make her out. She smiled when she saw my image, but only for a moment. "Blaine . . . you've looked better, dear man."

"I think I have. It's been an interesting morning. Oh . . . Jaelysana. She was helpful, but only in telling me what I didn't want to hear but probably needed to know."

"He seems clean down to the nanetic level. I've done a few inquiries of my own. The good doctor has made quite a name for himself. He's working behind the scenes to create a Center for the Study of Consciousness at the Institute. He *seems* very ethical."

"I notice a slight emphasis there."

Myndanori smiled. "I can't find a thing. That's what bothers me. There are no former lady friends, or men friends. There are no rumors. I even have to ask where you heard the rumor about the kept man."

I shrugged. "Jaelysana said the same thing. All Dyorr does is work at the Medical College. He's always where he should be, and when he's not, he's doing a good deed of some sort."

"He even waited until his fiancée had her degree before professing interest. You'll have to be very indirect here."

"I'm getting that impression. Oh, do you know anything about two other doctors? William Ruckless and Theodore Elsen?"

"Never heard of Ruckless. Elsen is an endocrinology resident. He's a samer. They say he's brilliant, but has an adiamante pump instead of a heart. Other than that . . . nothing."

"Jaelysana hinted that he was jealous of Dyorr."

Myndanori sniffed. "Most other physicians would be. Dyorr can charm people. All Ted Elsen can do is freeze them. If he hadn't discovered the glandular override cycle, he'd be in private practice in a west coast fishing village."

Myndanori had known more than she'd admitted. "He's hard on lovers, too?"

"I doubt he's had any recently."

Myndanori didn't have that much more to say.

Once she delinked, I studied the information the system had dredged up on doctors Ruckless and Elsen. Ruckless had been a fair-haired type in medical school at Vannes, and had some pubs to his credit, but there wasn't much there. From the record, it looked like he was the type to perform quietly, speak in vague generalities, emphasize professional ethics, and try to keep the waters calm. Elsen had a short stack of pubs—an impressive number for a junior doc on the faculty of the Medical College. Other than that, there was nothing.

I ignored all incoming vids and kept looking.

I did discover that Dyorr was giving a presentation to the Devantan Humanitas Foundation on the coming Miercen. The presentation was restricted to board members and their guests.

I used the vidlink code provided by Seldara Tozzi. I got a green screen and her voice.

"Please leave a message."

"This is Blaine Donne. I'd like to be present at Dr. Dyorr's presentation to the Humanitas Foundation on Miercen. I'm assuming that you could obtain a pass for me as a guest or an observer. Thank you."

Then I went back to look up some technical background on Lemmy's problem.

I was refreshing my very basic knowledge of jumpship generators and their commercial impact when Max sent an alert.

Incoming from Seldara Tozzi.

Accept.

The principessa wore deep maroon trousers and a matching vest, with a pleated white blouse. "Seignior Donne, I presume you have some reason for your request?"

"My reason is simple. I need to see Dr. Dyorr, and I also may need an entrée that seems rational. Seeing him give the presentation offers both."

"What rationale do you suggest I offer?"

With her wealth, I doubted she needed to provide any reason whatsoever. "You're known as a woman who is cautious with credits. That's one reason. The second, to be provided to your great-granddaughter, if necessary, is that, given her closeness to Dr. Dyorr, you wanted an independent assessment of his proposal."

A faint smile crossed her lips. "You will provide such?"

"I'll send you a short assessment, both onsystem and in hard copy."

"I am most certain I will find it interesting."

That meant it had better be good.

Seigniora Tozzi's smile vanished. "I will arrange your inclusion as a consultant observer."

"Thank you."

She didn't say more. The holo just collapsed.

I still didn't get all that much done for the rest of the day, except some technical briefing on Lemmy's problem, and that was hard enough given my burning eyes and pain-stabbed skull. It was almost afternoon five hour before the headache subsided, and I could see normally.

Lemmy's detector arrived by secure courier at that point. It wasn't much bigger than a stylus and looked like one. I tested it.

Interrogative test? I pulse-linked.

No emissions within two klicks, it replied.

Max . . . interrogative any other freqs or snoops?

That's negative, sir.

I left the device in a comm-blocked box that looked like a book on the library shelves in my study. I also gave Max instructions to monitor it.

I took my time getting ready for the evening with Odilia. I wore my version of an ancient dinner jacket and trousers—both were black and tailored more snugly than had once been the case. My cummerbund was dark brilliant silver, as was the bow tie, and the pleated shirt was pale silver. I wouldn't stoop to the ruffled shirts affected by some of the younger flashes. Or whatever was in vogue now. Ruffles were doubtless out. I hadn't been to a high social occasion in several months. Regardless, I'd certainly be out of style. That wouldn't disappoint Odilia. She expected my conservatism of appearance.

Then I made my way to the study, where I checked messages while I waited for my transportation. There were only a few recent messages—one from Krij asking to confirm that I had indeed filed an emended registry, one from Tony diVeau asking me to reconsider, and one from a Donacyr D'Azouza, requesting I return the vid at my convenience to discuss whether my services would be useful in resolving a particular problem.

The first I answered, to Krij's talking head, in the affirmative. The second I ignored, and the third I deferred. I'd get to it the next morning.

I left the study and headed across the entry foyer and down to the waiting limousine. I had originally arranged for a small special limousine to take me from the villa to Odilia's palacio, but after the day's events, I upgraded it to full-sized, both outbound and on the return. Even given what had happened so far, I'd be relatively safe at the opera—especially with Odilia. Afterward was another matter.

When I arrived at the palacio, the virtie servitor escorted me past the Angkorian temple and to the small formal dining room. This time, Odilia was waiting for me.

I entered and bowed. "Princesse."

"You do look daringly conservative, Seignior." Odilia inclined her head, her lips parted ever so slightly. The blue of her long-sleeved and full velvet gown accentuated the seemingly virginal impression of her impressively narrow waist and small but definite bosom. Definitely a woman figure without fault.

"The better to set off your delicate beauty." I hadn't noticed how large and childlike her eyes were, nor how they showed a shade that could only have been called "innocent blue." Such subtle and effective enhancements were anything but inexpensive.

She half turned, a clear invitation for me to seat her at the table. It was set just for two, but with DiNormand china and Iskling crystal.

As I seated her, all my comms and links went blank. We were surrounded by the kind of privacy screen that usually only showed up in SpecOps high command. My screens at the villa were good, but not that good. Only the city sisters and the very rich could afford screens such as Odilia's.

I said nothing as I slipped into the chair across from her.

"Here are the ground rules, Blaine." The smile was virginal. The eyes above it were not. "While we eat, I'll tell you what I know. You tell me what you know and what you'd like to find out. I'll tell you how far I'll go. After we leave the table, no business, no contracts. I've asked for the pleasure of your company for the evening, and I'd like to enjoy it."

"Agreed." I wasn't surprised. Behind the facade she had the same cupridium-hard mind as her mother Eleyna had had. But there was more than that to Odilia.

"That's one of the things I like about you the most. You're a realist, even if you have a core that's too idealistic for long-term survival in Thurene." She lifted her goblet. "To the evening ahead."

"To the evening ahead."

We sipped. That first wine was so white it was colorless, so smooth that it cut my throat like a razor, leaving the barest hint of lavender and mint-basil behind.

"Do you know why Legaar Eloi is so defensive about his operations?" I began.

"I would imagine that is because his success is based on so many little things. Everyone knows the basics of what he does. Anyone could copy those. Many have, and they all have failed, and not because Legaar has used force against them." Odilia smiled politely. "You are a danger to him. You, of all those who might investigate and research him, have the understanding and wit to discern what those small aspects underlying his success might be."

That might be true, but my understanding of such aspects didn't mean that my clients could ever replicate them. "Do you think that might be why he's agreed to back Judeon Maraniss?"

Odilia took another sip of wine before replying, then waited as an androgynous server placed a small plate before her, a similar one before me, and stepped back outside the privacy screen. "Legaar is successful because he will ally himself with anyone at the most advantageous moment, then leave or dispose of them as soon as practicable."

"What does Maraniss have that Legaar wants?"

"I don't know, except that it must be valuable." She picked up the delicate two-pronged silver fork. "Exceedingly valuable or something that will make Legaar more powerful."

On the small platter was a tiny bird's nest, except it had been infused with Berrigan Brothers honey, and within the nest were three leaves of Constantine Basil. No one had ever been able to describe why that honey, produced by special bees allowed access only to particular flowers, made all others seem either hypocritically sweet or suffused with a bitter aftertaste. When it came to natural organics, even after millennia, the synthesists and nanoformulators still couldn't replicate food well enough that a trained palate could not tell the difference.

I ate slowly, carefully, enjoying the tastes, before finally speaking again. "Maraniss must have some system that Legaar can exploit."

"If it were just a system, he'd merely steal it. Maraniss has something unique. No, I don't know what it is."

I misquoted one of the old standards:

"Elysium, heaven I know not where,
except with you, any isle is bliss and fair . . ."

Watching Odilia, I could catch no trace of a reaction to the word "Elysium," not a single one, and my enhancements were still among the best.

"You should have been a bard, Blaine."

"I'm adequate with words, and very inadequate with music. What do you know about Maraniss that you haven't told me?"

"I did invite him to a ball here last winter. He's good-looking, but his eyes are too blue. He dances well, but he doesn't converse well, except when he's talking about how cities and societies are structured. Aurelia didn't care for him. She said he just wanted to use women." Odilia laughed.

I didn't know Aurelia. "As if both men and women don't want to use each other?" I asked gently.

"You're a realist, Blaine. Behind their hard facades, most men are romantics. Those who aren't are usually hidden psychopaths."

"Like Legaar?"

"He makes the average darkside psychopath seem helpful and friendly."

"Have you ever had to deal with him?"

"Only when we were both on the Medical Research Board. All he was interested in was the nature of the research and to what commercial ends it could be turned. How it impacted people didn't seem to interest or affect him at all."

Coming from Odilia, who had been known to use a few people along the way, that was a total condemnation.

"Speaking of medicine, do you know anything about Dr. Guillaume Richard Dyorr?"

"The consciousness specialist? I've met him once or twice. Why?"

"I've been asked about him. What's he like?"

"I don't know. He's friendly, in an impartial way. He's brilliant, but doesn't flaunt it. He's not obviously a flaming straight or samer." She shrugged. "He wasn't the sort of person I'd be interested in. He seems more immersed in his work even than you."

"What about your neighbor's great-granddaughter—Dr. Marie Annette Tozzi?"

"Didn't I mention her before?"

"Only that she was the only one worth anything."

"I've scarcely seen more of her than of Dyorr. Marie's like her great-grandmother, I think. Charming on the surface, unyielding beyond that, and whatever her private desires are, no one will never know, even any lover she may have."

"She's engaged—or about to be—to Dyorr."

"From what I've seen, they'd make a good couple. Neither's excessively jealous, and they're both consumed by their profession."

At that moment, the servitor appeared and removed the first course, replacing it with the pisces argentia, lightly poached in cyanth. Their delicate scales still radiated all the lights of the visible spectrum. Each small mouthful set off a cascade of pinlike pricks of anise and dorium across my palate.

"Can Maraniss survive dealing with Legaar?" I'd learned all I was likely to about Dyorr and Tozzi.

"They're well suited to each other. Maraniss seems to see people as mobile pieces in a puzzle, and Legaar views them as disposable tools."

"You make them sound so charming. Do they have any redeeming qualities?"

"Their absence from any gathering is their best quality."

"Does anyone like them?"

"I wouldn't know who. Why do you think Legaar started Classic Images? He has a few of the women conditioned to respond to him. He never tells them that before they're biosculpted. The older ones don't tell the new ones because, that way, he spends less time with them. He's probably got a full-clone operation at his Time's End estate."

My initial impressions of Legaar Eloi weren't getting any better. "And you think Maraniss is nearly as bad?"

"He might be worse if he had the wealth and power Legaar has."

"Neither one has a listed residence."

"Legaar has the entire top floor of his Pier One building here in Thurene. It's well over a thousand square meters. That's in addition to Time's End. It's at the foot of the Nordmonts, and he calls it a small place, but it's ten klicks on a side. Part of it is where the restricted Classic Research lab is."

"And Maraniss?"

"Even I don't know where he hides." She stopped speaking and gestured for the servitor.

The next course was salad—mixed ferns from lower Tropianga, with crushed chazarian nuts and a drizzle of extra virgin olivepalm oil. I could tell that Odilia was emphasizing virginal themes even in the dinner.

After several bites, I persevered. "Have you ever been to Legaar's estate?"

"I had to go once. A benefit. He'd ushered away all the nymphs." She smiled politely. "His security is tighter than around the IS jumpport. More than a few flitters have been downed out there. All the deaths have been attributed to pilot error."

All that was interesting because none of it happened to be in any database I knew. I might be able to verify what she'd told me now that I knew. That's the way it often goes. "The pilots made an error in coming too close to his estate?"

"More or less." She smiled again, this time a hard bright expression. "Who's paying you to look into Legaar? Whatever it is, dearest Blaine, it isn't enough."

"It never is."

"You didn't say."

"I don't know. The client used a pseudofront and shielded ID. Made a direct credit transfer. They wanted to know the link between Maraniss and Legaar Eloi. Business has been slow. It sounded interesting."

"Suicide is interesting, but I don't recommend it."

"Who would want that connection exposed, whatever it is?"

"About half the aristos in Thurene, so long as it was embarrassing and would reduce Legaar's power and wealth, and so long as they weren't revealed."

That wasn't exactly a help. "Who most of all?"

"How deep is the ocean? How high the sky?"

With her questions came the servitor with the main course—Agneau de la Reine. Each rack of lamb had been steeped for days in a mint brandy marinade, then grilled so that the outside was not quite black, the inside warm bright pink. With the lamb was a choice of a blackberry mint or a lime rosemary sauce. Crisp green beans almondine circled the rack on the platter before me, each almond slivered precisely and butter-toasted golden. The next wine was a cabernet-merlot, Falconcrest Reserve.

I enjoyed the lamb and wine for a time before speaking. "I would have thought you, of all souls, dear Odilia, would have known more about the infamous Eloi brothers."

She raised her left eyebrow a millimeter. "When the evening is over, Blaine dear, you will know all that I can tell you."

If that weren't an ambiguous statement, I hadn't ever heard one. "In the meantime, what else can you tell me?"

"I understand that Judeon Maraniss likes black-eyed women in black. Legaar likes a greater variety. Interestingly enough, both prefer them teasingly subservient—at least in public."

I didn't believe the disclaimer in the last four words at all.

"Do they have partners or children?"

"Maraniss doesn't. Legaar had a wife years back. She obediently provided two sons, then departed. She lives in the Lamia system, well provided for."

"And the sons?"

"Legaar sent them off to school. I don't know where. I doubt anyone living on Devanta does, either."

Effectively, that was the end of what I learned at the table.

Dessert was a simple crème brûlée, accompanied by a pale amber dessert wine, Toad Hall Reserve. I doubted Odilia served anything that wasn't at least a reserve.

I took a bite of the crème brûlée. Flavor that was part pure vanilla and part cinnamon almost filled my senses, rich without being heavy, light without losing substance.

When we had finished, I looked to my hostess. "An exquisite dinner, Odilia. Truly enjoyable."

"Thank you." She rose from her chair, lifting the other eyebrow, less than a millimeter.

I understood. No more questions about the Elois and Maraniss. I knew a bit more, but not nearly what I'd hoped. Still, finding out anything when so much in Thurene was hidden in plain sight—and still invisible—was useful. Just not useful enough.

"I'll rejoin you in a moment," Odilia said. "You know where the guest facilities are."

I did. I used them, then waited for her.

We walked quietly to the portico, where a pale gold limousine waited. It was large enough to carry eight in the two semicircular couches of black permavelt in the rear compartment, and armored and shielded heavily enough to have held a combat groundcar to a draw. We sat across from each other, but at the far end, so that our knees almost touched.

"I've heard that Carreres Domingo is absolutely marvelous as Saturnus," she said as we were carried out though the cupridium gates.

"I've only seen *Hyperion* twice before, once with Kherrl Mylnes and once with Mykelj Farinelli."

"Which did you prefer?"

"Farinelli was better on the top, but he minced the role. Mylnes *was* Saturnus, but that's because he takes himself so seriously all the time anyway."

Odilia laughed. "It's best you don't write consulting reports on the opera."

I agreed with that.

"I would judge that Domingo has Farinelli's top and Mylnes's gravitas."

That might be worth seeing . . . and hearing.

Before long, the limousine pulled up at the entrance outside the upper entry foyer, used only by those who had boxes in the royaux row. A footman dressed as one of Apollo's minions held the door as we exited. I was of less import and status. I went first.

Those waiting inside the foyer looked at Odilia without seeming to. A few looked in my direction, less circumspectly. Two men stared.

"They're jealous, dear Blaine. Don't mind them."

I didn't.

Odilia steered us toward a blond woman in a clinging pale seafoam dress. While the garment covered everything from wrist to neck to ankle, it left little to the imagination. That was a waste of expensive fabric. Why use it like a surface coating? Paint would have done almost as well.

"Sephaniah, you look positively ravished," Odilia said in a honey-sweet voice. "I mean, ravishing. Have you met Blaine Donne?"

Sephaniah smiled at Odilia. "You always look so regal and distinguished. You certainly have managed to capture the look and spirit of the later Victoria, I mean, Victorian time frame." Sephaniah's blond hair was in long, perfect ringlets that curled forward across her shoulders and partly covered her almost nonexistent breasts, to which the seafoam fabric clung like a second skin, revealing every nuance. Clearly, the nymphet look was back. Rather, the nymphets-across-history look was back. Odilia was now merely a more conservative version of what Sephaniah flaunted.

The nymphet turned to me with a warm smile. "I'm pleased to meet you, Seignior Donne. You don't look like either the ancient poetic type or a searcher after truth in the shadows." Her hand almost touched my trousers, and my hip, not quite suggestively.

"I'm limited in both fields. Good poetry and truth are both difficult to discover," I replied.

"I doubt you're limited in areas where it matters most." She glanced toward Odilia. "Do enjoy the opera. It's said to be charmingly antiquarian." With a sidelong glance, she slipped away toward a tall and well-muscled gladiatorial type in black and gold. Maybe he was meant to be a god, but he looked more like a gladiator posing as one.

Odilia gave an amused laugh. "Sephaniah refuses to admit any intellect in public. She has a long listing of translations from lost languages, and she wrote the libretto for *Gilgamesh,* based on her own original translation from the Urdu or Sanskrit or whatever the clay tablets were written in. She also wrote the libretto for *The Lictor's Sword.* Have you ever met Laniel Greyspan? He's right over there."

"I know of him, but I've never had the pleasure." I turned slightly to see the angular figure talking to a shorter man and a woman who had clearly modeled herself after Titania. Greyspan had been the financial advisor to the city sisters for generations—and with his haggard face and thin gray hair, he looked it. He was one of the unfortunates for whom nanotech and telomeric therapy worked marginally. He'd had to rely on his own cloned organs to keep going. As his appearance revealed, that process had limits. He would reach them soon.

"Intellectually, it's a pleasure." Odilia left the rest unsaid.

She turned, and I stepped up to her side.

Out of the thousand plus in the opera house, there couldn't have been more than a dozen aristo women who did not look as though they were either nymphs, nymphets, or slightly older, and not more than twenty men who were not shaped in some semblance of youthful gods. My appearance was definitely on the older side. I hoped I didn't qualify as a satyr. I'd let a few wrinkles stay here and there, on the grounds that my various opponents and nameless enemies might underestimate me.

We walked across the foyer toward the middle, where Odilia had a private box, in the exact center of the royaux row. She extended her hand, and the door opened, keyed by her persona. I stepped forward and gestured for her to enter, since I could not actually open the faux goldenwood door. It closed behind me. I looked down. While I had been in other private boxes, I had not entered Odilia's before. The four seats directly behind the balcony rail were visible to the rest of the audience. That was where one sat to be seen. The second line was blurred from outside, but offered a clear view of the stage and the pit. That was where guests who wished to see the opera but not be seen sat. The two couches on the third level offered a restricted view of the stage, but were totally private.

Odilia eased down the steps toward the front, then gestured to the two seats in the middle of the first row. I seated her.

"Will anyone be joining us?" I had my doubts because there were only two programs laid out.

"*Hyperion* is very much a period piece these days, Blaine. Few in the Thurenen elite enjoy period pieces. They remind them too much of their mortality."

"You support the opera." I'd checked the program. Odilia was one of the larger donors. "Couldn't you change that?"

"I could, but a few period pieces are necessary. Contemporaneity for the sake of contemporaneity is even worse than senseless veneration of the past."

Was *Hyperion* senseless veneration of the past? It certainly was an ancient opera. At one time, I'd guess it had been considered futuristic, but it was merely derivative from one of the even more ancient poems written in proto-Anglo, which had been derived from even older myths. Not that either the story line or the music mattered, although I'd always been partial to the music. It, too, was derivative. Lamarque had evolved and improved melodies from someone called Lloyd-Veber, back before the collapse and Terran Diaspora.

When you get right down to it, everything anyone does is a pastiche based on the interaction of the past with present motives, civilization, and technology. I suppose it's always been that way.

The point of going to L'Opera was as much to be seen as

to see, to be heard as to hear. More than a few pairs of eyes strayed upward. Uncomfortable as it made me, I reminded myself that some visibility was necessary. It was a way to get clients. Not the only way, but easier than many, and far more pleasant. If I had to be visible, who better to be visible with than Princesse Odilia?

The murmurs died away as the first notes of the overture filled the theatre.

As the curtain rose, Saturnus sat under a glitter-tree, not exactly in a vale, and the notes came from the Naiad. "Far from the fiery noon, and eve's one star . . ."

I'd always liked those words, far better than the others mixed with them by time—the ones about the last day of life as we knew it and the carousing that followed.

Sitting beside Odilia, as the opera proceeded, I was aware of those lustful yet virginal pheromones she was exuding. Any normal male would have been, and in that respect I was very normal.

At the end of Act I, she turned and smiled at me. "There is a bottle of Angelique Blanche on ice on the sideboard. There are two goblets. If you would . . ."

"I would." I rose and bowed slightly to her.

Actually, there were two bottles of the Angelique on ice, but she had been right about the number of goblets.

When I turned, Odilia had reseated herself in the second row. I stepped down and extended the goblet to her, then sat down beside her.

I had a difficult—hard, really—time concentrating on Act II. Odilia's head was not quite on my shoulder, and I could feel and sense the palpable desire emanating from her. Yet she only looked at me in passing as she watched and listened to the conflict and desire on the stage below and before us, amplified by the lushness of the music.

We also finished the first bottle of Angelique. Rather, she finished most of it.

"Would you open the second bottle?" she asked after Act II.

"Of course."

She was on the couch when I turned after refilling her goblet. I knew what was coming, and I couldn't say that I was displeased. Anyone who says that pheromones boosting virginal lust is an oxymoron has no idea what they're talking about.

She took only one sip before setting the goblet aside and touching my cheek with those soft and slender fingers. The pheromones swept over me, and I was barely able to set down my own goblet before Odilia's arms went around me.

The world indeed lay before me like a land of dreams, and knowledgeable as we were about ignorant armies, still we filled that darkling plain with what certitude we could.

13

*One may describe experiences and events
in an absolutely factual fashion,
with concrete evidence to support that
description, and still lie.*

Odilia and I did manage to gather ourselves together before the applause at the finale died away. We actually looked presentable. I still was bemused at how easily she'd been able to shed all that faux-Victorian finery—and then redon it without looking disarrayed in the slightest. I felt disheveled and worse as we rode back to the palacio in her limousine.

I didn't love Odilia. I never would. She didn't love me, and never would. That might be because it is impossible to love and be wise. I have never been that wise, but we understood each other, and sometimes understanding and lust are an acceptable, if bittersweet, substitute for love. Why should we give all our bounty to the dead?

"Domingo wasn't as good as he has been," she said with a smile. "Or perhaps I was distracted."

"I believe the word is distracting, Princesse." I couldn't deny I had enjoyed the evening, and I was glad I hadn't been left loitering amid the sedge, hollow-eyed, where no birds sang.

When we reached the palacio, I walked her to the edge of the portico.

"Good evening, sweet knight of shadows." Odilia wrapped herself around me for a moment—and that was very out of character—providing a long and lingering kiss and some indiscreet fondling. As she stepped back, I realized she had slipped an envelope inside my cummerbund.

"I had a lovely evening, a truly lovely evening. Thank you." Her smile was seemingly without guile.

"Thank *you*."

Without another word, we parted. Sometimes, "good-byes" or "good nights" are redundant.

Her limousine had slipped away, but the full-sized special one I had engaged pulled up. My flashcode confirmed that it was my hire.

Once settled in the conveyance, I extracted the envelope. Inside was a miniature dataflat, and several printed sheets. I slipped the dataflat into my bodywallet, then leaned back, exhausted and involuntarily relaxed as I was, and began to read the sheets. I'd read halfway down the first when the limousine came to an abrupt halt.

"There's a wall . . . across the road." Drivers were supposed to be impassive. "Right across the end of Boudicca. It wasn't here fifteen minutes ago."

Walls didn't just get built across roads in minutes. Had the driver been suborned somehow?

I could feel a sudden pull, like a singularity beam focused just on me. Except such a beam would have been instantly fatal. I triggered the full nanoshield, just before a jolting twist ripped me out of the limousine and into swirling brilliant chaotic white. I closed my eyes, but they still burned. I could feel heat building around me, directed back at me by the shield.

Then the whiteness vanished, and I was falling. I didn't fall far, but the jolt, even inside the shield, was enough to immobilize me for a moment.

I dropped the nanoshield, but the relief wasn't that great. Even at eleven hour, under the stars of the Arm, I'd been dropped into a moist, almost junglelike environment. I was still on Devanta, because I caught a glimpse of the smoky red three-quarter disc of Bergerac in the east, but how could I have been moved and so quickly?

Not possible.

Sir? came the reply to my inadvertent comm.

Max, interrogative my location. Soonest.

Ten point three klicks at 326 degrees from Thurene city center.

That was close to the shielded IS installation above Glen Lake. The lake couldn't be that far . . . not with the humidity.

A whining rose behind me and grew into a shrill buzz.

I recognized it instantly. It wasn't a sound an operative ever forgot—nanogenetically modified Aswaran wasps. Nasty creatures. Near-immediate massive anaphylactic shock if they stung you. What were they doing outside of confinement? The entire swarm was almost on me when I triggered the shield again.

Frig! One was inside my jacket.

I contracted the shield, hoping to crush it—and that my shirt and undershirt and skin would protect me.

I sensed the crunch and eased the shield, enough to be able to move. I had to get clear of the swarm. I only had minutes before the shield cooked me, unless I went to partial porosity, and that would open me up to snipers. I headed downhill, toward where the locator said the lake was. It was off-limits, too.

The shield flared orange. I dropped to my knees. Someone—something—was firing at me. The particolaser had to have been a defense-response weapon. That meant I was inside the IS restricted area. *Double frig!*

I could sense even more heat building inside the shield, but partial porosity was definitely not an option. If I didn't get moving, I'd be out. I'd also exhaust my oxygen before long, even with the limited screen vibro-diffusion.

My systems had the lake at 143 degrees absolute at three hundred yards. I turned, centered myself, and started moving, trying to keep low, and out of sight line from the crystalline towers that held the response particolaser. I tried to keep an even pace. That delayed internal heat buildup.

The trees and vegetation ended a good forty yards from the water, and the low grass that sloped down to the lake was open to the towers and the laser. There was no help for it. I kept moving toward the water.

Another blast of light flared the shield and raised my temperature.

I jumped into the water. You don't dive when you don't know the depth, even within a shield, because if the shield hits anything hard, the shock still get transmitted. I went down, but only about a meter and a half before my shielded dress boots hit gooey mud.

Another blast struck shield and water, raising steam all around me. I lurched forward and tried an awkward surface dive. If I remained exposed, the tower laser would boil me alive. Underwater, there was no oxygen diffusion at all, and that was another problem, because the re-breather unit in my belt would only provide oxygen for a quarter stan. I'd already used some of that.

Still underwater, I cut off the nanoshield. I just hoped that the mechanism would stay dry. I didn't have much choice. If I left it on, I'd end up boiled in my own heat. The cool of the water around me was both a shock and refreshing. I kept swimming underwater. I hadn't had the water mods. Even if I had, I couldn't have kept them when I'd been retired.

I came up and took a quick breath, then dropped below the surface.

Light flared behind me, so close that I could feel the heat from the laser. I angled slightly to the right and kept swimming.

I finally managed to get to the overlook on the east side of the lake. It took a good quarter stan before I clambered out of the water.

Max . . . time check.

Eleven past eleven hour.

That was a only few minutes later than when I'd been sitting in the private limousine. How could that possibly be? I knew I'd spent a quarter stan swimming. I was soaked and tired.

I didn't have a chance to puzzle that over because a Garda flitter arrived and fixed me in its lights. Water was still dripping from my dinner jacket and trousers, and my boots were probably ruined.

"Walk toward the flitter. Keep your hands away from your body." The patroller's projected voice didn't sound like Javerr's. I was thankful for that.

"Stop."

My enhancements picked up all the sensors and remote probing. They didn't pick up anything, because there wasn't anything to detect. I'd gone to the opera, not out on an operation.

"Sensors confirm you are Blaine Donne, Fifty-One Cuarta Calle, Thurene."

"That's correct."

"Can you explain what you were doing in Glen Lake?"

"No, Officer. I cannot. You can verify that a few standard minutes ago I was in a limousine roughly at the intersection of Boudicca and Vallum. The next thing I knew I was at the edge of the lake on the far side with some very angry wasps chasing me. I ran into the water and swam here. I imagine that since the far side is an IS installation, that, if they choose, they can verify my appearance."

"How do you know that it's an IS installation?"

"I'm retired IS, Officer." I didn't mention the medically retired part.

"Glen Lake is a restricted water source. Bathing or swimming is forbidden."

"I understand that, Officer. I also know that even standing on the IS reservation is prohibited, and they have lasers. I just wanted to get away from there."

"I'll have to take you in, Seignior Donne."

The change in salutation was anything but good. He'd tapped into my dossier at the Garda.

The hatch behind the guidance section opened. The flitter was remote-operated. "Get into the flitter."

I did. The space was confined enough that my knees were tight against the bulkhead. The hatch closed, and the flitter lifted off. The flight back to the Garda station took less than five standard minutes. I spent the time gently easing the wasp carcass into a jacket pocket.

Within minutes of the time I stepped out of the flitter I was in an interrogation room across a table from an officer Donahew. The walls were a pale blue. That was a shade designed to relax. I didn't. There was a scarcely visible nanite shield between us.

"Swimming in reserved waters is an offense against the Codex, Seignior Donne." Donahew was stocky, dark-haired, and had pale green eyes. His voice was almost a bass.

"As I told you—or whoever was the RP on the flitter—that was the least dangerous alternative."

"Ah, yes." His lips curled into an amused smile. "We did check as you suggested. You were where you said you'd been when you said you'd been there. That raises a most interesting question. How did you manage to traverse ten klicks in a few minutes?"

"I told you. I don't know."

He consulted the miniature console I couldn't see. "Interesting."

I waited.

"For a space of five minutes a wall seemed to appear at the intersection of Boudicca and Vallum. What did you have to do with that?"

"The driver said it was there. Before I had a chance to look, I was on the IS reservation with wasps chasing me."

"That seems rather unlikely. Yet you're smart enough to know that we'd find it so. Why are you telling me that?"

"Because it's what happened, and if I tried to tell you what didn't happen, all those sensors focused on me would tell you that I was lying."

Donahew's smile grew broader. I didn't like the expression.

"Now how could someone—or how could you—hop out of that limo and get onto a flitterjet and reach the lake without registering on the satellite scans?"

"I don't know how any of it happened, Officer Donahew.

I only know that one minute I was in the limousine, and the next I was above the edge of the lake with wasps targeting me."

"Exactly what kind of wasps? Or do you know?"

"They sounded like Aswaran wasps."

"Nasty little creatures, but I haven't seen any in Thurene in years. They're interdicted, you know. I can't see as anyone would break the interdict just to have fun with a small-time regen spec-opper."

"You're absolutely right, Officer. Neither can I." I carefully eased the insect carcass out of the pocket of my damp jacket and onto the table. "This is one of them. I offer it to you."

Donahew looked at the insect and swallowed. His expression wasn't quite an old revolt from awe. More like disgust. The sensors refocused on the dead insect, playing over its black-and-red stripes, the shimmering, if now tattered, double wings, and the smooth long injector stinger.

"It *is* an Aswaran wasp." He shook his head. "That'll play Hades with the EPs." He paused, probably forwarding an alert to the environmental police. "You aren't exactly making this easier, Seignior Donne."

"I can't change what happened, Officer Donahew. Some windows are always broken when people play ugly Yahoo tricks."

He gave me an odd look, but then, it was an odd, if appropriate, old misquote.

"If I were the guessing type, Seignior Donne, I'd suspect that someone might be targeting you. You wouldn't care to speculate on that, now, would you?"

"Officer . . . I could speculate a great deal, but I have no idea who had the ability to carry me ten klicks without my even knowing how it happened." Donahew wasn't pressing me, not the way Javerr had, and yet he'd clearly accessed my Garda dossier. I wasn't about to ask why, but I made a mental note to keep that in mind.

In the end, Donahew sent me back to the villa in a Garda van—sealed. I'd still had to pay the fine—three thousand credits—for contaminating a public water source. The sisters have always frowned on that sort of thing, no matter what the reason. I did take the wasp carcass with me—in a case Donahew supplied after he entered the information into the files. He didn't want it anywhere around. That was also troubling.

Once I was inside my villa, I immediately went to my study and copied the dataflat's contents to a quarantined section of my systems, then stored the dataflat itself in the secure section below the study. I set Max to using the equipment on the lower level to dry and decipher what I hadn't read of the dossier Odilia had slipped me. I hoped he could do it. I had no idea if it were a summary or something new, and I was far too exhausted to try to make any sense of any of it until I got some sleep.

14

Selfless spirit glistens brightly whose selfish soul barters nightly.

Before the projection failed, I saw the shadow knight heading downhill toward the lake. He took one laserflash and kept moving. I knew Donne was fast, but he'd been wearing a full nanoshield and had it on even before the projection field had fully focused on him. I'd wanted to vanish him without a trace, but with the nanoshield in place I was rapidly losing control of the field, one of the inevitable consequences of attempting to focus the projection beam on a moving individual in a gravity well. Dropping a section of wall in front of his transport had reduced the motion vectors enough for the system to catch him initially. Even so, I'd had to precalculate the possible options, and trying to isolate a moving individual or locate one through defense screens verged on the impossible. That had meant using location B—dropping Donne into the nearby restricted area and the wasps onto him because they didn't take much power—and sending a coded alert through Legaar's system to the Garda. Javerr was reliable enough for that, and Shannon couldn't do much about it.

Donne might not even have made it to the lake. If he had, the various authorities would cause more difficulties for him, particularly explaining his movements and the presence of the wasps. Shadows can be stung.

In the darkness, I let myself out of my spaces in the laboratory and took the underground maglev back to the main estate complex. The entrance was hidden amid the statuary and the hedge maze below the pool, a mélange of the overendowed and overindulged in a setting of impeccable tastelessness. I could have walked around the overlarge pool, but at this time of evening, with no other real souls about, crossing the stone pavement was amusing.

A naked nymph with a perfect figure—in Legaar's estimation, at least—rose sinuously from a couch tucked inside a grotto just away from the pool itself. "Could I pleasure you, noble sir?" Blond hair with a tinge of green flowed over her shoulders.

"How would you pleasure me?"

"Any way you like, noble sir."

"Then lick my boots."

"As you wish, sir." Her voice remained sultry as she crouched to do as I had commanded. She moved her fundament suggestively, but not suggestively enough.

She licked the boots clean. "Is there anything else you wish?"

I thought about some variant on having her pleasure herself, but she didn't deserve anything that might cause her enjoyment. None of Legaar's nymphs did, but he'd conditioned them so any sexual encounter gave them pleasure.

"Hide in your grotto and defer your enjoyment until someone seeks you out."

That was an appropriate punishment for a wanton nymph, as well as a small frustration for Legaar, who enjoyed having his nymphs fawn over him. Besides, she was not Magdalena, who was serving her repentance, unlike this nymph who deserved no mercies, only dust and derision.

As she turned and retreated, I walked around the east end of the pool, constructed in the shape of an overlarge sycamore leaf, all too common on Devanta and anywhere else in the Assembly of Worlds—and even in the Frankan Alliance. Supposedly, Legaar had stipulated a maple leaf, extinct even on Old Earth, because of a distant ancestor, but the designer had come up with the sycamore. Legaar had the man biosculpted into a trollish dwarf of some sort, his intelligence burned out, and sent to Pelesian as a miner of red basalt.

As with everything Legaar did, it was excessive. There weren't ten people on Devanta who would have known the difference between a sycamore leaf or a maple leaf, and fewer than that would have cared—if they even had been able to see the oversized pool from an altitude sufficient to discern the shape. At that, their interest would have been far more centered on the naked nymphs and youthful and equally nude gods waiting to pleasure whoever requested their services.

Time's End was Legaar's pride, although I doubted he took joy in anything except bending others to his will, whereas I did take joy in Elysium, certainly a far-more-rewarding creation than a mere estate—for Elysium was an entire world time-backshaped into what it now was. Unfortunately, that would not have been possible without Time's End, as Legaar had so often reminded me.

I glanced up at the dark balcony of the suite assigned to me—overlooking the pool, not that I would bother to watch, not that the circular world would stand still.

15

*Humans require certainty to function
individually, and shared certainty to maintain
a viable society. Technology requires
knowledge, and knowledge enables
understanding. True understanding destroys
certainty.*

I slept a stan later on Sabaten morning. I also woke up with a headache and the half memories of nightmares, scarcely the tender grace of past days dead to me. Those days were still far too alive, for all the years they lay behind me.

Max . . . interrogative house and systems status?

All systems are green, sir. The repairs have also been completed. The villa operating account has been debited three thousand two hundred credits. You have ten pending messages.

Ten? Since the night before? I struggled into a steaming shower. No matter what anyone says, neither ultrasound nor nanite-scrubs give you the clean feeling of a good shower. They also don't help with headaches.

I ignored the messages until after I'd dressed, eaten, and drunk two cups of earlgrey. Max would have alerted me to anything urgent. The more I thought about it, the more puzzled and concerned I was about whatever had displaced me from the limousine to the edge of the reservoir. I could only think of three possibilities. I didn't like any of them. A fast flitter might have been able to transport me, but only if someone had literally suspended my thoughts and moved me and if they'd been able to avoid Special Ops surveillance. The second was that someone had some sort of technology that could literally lift someone from one place to another instantly—within a gravity well. The third alternative was that I'd imagined it all.

I walked from the breakfast room to my study. I could have accessed the messages anywhere in the villa, but I felt more professional in the study. The first was a confirmation that I'd been cited for trespassing in restricted waters and that I had paid my fine. It also contained a warning that a second trespassing offense within three years would not be a misdemeanor but a felony. That eliminated the third alternative. It didn't make me feel any better.

The second message was a request from my neighbor— Soror Celestina—that I reimburse her for the damage to her wall. I replied politely with a delayed response that since I was not responsible I could only refer her to my indemnifier, Gallian Re.

The third was another message from Tony diVeau, politely beefing that he felt that I was letting him down after he'd offered such a wonderful recreational opportunity. I deleted it and didn't reply.

The fourth was a reminder from Krij about brunch on Senen morning.

The fifth was a notice of a surcharge from the limo hire outfit because I'd left the limousine without notice—yet another suggestion of the impossibility of what had happened.

The sixth was a blank screen, with no return codes.

Max . . . the blank screen message . . . what about it?

That was an attempted penetration through the message system. So were the others not on the pending list. They had the format of sales presentations.

I had my doubts about that, but the defenses had dealt with them. Hadn't they? *Run a deep protocol and infiltration check.*

That has been done. Nothing detected.

That didn't mean that something hadn't gotten into my systems—only that Max hadn't detected them.

Contact InfoSec. Have them come out and run a full decon. Soonest.

Yes, sir.

Have them check the device that Lemel Jerome sent also. It's here in the bookcase comm-block.

I hated to spend those kinds of credits, but I'd hate even more to be done in through leaks bored into my system. I was just glad it wasn't Domen or Senen. End-days always meant a premium.

At that moment, the message system reminded me, *Return the vid from Donacyr D'Azouza.*

I didn't want to, but he had been talking about another assignment. With all the equipment Legaar or his AIs had destroyed, more work couldn't hurt. I laughed to myself. One of the reasons I never watched vidramas—even period historical ones—about private operators and consultants was that the protagonists never had more than one client at a time. Whoever wrote that crap didn't know anything about the business. One client at a time, and I'd have been out of business years before. It was about as accurate as doctors having one patient.

Connect.

The figure who appeared in the projection before me had light golden chocolate skin. His coppery brown hair curled into tight ringlets against his skull. Deep-set dark brown eyes separated by a strong nose slightly wider than optimal appeared to look at me. "I may or may not be here. Leave a message."

Honest as the talking head was, if it resembled him, I wasn't certain I wanted the job. Still . . . keeping up the villa and its equipment burned credits. I could always use more, and the harder I worked, the fewer the dreams.

"Blaine Donne, returning your vid."

The image vanished. It was replaced by a similar visage. The man who appeared looked the same, but for all the similarity, the "real" Donacyr carried an edginess, as well as some continued unreality.

"Seignior Donne, can you tell me where all past years are?"

"I wasn't the one who posed the question, slave as I may be to fate, chance, kings, and desperate men."

"Can you?" he pressed.

"No more than you can determine what wind serves to advance an honest mind." I didn't care much for games.

Even those I was forced to play by virtue of a presumed heritage.

"I have a proposition for you. It will arrive by secure courier shortly. You are not obliged to take it. I hope you will."

The projection vanished.

Max . . . back-trace.

That viddress no longer exists. It was a single-reply drop.

Whoever Donacyr D'Azouza might be, he or she had credits to burn. He or she wanted something done that was dangerous if it could be linked back. Either that or he/she was a privacy freak. The content suggested he also knew someone who'd been a former client of mine. I'd wait for the package and see what it contained.

In the meantime, I needed to work on the projects I had. Especially the Eloi-Maraniss commission. The full impact of what had happened hadn't really struck me until I'd started thinking about the total impossibility of what had happened after I'd left Odilia's.

I walked to the doors that led to the verandah and looked out, but turned back to the table desk and dropped into my chair. On the table was a duplicate of the hard-copy material that Odilia had slipped to me. I read it first.

Effectively, it was two sets of listings. The first was short, nine names of higher-ups in various Eloi Enterprise operations who had either vanished or been sent off-planet in the last three months. The second contained material on all the people who had crossed Legaar and Simeon Eloi . . . and what had happened to them. Most had been vanished. One architect was rumored to have been brain-burned and biosculpted into a troll and sent to a heavy planet as a laborer. A Garda lieutenant's stunner had exploded. The fragments had shredded his upper body so badly that while his physical form had survived, little else had. A forensic accountant who'd successfully prosecuted the director of Classic Investment for extortion that had resulted in market manipulation on securities held by Classic Investment had died when what appeared to have been a nickel-iron meteor smashed into his villa. A public advocate had prosecuted Classic Media for wavelength violations that had disrupted competitors' offerings. Her daughter and the daughter's husband had been drowned when a rogue wave had so thoroughly crushed their sailing craft that all safety equipment had been disabled. Her remaining daughter died of a raging infection three days later. The advocate had then walked into the courtroom and grabbed—or hugged—the director of Classic Media. Her nanoshield had crushed them both to death. She was clearly going to make someone pay, but Legaar hadn't been the one.

How could one blame the Elois for matters such as rogue waves and meteors? Except that nickel-iron meteor or asteroids were exceedingly rare in the Dominique system, and the planetary moons were too small for large tides, and there hadn't been a tsunami or any other wave action of that size in decades. The one factor common to all those was that they were improbable occurrences. Just like my removal from a sealed limousine.

I went back to the first list. Three of the nine had vanished without a trace, and six had theoretically been sent out to different sectors of the Assembly worlds to head "expansion efforts." That meant, I suspected, that they hadn't offended the Elois too badly, or that they were too well known or connected to be vanished immediately. Truly charming, the Eloi brothers, commoner than water, crueler than truth. Had they been the ones behind the morning's testing of my systems? How could they not have been?

Still wondering, I checked the miniature dataflat—through my quarantine system. It had more information about Legaar Eloi, an expanded version of his biography and a section with miscellaneous facts about Eloi Enterprises. Some of it I knew. Most I didn't, but there was no mention of anything about Elysium or Classic Research.

Before I got into more research, I tried a vidlink to William Ruckless. I got a talking head. I did with Theodore Elsen as well. I left messages with both.

Halfway though my studies, I moved out to the verandah

for a quarter stan or so while the InfoSec team swept the study. A good stan later, I leaned back in the chair, thinking. The more I studied about Legaar Eloi, the less I felt I knew him, but the more I detested him.

InfoSec has completed their decon, sir. Do you want to access the report?

I did.

There had been three sophisticated copy-and-divert traps. The intruders hadn't managed to break deep security, but they had been well on their way to building a shadow duplicate that would have managed to create close-to-replica results. I checked the InfoSec analysis, reading the key words. "Nova-class infiltration . . . highest-level expertise . . . top corpentity shadowsystems."

To me, that sounded like Legaar Eloi.

"Source . . . messages from Antonio diVeau . . ."

So . . . if Tony were the one fronting for Legaar, who else happened to be trying to get into my systems? And why now?

I kept reading. "Physical device attached to dress trousers, recently immersed in natural water, class II shielded passive beacon. Self-destructed prior to examination. Sephaniah! What had she wanted? And why?

Lemel's detection device had a burst sender, locator attached, but no snoop or infiltration equipment. That didn't surprise me. Lemmy wanted to know if his detector found any sign of the telltale emissions, whatever they were, and where. He didn't care much what I did, but he didn't totally trust me. In Thurene, I couldn't say I blamed him.

Max! Where's that beacon they found?

In the lower workroom, sir. In double comm-insulated isolation. It is nonfunctional now.

Leave it there. That could wait. I might as well try out Lemmy's gadget.

I went back to my own rooms, but through the courtyard garden, where I stopped to check the herbs, especially the lime rosemary and the emerald basil. I donned the gray jacket and trousers, and the matching shirt. The fabric had been nanetically designed to shift the reflected light to allow me to blend in against most backgrounds. A silver shadow in the light, a darker shadow in the night.

I used my own groundcar and drove to the carpark on the east end of the Left Bank. The vehicle could be destroyed but not tampered with. It was the third one I'd owned in five years. The indemnity corpentity hadn't been that thrilled with replacing the first two, and my premiums were near the max. Then, indemnity corpentities didn't care for any personally owned transport equipment. That was another reason I hired the special limousine when I knew there would be trouble. I reserved the real indemnity for the nightflitter.

There was no one else in the garage, and it was only a third full. Although it was already late afternoon, for the Left Bank, that was early. When I returned, I'd be lucky to see a single vacant space.

Unlike the South Bank, the Left Bank had no gardens, no topiary. The stone walk and the stone wall that formed the embankment were both gray granite. The walk was smooth; the embankment walls were rough-cut. Most of the buildings beyond Le Boulevard Nord, which flanked the walk, were also gray granite. The few splashes of color came from the awnings and from the flowers in the granite-edged beds in the Boulevard's median.

I headed west on the walk.

Ahead of me walked a couple. Both projected a muscular presence, but their movements were too delicate. They were using body-pak projectors, supposedly for protection.

I snorted. There wasn't that much smash-and-grab stuff in Thurene. The sat-screens and the miniscanners on the Garda net made the streets among the safest places in the city—at least for avoiding small-timers. The Garda couldn't stop it, but they almost always caught the malefactors. There weren't any repeat offenses by those malefactors.

There were multiple legal and/or undetected offenses in the privacy of homes and corpentities. There always have been, in any time and place, because homes and businesses are far more shadowy than anyone wants to admit. That has not changed over time, either.

The couple with the enhanced projected presence turned and waited, then crossed the Boulevard. They were headed toward the Banque du Sud. That confirmed their status.

The next intersection was Alois. I crossed the Boulevard and kept walking west. I nodded to the woman and her son coming toward me. She did not smile or return the gesture as we passed.

"That man there . . . he walked past the mirror, but I couldn't see him." The boy's words came from behind me.

"It's just another virtie, Louis. You've seen them before."

"Not on the street, maman."

"There's a first time for everything."

I couldn't help but smile inside. It didn't hurt to be taken for a virtie because weapons were useless against holo projections.

Ahead was Pier Two, an angular building a good hundred meters high that resembled an ancient warship's bow. It was one of the few without a stone facade. The green exterior captured the white-orange rays of the afternoon sun and turned them into a smoldering golden green illumination. Pier Two served as the center for commodities trades—or rather as the comm and info-storage hub for the system's commodity exchange. There were offices there, as well, because there was still a certain mystique about being located close to the trading center, not because it was necessary. Humans have always been like that. It hadn't changed in the thousands of years since the Terran Diaspora, and it wouldn't change in my lifetime.

Across the Rue du Plaisir from Pier Two was Pier One. Pier One was larger than Pier Two—another twenty meters higher and a third again as broad. It had a trapezoidal front facing the Nouvelle Seine, covered in pink granite with wide intelligent glass windows. The combination of sun-darkened glass and pink called to mind an aging courtesan of the past painted for the evening. That was certainly appropriate for the ostensible headquarters of Eloi Enterprises.

I crossed the river on the Pont de L'Ouest and walked the

South Bank back east. I had to go another quarter klick to use the east bridge. I've always hated retracing my way.

The carpark was almost full. The groundcar was untouched and untampered with. During my entire walk, Lemmy's detector had never let out a blip or a peep. Or anything. I hadn't expected that it would.

If you survive for long in SpecOps, you develop a certain sense about things. I'd survived there longer than most. I'd just pushed my luck too far too often.

I drove back to the villa, checking the systems and nets. Everything was quiet.

Even before I parked the vehicle in the underground security area, Max pulsed me.

Rapide Courier delivered a package for you, Max reported. *It scans clean. It's on your desk in the study. Dr. Ruckless returned your vid.*

Thank you.

I took the ramps up to the villa's main levels at a quick walk, then made my way to the study. The package contained a dataflat and a short note. I read the note.

Dear Seignior Donne:

I apologize for the game-playing upon your namesake, but it is one of the few pleasures left to me. The commission I offer is this. Locate the lady whose information is in the dataflat and assure yourself that she is safe and looks to remain so.

In departing, she requested that I never attempt to locate her. I will honor that request, but for my own selfish peace of mind, I would like the assurance that she is safe and—hopefully—happy. Your word is known to be good, and I will accept your assurance that she is safe.

If she is not, we need to discuss the matter to see if there is anything you can do to alleviate the situation, but under no circumstances are you to reveal information that would allow me to locate her.

If you wish to take the commission, flash the return code, and a retainer of Cr5,000 will be immediately sent.

I read it twice. Then I had Max do a data search on D'Azouza.

While he was searching and collating, I checked the vid-messages. The sole one of interest was from a woman—her talking head, properly—of indeterminate age. But then, weren't we all of indeterminate age, except for the handful of unfortunates like Greyspan?

"Seignior Donne, I have a simple commission for you. I'd like you to facilitate a transfer of assets . . . in a fashion that cannot be traced back to me. It must be done in a way that is absolutely legal and in accord with the Codex. If you wish to handle this, here is my return code."

That sounded like an inheritance to a child who had broken with parents or to a former disgruntled lover. Still . . . so long as it was legal and paid . . .

I activated the return code.

The image that appeared was that of a titian-haired young woman, clad in a blouse and cardigan sweater in a style that first dated from well before the Terran Diaspora. It was renewed periodically, as were most fashions. "Greetings, Seignior Donne. I'm glad my inquiry drew your attention. You may call me Nancy. I'm not exactly a secretive wooden lady, but I'd prefer to remain mysterious for now."

That might not bother me. It depended on what commission she had in mind. "You still haven't given me any details."

"The heiress in question is rather elusive. She used to have the identity of Stella Strong. She took another name later, but was most recently known as Maureen Gonne. I would like a bequest of ten million credits, approximately, in a portfolio held by the First Commerce Bank trust section, settled upon her."

"The Bank can do that. I can't."

"They will indeed, after you find her, verify her identity, and inform the contact at the Bank. The contact is Angelique deGritz. Here is the contact code."

The code flashed, and the system held it for me.

"Did Stella, or Maureen, refuse to marry William?" I asked.

"After a fashion. She is, or was, a samer."

Willa, then, I thought. "Do you have an image?"

"It's several years old. I'll send it, if you agree to take the commission."

"I'm not inexpensive, Nancy."

"If you take the commission, you'll receive five thousand credits as a retainer immediately."

"Who else wants her found? Or doesn't want her found?"

"The bequest will go to Vola Paulsky and her sibling, Relian Cru. I can't say if they know about the bequest."

"Who set up the bequest?"

"Their father."

I felt as though I were extracting deep-core samples with a syringe. "Who was he?"

"Clinton Jefferson Wayles."

The name was familiar to me, but I couldn't pin it down. *Quick search, Clinton Jefferson Wayles.* "Why didn't he just tell them?"

"No one knows. His spouse didn't know about the children, and they were never told about the bequest."

Clinton Jefferson Wayles, Max replied, *deceased 1337 C.D. Former Director, BCD, LLC . . . founded as Bretagne Consolidation and Development . . . Former Regional Governor, Bretagne 1306–1321. One son, Rodham Lee Wayles. Separated from spouse, Marthyl Owen Aheirne, never divorced . . .*

"What about his son, Rodham? How does he fit in? Does the bequest go to him if the others aren't located?"

"Rodham may know about the bequest, but it doesn't affect him one way or the other. If none of the three children is located within a specific time period, the bequest goes to the L'Institut Multitechnique in Thurene."

"How critical is time? You mentioned a time period."

Nancy laughed, politely. "It terminates a half century after the death of the last child or three hundred and one years from now, whichever is later."

If she spoke the truth, old Wayles hadn't wanted there to be much incentive for anyone to kill off all three. "Assuming you're correct in the terms of the bequest, is there any advantage to the latter siblings vanishing those earlier in line?"

"Obviously." The titian-haired talking head smiled. "Their situation is not unlike that of many in past history and fiction. That is why I do not wish to be informed of whether you are successful or not until after the bequest has been settled. Nor will you be able to contact me, except as a single-time return to a code, as you have now. I will contact you, periodically."

"You are convinced that if you know, the two others will find out?"

"That is a possibility I wish to foreclose totally. Will you take the commission?"

I didn't like it, but I'd done missing identities before. I either got horrendously overpaid or underpaid. No one was ever satisfied. But, given the way the year was going, I could see that I'd need the credits. "Yes."

"The funds are on their way, Seignior Donne. Good day."

Her holo projection vanished. The analysis suggested "Nancy" had been entirely virtie.

Before I contacted anyone, I put Max to work on a search of Stella Strong, Maureen Gonne, and possible connections to the late Clinton Jefferson Wayles. Then I checked the incomings. As "Nancy" had promised, I had received five thousand credits and an image that was more than a few years old. Stella—or Maureen—had been a student when the image had been caught. She'd been dark-haired, green-eyed, and somehow both petite and slightly stocky. I doubted that she looked anything like that now.

I also had information on both D'Azouza and Wayles.

I began with what Max had uncovered and routed to me about D'Azouza. Despite his appearance, Donacyr D'Azouza had to be pushing his third century. That was pressing his genetic heritage, the limits of medicine, and anti-gathic therapies. Not to mention luck. According to his bio, he'd had a number of careers, including being an entrepreneur in live theatre in Bresthavre, a furnishings designer with his own small corpentity, and a stipend stint in the Assembly IS, as a logistics officer. There were also large blocs of time unaccounted for. One problem was that I couldn't independently verify most of the material in his accessible bio, only the theatre and furnishings stints, which were the most recent. That bothered me. Anyone who blotted out parts of his past that thoroughly on the public and media records had something to hide. Or they hadn't ever been there. That almost certainly meant that D'Azouza was an alter ego.

The dataflat D'Azouza had sent was extensive. It included a good thirty images of a quietly beautiful woman. In the pictures, her hair ranged from a tight-curled honey blond to a short and straight light brown. Her eyes were hazel in all of them, and her build was athletically feminine. In some, her chin was almost elfin, but in what I took to be later images, it was just enough wider to remove the faerie impression.

The only name was Theresa McGerrie.

There was also a short bio.

I ran a check on it. The only item from the bio that matched with the records was a residence listing in South Bank from seven years ago, a single reference to a Terry McGerrie as an up-and-coming vid dramaturge—and credits for five full-length vidramas, the last in 1343. The name was a pseudonym . . . but D'Azouza must have known that. Or had he?

I could try. Besides . . . there was something in those images . . .

I sent the return code and decided to let what I'd learned stew in my subconscious while I reviewed the information on the other commission.

Material on the late seignior Wayles was anything but scarce. Most of it was less than illuminating. He'd lived most of his life in the Bretegne region, although he had graduated from L'Institut Multitechnique. He had an engineering background, but had clearly possessed great charm and significant powers of persuasion. His spouse had succeeded him, after a gap of some twenty years, as the regional governor. In fact, she still was. The two of them had succeeded in creating an economic and engineering climate that was lifting Vannes almost to the size and prestige of Thurene and past that of Avignes.

The quick search revealed almost nothing on Vola Paulsky, except that she had once created elaborate wish-fulfillment scenarios for an entertainment combine outside of Vannes before returning to the university for graduate studies in law. Relian Cru was listed as registered in Bresthavre, but with a privacy seal and no link codes.

There was no information on Stella Strong, but a Maureen Gonne had been a resident of Thurene until two years ago. She had been a senior information expediter for the Thurenean Fashion Alliance. There were no images of her under her name and no other revealing information.

I decided to start there.

I vidlinked to TFA and got a talking head. Dark brunette with tight curls framing a narrow face. Not my type, even in a virtie. "Thurenean Fashion Alliance."

"Maureen Gonne, please. This is Blaine Donne." I pulsed the short ID bloc through.

There was the briefest pause before the virtie replied. "There's no one here by that name."

"There used to be. Could I talk to whoever used to be her superior?"

"One moment, Seignior Donne."

The next image was that of an even-narrower-faced woman. Her hair was black, short, and plastered to her skull like paint. Black eyes and black brows against a pale face made me wonder if I wanted to see the next year's fashions. "Seignior Donne? How might I help you?"

"I'm trying to locate a Maureen Gonne."

"Maureen no longer works here."

That meant she had. "She was an information expediter, wasn't she? What do those duties entail?" I couldn't ask directly where she'd gone, because they couldn't legally answer. They could volunteer information.

"The position is the interface between the fashion media

links and the Alliance. The best expediters understand what the linkers need before they ask."

"I take it she was good, and that you'd have liked to have kept her."

The woman frowned, slightly. "She was on her way to being very good. If she'd stayed, she could have gone up the in-house media ramp. She made a good impression. She was quietly stylish."

I called up the image I had. "This is what she looked like several years before she came to work at TFA. Did she look anything like that?"

The woman laughed. "The eyes were the same, and she wasn't any taller." Another frown followed. After a moment, she nodded. "I can send you the image we have, because it was released in our annual report, and that's public."

I caught the sense of the incoming, but concentrated on the woman. "How long was she with TFA?"

"Not quite four years. I got the impression that was as much to boost her LS base as anything."

"That doesn't sound as though she intended to make fashion a career." Not if her reasons were just to boost her lifetime stipend.

"She was ambitious, but she was . . ."

". . . trying to combine security and speed in getting where she wanted to go? Did she ever say what she might want to do before she left?"

"No. She was more private than most. She gave the minimum notice necessary to avoid maroonlight."

"She didn't want anyone to know where she was going or call attention to it."

"I couldn't help you there if I wanted to, Seignior Donne. All she left was a one-way comm drop, and it was an Assembly-wide access code that had a one-year expiration— just enough to meet the minimums."

"Did she ever talk about family?"

"All she said—that I know of—was that her father was dead and that her mother lived in a small town outside Vannes, Degaulle, I think . . ."

Max . . . search Vannes and the area around Degaulle for possible matches to Stella Strong, the Fort or Forte surname, possibly . . .

Only possible match is Charlyse Forte . . . deceased 1349 C.D., noted mysticist and scholar. No known spouse. daughter Astrid . . . born 1315 C.D.

That *might* be a lead. I couldn't help but wonder if Charlyse's death a year or so earlier had something to do with everything. "Did she ever mention her mother's name?"

My question brought another frown.

I waited.

"I don't think she did. She did say once that her mother believed in the unbelievable." She gave me the polite closing smile. "I'm sorry I can't help you further. Good day."

After she broke the vidlink, I studied the TFA image. In it, Maureen was more slender. Her hair was a coppery blond that brought out the vivid green of her eyes. Her skin held a hint of bronze, and her nose was slightly smaller. Except for the eyes, the impression was far different. Then I noted the caption—Maureen M. Gonne, senior information expediter, with Gregory Coole, Media Director. The date was 1349, probably just before she left TFA.

Max . . . search for variations of Maureen Maud Gonne . . . and link to information specialties. Do the same for Astrid Forte . . .

That might get me more.

Next came Angelique deGritz—the purported contact at the bank. No one could make up a name like that. Not for a trust officer.

I didn't use Nancy's contact link. Rather, I made a direct inquiry to the First Commerce Bank's trust section. "Angelique deGritz."

The switch to the talking head was instantaneous—a statuesque redhead with flashing green eyes. Her figure was anything but sylphlike. "Greetings. Please state your interest plainly and clearly so that I can look into it and get back to you. Thank you." The voice was melodic but in the way a muted trumpet was.

Somehow, I didn't connect the ancient images of angels with this Angelique.

I broke the vidlink and searched for Angelique deGritz. All the systems confirmed that there was an Angelique deGritz employed by the First Commerce Bank. There were more than enough of the trivial details to confirm that identity

I leaned back in the chair and closed my eyes. Then I tried a return link for Dr. Ruckless. I actually got him.

He had a narrow oval face and deep-set eyes under dark brown hair, straight and cut moderately short. "I believe you contacted me, Seignior Donne. What can I do for you?"

"I'm looking for information, and unbiased opinions, Doctor. I'm going to have to evaluate a presentation on consciousness research next week."

"That's not my expertise." His voice was mild.

"Not directly, but you're considered an expert trauma surgeon. According to the numbers I've run, close to twenty percent of all severe trauma cases have some impact on consciousness."

Ruckless blinked. Then he offered a slow smile. "I'll give you points for reading at least some of my work. Exactly why do you want my views?"

"As I said, I'm being asked to evaluate a proposal on consciousness research. The proposal requests significant research funds. Or so I've been led to believe. Every credit that goes to one form of research doesn't go to another. I have to recommend whether this is a good proposal. Any considered medical expertise is always useful."

"I think I know about the proposal you're mentioning. That's all I know."

"I see. What is your considered view about this kind of research?"

Ruckless shrugged. "All well-designed medical research is useful. If the proposal is by the leading consciousness expert, it will feature a well-designed program of research. Until the research is conducted, evaluated, and the protocols, procedures, and results are peer-reviewed, the value cannot be determined."

"What about the comparative value of this field as compared to others?"

"That has been a matter of controversy for centuries. The exact nature of consciousness still eludes medical science. There are a number of theories, but none have been conclusively proved or disproved."

"You seem to be suggesting that such research remains . . . highly theoretical."

"I'm suggesting nothing. I've given you the facts."

"Do you think that what research gets greater funding is as much a function of the fund-raising ability of the researcher as the validity of the research itself?"

Ruckless laughed. There was the slightest edge to his laughter. "That's always been true. There's no reason to suggest that will change." He shrugged again. "Sometimes, those with that gift are also great scientists. Certainly, some solid work has been done here on consciousness studies." He smiled. "I'm afraid that's really all I can say. As I mentioned earlier, it's not my field."

"Thank you. You've been helpful."

His image vanished.

I took a deep breath. If I'd read Ruckless right, he wasn't that happy with Dyorr's proposal, but he respected him. He wasn't about to undercut him.

I decided not to press Elsen, not until after the end-days. I had more than enough to handle. Besides the new clients, I still had to figure out how to deal with Tony diVeau and Sephaniah. I also had to see what their connections to Legaar Eloi might be. Beyond that I needed to find out if there was even a theoretical way I could have been moved from one point on the planet's surface to another.

16

Speed and concealment beat power on all occasions . . . except the last one.

Once it got dark, the next step was to use the nightflitter. With the kind of technology *someone* had used on me, I needed to scout out Legaar's estate . . . carefully.

Obtaining the nightflitter had been difficult. Having it was half luxury, half necessity. No one hired out flitters without their own pilots as part of the hire, and no one hired out combat nightflitters. Mine was one templated for the ill-fated Christos Republic by Thurenan Arms. TA had done all the design work and templating for thirty comparatively low-tech flitters that no one wanted. I'd bid just enough for one so that they could recover some costs, and get a write-off that they wouldn't have if they hadn't actually nanofactured at least one. They'd accepted my bid, and I'd had to borrow five million creds, mostly from financiers Krij knew. It took me five years to pay off the flitter and the improvements. The Civitas Sorores had been less than pleased, and months had passed before I'd obtained all the permits— with the stipulation that no offensive weapons systems were to be installed. I hadn't, but the shield systems were very innovative. Except for fam rides and learning the systems, I'd only used it a few times, but I'd gotten it on the basis that, if I ever needed it, I wouldn't have time to get it.

Besides, I liked having it.

I went to my quarters in the villa and donned the boots and gray flight suit. The flight suit met all my requirements. Besides providing the interface with the nightflitter, it could handle temperature extremes, gee forces, and would provide visual camouflage should I have to set down somewhere.

Then I took the concealed circular staircase from the office study down two levels to the small hangar. The lights were red there. The reflections off the nightflitter cast shifting patterns on the gray walls and overhead.

The nightflitter was just under twenty meters in length and three in width at its narrowest, six at the widest point of the lifting body. Especially at night or in dim light, looking at the curved black surface planes twisted your eyes. Doing it twisted mine, anyway. The engines were nanojets and burned the same restructured hydrocarbons that all high-performance atmospheric craft did. The one drawback of all flitters was that, like ancient sharks, they couldn't remain motionless for long, because power was generated by a boosted by-bleed from the engines before the exhaust vector stage.

There weren't that many piloted atmospheric military craft, not when most of them could be handled by commlinks—without the weight and vulnerability of a pilot. But a piloted craft had one advantage. It was self-contained with the most adaptable guidance system available. No one could fry the commlinks or locate the craft through links or guidance systems. The stealth configuration and selective absorption/reradiation properties of the airframe made it effectively invisible, particularly at night, except to the highest-level military systems.

I installed Lemmy's device in the remote-link section. It checked, and I hoped it would continue to work. Then I climbed into the cockpit, put on the lightweight helmet, secured the links between the flitter and flight suit, and suit and helmet. I lowered the visor and went through the checklist—manual, but projected on the visor. All systems were go. Including the self-destruct system. I hating having it, but there might well be times when losing six million credits of nightflitter was preferable to having it inspected or confiscated by unfriendly souls.

Light-off one.
One on-line.
With one generator up, the flitter came to full life.

Hangar doors open. With that command all the lights went out.

I taxied up the ramp and out through the doors into the courtyard. Once the tail was clear, I sent the command to close the hangar doors. Next came the unavoidable part. I clicked into ACS, requesting a departure vector at low altitude. Over Thurene, even private air traffic was controlled. If I went stealth all the way, I probably could have avoided detection. That would have been illegal, and if Javerr and the Garda ever found out, they would have caused trouble and petitioned for a reformatting of my thought processes.

I inputted Carcassonne as my intermediate destination with a late return to Thurene. In less than a minute, I had a departure vector.

Shadow-one, lifting off on departure vector.

Cleared to ACS boundary on departure vector two eight one, immediate climb to one thousand AGL.

Accept-affirm. One thousand meters was higher than I preferred, but the city sisters disliked extremely low-flying craft, especially those on modified manual, even with a transponder.

Light-off two.

With both engines online, I fed all power to the diverters. The nightflitter eased skyward vertically, burning power like credits spent on the South Bank until I dropped the nose slightly and began to transition to forward flight, turning to the northwest in a gentle bank. I leveled out on my departure vector, at exactly 1,001 AGL.

Below me, the city spread out like light-jewels sprinkled on black velvet. The Nouvelle Seine shimmered like a shiny black ribbon, and Bergerac lay just above the western horizon, almost baleful in its redness. I concentrated on the scanner reads, but the air was mostly clear. A long-haul scrammer was setting down at Esthavre.

Once clear of Thurene ACS, I went manual, blanked the

transponder, and activated the stealth active features. Then I banked into a snap turn that left me on a heading of 015. I didn't want to go there, but those hills were the closest.

After twenty minutes, I dropped to 500 AGL and slid around the Piedmont Hills and into the Somme Valley, following the river back eastward. The ACS tracking system had doubtless alerted the satellite scan and accessed their feeds what I'd done when I'd gone stealth. That wouldn't help. Nothing short of IS or Assembly SpecOps tech would have even had a chance of detecting me. And my acts weren't illegal. Just out of the ordinary.

The lights along the Somme were spread apart, like the stars on the fringe, and the hillside vineyards and the forests above were dark.

I checked course line and plot, called both up for a visual check. Fifteen minutes to the southwest corner of Eloi's Time's End estate. I couldn't help but wonder whose time.

Satellite scan detected and neutralized.

I smiled at that. If Officer Javerr wanted to check satellite feeds, he'd find nothing there.

The nightflitter and I slipped through the shadows of darkness.

ETA in five.

I checked the plot. Right on course.

Bandits on intercept!

Intercept? How? I'd tested the nightflitter against the best WDF alert systems, and they'd never detected me. I pushed that thought away and checked the vectors.

Three combat flitters with the low profile of RPs were definitely screaming toward me. I'd worry about the detection later.

I checked the terrain profile, then ran a quick calculation. The three had moved into a reverse V—an enveloping maneuver, designed to force me down into the terrain. That was fine with me. I dived for the deck and activated full restraints.

The lead flitter followed but stayed above me. They wouldn't use missiles or cannon. Not at first. They'd be programmed to force an "accident." That would mean using nanoshields or something to force "controlled flight into terrain," as the old, old phrase went. I leveled out at less than a hundred meters above the ground. Above the tree-tops, really.

As the lead RPF accelerated toward my tail, I deployed the air brakes—nanetic extensions of my shields—then waited just enough that the RPF overlapped my shields, before I dropped the brakes and accelerated up.

I slammed into the trailing edge of the RPF's shields. The RPF automatically shrank its shields to avoid being destabilized. That allowed me to get on top and behind. My shields were stronger, and my engines more powerful. In instants, the first RPF pinwheeled downward. The stabilization systems operated well enough that it hit flat, making an oval depression in the pine forest. Before long, flames would be flashing skyward.

Still playing prey, I turned southeast, toward a low ridge-line.

Instants before I should have crashed into the trees at the crest, I angle-banked right, then flipped back left behind the ridge before accelerating almost out of the trees at the flanking flitter. My course looked like a collision course, and that would have been fine with the operator/system controlling the RPF. Except . . . at the last instant, as programmed and executed by my systems—even my reflexes aren't that fast—the nightflitter angled left and extended shields.

The impact unbalanced the RPF enough that it slewed and lost lift. Losing lift at a hundred meters AGL at that velocity is usually cause for an impact resulting in maximum structural damage to the airframe. That occurred with a satisfactory shock wave.

The third RPF immediately turned and tried to accelerate back toward Time's End.

That didn't work either, because the nightflitter was faster.

I just gained enough altitude to use my shields to pancake it into another stand of trees.

With the three flitters out of the way, I banked the night-flitter and dropped to less than a hundred meters AGL and swept along the southern perimeter of the estate. The readings from the remote links indicated that Lemmy's gadget was detecting something, but there were also massive energy sources on the estate. They read like they were dreadnought emanations, or even almost miniature black hole generators.

As soon as I had what I needed, I banked back south and screamed toward Thurene. There was no point in seeing what other defenses Time's End had. Not yet. Not when every muscle in my body was sore from the gee forces I'd pulled and when my head was throbbing as if being pounded by a heavy rubber mallet.

I left behind three fires burning in the pines. They'd be traced to Eloi's flitters, and that meant he'd have to pay for containing the fires and/or explain what he was doing with three military-class RPFs. At least, I hoped he would. That wasn't something I was counting on, though.

As I headed back to Thurene and the villa, I had to consider four factors. First, I'd been detected—and I'd been detected from a goodly distance. Second, the detector had confirmed that Legaar was using equipment that infringed on Lemmy's patents. Third, there was a massive energy-generation facility on the estate. Fourth, from detection to the RP attack flitters, high-level military equipment was being used. I'd have bet it wasn't from Devantan or Assembly sources, either.

The results from the energy detectors supported the fact that the research center was no shell. Hidden somewhere on Legaar's estate was a facility producing enough energy to power half of Thurene. Energy generation of that magnitude didn't take place unless someone was using it.

Another thing struck me. Why had it been so easy for me to take down the RPFs when they'd been able to detect me so early? Their maneuvering suggested human operators rather than instant AIs, and that didn't seem to make sense. The other problem was that, if Legaar or his henchmen could remove me from a limo . . . why not from a nightflitter?

It did make some sense for Legaar to locate whatever he

had going with Classic Research at Time's End. If you're going to break the law, do it where no one can prove it. What bothered me about the setup was something else. Legaar Eloi had more than enough credits to pay royalty fees—even exorbitant ones. Why hadn't he? From what I'd discovered so far, he wasn't given to willful lawbreaking. In fact, all the filings and records suggested that he'd gone to great length to keep everything legitimate.

All of that suggested I'd gotten involved in far more than I'd ever anticipated.

As I approached the ACS boundary, I de-stealthed the nightflitter and climbed back to 1000 meters AGL. Then I requested an inbound vector.

Interrogative origin?

Thurene. Completion round-trip flight. No landings. Plan on file.

The system might hiccup inconsistencies to real controllers, but what could anyone say? I had done a round-trip. I was returning docilely to the fold.

As I settled the flitter back down into the courtyard, I vowed I wasn't about to go anywhere on Domen. Not when I was going to need most of Domen to recover from the stress I'd put on my body and system.

17

*Elysium's grace exceeds them all, the price
far higher than fair Satan's fall.*

Despite the freshness and fragrance of the light wind blowing out of the west, I'd closed the balcony doors in order to concentrate on the energy-balance calculations. The sounds of the nymphs and satyrs in the sycamore pool—and those with whom they played and pleasured—had been more than a little distracting. I much preferred the gently teasing invitations of Magdalena, far more entreating than the roistering of the pseudo-Grecians, but my personal enjoyments waited on the necessities posed by the projections hanging in the air of the suite before me, for I did not ever intend to be held green and dying, screaming in my chains like the sea of time beyond the branes of the present.

The prime sub-brane core system remained stable, but that stability was maintained only by the power links between the fusactors on Time's End and the one that supplied power to Elysium. Any expansion of the sub-brane required a full Hawking system, and even Legaar couldn't supply anything like that, and for that reason we waited on the off-system delivery of just that system.

Maraniss, get down here now! Legaar's words burned through the implant and my thoughts like fire.

Down where?

The defense control center, idiot!

I'll be right there. Or as soon as I could get there, although I wondered what was so critical that Legaar was fuming and fretting in the estate defense center. I wasn't about to argue over the link. When an Eloi was angry, there was no reasoning anyway. Sweet reason overwhelmed by virtue's passion—or the passion of what he felt was virtue, which was not exactly the same thing, except in what passed for his mind.

The nymphs must have sensed my anger, or they were all occupied with Legaar's guests, mostly rank and file representatives elected to the planetary forum that advised the sisters, because I got to the grotto that held the maglev without being accosted by the curdling folly of the girls of Legaar's lights.

I'd had barely gotten to the top of the ramp in the defense center and stepped through the doors, when Legaar turned.

"You took too damned long! Idiot! You're a complete idiot! You're a slow idiot! Where are you when you're needed?"

"I was in the quarters you supplied, going over what's necessary to implement the next phase. What happened?"

Legaar glared at me, but I just waited for his reply.

"Your detectors picked up an incoming craft. It didn't register on the standard screens. That means it had to be military. The defense system launched three RP flitters. Because the standard detectors couldn't pick them up, we had to override and transfer input location, using the projection field detectors. That created response delays. I've played back all the data, but the attacker took out all three RPFs, somehow without any energy discharges. I tried to use your beam gadget, but the attacker was gone—or off the farscreens—before I got the hang of it. If you'd been here, it wouldn't have happened."

"Legaar . . ." I kept my voice calm, although with his irrational childishness, it was more than a little difficult. "I was here almost all day. I need quiet and no distractions to plan the logistics and implementation. I don't get it here. That was why I instructed you and Chief Tech Dylane on how to use the beam for defense."

"Who in the planetary self-defense force had any idea about the project? Who did you let it slip to?" His voice was querulous.

If anyone had let matters slip, it was likely to have been Legaar, but there was little point in making that comment. "I've been here for days or in Elysium. Exactly when could I have let anything slip?" Before he could answer, I went on. "Can we be sure it was the PDF? What about Assembly Special Operations or the Assembly space force?"

"They can't interfere with planetary governments."

"They can if they suspect other systems are involved. If someone has let it out that the Frankans . . ."

"No! Don't even mention the name. Idiot!"

I was more than a little tired of his paranoia, but I needed him—as did the Frankans. "It's more likely to be a corpentity recon, possibly trying to get you to react."

He stopped, and his eyes glazed. Unlike most intelligent beings, Legaar could not walk and do anything else at the same time, let alone link to his system.

Again, I waited.

His eyes focused. "You were right. We got a backlink and a pattern. It was in the system all the time. We've even identified the source, but not the operator. It doesn't matter, though. This time, we'll take care of the head, not the fingers."

"A corpentity?"

"The head of a corpentity. I've got removals looking into a vanishing."

"Just for snooping?"

"I should have done it sooner. I've also contacted Lamoignon. The RPFs went down on Thierry land, and RT will press for damages."

"Guillaume Lamoignon?"

"Why not? It's better to have him representing Classic Research than attacking us. He's more ancient régime than any other opponents of the sisters."

"I see." I had my doubts, and I'd always had them where Legaar was concerned, but whether I had doubts or not, he was the vehicle necessary to assure the eternal solidity of Elysium. More important, once the Hawking system was linked and powered up, I would control Elysium—and its future.

18

Knowledge is not understanding; that's why so many pedants are idiots.

Most of my body was sore when I woke on Domen morning. That was despite a hot shower and autotherapy in the villa's medcenter the night before. High-gee maneuvers against RPFs did have a price for the pilot. Another hot shower helped—some.

I ate breakfast in the sheltered garden corner of the courtyard, watching the holoscans of news and items Max thought would interest me. The only news that really intrigued me was one particular blurb, accompanying a talking head.

> "... last night three surveillance vehicles suffered major systems malfunctions and crashed north of the Somme on forest lands owned and managed by Rothschild Thierry. RT explained that the fires had been controlled and that those responsible had already indemnified RT ..."

That was all.

Just what was going on at Time's End? I only had a tenuous and rumored connection between Legaar Eloi and Judeon Maraniss, and nothing at all that would link them to something called Elysium. I didn't even know what Elysium might be, except a guess that it was a project of some sort being undertaken by Classic Research requiring more energy than a handful of deep-space battle cruisers and that

Maraniss had some special expertise necessary for the success of the project.

Then there were the complications from both Sephaniah and Tony diVeau. I'd neglected following up on them to see what connections they might have with Legaar. Their attempts to snoop and crash my systems hadn't happened until I'd gotten involved with Seigniora Reynarda's Elysium commission. I've never been a believer in coincidences. I still wasn't.

The "transfer" business from the limo to the reservoir also still nagged at me. If Legaar or Maraniss had done it, why hadn't they used it against the nightflitter? If they hadn't, who had? And why?

I was also still stiff and sore. The soreness would have made it somewhat easier to keep my vow not to get consumed with pending projects—until early afternoon, perhaps. But I didn't get that choice. I'd only finished handwriting a polite but warm note to Odilia and arranged for Max to send it by courier when the system alerted me.

Incoming from Lemel Jerome.

Have him wait one. I'll be right there. I swallowed the last of the earlgrey and stood, trying not to wince. Then I crossed the courtyard to the study.

I'm a creature of habit. I prefer to handle business in the proper setting.

Once in the study, I pulsed Max. *Link.*

Lemmy appeared before me. His black hair was plastered back. He was grinning. His brown eyes still looked flat. "You did it, Blaine. The conveyer of carnality is employing my patents, and I've got proof."

"You got all that from the detector?" I knew Lemmy was bright, but applied science bright? "And you backlinked a burst transmitter direct to you?"

"How else would I find out?"

Lemmy might be science bright, legal bright, maybe even gadget bright. He wasn't survival bright. "Legaar could track that back to you, unless you used remotes, with drop filters."

"So? Why would he bother? He can pay the royalties.

He's got a massive jump-generator there, or something so close to it that it makes no difference."

"Lemmy . . . you can't operate a jump-generator on a planetary surface. Not without—"

Oversurge! reported Max.

The link was gone. So was a good chunk of system over-load protectors, but that was what they were for. I also had a strong feeling that poor Lemmy was also past tense, cour-tesy of Legaar Eloi. I had a stronger feeling that I had best be very careful. Lemmy's detector needed to be thoroughly insulated—and then some. Immediately.

Max, status of Lemel Jerome's detector?

Isolated and damped, as you ordered, sir.

I *thought* I'd done that, but I needed to make sure. *Moni-tor all news sources for breaking information on Lemel Jerome. Inform me immediately.*

I tried a relink to Lemmy. All I got was a stiff talking head that stated, "The link locale you have contacted is not responding."

I knew that. My system would have reconnected auto-matically if it had been possible. Whatever had knocked Lemmy out of link—and probably worse—had to have come from Legaar. Legaar was doing something connected to Lemmy's patents. Lemmy had said that Legaar had a jumpship generator at Time's End, but jumpship generators couldn't operate in a gravity well—or even near one. Not without the power of a Hawking system. If Legaar did have a Hawking system, it would have registered on the nightflit-ter's systems.

Still . . . it made me nervous. Very nervous, because if someone had actually operated a jumpship generator in a gravity well, particularly a planetary gravity well, powered with a Hawking field, the result would have been instant obliteration, for the planet and a goodly chunk of space around it. Not obliteration, exactly, just the transformation of all matter into energy. That equated to obliteration for entities nearby. That included me and Krij and the Civitas Sorores.

That had been the fate of Salem. The Vishni Confederacy

hadn't bothered with sending conventional warships against the rebel Christos Republic. They'd just assembled a Hawking system on the back side of an inner planet, linked it to two jumpship generators, and triggered both generators. Instant flare-nova, along with the destruction of the inner planet. That was the reason why the Assembly used EDI detectors to scan continually all its inhabited planetary systems. Hawking systems could be built anywhere in space, although they were too large and too unstable for continued jumpship usage, and the energy concentrations necessary for full operation took days to build before the system was stable and usable.

I knew the Assembly IS was continually monitoring for such a possibility. That knowledge didn't make me any happier.

Telling the Garda—even Colonel Shannon—about what Legaar Eloi had on his estate wasn't an option. They couldn't do anything because what Legaar had done, so far, wasn't illegal. Even informing them anonymously wouldn't be either anonymous or safe, because Shannon and Javerr would know I was the informer. They'd try to pin the destruction of the RPFs on me. Or Javerr would, and he'd inform Legaar. I already had enough trouble on my hands as it was without even greater interest and animosity from the Eloi group.

There was another option. It would take time, but I needed to use it.

I leaned forward and took out the stylus. Nothing was going into my system, anywhere, until the delays and blind links were set up. I had to call on old memories and near-forgotten codes. They'd be outdated, but that alone would create some attention.

In the end, the message was simple.

CODE RED OMEGA TWO

Modified jumpship generator located within confines of Time's End on Devanta. Coordinates follow. Area guarded by military-level RPFs and surveillance systems.

Massive power-generation system also in place. Currently exhibiting less power than a Hawking system.

AUTHENTICATE:Σ ç Π-74

It went enrypt/unencrypt/re-encrypt through four blind links, two erase-delays to a temporarily co-opted burst sender belonging to a small commerce bank. From there, it went to the regional Assembly SpecOps HQ. Behind it, the tracks of its passage erased themselves.

For a moment, I leaned back in the chair and looked out the east windows.

I still had more work to do on the D'Azouza and Stella Strong commissions, as well as on the Tozzi case—and a great deal more on the Elysium contract, if I could only figure out what else to do that wouldn't make me even more of a target.

I also needed to increase the security levels around the villa and in the comm system.

19

What one knows and what one thinks one knows are the same only for a fool.

By the time midmorning on Senen arrived, I'd tried several more times to reach Lemmy. I got the same response. Since I'd never known his physical locale, I couldn't go around to investigate, either. I worried, though.

I had also spent well into the evening on Domen trying to dig up more on the mysterious Stella Strong/Maureen Gonne and on Theresa McGerrie. I'd found little enough more on either, except several old-style text mysteries published under the name of Terrence McGerrie, one of which was entitled *Coeur Rouge*. I'd even paid for copies of the books and then scanned them. The bio was short.

Terrence McGerrie is the pseudonym of a professional whose work has much to do with the subjects portrayed in those novels but nothing to do with those for whom and with whom McGerrie works. McGerrie admits to living in the area of Thurene, but to little else.

There was no picture.

I read the novel—scan-quick. It seemed to be rather dark and obscure, requiring illumination and something more to bind it together. Then, that just might have been my view. I tend to like works—operas, dramas, books—where there's a bit more than a mere shred of hope at the end. As for its subject . . . so far as I could determine, it was about a man trapped in the intricacies of his work as an advocate for the

Civitas Sorores. When he recognized this and that he had done nothing of real value in his life, he looked around and saw that his nephew was about to do the same. He took all his savings and sent the nephew on a grand tour of the Gallian sector, hoping to open the eyes of the younger man. Yet the young man returned, politely thanked his uncle, and became an advocate in the same specialty as his uncle.

Depressing. It was meant to be, but I wasn't about to read another one. The others had the same author bio. I couldn't help but wonder if Terrence had switched genders to become Terry, and if D'Azouza had been his lover before the switch. For a samer to transex certainly wasn't unheard of. For some it made sense because they weren't really samers, but physio-psychically the "wrong" sex. For the others, such a switch merely compounded their difficulties.

I put in a vidlink to the Authors' Centrality, but on an end-day, I got what I expected, a talking head that only referred me to the same bio I'd already read. I'd have to get back to the Centrality when I had a chance to reach real people.

Both commissions bothered me, if for different reasons. Each involved elaborate game-playing, and there was more behind each game.

Why had "Nancy" tasked me to find Stella/Maureen without a report back to her? There were more than a few possibilities. She could be worried that, if she attempted to find Stella, adverse consequences might befall her. She might feel guilty but simply be so well-off she didn't want to bother tracking down Stella. She might somehow be setting me up. Or setting up Stella. Or she might not have the ability and resources to track down Stella. The last one was the simplest and most logical. I doubted it was the right one. No matter what they say, few people do the simple and logical.

Donacyr D'Azouza's commission was even more improbable. Just find a woman and make sure that she was all right? If D'Azouza didn't happen to be a sex-change-jilted lover, then the situation sounded like McGerrie wasn't all right, not in the slightest. I'd end up entangled in a web I wouldn't have wanted to be in. Yet both clients had paid well in advance. That didn't fit, either. Not unless a great deal more was at stake than I'd been told.

That was all too often the case.

But what?

I put in another two hours on Senen morning trying even more offbeat searches. I found nothing.

Then I began searches on Antonio diVeau and the woman called Sephaniah. I didn't even know her last name. With Odilia's references to her translations, especially the musty Wolfe *Lictor* work, I discovered that she was Sephaniah Dylan-Zimmer. She was also a classics professor at Sur-malle Université, just northeast of Thurene. I used the university link and got a virtie image. It was hers—or that of the Sephaniah who had accosted me at the opera. Unlike her state of near undress of that evening, the virtie image showed her attired in gray jacket and trousers far more decorous than she had worn at the opera. Before the talking head even delivered a spiel, I cut off the image. That could come later. I now knew where to find her.

I'd known that Tony diVeau was the vice director of entertainment and leisure lending at Banque de L'Ouest from a previous commission. He'd occasionally linked, once to offer me a line of credit at the bank. I'd declined, but politely. Krij's contact at Trapeze Zaphir—Rennos Zaphiropoulos—had been far too good to me to leave for a glad-hander like Tony. Besides, I trusted the old Greek. I did even more now that it appeared that Tony was even more closely linked to the "entertainment" industry. I ran a search on Antonio diVeau . . . and on Banque de L'Ouest. I didn't finish reading it all by the time I needed to leave for Krij's, but I was more than ready to leave all my pending commissions behind, if temporarily.

I took my own groundcar. It was armored and shielded, but not armed. I couldn't have afforded the indemnity coverages—nor to do without them. Cuarta Calle was nearly without traffic, and even Le Boulevard had only a scattering of vehicles. I began to run into bicycles once I neared the

Narrows. They'd made a comeback among the nature exercise types who lived there. I wouldn't have been totally surprised to learn that Krij had bought one.

She didn't have a villa, but a comparatively narrow town house in the older section of Thurene on the hill to the west of the Narrows. All the dwellings there dated back three centuries or more. Their walls did, anyway. The interiors had been changed often.

Krij lived just a block down from the historical Doherty Torcastle on VanGelder Way, more of a lane or an alley. It was so narrow that it could only take a single groundcar—one-way only. There was barely enough space to squeeze the groundcar into the single space before her old-style garage. I couldn't even open the door fully and had to ease out and along the side of the vehicle to the street-level landing. The steps up to the main level were brick that had been coated with some sort of permatex that matched both the color and texture of the original finish. Except it wouldn't wear out.

The sunlight flickered as I started up the steps, dimming slightly. The solar screens had adjusted again.

Krij met me at the door. She wore a scoop-necked blouse of green velvet that matched her eyes—and black trousers and boots. A gold chain around her neck held a gold pendant with a large pear-shaped emerald—synth, of course, but striking.

She gave me a smile and warm hug, one that I returned.

"I asked a few others here. I hope you don't mind."

"How many eligible women?"

She smiled, not quite in a superior fashion. "I knew you'd ask that. They're all eligible, but they're with someone else." There was a hint of mischief in both her smile and her eyes. "Andrea won't be here, either. She's with her father."

Krij had always been like that with me. Behind the professional demeanor was a quietly playful sense of humor.

"Besides," she went on, "you value your freedom too much. As the old saying goes, 'The most ordinary cause of a single life is liberty.'" She led me from the foyer to the archway into the parlor. A selection of natural wines was set on the sideboard. I could hear voices from the library-study beyond.

"You're cruel, sister dear."

"Accuracy often is." She laughed, far from cruelly.

"At least, let us agree to a short armistice with truth." Before she could say more, I asked, "Do you know what the connection might be between Judeon Maraniss and Legaar Eloi?"

Krij shook her head. "I don't know of one." She smiled wryly. "That could be because I've never heard of Maraniss until you mentioned him. I do know that I wouldn't want to deal with either Eloi. Legaar's worse than Simeon, but there's little to choose between the two of them."

"What about the Elysium Project?"

"What's that?"

"I don't know. I think it's a project of Legaar's. He's using Classic Research to fund and develop it. It's taken a lot of creds and even more power." Those were guesses on my part.

"They have a lot of credits."

"Gotten in ways I can't say I admire."

"You don't admire many in Thurene, Blaine." She grinned. "What other contracts are you pursuing where I might be of more help?"

"The rumor of sordidity and fortune hunting involving a well-known physician and two separate cases of missing people. One's an heiress named Stella Strong or Maureen Gonne or who knows what else. The other's name I don't even know, not for real. He or she used the pseudonym McGerrie years ago. The client's convinced she's a she, but I'm wondering if she used to be he."

"Gonne? As in Maud Gonne—the old Earth mythical heroine?"

"The same."

"I don't think I can help with either missing soul. What about the sordid business?" Krij steered me toward the sideboard.

"Seldara Tozzi fears that a Dr. Guillaume Richard Dyorr is not what he seems and is after her daughter's inheritance."

"Seems like a perfect match. They're both doctors, both respected, both friendly, and neither shows much passion beyond medicine."

"How do you know so much?"

"We have the research account for the Medical College of the Institute," Krij replied dryly.

"Do you have all the important accounts in Thurene?"

"We have a few—just the ones that require some technical understanding for the accounts to make sense."

"What about Dyorr?"

"He's brilliant, and from what we see, as honest as the sun isn't. I don't know more than that. I've never met him, just audited his accounts. They're meticulous."

"And Tozzi?"

"She's a former korfball star who's as bright as she was athletic. All the beauty credits and genes can provide, and the same drive as her great-grandmother. Pleasant and cool. I've met her twice. I'd want her as a surgeon, but not as a friend."

"Any reason why?"

"Nothing I could put a finger on. Siendra has better judgment about people than I do, and she agrees. Marie Annette would never do anything illegal, though, or anything close to it. Not with that family and background." Krij pointed. "I think you ought to try the primitiva grigio."

That was one of her ways of closing a subject. I just poured a quarter of a goblet. The parlor was spare, with a sideboard on the north wall and a settee flanked by wooden armchairs on the south. Between them, over the sarcenan wood floor, lay the amber-and-green woolen rug Krij had inherited from our mother.

"If you'll excuse me for a bit . . . I need to check in the kitchen."

"You're doing it natural and yourself?"

"You didn't expect otherwise, did you?"

I laughed. I hadn't been thinking. "Go." I turned and crossed the parlor, stopping just inside the library, far warmer with the wooden shelves and the books that ran from floor to ceiling. The carpet was a Sacrestan, with soft reds and golden browns in circular geometric patterns. I'd given it to Krij because she'd liked it.

The first person I saw was Siendra. She barely glanced at me, engaged as she was in talking to a tall and overmuscled type who had clearly gotten himself biosculpted into young god format. Siendra looked the same as always, wearing a warm tan jacket and cream shirt above darker khaki trousers. As usual, she appeared competent and quietly feminine.

The other couple I didn't recognize. One was petite and slender. At least, she had a figure. Her companion was another woman, wearing brilliant flowing red that failed to conceal that she was voluptuously endowed. Both turned to me.

Krij reappeared, carrying a small tray. "Blaine, I'd like you to meet Deiphne and Galyanna." She turned to them. "This is my younger brother Blaine."

"Seignior Donne," murmured the petite Deiphne.

Galyanna nodded pleasantly. "It's good to put a face to the name, especially such a respected name."

"Krij has the respected name. If mine's respected, it's only because of her."

Krij raised her eyebrows but extended the tray. "Have a stuffed mushroom. They're fresh hijatis."

I took two, all that I could manage with one hand. Krij carried the tray to Siendra and her escort.

"You're the one who takes on the strange commissions, aren't you?" Galyanna's voice was as ripe as her figure but with a hint of huskiness.

"The strange ones pay the bills," I said, after finishing off the first hijati. The cheese filling was better than the fungal exterior. "What are your interests?"

"We're dynamic re-creators," offered Deiphne. "We specialize in early interstellar."

"Particularly the Saint and Fundie exoduses," added Galyanna. "And their attempt to find or create their own paradises . . ."

I had to wonder about that. How could any culture create

a paradise when the only paradises were those we had lost? I smiled and let them talk about the period and their work in supplying authenticity to Net-REAL. I wasn't sure it was realism.

After a time, I decided Siendra's pseudoyoung god couldn't be any less interesting. I waited until they asked if I want to join them in refilling their goblets. "I'm still doing fine."

They turned toward the parlor. I eased toward the other couple.

Siendra inclined her head, politely, but neither warmly nor coolly. "Blaine, I'd like you to meet Markus. He teaches at the Lyceum."

"What subjects?" I didn't really care, but thought I should ask.

"Economics. My specialty is postindustrial and early-info-age transactional transformations." Markus beamed broadly, a smile too wide to belong to someone as young as the body he wore signified.

"What would be an example of a transactional transformation?"

"The movement from credit based on present earnings as the basis for repayment to future earnings eventually to credit based on projected changes in personally-linked asset values."

In practical terms, those sounded like merely different methods of assessing ability to repay. "Wouldn't it have been a greater transactional transformation when people moved from using existing assets to purchase capital goods to credit itself?"

"Of course. Of course, but that was merely the first step in a series of transformations basing credit-worthiness assessment more on future reality than upon past reality . . ."

I listened. I did wonder how "future reality" could possibly be more reliable than past reality, since the past had happened, and the future hadn't. That was like worshipping gods of a marketplace that hadn't been built who promised beautiful things that hadn't yet been created.

Siendra smiled faintly, and I had the sense she was as bored as I was. I didn't need a lecture upon the shadows of finance and transactions.

Galyanna and Deiphne returned with goblets refreshed and refilled, and Markus turned toward them.

I stepped back, slightly.

As Markus began to declaim to the other couple, I eased back to the sideboard in the parlor and refilled my goblet. Half-full, this time. I almost didn't notice Siendra's approach. "You're always so quiet, Siendra. I suppose that's part of what makes you so effective."

"That only works if you have a partner like Krij. Quiet by itself can leave you ignored or a target."

"Because people mistake quiet for vulnerability?" I gestured toward the wines.

"Some do. The smarter ones don't." The faintest hint of a smile came and went. "The primitiva grigio, if you would."

I poured her a third of a goblet. Then I asked, "Have you ever heard of something called Elysium, connected to either Judeon Maraniss or Legaar Eloi?"

Siendra's brow furrowed slightly as she concentrated. "Maraniss . . . he's a civic patterner, or he was. I think he gave a lecture some years back, something on designing the ideal city and culture. He radiated arrogance." The frown vanished. "That's all I know about him. Krij may know more than I do about the Elois. The financial and operations sides, anyway." An expression between cynicism and amusement flitted across her lips. "That's not a business that needs our services. We're both grateful we don't have to decline their credits."

"I can imagine."

"Blaine, Siendra." Krij appeared almost beside us. "If you'd head toward the dining room, brunch is ready."

I was hungry, I realized, as I walked beside Siendra toward the dining room that lay behind the study. Markus and the other couple were already seating themselves at the table that could not have held more than eight. Not comfortably.

Warm fall sunlight angled through the skylight. It gave the dining room a lightness that contrasted with the dark wood of the table and chairs.

My place was between Krij and Galyanna.

I knew who I'd be talking to for the duration of the meal, and that was more than all right with me. I wouldn't have minded talking to Siendra either, quiet as she was. Even so, during the meal itself, I enjoyed talking to Krij. We didn't discuss anything particularly important. It was a relief not having to be on guard all the time. Even so, I still couldn't help but fret about what had probably happened to Lemmy.

After the apple tart dessert and coffee and tea, the samer couple left first. Not long after that Markus and Siendra departed. Siendra wished me well, quietly.

I stayed for another stan, then drove back to the villa and went back to work on my commissions.

I tried to contact Lemmy. The system continued to tell me that a link was impossible because of technical impediments.

With some reluctance, I started in on the material about Tony diVeau. There was a great deal that mentioned him in passing, with the emphasis on Banque de L'Ouest. None of that revealed much about Tony. The professional and personal information available in public files was much more limited. He'd gotten an advanced degree in finance from the College of Business at Dartmoor Institute. After graduation, he'd left the southern hemisphere for good and come to Thurene. He started with the First Commerce Bank. Once he'd married Lylette duParc, he'd been offered the position of assistant vice director at Banque de L'Ouest. That wasn't surprising. Her father was the senior managing director. Tony and Lylette had two children, and she was a curator at the Musée Toklas.

Tony deserved a very personal visit—at the bank, and I needed to contact Sephaniah as well, but at the university. I couldn't do either on an end-day.

I tried a search for what amounted to immediate point-to-point transportation. The only systems were variations on

Hawking wormholes, jumpshift generators, and other interstellar systems. There were no references—even theoretical ones—to such a system that would work in a gravity well.

So I spent the rest of the afternoon working on special indirect search routines. That was because the direct searches hadn't worked in the slightest in obtaining any additional information.

20

Hatred is a form of faith, distilled by passion to remove all rationality.

The north end of Thurene holds the River Crescent, with its mosques and markets. There is brass hammered in the ancient fashion, for those who believe that those who fail to learn the lessons of history are doomed to repeat it. There is also brass nanoformed into intricate lace patterns for those who believe that history is bunk, and for them the future is always different and now.

The wind always swirled out of the north in the River Crescent, but it was colder and harsher this night. Even the unlit waters of the Nouvelle Seine showed small whitecaps beyond the three piers that held dhows, tied fast to bollards carved with curved and intricate symbols praising the only God. Despite the wind, the perfume of cooking oil and roasting fowl and lamb permeated the streets and alleys. It wasn't unpleasant, merely pervasive.

In my shadow grays, I eased down the stone alley. Beyond the gray-green sandstone walls to the right lay the back wall of the weavers' market. There I had found rugs of all types, including the artisan quality Sacrestan that I had given to my sister. Among the dross one could find great artistry, surprisingly often, because what was popular in the salons of the palacios and villas of Thurene had little to do with excellence.

Why was I in the River Crescent, where no sane outsider ventured in the late evening?

I deferred that question, my senses and implants alert. I was seeking someone in trouble, anyone in real difficulty.

From the weavers' market I slipped westward along Falange Way, two blocks back from the river. From there I followed another unnamed alley back toward the Nouvelle Seine, slowing as I sensed someone ahead.

An old man walked slowly along the side of the alley with the narrow sidewalk. In the dimness I could see the thin silver-gray of his hair above the gray-and-black woolen poncho-cape draped over his stooped frame. Old age fell more heavily upon those in the ethnic areas such as the River Crescent and western hill barrios. They lacked the resources to hold age at bay. Some also felt that there was a vague obscenity in seemingly eternal youth, particularly as displayed by the aristos of Thurene. But then, much of what was displayed by the aristos in any society was vaguely obscene, if not more so.

The old man stepped around a cart chained to a faux wrought-iron grill. Ahead of him, a small girl sat huddled on the stone curb where the alley intersected a narrow way. She was bathed in the dim light of an antique streetlamp.

"Little girl . . . are you all right?" His voice didn't sound that old, despite his stooped frame.

She did not respond.

I could sense the youths in the alleyway ahead, and I could hear whispers. The old man should have as well.

"Are you feeling well?" He touched the girl's blanket with his walking stick. The stick went through the holo projection.

At that moment, the seven youths charged from behind a stone stoop just up the narrow way. The old man did not attempt to flee as they encircled him. The image of the small girl vanished.

I waited. I had a feeling that all was not as it appeared.

"You want to help us, don't you, old man?" The leader of the group stood slightly forward. He wore a pseudo gold-mesh jacket over maroon leather trousers that were form-fitting down to the knee and broadly flared below above matching maroon boots. The others were attired in the same style. Two were muscular girls with hair cut even shorter than that of the young men. All had black hair streaked with luminescent gold.

"The Garda will see what you're doing," suggested the man.

"No, they won't. We're feeding a false holo over a shroud."

That rang true enough. It didn't seem to bother the chosen victim.

"What do you want?"

"Just some entertainment, old man. And your creds."

That was another difference in River Crescent. Many of the inhabitants still carried actual credits. They distrusted the banking system. They also didn't want the sisters to know what transactions took place between whom. That's been a universal constant since the first staters or shekels . . . or whatever . . . were minted.

"Entertainment?" There was no puzzlement in the man's voice. There should have been.

"You're going to dance for us. You fall down, and we'll use these to help you up." A long wooden wand appeared in the leader's hand. Similar wands appeared in the hands of the others.

The old man straightened. An electrolash flashed in his hand, taking the place of the walking stick. A flare of light appeared, and one of the youths went down. Another charged the man, but the lash struck her in the chest. She screamed, then convulsed.

I forced myself to wait until all seven were down. That took only moments.

The old man began to repeat using the lash, starting with the leader.

The youngsters probably deserved what they were getting, but those on the stone pavement would be dead before long at the intensity their would-be victim had programmed into the lash.

"Enough." My voice carried. "They've had enough."

The man turned. Behind the plastiflesh, I could sense the

rage. And the fact that he was neither old nor young. That was before the electrolash flew toward me.

I dove forward into a forward roll. Most people make the mistake of trying to escape a lash, but a lash can extend it-self far more easily than it can retract into close quarters. I came out of the roll almost chest to chest with him, for the moment it took to knock the weapon out of his hand.

His other hand went for the belt knife, but I kneed him and palmed his chin. Hard. Then I snapped the knife out of the sheath. He went down on top of the gang leader, who was beginning to twitch.

I followed the energy trails to the shroud unit and projec-tor, set at the base of the stoop where the seven had waited. Not exactly the magnificent seven. I crushed the equipment with my boot, then walked back to the pile of bodies and hoisted the pseudo-old man to his feet.

"Come along. You really don't want to be found here when the Garda arrives."

For the first time, he looked at me. Not that he could re-ally see my face, not with the shadows that accompany me.

He shuddered. "Are you . . . ?"

"No." I kept him walking until we were on the street that bordered the river. "You're on your own from here on in."

Behind us I could sense the approaching Garda flitter. It would be a remote. They always were in the ethnic areas.

I turned and hurried westward, leaving the man standing there.

Even in the River Crescent, nothing was quite as it seemed. Just like everything else in Thurene.

For me, in the shadows, so much was clearer than in the bright illumination of Thurene. The city's brilliance con-cealed so much more than it revealed. Was that why I took refuge in doing what I could in the shadows?

21

The distinction between precision in speech and obfuscation can only be made by the listener.

First thing on Lunen morning—after my workout—I made an appointment, under a misleading name and false pretenses, to meet with Angelique deGritz early in the afternoon. Then I went back to working on my three commissions. This time I began to access my network of contacts and acquaintances—those I could reach.

I started with Shannon at the Garda.

"Colonel . . ."

"What are you up to now, Donne?" Flat brown eyes glared at me from under his jutting brow. Why he'd kept the residual ape-brows I had to wonder.

"Just asking around. Trying to locate people. Either a Maureen Gonne or a Terrie McGerrie. You know either?"

"I'm happy to say that I don't. Why are you asking?"

"Lost relations. One's an heiress. Can you tell me if either's been reported as missing? That's a public record," I reminded him.

"Maureen Gonne or Terrie McGerrie?" Shannon didn't look happy, but after a moment, replied, "Neither one. No record of death, either, or anything on the public record."

"Thank you, Colonel. I appreciate it. Does the name Elysium Project mean anything?"

I doubted that Shannon could have counterfeited the fractionally blank expression of incomprehension before he replied. "Never heard of it. What is it?"

"I don't know, either. I heard it in connection with a civic planner named Maraniss, but no context. So far as I know, there's nothing illegal even rumored about it."

"Maraniss . . ." Shannon frowned. "He was on the advisory board for the Civitas Sorores four, five years back. Sort of arrogant. He told the Soror Prima that Thurene could have been an ideal city." He smiled, wryly. "Elysium . . . that was the word he used. Said Thurene could have been Elysium if the sisters weren't so obtuse. Should have remembered that."

"Did he say anything else?"

Shannon laughed. "He couldn't. The Soror Prima dismissed him on the spot. Said he was out of line. Had everything he said struck from the record."

So that was why there was nothing in the data systems.

"Nothing to do with the Sorores after that," Shannon went on. "No media, either."

I nodded. "Thanks."

"I'll be in touch when I need something you might know."

Shannon had even less subtlety than I did. "You know where to find me, Colonel."

After Shannon, I began vid-calls to those who owed me—or who might tell me anyway.

J. William Smith preferred to be called William. I usually called him Jay or Bill. That depended on how much I wanted him on edge. He was an advocate on the lower fringe. He had to actually work at providing services for those who could barely pay.

"Jay, how's the advocacy racket?"

"Blaine, how you can use such crude language with antecedents such as yours is a matter that even the ancient gods with their all-too-human foibles would scarcely have tolerated." His appearance was Old Earth courtly, with gray sideburns. That was an affectation. So was his language.

"How are you faring in the conduct of your most ancient and plutocratic profession?"

"Scoffer."

He was right about that. "I admit it. I need some information. I'll add to your coffers if you can tell me. As always, if it involves a client of yours, it's off-limits."

"Remuneration would be acceptable." He beamed from behind the wide mahogany desk that was a virtie superimposition.

"Have you ever heard of something called the Elysium Project?"

"Alas, I must confess that there are many, all rather sordid, although the only one with which I have had any contact was an establishment in the nether reaches of Thurene. That would have been the Elysian Pleasure Fields, but it was renamed three years ago after it suffered some damage from unexplained causes."

"Competition for the Classic enterprises of the Elois?"

"Far too sordid, I fear, to even approximate competition, Seignior Donne."

"So it wasn't owned by the Elois?"

"No. The proprietress was originally from Nantes. I assisted her in pursuing recompense. Once she received it, she divested herself of the enterprise to another individual."

"Not Eloi?"

"No . . . I now believe it is operated as an institution professing to deal with less intimate bodily functions—mere massage and the like."

"Anything else about Elysium?"

"I have disclosed all that I can recollect."

"What about a Judeon Maraniss?"

"A most obnoxious and arrogant example of an individual whose intellectual capabilities have convinced him all others are so far beneath him that they merit less than condescension."

"Do you know him?"

"Not in the slightest. I have encountered him upon a handful of occasions, all of them passing, and none of them pleasant."

"If you hardly know him, why do you dislike him so much?"

Jay spread his hands. "I admit to a totally visceral and intellectually unfounded immediate detestation."

"Another case. A Dr. Guillaume Richard Dyorr."

Jay snorted. "An expert. A pain-in-the-ass expert. Solid and friendly."

"I take it he was an expert against one of your clients?"

"He was. We lost. Nothing more to say."

With his tone, I wasn't about to pursue Dyorr. Besides, he'd told me the important stuff.

"Different case. Stella Strong and Maureen Gonne. Same person, different names."

"My knowledge of either appellation or the personage behind either is nonexistent."

"Astrid Forte or Charlyse Forte?"

"Likewise . . ." Jay shook his head. "No . . . Charlyse Forte was a mysticist, I think. I met her at a friend's party near Vannes years ago. Heard she died a while back. Only encountered her in passing. Attractive woman, though. I know nothing more and have never since encountered her or her appellation."

"Terrie McGerrie, or variations on the name?"

"Ah . . . I do have some minimal knowledge. That is the pseudonym of a professional who has authored a number of dramas. She is and has always been female, and is currently creating—albeit it at a less prolific rate—under the pseudonym of Carey Douglass."

"Do you know her personally?"

"I have never met the lady, even in a virtual sense. The information came to me through my accounting compliance auditor."

"Who might that be?"

"Corey Richarde."

Once I finished with Jay, I tried a vidlink to the accounting compliance auditor.

All I could say about Corey Richarde was that her virtie appearance was best described as glittering in a shifting silver jacket and trousers, yet imperially slim.

"Blaine Donne, for Corey Richarde."

The holo flickered, and a slightly different image appeared. This time, the jacket and trousers were glittering gold. "Seignior Donne. You must be pursuing information.

With your sister handling your compliance affairs, you scarcely would need my services."

"I am. I'm trying to find the personage behind the names of Terrie McGerrie and Carey Douglass."

She nodded. The virtie shifted slightly. The gold was a superimposition. "I can only tell you that the personage is alive and doing well. Other than that . . ."

"Client confidential?"

She laughed. "To admit or deny that would provide you with more information than I should."

"I understand. What about the names Stella Strong and Maureen Gonne?"

She shook her head.

"The Elysium Project?"

"That sounds less than savory, but I've never heard of it."

"Judeon Maraniss?"

"He's a civic planner of some sort. I met him briefly at a Civitas Sorores hearing a number of years ago. Briefly was too long."

That was all I got from Corey Richarde.

I made three more vidlinks before Max flashed me.

Incoming from Theodore Elsen.

Accept.

Elsen was angular and spare, with short disheveled brown hair. He didn't look all that big either. He didn't even offer a greeting. "What are you chasing down, Seignior Donne?"

"Medical research. I've been asked to evaluate a research proposal."

"And you're looking for dirt and inside expertise. You always do. You think you know how things work, but you've got a lot to learn."

"What do you think about the state of consciousness research?"

"It's still fortune-telling based on the alchemy of quantum biological effects that may not have any impact on brain function at all."

"Why does it get funded, then?"

"Why does anything get funded? It isn't enough to be a

good scientist and outstanding medical researcher. You've also got to be personable, friendly, persuasive, and well-connected."

"By planned marriage?" That was a gamble, but I thought he might react.

"By whatever works. Medical centers want docs to produce. We either do high-credit and high-visibility medical procedures or glamorous research. Some have found that glamorous research doesn't have to be all that rigorous scientifically."

"Like consciousness research?"

"Draw your own conclusions, Donne. I drew mine a long time ago. Even the best scientist in the field can always use more friends, family, and credits."

"What else can you tell me?"

"Your report won't change a thing."

"Then why did you return my link?"

"I just wanted to see what a knight looked like in person. You're better in the shadows."

With that he was gone.

For personal charm, Theodore Elsen was right up there with Legaar Eloi and Judeon Maraniss. But he had told me a few things in passing. While he didn't like Dyorr, he gave him grudging respect. He also had implied that Dyorr wasn't just fortune hunting.

So why did Seldara Tozzi think so?

I went back to trying to contact people.

I made seventeen more vidlinks and got nothing I didn't know already. I got less than nothing because I'd used up goodwill and access to no good end.

After that, I used my system links to do a virtie search of the city records for building and construction permit requests, but there was nothing there about either Elysium or Maraniss, and the Eloi and Classic permits over the past ten years were for minor alterations or additions—all but one. That was the Classic Research center at Time's End. Construction had begun on that slightly over three years before.

In the end, Maraniss's words suggested a linkage between

him and Elysium. The timing of the building of the new research center suggested a link between Maraniss and Legaar Eloi, but I still had nothing that remotely resembled proof.

By then it was time to drive to my appointment with Angelique deGritz. Traffic was light. It always was, what with the taxes and usage fees.

The First Commerce Bank was located on the east end of the Left Bank, three long blocks from the river. The building was a brownstone with a design far more appropriate for a city in the Columbian sector of the Assembly. The receptionist was not a virtie, but real. She could have once been a special operative or an IS commando. I'd have bet commando.

"Kinnal Galwaie. I have an appointment with Angelique deGritz." I proffered the perfectly legitimate alternate identity card.

She scanned it, then pulsed the commnet. My implant systems could detect the energies but not decrypt the protocols.

"Take the ramp to your left. Her office is the second door on the left on the lower level."

"Thank you."

The ramp was only fifteen meters long. The doorways beyond were close together. The second door slid open as I approached. I stepped through.

Angelique deGritz looked up from a small console in an office not much larger than my desk. Her hair was a luminous mahogany flame, but her eyes were emerald-metal hard. They bored through me. "You're not Kinnal Galwaie. You're Blaine Donne. You're not here to set up a trust. If you can't explain quickly why whatever you want is both legal and in the Bank's interest, I suggest that you leave— immediately."

Her words were sharp enough to draw blood. Whether she'd actually recognized me or whether she had a comparator system that had identified me didn't matter.

"I've been retained to locate a woman. I've been told that she may be the heir to a bequest that is administered by the

Bank, and I was given your name as the contact, once I located her, but I frankly don't want to spend time chasing down someone under false pretenses."

"That's rather general. It sounds legal, but we cannot offer any names." The sharpness diffused into boredom. I didn't believe it.

"I'm told that the bequest is from a Clinton Jefferson Wayles to children he had with women who were not his wife. I've been commissioned to find a Stella Strong. She supposedly also went by the name of Maureen Gonne."

Angelique nodded politely. I could sense the links.

"I can only confirm there is a bequest from the estate of one Clinton Jefferson Wayles. The terms of the bequest cannot be made public, nor can the identities of the beneficiaries."

I had to frown at that. "I thought bequests, once registered, were public documents."

"They are, Seignior Donne. They cannot be officially registered until the identity of the beneficiary is known, confirmed, and certified. Was that not why you were retained?"

"Why couldn't the beneficiary just appear before you and certify her identity?"

"Such an individual certainly could. It would be far easier for everyone."

"If there is more than one beneficiary, and only one appears and is certified," I asked cautiously, "are the terms of the bequest made public at that time?"

"No. We have to make public that such a bequest exists, but in the case of multiple or contingent beneficiaries, none of the beneficiaries' names are made public until all primary beneficiaries are certified or otherwise accounted for."

"Otherwise accounted for meaning deceased."

"Usually. Or legally ineligible, as in the case of felons who might benefit from a crime."

"Offspring who murder to get the inheritance? That sort of thing?"

"That's one class of ineligibility. The others are listed in the Codex."

Cold and precise as she was, there was no sense of deception about her. That meant she'd offered no untruths but left much undisclosed. That was the way angels lied, I figured. Assuming there ever had been angels.

"You don't hold off disbursing until everyone is found? If they're not, that could be a long wait," I pointed out. "Hundreds of years."

"The maximum is three centuries and a year, the minimum fifty years. We disburse what is possible as soon as the legalities are satisfied."

"Assuming I find this woman, what do you need to certify her?"

"Her proper Gallian identity, her birth record, and gene-certified record of parentage or, if she is not genetically related, the legal record establishing equivalency of parentage."

I nodded politely. Angelique had as much as confirmed the bequest did go to children.

"Did you ever know a Terrence or Therese McGerrie?"

"The dramaturge? Not personally or professionally. I've seen one or two of her works."

"Carey Douglass?"

"No." Angelique smiled coldly. "I think there's little more for us to discuss, Seignior Donne. Good day."

I left. I'd never even had the chance to sit down.

22

*Bartered bastard bride of dead suns bares
her beauty while hot blood runs.*

Legaar stood in the doorway to the suite, looking almost disappointed that I was unaccompanied by one of his nymphs, but I've never had much use for sycophants, especially for sexual sycophants. Magdalena was compliantly understanding, not falsely flattering, and there was a difference between the two.

Yet sometimes, I wondered about Magdalena. Should I have let her loose? Was indeed everything spoiled by use?

"I want to see the projections." Legaar's words weren't a request because he never requested anything when he could order someone around. His brother Simeon was just the opposite, and the more quietly Simeon requested something, the angrier and more dangerous he was. Legaar was bullying and dangerous all the time.

"What about the shadow knight and the Fox?" I didn't really care about either, but Legaar did. Besides, it was a way of keeping him off-balance, and that was necessary with his calculating and predatory personality. "Has the Garda found the trails your agents planted from Jerome to Donne?"

"The Garda's still looking into the matter. They'll have trouble with the time displacement." Legaar frowned. "We should have taken care of Jerome when you first realized the application of his work."

I'd suggested that, but Legaar had thought Jerome wouldn't even notice the use of one modified jump-generator out of the thousands in use across the Galaxy. I wasn't about to remind Legaar that I'd warned him. "What about the shadow?"

"The shadow's been quiet ever since you shook him up. Hasn't even been haunting the back streets or the South Bank. This will tie him up further. Nothing new on the Fox. That could just be a rumor or a false lead for us."

"Is that from your friends on the Garda?"

"And some others."

"Do you want me to try with the field again?"

"No. It's too complicated and uncertain planetside. And it's slow. Besides, the local Assembly IS agents found out about the anomalies and the energy use, and they've beefed up satellite and local EDI surveillance. Now, they might be able to pinpoint the source. Unless the shadow comes out after us directly and without shields, it's better not to use the projection field. The shadow can't do that much anyway, but I don't want the Assembly sending in a fleet. Our . . . allies might disassociate themselves if that occurred."

"How are the defenses?"

"We got more RPFs. They'll take care of anything local." Legaar waved his arms. "We're set. Stop chewing the air and show me the projections."

I called up the first projection, positioned so that the entire system hung between us, with Devanta a point of green, and the sun reddish orange. "The nodes are the fuchsia points. They're really MDLs."

"Stop using all your acronyms." Legaar snapped. "They're just glorified knots in underspace."

"Overspace. They're multidimensional loci."

"They have enough twists that they're knots. Call them that."

Before he agreed to the project, Legaar wouldn't have known an MDL from a Hawking wormhole or sintered black hole or white hole. His interests lay in the credits produced from much shallower and more mundane depths and darknesses.

"Voltaire's the fulcrum," Legaar said. "Do you have all the vectors and field positions calculated?"

That was another stupid statement followed by an even stupider question. I'd already reported that the calculations were as complete as they could be until the field was operational. For the system to work optimally, the sun and the target moon had to be on opposite sides of Devanta, and we couldn't make all the adjustments at the last minute. That's why as much as possible was precalculated. I'd told him that at least three times.

"Wipe that condescending look off your face, Maraniss. Unless you want to finish this operation as a brain-conditioned nymph."

"I wasn't being condescending, Legaar." I smiled politely. "I was just thinking about what was coming to the sisters." Legaar's words were a bluff. After the operation . . . then it would be a real possibility . . . except that I wouldn't be anywhere that Legaar could reach. Matters were so far along that I could complete the project—if necessary—without the Hawking complex, but it would be messy, and the inflation would be less than ideal, not that it would matter in any lifetime I had. It would also leave traces of the methodology, and I didn't want to leave anything for the thoughtless and ungrateful Assembly.

Or for the Elois, except they wouldn't find anything.

The Civitas Sorores and all those who fawned over the sisters wouldn't get all that they deserved, but they'd get enough, and it would probably be sufficient for reformulation—assuming that there was anyone left to be governed. In any case, total revenge had to be secondary to my success. Legaar and Simeon would get their rewards as well, and that, too, would be as it should be, for a process in the weather of the world would blow the moon into the sun, figuratively, of course, and worlds would hang on the trees of time and gape, unable to act.

"It's not about revenge, Maraniss. It's about creds and power. Those are what count."

I nodded. He was half-right.

"The next projection, frig it! Get moving."

I called up the stress lines that would extend all across

the Gallian sector. At this point, the projection went to modified scale, but that was good enough for Legaar to study and gloat.

"Bastards on Dreyfus . . . they'll get theirs, too."

That was indubitably true, assuming one meant dying a slow and lingering death was "getting theirs." The other systems in the Gallian sector were too distant for more than minor disruptions to their heliospheres.

"Next projection."

"Did you ever discover who sent the military flitter to do recon on Time's End the other night?"

"Javerr did some checking. There was no record from ACS of any flitters headed northeast out of Thurene. Our systems had it coming due east. There's a SpecOps base east of Vannes, and it'd be a straight flight from there. The maneuvers were SpecOps, according to the analysis."

"Special Operations? They're not supposed to be operating planetside."

"Doesn't matter. They didn't get inside, and the outside scan they did won't tell them anything."

"No, but they still shouldn't be planetside."

"You want to tell them, Maraniss?"

I didn't, but in three weeks it wouldn't matter, not when I would have fostered the golden white light of Elysium and veiled the man-shaped galaxy that had spawned and rejected me.

23

It had taken some effort, but by late midafternoon on Lunen, I'd found Tony's groundcar in the restricted parking area for bank officials. I hadn't been able to get that close, but I'd used an airbolt projector to dust it with nanosnoops, placed so that some would sift inside when the doors were open. I was assuming that the vehicle parked in the space marked for the VICE DIRECTOR, E&L, was his. The carpark was beneath the pseudogranite, faux-classical structure that housed the bank. The public section was on a different level, but I just walked down a ramp.

To any snoops or onlookers, I would have appeared curious. I just pointed at one vehicle, then turned away. The projector was hidden in my sleeve.

Then I walked briskly up the pedestrian ramps and through the main entrance to Banque de L'Ouest, guarded by two virties and a virtie receptionist. The guard images were symbolic of the nanobarriers that blocked unauthorized entrance to the Banque's business offices.

"Blaine Donne to see Antonio diVeau."

"One moment, ser." The virtie receptionist smiled warmly. Her brown eyes were supposed to show trust. They just looked flat to me.

As she checked, I looked past her image. The decor was a cross between brass rococo and green marble, with handpainted replicas of ancient Old Earth French pastoral oils. The walls were paneled in dark pseudocherry. The handful of desks in the open area held young-looking men and women in severe gray suits and pin-striped shirts. The only color was modestly colored scarves for the women and fine-striped ties for the men. I hadn't seen such a living montage of antiquity in years.

"It will be a few minutes, ser. Would you like a seat in the waiting area?" The virtie gestured to a period love seat against the wall just past her console desk.

"Thank you." I settled myself in to wait. I let my implants scan the energy flows. I was careful not to attempt to crack them. The temptation was strong because they were as obsolete as the decor and about as effective.

None of the pin-striped young bankers looked at me. All appeared fixated on the vid-holos before them. I had no idea what they were doing and less interest in learning. I waited almost fifteen minutes.

"Seignior Donne, Directeur diVeau will see you now. His office is the second door on the left."

Directeur? That usage had gone out with the decor. Except in Banque de L'Ouest, I gathered. "Thank you." I stood and walked to the second door. I opened it, stepped inside, and closed it. The office beyond was small, no more than three and a half meters square.

Tony diVeau stood after I closed the door. He had an oval and round, friendly face, a short, muscular neck, broad shoulders and a heavy torso emphasized by a gray pin-striped suit jacket that was a shade too small. His smile was the warm and welcoming type perfected by all effective bankers since the creation of banks. His hair was brown, of moderate length, and slightly wavy.

"Blaine . . . I thought I wasn't going to hear from you." Tony gestured to the straight-backed chair across from the unnecessary cherry desk with its equally unnecessary drawers. "I hoped you would. Can I count on you for that cataract trip to Pays du Sud in Novem . . ."

"There are reasons for that." I didn't sit down. I offered a smile meant to be furtive. "Tony . . . I need a moment of your time."

"You can have all the time you need, Blaine."

"If you'd just take a walk with me. Just across to the plaza or around the block."

The barest hint of puzzlement flickered in his eyes. Then they went blank, as he linked to the bank's comm system. I could sense the energy flows. Again, I refrained from attempting to eavesdrop on the link. Even so, I caught some of it through the leakage of a sloppy system.

". . . need to take a walk with a client . . . not more than half a stan . . ."

Tony's smile returned. "If it makes you feel more comfortable, we can certainly do that." He stepped from behind the desk.

I let him lead the way out of the office and past the unseen security barriers. We crossed the lightly traveled Rue de Paix and began a stroll around the statue of the second Soror Prima. I'd never learned her name. That kind of history didn't appeal to me.

"What did you want to talk about, Blaine? I can guess it's not about cataract trips." He laughed heartily. "A credit line . . . some sort of . . . special financial arrangement?"

"You make those sorts of arrangements?" I tried to let just a hint of tentativeness enter my voice.

"We try to be helpful to everyone." Tony smiled more broadly.

"I'm not in the entertainment and leisure lines."

"If it's something I can't handle, Blaine, I'll make sure you get someone who can."

I nodded. "I'm curious . . . about . . . how this sort of thing is structured. I assume the interest is tied to . . . risk."

"That's the usual way."

"So . . . if it's an unusual business, say, like the Classic Escort Service, you look at the risks?" I laughed. "I don't imagine that's all that risky. It's an old line of business."

There was the slightest pause. "It's a legitimate form of entertainment. We assess it like any other. What did you have in mind?"

"How well do you know Legaar Eloi?"

Tony laughed, genially. "No one knows the Elois, not even their bankers."

"You're in the entertainment sector, and you're vice director. Don't tell me you haven't met them."

He shrugged his wide, almost beefy shoulders. "I wouldn't say that. Directeur Eloi has always been most businesslike."

"How long have you been dealing with him?"

Tony stopped and looked sidewise at me. "I don't think I ever said I had been. His manner's always been businesslike, even at receptions."

"I've heard that." Tony had still confirmed that he knew Legaar on a more-than-casual basis. "Do you know who first bankrolled him?"

"There are all sorts of rumors." Tony laughed again, but there was a nervous edge to the sound. "I wouldn't believe them. We certainly didn't."

"There are more than a few. Like the fact that he has people spy and snoop for him. Or that top people who aren't successful disappear." I laughed again. "I'd thought about getting into a competing business, but talking to you, Tony, tells me that it's not a good idea. I'd just want to disappear people who did those sorts of things, and that just creates problems." I smiled. "It's been good talking to you. I thought you'd be just like you are. And I appreciated the cataract offer, but I'm better at other things than swimming." I stopped and smiled again. "Take care, Tony. You've got a good family."

"Blaine . . ." He almost made my name sound like an expletive.

"Let's leave it at that, Tony. I don't like snoops dumped on me, and you don't want trouble."

Before he could say more, I turned and walked away. I had my implants on full, but we were in a publicly monitored space. Tony wasn't stupid.

I walked back to my own groundcar. I couldn't help but think how much Tony reminded me of Lawrence Luchesi in *The Financiers*. The satire-drama had been ridiculous. Yet I could still smile at the idea of bankers with selectively adapted vampiritic and shark tissue implants. That idea had been around since the first Clone Conflicts back on Old Earth. It had almost been more satirized than the absurdity of intelligent design.

Once in my groundcar, I tapped into the snoops I'd planted on and around Tony. Then I started back toward the villa. I was almost there before the first signals came back.

". . . who does he think he is . . . just walk in and pressure me . . . see how he likes being squeezed . . ."

Those remarks cut off. I was pulling into the garage when the signals resumed.

"Ser Daglione . . . it's a pleasure to hear from you. Yes, I know I linked you. It's about your line of credit . . . oh, we certainly do want to work with you, but there is a certain risk to the kinds of transactions you specialize in . . . we have to take that into account when we set the rate . . . I might be able to come down a bit . . . you've been a good customer . . . we're limited. There are certain guidelines set by the sisters, and we can't do much about them . . . Yes, I know . . ."

Tony went on for another ten minutes before he broke the link. I could tell he was doing something, but it was nonverbal.

Abruptly, he began to speak, his voice low.

"Pass it on . . . Blaine Donne. This guy Donne is onto something. He's fishing, and he knows where I stand. How? I don't know. No . . . a meeting won't do any good. He might even be watching and tailing me. That's one of the things he does. I said . . . just pass it on."

Another silence followed.

". . . ought to take care of him . . . threaten me . . . even veiled . . ."

Tony's remarks validated my earlier opinion of him and my suspicions of his links to Legaar Eloi. Again, I had no usable proof, not the kind I could take to the Garda or the justiciary. That didn't make the connection less real.

24

Too often, predators forget they are also prey.

By the time I got to my study on Marten morning, all my snoops on Tony had expired or been swept. His mutterings and the verbal sides of his vidlinks hadn't revealed more than what I'd already suspected. They also hadn't led to anything of a firm and provable nature.

I hadn't discovered that much more on Sephaniah Dylan-Zimmer, either. I'd found additional publications, citations of her work by other scholars, and more published research, but the professor led a very private life. That was understandable. It wasn't helpful.

I had a few minutes before I had to leave for Dyorr's presentation to the Devantan Humanitas Foundation. I could only try the direct approach. I used the vidlink.

This time the talking head was wearing dark green. The color was more becoming. It also showed a sophisticated programming.

"You've reached my office at the university. As you may know, I'll be on sabbatical until Triem and will be unavailable until then. Messages will not be forwarded unless they are of an urgent nature, and that requires contact with the university administration."

After those words, the image froze in place.

Messages not being forwarded strongly suggested that she was out-system somewhere. Doing research on Old Earth? I linked to the administration vid-codes. After a good minute,

I got another virtie. This one was synth rather than replica. She was politely clean-looking and blond.

"I'm looking for someone who can authorize an urgent message to Professor Dylan-Zimmer."

Almost immediately another face appeared. Unlined, but narrow and severe under hair too dark for her pale skin. "I'm Subprovost Harras. You indicated an urgent message for Professor Dylan-Zimmer."

"Blaine Donne. I've been trying to reach Professor Dylan-Zimmer, but all I've gotten is a message that she's on sabbatical and won't be back for another three months."

"I'm sorry, Ser Donne. That's all I can really tell you."

"When did she leave? That's not a secret, I assume."

The severe-faced woman did not answer.

"How long is the minimum standard sabbatical? That can't be confidential."

"Six months." Even those words came out distastefully.

"Thank you. Then the woman who met me last week here in Thurene, claiming to be her, was unlikely to have been."

"That would have been impossible. Do you have a message?"

"No. I was just trying to verify an identity. You've been most helpful. Thank you."

"Is that all?"

"It is, thank you."

"Good day, Ser Donne."

The projected image vanished. I leaned back in my chair. Had Odilia known?

After a moment, I tried a vidlink to the princesse.

She actually appeared. She was wearing dark crimson, not maroon, with a wide black belt that emphasized her impossibly narrow waist.

"Blaine . . . I only have a moment . . ."

"I just had a question. How well do you know Sephaniah Dylan-Zimmer?"

Odilia frowned. "Not that well at all. I only see her at the opera, and that's only once or twice a year. I understand an occasional appearance at the opera is her one luxury. I like her work, but we're not really even acquaintances. In person, she's very different from professionally. I like the professional side, not the personal side."

"I just found out that she's been on sabbatical for more than two months. Out-system."

"That can't be. We saw her . . ."

"We saw someone . . . It wasn't her."

"I'm rather late, Blaine dear. I'll have to think about that." She blew me a kiss, and the image went blank.

I collapsed my projection.

How much did Odilia know? I thought she'd looked surprised for the faintest instant. Stunned, almost. But had that been at my revelation? Or at the deception of the false Sephaniah? That also assumed that the "opera" Sephaniah had been false. But why would a professor intimate she was off-planet, then flaunt herself at the opera? That verged on false representation and dishonesty. Professors had lost their positions for far less. Even tenured ones.

Yet . . .

I shook my head. I'd have to let my subconscious ruminate on that. In the meantime, I had to get moving.

I barely made it to the large conference room at Banque du Sud by quarter to eleven.

There were guards, both with low-porosity nanite shields, and stunners. They looked at me.

"Blaine Donne. I'm a consultant, here at the request of Seigniora Tozzi."

"ID confirmation, ser?"

I flashed the codes, and the small scanner studied me. The skeptical expressions were replaced with ones of boredom.

"You're cleared, ser. Observers in the last row, please."

The aide standing beside the guards handed me a booklet and a dataflat. "Here are the briefing materials, Seignior Donne."

"Thank you."

The conference room was of moderate size, perhaps twelve meters wide and ten deep. In the front was a low dais with a podium set on the left. Below the dais were rows of chairs.

I had the last row almost to myself. I sat on the far right end. That way I had some chance of at least catching profiles of those in the rows closer to the front. There were two others in back with me. One was a muscular woman verging on stockiness and the other a youngish-looking media linker. Neither looked in my direction.

Dr. Dyorr stood on one side of the dais, beside the podium, talking quietly to a woman I'd never seen. Dr. Marie Tozzi sat in the first row of chairs on the far left-hand side. Her eyes were not on Dyorr, but on a striking brunette. The brunette was obviously an assistant to an older man in a dark suit because he would turn and tell her something before resuming his conversation with another woman.

I didn't try to read everything in the booklet, but I did skim through it very quickly before turning my attention to the various individuals. Not counting Dr. Tozzi, there were nine people in the center of the first row of seats, with four or five empty chairs on each side. About half of those in the first row had assistants in the second row. No one was in the third row. The fourth row was where I was.

The distinguished man with the striking assistant stood. "For those of you who don't know me, I'm Pietr vonGarodyn, the chairman of the Humanitas Board. The only business at this meeting is to hear a presentation by the distinguished Dr. Guillaume Richard Dyorr, the director of consciousness programs at the Medical College of L'Institut Multitechnique. I won't belabor his credentials . . ."

Unfortunately, vonGarodyn then proceeded to state all the professional background on Dyorr. It was all in the handouts, but that didn't seem to matter.

While he talked, I watched. Just as Dr. Tozzi watched the brunette, a petite blond woman studied Marie Annette, if not so obviously. She was also an observer, at the far end of the row. I hadn't noticed her initially, but she was more than passingly pretty.

Eventually, Dyorr took the podium. He paused, not rushing. Then he spoke. His voice was a pleasant but not striking baritone. "I would like to thank the Board members, and indeed everyone here, for being kind and gracious enough to afford the Medical College the opportunity to present this proposal." He smiled. "Consciousness has been termed the last great area of medical uncertainty. It most definitely is. It is, or it represents, a combination of physiological and mental processes so involved and intricate that it has yet to be understood or replicated outside the construct of a human brain. Yet, after all these centuries and all the planets we have occupied and transformed, we cannot define or replicate the very process that has made our history as a species possible. To gain a greater understanding of this physiological miracle is the goal of the research proposed . . ."

The presentation lasted exactly twenty-one minutes, almost to the second.

During the entire time, not a single Board member looked away from Dyorr. Tozzi looked mostly at them rather than Dyorr.

There were no questions.

Then Pietr vonGarodyn stood again. "At this time, we would like to request that all those who are not sitting members of the Board leave."

Marie Annette joined the personal assistants and those of us classed as observers in leaving the room. Dyorr remained behind.

I eased toward Marie Annette. "Dr. Tozzi?"

She turned. I hadn't realized that she was almost as tall as I was. Her gray eyes were wide-set and penetrating, her skin flawless. She wore a dark gray medical singlesuit, with a pale blue jacket over it. "Yes?"

"I'm Blaine Donne, and I've been tasked with covering the presentation." I shrugged. "Some of what Dr. Dyorr said was . . . shall we say . . . daunting, and I have a technical background."

"The proposal outlines a first step in a graduated effort." She was close enough that I could sense her pheromones. They were damped to levels that proclaimed her female— and uninterested. I suspected that was probably the norm for a surgeon. "Dr. Dyorr is a careful and patient scientist."

"He seems quite dedicated. How did you become involved in the project?"

"I'm a surgical resident. I intend to specialize in neural net surgery." Her smile was icy. "Why did my great-grandmother request that you evaluate the proposal?"

"I can't speak to motives, Doctor. I only know that I was hired to do the evaluation and to submit a report."

"What will you report?"

"My evaluation of the proposal." I smiled. "What should I report?"

"That it's one of the few true pure research projects being attempted and well worth the funding."

"It does seem strange that so little progress has been made in the area."

"That's because people don't want to know about consciousness, just like they didn't want to know about evolution and pan-gaiean life seeds before the Diaspora. When dearly held and illogical beliefs conflict with science, science usually loses." Her smile was polite. "Good day, Seignior."

She turned and left, and the only ones outside the conference room were the two guards and the aide who had given me the handouts.

I turned to the aide. "There was a blond woman, one of the observers. I was supposed to meet her afterward, but I got tied up with Dr. Tozzi . . ." I tried to look embarrassed.

"Oh . . . that must have been Daryla Rettek. She's the scientific media linkster."

"Thank you."

On the way back to the villa, I thought about Dyorr and Tozzi. He was certainly committed to his research. He hadn't even so much as glanced at his fiancée during the presentation. She had occasionally looked at him, and she certainly believed in his research. But I wasn't getting the impression that he was turning the heavens to get to her eventual inheritance. That could mean he was a far better dissembler than I was a discoverer. I didn't think so.

When I finally returned to the villa, I drafted a report on

the presentation. I had to conclude that it was well organized and that Dyorr had made a convincing case for his research.

I also ran checks on vonGarodyn, not because I cared about him but because I wanted to know about his aide. In the end, I discovered that she was Cecilia vonKuhrs, the staff director of the foundation, married three times, with two grown children.

There was very little on Daryla Rettek. In fact, there was nothing except her identification as the science media linkster for L'Institut Multitechnique.

I decided to link Myndanori, but she was out. I left a message requesting she backlink.

Then I went back to other varied searches.

Two stans later, all I'd found was more dead ends. By then, I wasn't sure I could find any more of even those. I'd had five commissions. One of the clients was most likely dead, and he'd never even paid a retainer. Worse, my use of his detector had probably led to his death, either directly or sooner than otherwise would have been the case.

Even after Dyorr's proposal, almost everything I'd discovered in the other three cases was based on hints, indirect implications, in fact barely more than nothing mixed with supposition. Scarcely more than a certain slant of light after dawn, or before twilight, even more uncertain than the shadows of Thurene.

What could I do?

Given what Angelique deGritz had told me, I did run checks on the status of Stella Strong/Maureen Gonne, Vola Paulsky, and Relian Cru, but none showed up as deceased or in the status of the incarcerated or the civilly limited. I also tried on Astrid Forte, although I had no real link that indicated she might be the same individual as Stella Strong, but there was nothing on her except a blanked identity in Vannes.

I began another round of vidlinks, starting with the Artists' Centrality. I'd only gotten talking heads the last time, and not a one had gotten back to me. Three talking heads later, I was linked to a real person, a Carthon Wills. He had a boyish and bespectacled look, even without the spectacles affected by the retrowriters.

"Seignior Donne, I don't believe I know you. What have you created?"

Chaos mostly, or so it was seeming. "I'm not a creator. I'm trying to track down a creator for a project."

"What sort of creator? I'd have to know the scope of what you have in mind, and a budget estimate would help . . ." His smile was singularly unhelpful.

"I'm trying to track down a Terrie McGerrie. I think she also uses the name Carey Douglass."

"She does not take inquiries or unsolicited commissions, Seignior . . . uh . . ."

"Donne. Blaine Donne. I'm not inquiring about productions. I'm inquiring about her. I'm trying to get in touch with her."

He or his image drew itself up in a poor imitation of an offended cat. "The Artists' Centrality is not an acquaintance linknet."

"I'm not looking for her for that reason."

"I have heard that too often, Seignior . . ."

"Donne."

"If you have a commission, or if you would like to leave your contact information, it is up to each artist to make a decision as to whether to return a link." A sniff followed the announcement.

I had the feeling I wasn't about to get much more from Carthon Wills. "Here's my contact link." I flashed it across, with a brief message requesting that Terrie McGerrie return the vidlink. I doubted that she would.

I sat at the table desk, not even really thinking. I was just wondering if I'd ever had to deal with so many ambiguous commissions at the same time before.

Seigniora Reynarda, requesting an appointment here in one stan, sir.

She doesn't just want to vidlink? That was odd.

It was just a coded request.

I'll see her. It couldn't hurt.

While I waited, I sat down and set up several more different search routines. I used the systems to draft a quick hard-copy report for Seigniora Elisabetta Reynarda. I ended up revising it twice before I had it printed out and set on the desk. Then I checked the search results. They added nothing new.

In the few minutes after that, I half thought and half let my mind wander, trying to see if it might offer some brilliant insight that I could offer Seigniora Reynarda.

It didn't.

When Seigniora Reynarda entered the study at quarter past eleven, she looked almost the same as she had when she had appeared weeks earlier. The natural stormy blond hair was perfectly in place. This time she was wearing a fitted black singlesuit, with black boots, and a lighter gray short jacket. She wore neither a scarf nor ear jewelry, and only a single silver-gray pin on the lapel of her jacket. The pin was a silver fox.

Was she claiming ancestry or affinity?

I moved out from the desk. "Seigniora . . ."

Before I could say more, her black eyes raked me. She stopped a good two yards away from me. "Seignior Donne. For a man with your background and reputation, you don't seem to have accomplished much—except get a citation for swimming in the city reservoir. That does not come under covered expenses, Seignior Donne."

"The swimming, no. The citation, probably not. Escaping a swarm of Arswaran wasps, yes."

She pulled the single-eyebrow trick She was good at it. That I had to admit.

I half turned and lifted the clear case from the corner of the desk, then handed it to her. "One Arswaran wasp. It's time-dated. If you can persuade the Garda, they could also confirm it."

She took the wasp and handed the case back to me. "Exactly what have you discovered?"

I handed her the hard-copy report. "I could give you a linked one."

"This is most suitable . . . in format." She read the three pages quickly, then looked up. "From what I can tell, you have managed to alert the Elois to your presence and interest without finding out more than Maraniss is engaged in something with them, and that Classic Research is involved in a hidden effort on Legaar's estate requiring a massive amount of power."

"Also that the Elois have a measure of effective control over what the Garda in Thurene observes and whom they harass, and that they have snoops and taps in almost every aspect of the record system of the Civitas Sorores."

"You have found nothing about a link to Elysium?"

"Only the probability that it is the project being undertaken at Time's End and that I've observed at least three military-style RPFs patrolling that perimeter."

She offered a snort. It wasn't that good an expression of disgust. "You've established that they're probably doing something illegal but without enough proof for the Garda or anyone else to act. But then, they always are. That's their methodology. Just to show my goodwill, I'll even provide another five thousand as remuneration for what little you have discovered, and for your difficulties with the wasps. I think ten thousand credits should be sufficient for your time and even the cost of the citation."

Before I could speak, Max verified that the receipts account had accepted another five thousand credits.

The black eyes fixed on me again. "If you wish to investigate further, and if you find more, you'll do it without any more advances. I'll contact you later. If you can find a definite link, I'll pay another ten thousand credits. Otherwise, I'll pay nothing."

"I'll see what more I can find out." How hard I'd try was another question. Still, it was worth a few more stans of work.

"Good day, Seignior."

I watched her go. I had a very uneasy feeling. Feminine as my scans and systems showed her to be, she still exuded no pheromones. I could only hope that some of the nanotraps from the desk and the case were sticking tight.

She was barely into the private limousine before Max informed me, *Incoming from Del Shannon.*

Accept.

The colonel appeared in the space before the study desk. "Donne."

"Yes, Colonel. What can I do for you?"

"You can talk to Officer Javerr when he arrives, for one thing."

That was one of the last things I'd prefer to do, but I couldn't very well play runaway. "Could you tell me what we'll be talking about?"

"I'm sure Javerr can explain it, Donne." Shannon smiled. It wasn't a friendly expression. "If you'd rather, we could insist on your coming here to headquarters."

"I'll be happy to talk to Officer Javerr, Colonel."

"I thought you would be. You've always been reasonable."

"Can you at least tell me when to expect him? I'd rather not miss him."

"Very shortly." The colonel broke the link.

Shannon had never been so cold, not even when we'd had to deal with the Frankan incursion in the Grenadan sector, where we'd initially been hammered.

Shortly turned out to be less than a quarter stan.

Garda flitter incoming, sir, announced Max.

Hold the defenses.

Javerr dropped his flitter right into the courtyard, almost at the base of the steps. The armament was aimed at my front door. What the Garda carried wouldn't have done much damage, but there was no point in letting them know that. He walked up my front steps as if he owned them.

I met him at the top, just outside the columns framing the main entry. "Would you care to come into the study, Officer?"

"Not especially, Seignior Donne, but it would make the most sense."

He followed me across the entry hallway, trying to record everything in sight. There wasn't much there.

The door closed behind us, and he took two more steps before stopping and turning. "Where were you on Domen morning, Seignior Donne?" Javerr made "seignior" sound like a curse.

"I was here in the villa, Officer."

"You were here all day?"

"I certainly was."

"And I suppose you were here all day Senen as well?"

"No. I went to brunch at my sister's house."

"Just the two of you, I suppose?"

"No. There were four other people there."

"Close friends?"

"Three of them I'd never met before, Officer."

That upset Javerr, or at least surprised him.

"Who were they?"

"My sister and her business partner, an academic economist from the university, and two dynamic re-creators who provide stories out of the early interstellar period."

"How long were you there?"

"Until midafternoon."

"Then where did you go?"

"I came back here. I had work to do."

"I understand you have a connection to Lemel Jerome."

"That's certainly no secret. He occasionally engages me to provide information for his various projects."

"Are you working on one now?"

"I have in the past, Officer Javerr. I am now."

"On what?" He didn't quite snap.

"You'd have to get his permission for me to reveal the exact nature of the project. I can say that every commission he has given me has dealt with information on whether some individual or corpentity might have been infringing on one of his patents."

"You won't tell me?"

"Not without his permission, no." I paused. "Could you tell me what this is all about, Officer?"

A quick hint of indecision flickered about him before he spoke. "There's no reason not to, now. Lemel Jerome was killed in an explosion in his dwelling sometime after mid-morning on Senen."

On Senen? The energy surge I'd felt when he'd been cut off occurred the day before, on Domen. "Lemmy? Killed? On Senen?"

"That's what all the evidence shows. There wasn't much left of his dwelling, and less of him."

Was I losing my mind? If Legaar or someone else had destroyed Lemmy's place a day after the vidlink had crashed, then what had caused the crash? Why hadn't I heard something? Or had Lemmy set up something to throw Legaar Eloi off his trail? Or was Javerr trying to mislead me?

Javerr watched me. "You really didn't know, did you?"

"About his death on Senen?" I shook my head. "I knew there was something wrong because when I tried to link him to give him a status report, I got a system talking head. I kept getting it."

"You didn't go looking?"

"I've never known where he lived or worked. That's often true of my clients and commissions."

Javerr kept battering me with questions, all from the same angle, but after close to a stan, he quit. It wasn't a surrender, but more like an armistice until he could find another weakness.

After he departed, I wandered across the study and looked out on the verandah. The late-morning light appeared chill.

Incoming from Terrie McGerrie, Max announced.

Accept and record.

The holo image that appeared in the air in front of my table desk was that of a small blond woman, with fine features and gray eyes. Her chin was slightly pointed. She turned, as if to face me. I could tell it was an altered image, not by anything obvious, but by the smoothness and directness of the motions. "I believe you vidlinked seeking me. I wish to inform you that I accept neither unsolicited commissions nor inquiries. Nor do I respond, except in this fashion, to such. Good day."

The holo image vanished. Another dead end.

Except there was something . . . something about her. Or had it been her words or her way of speaking?

Try as I might, I couldn't dig out what it might have been. I set that thought aside. I needed to check on what the snoops I'd placed on Seigniora Reynarda had found. If anything.

25

*A man belittled has almost the fury of a
woman scorned—almost.*

Once the seigniora left the villa, I discovered that she'd immediately neutralized all the snoops. I couldn't hear what was going on, but I could still follow the tracking patterns. The limousine made its way to the Boutique, where Reynarda apparently wandered through the shops around Maiden Lane. Then she and all traces of the snoops vanished. One moment, her location was registering normally. The next, there were no signals. That alone confirmed my uneasy feeling.

Who was Seigniora Reynarda? Someone had clearly borrowed the name, if not the methods of the Fox. Was it some government entity? Neither Special Operations nor any Assembly-level unit would risk having the commander court-martialed, not to mention facing planetary charges. Meddling with local citizens, or even with a former special operative, couldn't be worth that kind of risk. And I couldn't see why the sisters would bother with using a front like the seigniora. They could monitor me through the Garda in any public place and track any public act I did.

Whom did that leave? Another corpentity? I snorted. Who else could it be? Who else wanted to expose Legaar and not leave any traces? The problem was that, if I wanted to track those behind the female facade, I could be looking at almost any corpentity in Thurene, if not from even more distant stars and climes. Except that I had the feeling that the seigniora's feminine form had merely concealed another woman, probably a samer, but that was far from certain.

Did I want to pursue the Elysium contract on her terms? Not really, but I had the feeling that, dangerous as it had been and might be, not tracking Legaar might prove even more dangerous, now that he and his systems knew I was interested. By dealing with Tony diVeau I'd emphasized that. But I'd hated the idea of a glad-handing sleazy banker snooping my systems. I couldn't let that go. Not if I wanted to retain any effectiveness in my line of work.

More to the point, credits were credits, especially with my level of expenses.

I frowned. I'd been concentrating on the Elois and on Maraniss. That hadn't gotten me anywhere. What about tracking more information on those around them?

Max, search all names associated with the various Classic corpentities . . . or with Eloi Enterprises. As possible, match names with jobs. Limit search to this past calendar year. Then I recalled that Odilia had also provided lists in the dataflat she had slipped to me. I added those names to the search.

I tried a link with Krij. She wasn't taking links. I left a message with her talking head and finalized my draft report on Dyorr's research proposal. Basically, I made several points. First, his research was long-term and expensive. Second, it would benefit a limited number of people, but they were those who could not be helped by existing medical technologies. Third, it would greatly deepen true understanding of what comprised intelligence. Fourth, if successful, it could lead to even more potentially socially disturbing implications than present psych-conditioning used by existing less-than-savory commercial applications. Fifth, it would upset every established religion. Finally, sooner or later, someone was going to do it, and Dyorr's proposal was likely to provide Devanta and the Assembly with greater oversight and control than anything else. Seldara Tozzi wouldn't like the report, but she'd regret my not telling her what she didn't want to hear even less.

I hoped it wouldn't be that long before Myndanori got back to me, but she would when she did, and not when I wished.

With that task done, I began to study the Eloi-related search results.

Max had come up with 611 matches, linked to 203 individual names. First I read through them and set aside those that were clearly "social" or irrelevant matches. Those were the ones that mentioned the spouse of someone attached to one of the Eloi Enterprises in a different context, such as attending a benefit or leading a volunteer or charitable effort. Then I dug in and began to study the rest.

After another hour I had a short list of eleven names. What was interesting about them was that all of them were still alive and that none was presently on Devanta.

Incoming from Krij.

Accept.

Krij's image appeared before the desk. Her smile was warm. For that I was glad. She tossed back her head slightly and flipped a short lock of shimmering jet-black hair back off her forehead. "You left a message, brother dear."

"I'm still working on the Eloi project, and I've got some names I thought I'd run past you."

"Before you do that . . . I need to ask . . . what did you do to piss off Banque de L'Ouest?"

"I told Antonio diVeau I didn't appreciate his trying to snoop and crash my systems under the guise of inviting me on a cataract rafting trip. Why? What did he do?"

"We keep running dossiers on all our clients. You're one of them. This morning we got an alert that you'd been credit-denied by Banque de L'Ouest. The notation with it indicated you were close to bankruptcy. Since you have this phobia about debt, and since we audit your books, I know that's somewhere between highly unlikely and impossible."

"He's been suborned by Legaar Eloi."

Krij sighed. "We'll file a reg-comp denial and issue a counternotice, with an intent to request documentation in support of their notice."

"You'd better bill me on this."

"We'll see. I hate bankers almost as much as you do. Now . . . what about those names? I've got to meet a client here in a quarter stan."

"What do you know about Laisyn Welles?"

"Besides being the director of Classic Investment?" Krij smiled. "Not all that much. The Vallum Streeters think that he's the reason why Eloi Enterprises is so successful in the financial markets."

"Then why did Legaar send him to the Abssenya systems last month?"

"He probably said something Legaar didn't like. That's a real danger."

"You know anything else?"

She shook her head.

"What about Willa Ching?"

Krij offered a rueful smile. Her green eyes softened slightly. "You know I've always been better with the numbers and the regs. People are what Siendra would know more about. She deals more with personnel management. She's here. Would you mind talking to her?"

"Mind? Why would I mind?"

"You seem to avoid her. In a polite way, that is."

"I've nothing against her. I just don't know her well, and she's so reserved around me . . ."

Krij's laughter filled the study. Before it died away, her image was replaced by that of Siendra, wearing a dark brown jacket over shimmering white shirt. She was smiling, as if amused at something.

"Siendra."

"Blaine." She paused. "Krij said that you wanted to know about people in Eloi Enterprises. You're interested in Willa Ching?"

"Among others," I admitted.

"Ching has a talent absent from the Elois. She can make people feel wanted and valued."

"She was sent to Frydrich in the Prussian system," I pointed out.

"That would make sense if they're expanding in that area. You'd want a people person, particularly there." She tilted her head slightly, thinking, and probably linking to her own systems.

I waited, but I couldn't help but note that she looked more alive in that unguarded linking moment. Most people didn't.

"Eloi Enterprises' annual report notes increased revenues from the Prussian systems," she added. "They don't give details, but they wouldn't mention it if the numbers weren't significant."

Left unsaid was that the city sisters would be on them for felonious misrepresentation for failure to at least note an area of markedly increased revenues.

"What about Laisyn Welles?"

"A true financial genius. He turned Spectrum around in less than a year. That was when the Elois took him aboard. Classic Investment had scarcely ever made much. It was operated more as a capital pool and low-risk hedge fund. Within a year, he had it almost as profitable as Classic Media, and within two it was nearly as profitable as the escort operation."

"But why would Legaar send him to Abssenya?"

"To make more credits. The one thing the Elois like more than anything is credits."

That might be, but sending all the names on my list out-system didn't make sense. "Do these names mean anything to you?" I began to read them. "Valera N'gao, Mahmed Kemal . . ." When I finished, I waited again.

Siendra smiled. "They're among the best people the Elois have."

"Every one of them has been sent out-system in the last year. They haven't returned."

"I'll have to ask Krij what she thinks, but it looks to me like they're trying to expand into true multisystem operations. You know that they've clashed with the Civitas Sorores repeatedly. It could be that they just want to move their operations elsewhere and that they're expanding as quickly as practicable."

I hadn't thought of that. Was Elysium Legaar's plan for bailing out of Devanta? Or was Elysium just coincident with expanding operations? Or something else altogether?

"Send me the list, Blaine, and I'll see what we can find out."

I flashlinked it to her. I also included the names of Sephaniah Dylan-Zimmer's and Antonio diVeau, as well as Seldara and Marie Tozzi, Dr. Guillaume Richard Dyorr, Cecilia vonKuhrs, and Darlya Rettek.

"There's one other thing where you might be able to help, if you would," I ventured. "I was trying to locate a dramaturge named Terrie McGerrie through the Authors' Centrality, but they weren't much help."

"I don't imagine they would have been." Siendra laughed softly. "They're not supposed to be helpful in that regard. More than a few of the dramaturges and creators use pseudonyms and don't want to be traced, even to a pseudonymous talking head. For some, the way words are used in direct vidlinks is as much an indication of identity as their face or name might be."

"What are they hiding from?"

"If you'd written *The Exciting Escapades of Dragoon and Dirt,* would you want to talk to anyone?"

"Someone wrote *that*?"

"It's a spoof of an ancient spoof, and it lase-burns more than a few pretentious types in the Gallian sector. In literary terms, it's somewhere between bad and truly terrible. That's according to those who have read it."

"Which? The original or the latest spoof?"

"I doubt either is that great, but I've read neither," Siendra confessed.

"Somehow I don't think that's why people hide their creative identities."

"What if you'd written *The Universe According to Sister Incognita*?"

"Was it that accurate in depicting the inner workings of the Civitas Sorores?" I asked.

"Accurate enough that the sisters attempted to suppress it," Siendra pointed out. "Accurate enough that all the security systems were changed and the points of system and physical access were modified."

"And all these creators think they'd lose their freedom of expression if their identities were known?"

"I doubt that most think of it in those terms, Blaine, but they wouldn't be comfortable without some identity shield. Nor would you, were you in their position. They're either notorious, or nonentities, or professionals who don't want their more lucrative major careers undermined by their minor literary and dramatic efforts."

"I suppose not. Did I ask you about Maureen Gonne or Stella Strong?"

"Krij asked me. I've never run across either name. Our databases don't show them either, except that Gonne was with TFA for not quite four years, but you knew that."

"What about Astrid Forte?" I had trouble remembering to use that name, although there was no certainty it was even connected to Strong/Gonne.

"Let me see."

After a moment, her eyes widened. "That's a registered legal identity."

"What does that mean? Everyone has a legal identity."

"One that's registered means that it's not only reserved, but that its use by any other individual is a felony." She smiled. "Registered identities are limited to the directors of major corpentities, justicers, and elected officials above the local level. They're also allowed to certain other individuals if a petition is approved by the Civitas Sorores."

"What kind of individuals?"

"Security personnel, prominent artists, people whose fame or notoriety might make them vulnerable to ID theft."

That left me concerned and puzzled.

"Blaine?"

I shook my head. "It doesn't make sense, but I'll have to think about it." She and Krij had given me what they could.

I supposed that I should have gone back to the commissions immediately. I didn't. I felt that breaking the link so quickly would have been bad manners. So I asked, "If I'm not intruding, what did you do before you worked with Krij?"

She shrugged. "I spent two tours as a line officer with the Assembly Interstellar Service. That was enough. Piloting was the only good part, and that didn't make up for the rest of it. I didn't see much combat. That was before the Frankans started getting restive. After that, I tried being an administrative resources director and a few other things. The service and the corpentity stints confirmed that, while I could handle military and administrative bureaucracies, I was severely less than pleased in doing either. I met Krij when she was on an assignment and persuaded her that my expertise was better as a consultant than as a bureaucrat. I haven't regretted it."

"She's done better with you."

"I'd like to think so." She frowned. "Why didn't you join her after you left Special Operations? Your talents and hers would be formidable together."

They might be, but I needed distance. Krij could be formidable all by herself. I laughed. "I'm more of a shadowy character. She's a creature of the light."

"That sounds more like a reason to work together rather than separately." She gave the slightest headshake. "Krij just flashed me. Our client is arriving."

"You'd better go. Thank you."

Her image vanished.

Two tours in the Assembly IS? She'd said she'd liked the piloting best. That meant she was deep-space qualified. I'd never gotten to that, just in-system small craft.

I still didn't have much more to go on for any of my commissions.

Then . . . something Siendra had said struck me. If word usage were a signature, couldn't I use that to search? It took me almost a stan to set up a search routine that compared elements of style, subject, and presentation. I turned it loose on all literature and vid-dramas created in the past year on Devanta. The systems promptly informed me that the expected time of completion would be some thirteen standard hours. I'd suspected it would take a while, but that long?

There was no help for it. So I tapped into the current news, then had it play out with holo and audio. The image appeared in the space before my desk.

". . . the alien spacecraft mystery deepens . . ."

How could it deepen? It was alien and billions of years old, as I recalled.

". . . University of Muriami technarcheologists have confirmed that the spacecraft discovered last month in the Drift is indeed more than a billion standard years old. Yet it appears to be almost an exact duplicate of a current non-Assembly military craft . . . buried in the middle of a constructed asteroid with a large and inactive power source . . . one expedition member suggested it might be some sort of burial monument . . ."

I laughed out loud. It had to be a fraud of some sort. Humans hadn't been around millions of years, let alone a billion, and the odds of another race producing a similar craft were statistically improbable. It was more than a little unlikely that humans had copied the alien craft, either, since spacecraft development had been progressing for thousands of years. Progressing far too slowly to have gotten an infusion of alien technology. As for a burial monument in deep space . . . I snorted.

I thought about blanking the audio as another image flicked up into a holo projection. I didn't look, but half listened.

"Assembly Premier Ferraro met earlier this week with the special envoy from the Shiite League in an effort to slow the escalation of military buildups in between the

Frankans and the League in the Sack area of the Trailing Arm. . . .

"The Assembly's Gallian Sector Four Fleet completed its deep-space maneuvers without any additional encounters with unidentified forces . . . earlier, rumored contacts had been laid to Frankan or Argenti vessels.

"The Assembly Ministry of Government Affairs has released the revised standards for planetary government reformulation. The principal change in the policy and guidelines was to clarify the language defining nonconsensual, nonrepresentative planetary governments . . . Devantan libertarian critic Alesandro Hamilcar praised the MGA revisions as long overdue. He pointed out that in many respects the Civitas Sorores of Devanta might well be included in the definition of repressive planetary governments . . ."

The dear sisters? I couldn't say that I was that fond of the Civitas Sorores. They were anything but representative, despite the facades erected around them and the illusions of representation fostered by the elected advisory representatives. But I'd never been that fond of popular democracy either, and I certainly didn't want the MGA policy revisions to be used as a tool to demand reformulation of Devantan planetary government structures—or the lack thereof. Why were people always meddling with what worked?

"The Masculist Forum has released a statement denouncing the use of medical technology to 'artificially' establish the sexual orientation and gender of human fetuses in utero . . . Masculist spokesman Josiah Brigham called Thurene the Gehenna of a doomed culture . . ."

I winced at that. The law already prohibited prebirth sexual manipulation, except in cases determined medically necessary. Why were the Masculists digging up that legal corpse? No judiciary would change the law, and the sisters certainly wouldn't.

"On a happier note, the PostColonial Museum in Vannes has just opened a totally new exhibit featuring the first sisters of Devanta . . .

"In Devantan legal news . . . yesterday EsClox Limited filed for a preliminary injunction against the just-enacted charter amendment requiring mandatory licensing of defense-related technologies . . . The EsClox motion claims that the definition of "defense-related technologies" is so broad that it could include all advanced systems . . . The Soror Tertia of Devanta expressed confidence that the motion would be rejected in a matter of weeks. She said it was merely a delaying tactic. No charter amendment has ever been overturned by the Sector Judiciary . . ."

Something about that nagged at me. I couldn't have said why.

Max . . . quick background on EsClox.

Within minutes, Max had something. I blanked the news and read the short paragraph off the holo projection.

"EsClox . . . nanodesign specialty firm from Bretcote . . . provides quantum synchronization equalizers and other equipment of a similar nature . . . ownership has remained private, but one third of capitalization was provided by Classic Investment in return for a semiexclusive, long-term technology-sharing agreement . . ."

That brought me up short. *Max . . . search high-tech Gallian sector corpentities with technology-sharing agreements with either Classic or Eloi enterprises.*

There were thirty-seven—all on Devanta. None had any name remotely similar to Elysium. I had to hand it to the Eloi boys. They had access to a lot of new technology. Why Legaar and Simeon would need it in their businesses I couldn't understand. What I could understand was that EsClox was pursuing a legal challenge to buy time. That suggested Legaar clearly had something going on with Classic

Research that he didn't want to license to the Sorores. Or not until he cleaned up matters, such as his use of Lemmy's technology. Yet . . . with all the tech-sharing, Eloi was expanding elsewhere?

I was learning more than I'd ever wanted about Eloi Enterprises, but not much of it pointed to Maraniss or to whatever Elysium might be. Not that I could see. Not yet, anyway.

26

*Indirection offered with care can be far more
useful than unthinking directness.*

From as soon as I'd stepped into my study on Miercen morning, I'd gotten to work on setting up more indirect searches for my pending commissions, based on variations of what I'd set up for Terrie McGerrie the day before.

The style comparator routine had come up with another possible pseudonym for Terrie McGerrie. The probability was over seventy-seven percent that a newer dramaturge with the pen name of Marley Louis was also Carey Douglass/Terrie McGerrie. Louis's latest work was entitled *The Endeavor Affair.* Except for the name, the bio was close to identical to those for Douglass and McGerrie. I sent a mental and silent thank-you to Siendra. I was beginning to see why Krij was more successful with Siendra as a partner.

With a smile, I went back to work, this time setting up a modified routine to compare biographies among those registered in the Artists' Centrality, plus those listed in the various works. Then I set it running while I studied the results from my earlier work that morning.

Unlike the dramaturge search, those for the Elois and Stella Strong were less successful. The results told me nothing I hadn't already known. There was absolutely nothing else on Astrid Forte, either. Obviously, Siendra and Krij had access to sources I didn't.

Over the past weeks, I'd learned a great deal about Eloi Enterprises and its Classic subsidiaries. The problem was that I had no idea what was relevant. I'd learned some about

Terrie McGerrie/Carey Douglass/Marley Louis, mainly
that she was clearly a most talented—and reclusive—writer
and that she lived somewhere in Thurene. And, on the other
hand, I'd learned virtually nothing about either Stella
Strong/Maureen Gonne/Astrid Forte. Nor had I discovered
anything close to what Seldara Tozzi was seeking.

Incoming from Odilia Ottewyn.

Accept. Why was she vidlinking? She said she detested
virtie-comm.

Odilia remained slim, dark-haired, and seemingly virginal. She wore a velvet jacket shaded to the cranberry with
a cream blouse. "Blaine, I just read your charming note. You
were so sweet to handwrite it."

She'd never mentioned that the day before. I didn't push.
"I could do no less after such a warm and wonderful evening at the opera, Princesse."

"I would have responded in kind, dear man, but I'm
rather pressed for time. We're leaving on *L'Etoile* in the
morning."

"You mean I won't have another chance to accompany
you to the opera this season?" That would have been unlikely, but I had to say something.

"I fear not, Blaine. Amelia insists she must go to the
ball—the midwinter ball on Firenza. When one's daughter's
future might be determined by her presence at such festivi-
ties, what can a mother do?"

I'd never heard Odilia mention her daughter, or any child.
"That sounds like a long visit to Firenza. I hope that you enjoy every moment of it." I smiled. "Or that Amelia does."

"I'm most certain that she will, dear Blaine. I do wish
that you could be there on Firenza when all the fireworks go
off. The midwinter festivals there do so much to lift one's
spirits. At times, even the most shadowy of individuals
needs to get away and bask in the light."

Fireworks? I set the system to do a quick search of
Firenza and its winter holidays, with a query on fireworks.
"I fear you have me, Princesse. I bow to your kindness, and
to your warmth." I did bow and smile.

"We'll be in the Palacio di Soleil, should you choose to grace us with your presence."

"Thank you."

With a smile, her image vanished.

I swallowed and read over the console display set into the desk surface.

Firenza did have midwinter holidays. There were three of them, each a week apart. They were lavish, social, and extravagant, especially for those with wealth, who took turns as acting as the duke—or duchess—of merriment. There were incredible light shows. Fireworks were banned.

Odilia had to have known that. She was warning me that fireworks were about to go off around me. And that she wasn't about to remain on Devanta. She'd linked one day after I'd told her that the Sephaniah at the opera was a fraud. Was that also a factor?

Incoming from Siendra Albryt.

For a moment I hesitated before recognizing her surname. Krij had introduced her once, and from then on, she'd just been Siendra. *Accept.*

As usual, she wore an earth-toned jacket. This one was somewhere between tan and khaki, but with its collar and lapels trimmed in a thin green piping. That touch of green combined with the soft shimmering cream blouse somehow made the hazel of her eyes more vivid.

"Blaine, Krij and I undertook some information surveillance. You may be onto something. Eloi Enterprises has been transferring credits off Devanta for almost a year. They've also sold most of their real estate and are leasing it back from the new owners. It's been very gradual."

"Are they in financial trouble?" That didn't seem likely, but I'd learned a long time back that corpentities could be more than slightly deceptive as they approached financial collapse.

"We don't think so. It looks more like they're tired of dealing with the sisters and are trying to ease out. If anyone knew they wanted to relocate most of their operations, people would bargain for better deals. They've also set up full-scale escort and entertainment services in Abssennya, Frydrich, and Neuiravia."

"That's not a sign of financial weakness."

"Neither of weakness nor of indecision."

"Why now?" I couldn't help musing.

"Their relations with the Civitas Sorores have been getting worse. The sisters have brought four civil complaints and motions against Eloi Enterprises in the last year. In three cases, the Sector Judiciary upheld the System Judiciary against the Elois. The fourth is pending."

"What about the Assembly revisions in the definitions of repressive governments? Would that be a factor?"

Siendra paused, tilting her head slightly. "Generally, repressive governments are harder on operations such as the Elois'. A less repressive government would benefit them."

"Only after the reformulation," I pointed out. "Values of real estate could decline in the interim as well."

"The sisters aren't anywhere as repressive as most governments the Assembly has determined worthy of reformulation."

I shrugged. "It was just a thought."

"I'll ask Krij. She may know something."

"Thank you."

"Oh . . . on those non-Eloi names. The banker secured subsidiary financing for his employer from Classic Finance. It likely saved Banque de L'Ouest from an unfriendly takeover. That confirms your belief in his position. We've filed a denial of his credit notice against you, and demanded documentation, but there's been no response yet. The other is just what she seems, but she's been doing research on Old Earth for at least the past four months. Very noted scholar. One of her daughters is employed by Classic Media. That's all we could find out that we didn't discuss earlier.

"Now . . . about the Tozzis and Dr. Dyorr. There's a lot there, but nothing in the slightest out of the ordinary, except for one thing."

"What's that?"

"There's absolutely no information on any romantic or

other personal attachments for either Dr. Tozzi or Dr. Dyorr. Krij had mentioned you were interested in that aspect for him, but I thought it might be worth checking on her as well."

I nodded. "I appreciate that."

"Cecilia vonKuhrs comes from an old, old, Old Earth family, but she's a most effective foundation administrator." Siendra smiled. "She has what one might call a catholic taste in men, but she's always used it to her advantage."

"With women, too?"

"I couldn't say from the record, but given some of her known liaisons, I'd doubt it. There's nothing at all except the bare basics on Darlya Rettek."

"Thank you. Is there anything else I should know?"

"At the moment, I can't think of anything."

"Send an invoice for whatever I owe you."

"Krij said to tell you that the information value is more than worth our time."

It must have been. Krij had never hesitated to invoice me, if at discounted rates. "Thank you . . . and her."

Once Siendra broke the link, I sat back behind the table desk, thinking. I didn't get far.

Incoming from Myndanori.

Accept.

"Blaine, dear man. To what did I owe your link?" She was wearing a soft purple blouse and an off-black vest. The combination of that sort should have clashed with her hair and complexion. It didn't.

"I'm still working on various commissions. You remember Dr. Dyorr?"

"My mind isn't that scattered. Your client has this impression that Dyorr's some sort of hidden samer. If he is, he's so hidden that he'll never find himself, let alone another samer." Her laugh was light and cruel.

"That's probably true, but it raises another question. Could you ask around about a semihidden samer named Marie Annette . . ."

"Last name? Or is this Dr. Tozzi? Blaine, you have a devious mind."

"I'd appreciate it if you ask around only using the first names. If I'm wrong, I get some protection. So does she. Besides, I'm not sure what name she might be using, if she is. Fairly tall woman—"

"Black-haired with gray eyes, severely beautiful, if a touch muscular," Myndanori finished. "If she's been around, someone will know."

"Also . . . I'm interested in what you might know about a Daryla Rettek. She's the science media linkster at the Institute."

"I should know her . . ."

"Petite blonde . . . pretty, not beautiful, but still good-looking."

"I'll have to think about that. You'll owe me for these."

"I always do."

She laughed—and broke the vidlink.

I hoped Myndanori could come up with something. If she couldn't, then I'd have to consider other alternatives. What those might be, I had no idea.

For the moment, I was far more worried about what was happening with Maraniss and the Elois. Odilia had almost never vidlinked with me, but she'd gone out of her way to let me know she was leaving Devanta for at least half a year for a system scarcely that close to Devanta, and that her departure hadn't been planned for that long. It might not even have been planned the day before. She as much as told me that fireworks, or something was going to happen on Devanta. Her indirection suggested that she was also certain that either my system or hers had been compromised. She was leaving Devanta as quickly as possible. She was worried, if not frightened, and that was a side of Odilia I'd never seen.

On top of that, the Elois were liquidating assets and transferring funds out-system and had been for at least a year. Legaar had the equivalent of a jumpship generator at Time's End, and Lemmy had been killed when someone had discovered he had traced the use of that set of patents to Time's

End. Legaar also had the equivalent of military-level RPFs guarding his estate.

More than one thing still didn't make sense. Why had Sephaniah snooped me in a way that was bound to be discovered? So that I would tell Odilia? So that Odilia got a message indirectly? But Odilia claimed she scarcely knew Sephaniah.

Either way, that suggested someone besides Legaar.

The other thing was my near-instant transport from the limo. That suggested a tool with incredible possibilities . . . yet all that I'd seen was a section of a wall dropped and . . .

Of course! Whatever the device or technology was, it was complex and had limits. The wall had been dropped to stop the limo. That suggested the device wasn't that good at handling moving targets. The fact that I hadn't been moved or killed while sleeping suggested that it was limited by defense screens as well. For now, at least. Technology always got better.

The week before I'd been intrigued and mildly concerned. I was more than that now. Much more.

27

All patterns have their sources—and their consequences.

I tried to go to bed early on Mercien evening. I didn't sleep. Not immediately. Half-formed thoughts swirled through my mind, and most dealt with the Elois, except for a phrase Siendra had said. Even half-asleep, I recalled it exactly: "Neither of weakness nor of indecision." Why that phrase?

I drifted into an uneasy sleep, with those words reverberating somewhere.

Three hour and a quarter.

I shuddered awake. I hated getting up when it was dark, especially when it was going to be dark for another three stans. A quick hot shower helped, as did a mug of SpecOps Sustain. It was legitimate to buy it, but who would want to, the way it tasted? It was good for jumpshifting a sluggish metabolism. Mine was, at least when jolted out of settled routines. I put on the gray flight suit last, along with the flight boots.

Before I headed down to the nightflitter, I ran a quick news scan, sifting through the stories.

". . . Frankan foreign secretary Chartrand denied reports that two Gallian media commentators had been summarily detained for attempting to reveal interstellar military deployment patterns . . ."

". . . demographic sociologists at the L'Institut Multitechnique revealed an algorithmic population distribution optimizing methodology with multiple uses for civic master patterners . . ."

Just what we all needed—another mathematical model that treated individuals as discrete volitionless lumps, as if one model or one size applied equally to all.

". . . a team of atmospheric scientists from L'Université de Vannes reported yesterday that they had succeeded in mapping previously undetected magnetic field anomalies over the midhemispheric latitudes . . . particularly strong in areas to the north of the Somme . . ."

Was that the result of whatever the Elois and Maraniss were doing at the Classic Research center at Time's End? Was what they were doing linked to Odilia's decision to flee? Or was I just jumping to unwarranted conclusions?

Either way, I'd had enough. I cut off the news feed.

I couldn't just flee to Firenza on suspicion. Jumpship passages to places like that cost as much as a good dwelling in the area where Krij lived. Even what I could get for my villa would only have paid for a handful of passages.

After making a last check of the systems integrated into my gray flight suit, I walked along the inside corridor from the villa's kitchen back to my study. From there, I took the circular staircase hidden behind the bookcase down to the lower level. I went to the hidden locker that held all the gear I'd kept saying for years that I wouldn't use. I'd thought about calling it my inner sanctum, but it was really a lower sanctum, and that didn't roll off the tongue. It just sounded vaguely vulgar.

I selected the enhanced opticals, the vibrodetects, and two dayration paks. No weapons. Not for this mission. Not this time. Then I crossed the red-lit hangar to the nightflitter, squinting for a moment as the shifting light patterns from the craft's curved angularities tried to twist my eyes away from its twenty-meter length.

After storing equipment and rations in the small locker beneath the pilot's couch, I eased up and into the cockpit. Once I had my helmet on, I checked all the links, then lowered the visor and ran through the checklist.

Light-off one.
One online.
Number one generator brought all the flitter systems online.

Once the hangar doors irised open and the lights went out, I taxied the flitter up the ramp and out the courtyard. This time, I requested a departure vector from ACS to Vannes via Carcassonne.

Suggest routing through Lyons via Carcassonne.
Accept.
Cleared to lift off.
Shadow-one, lifting off on departure vector.
Cleared to ACS boundary on departure vector two six three, immediate climb to one thousand AGL.
Accept-affirm. I lit off the second engine, then fed all power to the diverters. The nightflitter rose vertically until I was clear of structures, particularly my villa, when I nosed down slightly and transitioned into forward flight, I turned just south of due west to hold my vector, climbing and leveling out at my cleared departure altitude.

This time I waited until I was well clear of the ACS boundary before I went stealth, banking into a descending turn and steadying on 020, angling back to the western end of the Piedmont Hills. The lights of the various towns and villages to the north of Thurene were dimmer. A thin ground fog was forming. It often did in late fall and early winter.

Within minutes I was nearing the west end of the Somme Valley. There the ground fog was thicker. I stayed just above it even after I turned north toward Time's End.

At that moment, for an instant, the detector system flared. Whatever it had been had passed over or by me. I ran the signal back. It had come from above, either from a superstrat recon or a satellite, but it hadn't lingered long enough for a lock. More of a random sweep. Those were always possible.

Even so, I angled west for the next several minutes, then dropped even lower, almost hugging the treetops. Once I left the lower ground near the river, the fog thinned. Another twenty klicks, and I swung back northeast, keeping just above the treetops and using the terrain to shield me from the surveillance sensors at Classic Research until the very end.

Then I slipped the flitter around the east side of the tallest hill on the Rothschild Thierry lands—several klicks north of a light I thought might be an RT field station—and eased down into a cleared area on the north side. Most of my emissions would have been masked by the nightflitter's stealth capabilities, and even Special Ops would have had a hard time locating me from minimal emissions for such a short period.

Even so, I was cautious. I shut down one engine immediately. While I waited, I used a burst-bounce relay to amend my flight plan, canceling the last legs and claiming that I'd set down in Villedumont. That way, no one would be asking why I hadn't shown up in Vannes.

After ten minutes, I shut down both engines, damped all emissions, and used the fuel cell to power the single passive detector that monitored all freqs and energy sources. For the next two hours all I had to do was watch the detector. That, and think.

Bergerac's smoky red light lent a surrealistic sheen to the curved angularity of the exterior surfaces of the nightflitter. Voltaire was but a crescent in the western sky and would set before dawn.

I took a deep breath and concentrated on the detector.

I still wondered what my subconscious was trying to tell me with the perseverating repetition of the phrase Siendra had used. "Neither of weakness nor of indecision." All she'd meant was that the Elois hadn't been operating out of weakness or indecision. I knew that. What else was there in the words?

I pushed the question away. I'd wrestled enough with the phrase. My subconscious had brought it up, and my subconscious was either going to resolve it or forget it.

28

*Those souls who fill the city's halls pay more
than gold to guard its walls.*

I was dozing, dreaming of Magdalena, when the message jolted me—most rudely—from that bliss of secondary sensuality.

Ser Maraniss . . . Ser Maraniss . . . Director Eloi would like to see you in the operations center immediately.

I jerked up into a sitting position, trying to reorient myself in the darkness of the bedchamber, but no light broke where no sun shone. There was no low golden light from the skies, confirming that I was indeed at Time's End and not in Elysium.

Time?

Five fifty-three, ser.

What did Legaar want? He was sadistic, but not without purpose. He also wasn't exactly prone to rising before the sun, and his presence in the operations center so early suggested more trouble because the Frankan forces couldn't have arrived even well beyond the system in the time since we'd last discussed matters.

Should I consider my alternatives?

Not yet. I feared not the working world of the Elois, nor their flat synthetic souls and blood.

I pulled on a singlesuit, gray and wrinkled, but clean, and splashed cold water on my face. I was almost out the door before I realized I was barefoot. I added socks and boots, then made my way down to the maglev. I only saw one sleepy nymph—red-haired and as blowzy as a naked yet shapely figure could be. She was about as far from my tastes as possible. I missed Magdalena's compliant elegance.

Legaar was waiting in the Research operations center, pacing in a long oval path, his boots pounding the resilient floor. He looked up, even more disheveled and tired than I felt, stuffed as he was into an off-blue singlesuit. His boots were scuffed and gray, and he was unshaven and bleary-eyed.

"Someone's out there spying. They're less than a klick from the perimeter. The monitors detected another anomalous burst of energy at four fifty-seven. There was the faintest trace of elevated thermal radiation. Now . . . there's nothing. They're just waiting."

What was I supposed to do about that? His system and people were in charge of security. "Elevated thermal radiation for a short time? It could be a flitter engine shutting down. Or it could be some foresting or logging crew opening a bunch of thermal-pak meals." Or a lightning strike fire fizzling out, or . . .

"It doesn't match any of the parameters except a flitter engine, sers. It is a military-style flitter." The system ops voice was well modulated, far too well modulated to be human so early in the morning.

"Where is it?" I finally asked.

"I told you," snapped Legaar. "Less than a klick beyond the perimeter, on a hilltop that offers a line-of-sight view of the dwelling complex and a direct access to the front of the research center."

"That won't show anything, not with passive observation, and if they use energy-based scanners, the shields are more than adequate. Let them look. Nothing's going to happen for days, and it could be longer than that."

"I don't like it, not after that military flyby earlier."

"Are you sure it was military or Special Operations? Could it be the Fox clone? Or the shadow? Could he be a covert agent of the sisters?"

"Later today, I can check. We can't wait for that, though. I'm sending out a surveillance team once they're assembled."

"Onto RT lands?"

"RT won't ever know."

"Like they didn't last time?" I shouldn't have said that. I was still sleep-fogged.

Legaar glared at me.

I managed an apologetic shrug.

He kept glaring, and that suggested that I needed to say something. "Won't that reveal that we're hiding something?"

"They wouldn't be out there if they already didn't know that."

"They might be trying to provoke us into revealing the importance of Time's End."

"That could be, but if whoever's watching doesn't return, it doesn't matter."

What he was leaving unsaid was that he didn't want to unleash the RPFs again, or not so soon, against a target on Rothschild Thierry lands. Using his personal commando unit would be far less obvious, no matter how it turned out. Also, if the Civitas Sorores or Assembly Special Operations were involved, if the commandos didn't use proscribed weapons or equipment, that would make it more difficult to obtain an inspection warrant, without a lengthy and obvious process that could become politically rather difficult for the authorities.

"There's not much else I can do right now," I pointed out.

Legaar scowled. Then he nodded. "There'll be more for you later, Maraniss. Go get some sleep."

His words were more order than concession, but, for the moment, it didn't matter.

29

Over the next stan, as I waited in the darkness in the night-flitter and monitored the detectors, there were no untoward energy emissions, and no launches of RPFs from Time's End. My earlier foray had produced an instant attack-response. The lack of a response suggested that my approach and landing had not triggered those defenses.

I kept monitoring the detectors, but they indicated nothing.

My thoughts kept returning to my other two unresolved commissions.

Why Terrie McGerrie remained hidden was more than obvious. Why someone wanted to find her, yet not be informed, was less than obvious. Far less, unless they had full access to my systems, and with all that I'd expended on security, that seemed unlikely. Honest concern? I snorted. Unlikely. Jealousy? A desire to know she was worse off? More likely. I hated taking credits under those conditions, but . . . my expenses were considerable.

Why wouldn't someone like Stella Strong wish to come forward and claim a substantial bequest? Or were there terms in it that had not been made public? If so, what were they? If not, why was everything so shrouded in secrecy? Who really was behind the facade that was "Nancy"? What was hidden behind the overt agenda suggested by Seldara Tozzi's inquiry? Why hadn't I asked those questions before?

In the dimness of the cockpit, I reflected. Most of my

commissions before this had involved seeking obscure information or in dealing with unsavory individuals whose locations and motivations had been relatively transparent. Or in finding "lost" children, missing spouses, or properties mislaid as a result of multiple spouses and subsequent deaths and readjustments. A few times, I'd been retained merely for the sake of appearances. Once or twice, I'd actually been in real danger.

My thinking had gotten sloppy, and I hadn't even realized it as I'd relied on easy access to convenient information and upon my physical training and talents.

That burst of realization was bitter, and I couldn't push it away easily. Was that why I haunted the shadowed streets of Thurene? Because I needed to prove, if only to myself, that I provided some service of worth and value?

Slightly before dawn, I left the flitter and headed for a particular tree on the south side of the cleared area, a sycamore—adapted, of course. They kept their leaves later, but they also were easy to climb, provided I didn't go too high into the crown. The wood was softer and weaker than oak. Even so, at close to twenty-five meters above the ground, I looked down. I decided not to do that again. How I could fly aircraft and yet worry about how high I was in a tree was a paradox I deferred exploring. Until I was out of the sycamore, anyway.

I settled into place, straddling a limb, with my back to the trunk, and began training my optical and other passive detection gear on Legaar's estate to the north. Passive detection gear had the advantage of not revealing the observer through energy emissions. I was hoping that a longer surveillance might tell me more than what I knew. Data and system searches, aerial surveillance, and everything else I'd done only went so far. Whatever was happening—or about to happen—involving Legaar Eloi and Judeon Maraniss was going to occur at Time's End. I *knew* that. Proving it was another matter. Even getting a hint of what it might be was going to be difficult.

Before I completed setting up and focusing my gear, the

sun had climbed just above the seemingly endless expanse of mixed forest that extended both east and west of me—a canopy of green, dotted with yellow, orange, and red. I had a relatively clear view of Time's End from my near-hilltop vista. I could see the operations center directly, and to the northeast, the west side of the main mansion, as well as sections of the pleasure pool beneath and to the southwest of the main structures. So soon after dawn I didn't expect to see anyone moving around.

Except for a brief glimpse of one naked nymph, I didn't. There was no motion around the flat front of the Classic Research structure or in the grassy expanse to either side.

I settled back to wait. It was likely to be several standard hours before activity at Time's End picked up, and I probably had a long and boring day ahead. Still . . . what else could I do? The passive energy detector registered a high level of damped emissions from the research center and a lower but significant level from the mansion complex. Neither was unexpected, and the readouts didn't show increases in the energy levels from the fusactor power plant that was somewhere to the north of the two complexes. The baseline level remained high enough to be disturbing, and I had trouble believing that no one else had noted all that power being generated. How had the Elois explained it? Or had anyone even asked?

I'd only been watching for a short time when I caught sight of movement around the pleasure pool. That was almost at the limit of clear range, even with enhanced opticals.

Maraniss—or someone very like him—was walking away from an irregular patch of darkness, most likely an artificial cave. He was wearing a very unstylish singlesuit and boots. Had he spent the night with one of the shapely nymphs?

Given his clothing, I didn't think so. Rather, he looked as though he'd had a long and hard night at something else. As for the cave, it had to be an entrance. My guess was that the cave concealed some sort of transit system from the mansion to the Classic Research facility. Probably a small maglev to

cover the three klicks. The combination of hidden transport
and a tired Maraniss suggested I might not be waiting long
for something to happen. I hoped I was wrong.

Less than half a stan later came a *bleep* on the passive
comparator, suggesting limited energy usage. I focused
the opticals on the area indicated by the comparator. The
ground seemed to waver, if slightly, and the passive detector
kept showing energy usage just above background. Someone was using a concealment screen, and moving south-
ward across the low grassy area that marked the perimeter
of the estate.

Another energy shift marked the point when the estate's
defenses were shunted around the concealed vehicles. By
studying the grass behind the concealment shield, I could
make out traces of at least two wide-tired vehicles. Tires
were far quieter than using ground effect vehicles. All of
them were headed in my direction.

Much as I would have liked to continue surveillance,
it was time to depart—quickly. Climbing down a large
sycamore takes time. That is, if you're carrying equipment
that can be traced back to you if left behind and if you intend to walk away from the trunk of the tree under your own
power.

Eloi's team was less than two hundred yards away by
the time I scrambled back into the nightflitter. At that moment, the entire Time's End complex bristled with energy
and active surveillance. Someone was waiting for me to
take flight.

I paused for a moment, thinking. I should have thought
more and sooner.

I didn't light off the engines, because, I realized, if I did,
I'd likely be a grounded loon, if not cooked or fried. Eloi
knew about where I was. He'd shown no reservations about
destroying the landscape of his neighbors. His team was
close enough that they'd easily see and hear a liftoff—
perhaps even lighting off the engines. They were also
doubtless armed with missiles or other items likely to be
rather hard on the nightflitter at close range. The flitter's

shields would only be partly effective on the ground. That didn't even count what Legaar might launch or direct at me from Time's End.

Reluctantly, but quickly, I climbed out of the cockpit and dropped to the ground. The gray flight suit held the same attributes as my shadow grays, and I hadn't brought personal weapons. My own attributes and training would only be good at close range. That assumed Eloi's team wore "standard" nanite-reinforced uniforms and helmets.

After leaving the canopy just barely ajar, I slipped beside one of the wheels, standing in the shadow. My upper body was concealed in the wheel well, and my legs blended into the undercarriage. The best idea was to take out the team—if I could—quietly, and then lift off. It wasn't a very good idea. But then, I hadn't expected close to a two-hour delay in response, either. Or how frigging long it had taken to climb down the tree.

As soon as the nanite camouflage barrier—now looking like pine undergrowth—appeared at the edge of the clearing, someone opened up with a slug thrower. He had to have been using fragmenting osmiridian shells—or some generic equivalent. One long burst shredded the cockpit area.

The idiots hadn't even bothered to check the flitter.

By then, I was moving into the trees. I dropped behind a large-trunked fir and peered over a ridged root back toward the doomed nightflitter. Much as I hated to do it, I sent a quick link to the self-destruct system. I was close enough that the flitter system acknowledged the arming signal.

The firing patterns disrupted the projection shield enough that I could make out the team from Time's End. There were only four Classic Research commandos on two TCs. Technically, the vehicles were full terrain capable or VFTCs. At higher speeds, they were terrain choppers. That name had stuck years before, despite all the military efforts to change it.

Another burst from the weapons type on the leading TC took out the aft section of the nightflitter.

The two TCs were within fifty yards of the craft, getting

ready to fire more of the fragmenting shells. At that rate, there wouldn't be any arming system left.

Shadowflare Omega. I flattened myself behind the roots of the fir even before I finished triggering the self-destruct system and activating my personal nanite shield.

Whummptt!

The ground shuddered. Energy and pieces of all manner of objects sheeted above me. Large and heavy projectiles slammed into me.

So did darkness.

When I woke up, I could feel a burning sense of agony—and immobility—in my left forearm. It was pinned under a small log. Maybe it was a limb from a nearby oak. It was heavy enough that I couldn't budge it. From where I was sprawled, I couldn't get my legs or shoulders under it, either.

The nanite shield had protected me from the worst before it had gone semipermeable, then burned out. That was a limited consolation in the position in which I found myself.

In the end, by contorting myself and using a small belt knife, I dug enough in the way of needles and dirt from underneath the arm to free it—after I passed out from the pain that had been blocked by the compression of the arm against the ground. I thought I heard a whispering somewhere, but the only sounds that remained when I regained consciousness were those of insects, and rough cawinglike sounds, except they sounded more like "kaugh." Even in my state, it sounded raw and ugly.

Obviously, no one else was alive nearby—except for an unkindness of ravens and more than a few insects, including a persistent deerfly. The ravens were busy enough that they paid me little heed. The deerfly paid me far too much attention.

Almost another half stan passed before I managed to immobilize the arm between two lengths of fir and tie strips of the flight suit's sleeve into a sort of sling.

When I did manage to get to my feet and peer around the tree, I swallowed. The entire clearing was a mass of shredded and tangled wood, vegetation, and shredded composites.

Thurenan Arms had clearly designed the self-destruct mechanism to assure that nothing usable remained anywhere close to the nightflitter. At least, nothing usable except to the ravens and eventually the carrion beetles.

That suggested that I depart immediately. At the same time, I couldn't help but wonder why a follow-up team hadn't been dispatched. Maybe Eloi only had one team on standby. Still, remaining seemed unwise.

If . . . if I recalled correctly, there was some sort of RT station around three klicks south. Time's End was closer, but that wasn't an option.

I swallowed and started walking away from the devastation. My steps were cautious. I couldn't afford to trip or fall.

Sometimes, my arm throbbed. That was when it hurt less. I kept walking.

I'd gotten to the other side of the hill and found what once might have been a path, when I realized that something about the uniforms worn by Eloi's commandos nagged at me. They hadn't worn insignia, and the colors had been forest camouflage, but . . . the cut, the design . . . something.

I couldn't figure what it might have been.

Despite the intermittent cool gusts of wind, and a patch or two of frost in the shade under a few trees, I didn't feel that cold. My mouth was dry.

I kept walking.

30

*Those who planned the city's skies
Also dreamt its pleasures' lies.*

I have never been a human being who glories in naps or in catching sleep at odd intervals. Rather I have always followed sleep who kissed me in the brain so as to drop into dreaming. With such effort in attaining a second sky far from the mundane stars, I had barely reached the cloud coast, seeking Magdalena, when the link slammed me back into full awareness.

Ser Maraniss . . . Director Eloi would like you back at the operations center. He apologizes, but something has come up.

I'll be there shortly.

Of course something had come up. With Legaar, and with most of those who inhabited and structured modern corpentities, any nonfinancial contingency was unexpected and unwelcome, something to be avoided or eliminated. Their creativity was like the fabled emperor of ice cream, invariably melting under the heat of either stress or sensuality, yet for them, even when they dawdled with their nymphs and wenches in such undress, sex was as coolly concupiscent as a chilled confectionery, and even less pleasing, though they knew it not.

He would appreciate it.

That was something I seriously doubted, since Legaar was not the sort to appreciate anything provided by other individuals. He regarded all services as his due, and, in time, I would provide him just that.

For that reason alone, I did take a little time to shower and clean up.

Legaar was once more pacing when I reached the operations center. Despite the climate control systems, the air was acrid, permeated by the odor of his perspiration and stress emanations.

"You took your time."

"You didn't say that it was urgent," I replied. "I was showering when you linked. I didn't think you wanted me to arrive here in that state. Besides, your nymphs might have waylaid me along the way."

"That might have done some good."

Not for me, since none of them happened to be anywhere as close to perfection as Magdalena, a creature who matched Elysium for grace and beauty.

"I shouldn't have let you create her."

I ignored his reference to Magdalena, obvious as my reactions must have been. "What did you want?"

"The surveillance team never reported back. Less than a stan after they should have reached the target location, there was another energy burst. That made two in less than three stans," Legaar said. "One was at four fifty-seven this morning, and the other at seven nineteen. The second one was explosive in nature."

Since his commando team hadn't returned, that certainly made a direct and crude kind of sense. "So someone else has decided to reply in kind. Do you know who?"

"We had no reports from the team after the explosion. We launched an RPF for surveillance. There's a seared area in a clearing on the hillside on RT lands. There's some debris. It appears to be what's left of the TCs and some sort of aircraft, although the sections are too small and too scattered to determine the type and source from the RPF scans."

"You're not sending anyone out to recover the TCs?"

Legaar shook his head. "There's no reason to. The team didn't carry anything that would link them to Time's End. If they were stupid enough to walk into a trap, that was their problem. They took out the aircraft, and it was positioned to do surveillance. We didn't detect ongoing emissions, and that means it was set up for long-term passive observation. We've stopped that for now."

"You'll just leave everything there?"

"We'll let RT deal with it. For all we know, it was just an aircraft crash. It didn't occur here, and that's not our problem."

If what Legaar said happened to be correct, his judgment was right. "That makes sense. But why did you ask me to come back here?"

"I had my reasons."

He always did, but I wasn't about to ask directly. That was what he wanted. "What did you find out about the shadow?"

"He flew out to Villedumont last night. That's not all that far from the Special Operations base. He was medically retired from Special Ops."

"That sounds like he still might have ties there. Could he be a covert agent of theirs?"

Legaar laughed. "I'd love to prove that. Special Operations can't employ their techniques and equipment against Assembly citizens on Assembly worlds. They can do training, but that's limited to weapons training on their own reservations and nonspecific surveillance."

Nonspecific surveillance sounded like an oxymoron or, more politely, a military contradiction in terms. "There's no reservation near here. Did any of the debris suggest Special Operations?"

"From an RPF scan? How could we tell? Once RT looks into it, I'll have sources suggest that they probe the possibility of SpecOps involvement. Right now, that shouldn't come from me."

"Are your other . . . arrangements . . . in place?"

He ignored the question. "I have a small task for you, Maraniss. I do believe it's within your capabilities. You'll need to return to Thurene for the next few days."

I didn't like that at all. I could return to Time's End in less than a stan using the projection field, but that would alert the sisters prematurely. "What can I do there that you don't have far better tools for?"

"They're known as tools. You're not. You're known as a civic planner and patterner, if a rather unreliable and eccentric one. I want you to talk to a few people. You know who. Suggest that you've been relaxing at Time's End, but that you've seen or heard strange aircraft more than once and that some of them seemed to be Assembly craft rather than planetary or system craft."

"No one who knows anything will tell me anything."

"That's not the point. What we want to do is get other people to start asking questions."

Upon occasion, Legaar was even close to logical, and this appeared to be one of those occasions. That I found it so nagged at me, so much so that I still didn't like it, neither being separated from Magdalena nor from quick transit-access to Elysium.

I also didn't like the idea of Special Operations getting interested. Unlike the Civitas Sorores, whose competence and foresight were limited, not to mention their assets and technology, Special Operations had greater competence and, more important, direct access to the Assembly space service—and they did have the resources to affect my plans for Elysium.

31

Torture and forced interrogations are for the incompetent; manners and civility are far more effective . . . and deadly.

I walked only three or four klicks to the RT field station. It felt like ten, and it took me more than two stans before I staggered across a wide expanse of grass toward the old-style log dwelling. Behind it was a long shed that had to have contained far more modern equipment than its broad plank exterior walls suggested.

The woman who stood on the narrow covered porch of the dwelling wore RT field greens. She greeted me with opaque brown eyes and an immobilizer aimed directly at me. I'd have been trussed up in intelligent expanded foam in instants if she triggered the truncheonlike device. "What the frig are you doing here? This is a restricted watershed." Her eyes dropped to the crude sling and splint on my left forearm. "How did that happen?"

"I thought you might know." I tried not to wince. "I was overflying the area just north of here. I had a flitter, and something went wrong. I set down. I was checking the flitter when some commando types in TCs charged out of the woods and started firing. I scrambled behind some trees, and everything exploded." All of what I said was true, if not necessarily in that order or with the implications my sequence suggested.

Her face tightened. She forced it to relax. "Who are you?"

"Blaine Donne. I live in Thurene. You can check that."

"Blaine Donne?"

"D-O-N-N-E, that's right."

She studied my face. "You're in a lot of pain."

"Some," I admitted.

"Sit down on the bench there. Don't move until I come back."

I sat. It was a relief to get off my feet. Despite being fall, the day was warm enough that being in the shade didn't bother me.

She returned in less than five minutes. Another woman in the RT field greens now held the immobilizer. The first woman held a portable diagnostic until and a medkit.

I barely managed to stay conscious while she did the diagnostics, then immobilized the arm in a temporary cast.

"You'll need some better work on that, but this will keep it from getting worse," she explained. "RT will be sending a transport. They may bill you for it."

I hadn't expected less.

All in all, I waited almost two stans. It was a long two stans because the field foresters had clearly been instructed not to converse with me any more than absolutely necessary. Finally, a pair of RT flitters appeared in the cloudless afternoon sky. One was a standard transport flitter, the smaller variety, almost bulbous. The other was a deadlier and sleeker version. It didn't have stealth features. With the shields and armament it carried, it probably didn't need them.

Both set down on the open space to the north of the porch where I waited.

A slender but muscular individual emerged from the transport flitter and strode across the grass to where I sat in a more comfortable chair than the green bench where I'd first been. The newcomer wore the royal green of the RT private forces. Her hair was so blond it was almost silver, but it was cut even shorter than Krij's was.

I stood although I didn't feel like it.

Her eyes took in my tattered and ragged flight suit and the bulky temp-cast on my forearm. "Why don't you sit down, Seignior Donne? You're a long way from your villa and the shadows of Thurene, and you look like you've had a difficult time. Oh, I'm Fiorina Carle, and I'm an information specialist with RT."

Her obvious concern and manners—as well as her knowledge about my background—chilled me more than Javerr's arrogance ever had. I did seat myself.

She turned and walked to the far side of the porch, where she lifted the other chair and carried it back toward me. Then she placed the chair just outside the edge of my personal comfort space. She settled into it with a studied ease that bothered me even more. "We've had the report from the forester, but I'd appreciate it if you'd tell me what happened in your own words. We're not exactly pleased when innocent pilots"—she smiled humorously—"not that many would claim innocence as one of your characteristics—find their flitters destroyed on RT lands. We also don't like it because this land is the watershed for the springs that feed our waters and vineyards. We take contamination seriously." She laughed, sympathetically and warmly. "I can understand that you're more likely to be concerned about your injuries and those who caused them, and we're concerned about that as well. If you wouldn't mind . . ."

Exactly how much should I tell her?

The more I could without compromising my own situation, the better. She was clearly one of RT's best, and that might be why it had taken two stans for before the two flitters had reached the station on what was a flight of less than one stan from Thurene.

I frowned. "You obviously know who I am, and what I do. I hope you'll understand if I don't name names."

"Why don't you tell me what's comfortable?" She didn't smile, just nodded sympathetically.

"The bare bones of what never yet was heard in tale or song?" I asked with a grin.

"That to the service of this house belongs," she countered.

She was well-read, and that made her all the more dangerous, but perhaps not to me. "I have a client who paid me to discover the connection between several individuals. Not any dirt. I wasn't asked to delve into possible illegalities, but everything seemed to lead toward the property to the north of here. That became especially interesting after I discovered that several RPFs from that property crashed on RT lands recently. The news didn't give much in the way of details, but I thought it might be worth looking into. So I flew out here, but I found myself having difficulties, and I set down in a cleared area on the other side of the hills to the north. I was outside my flitter when my detectors alerted me to energy concentrations moving toward me. I tend to be suspicious, Lady Carle—"

"Fiorina, please."

"As I said, I tend to be suspicious, and since my flitter wasn't going anywhere, I ducked behind a tree. I don't know what they used, but there were fragments of flitter going everywhere. Then there was an explosion. I was flattened. When I came to, there was a limb pinning my left arm to the ground. I couldn't move it—the tree—but I did manage to use my belt knife to scrape away enough under the arm to slide it out. I have to say that I passed out. I managed to splint it and tie together a sling. Then I started walking."

"You were closer to Time's End. Why didn't you head there?" The question was delivered warmly and rhetorically. She already knew my answer.

"I had the feeling that whoever had been shooting at me had come from there. Somehow, Time's End didn't seem like a good idea. I have my little vices and limitations, but I try to avoid complete stupidity."

"The satellite scans didn't show your arrival over RT lands, though," she mused.

"I came in very low," I admitted, "and the flitter did have some rudimentary stealth features. Obviously not enough to avoid detection by someone."

"What time did you set down?"

I smiled. "In the dark before dawn. I'd thought that very early morning would have been less dangerous. I was wrong."

"Do you recall exactly when?"

"Not exactly. You don't think about time under those circumstances."

"With your passion for detail, Seignior Donne?" She raised her eyebrows. The effect was less because they were so pale.

"Detail tends to get lost when things go wrong quickly. I'd say it was somewhere around six hour, but that's a guess."

She was very quiet, very professional, very thorough, and very insistent. She spent two long standard hours talking to me. I gave up more than I'd hoped and less than I could have, and that was about the best I could have expected.

Then she smiled once more. "You've been very helpful, Seignior Donne, and I do appreciate your patience at a time when you cannot have been that comfortable."

"I've told you what I can, and I appreciate your professional approach." I still didn't want to call her Fiorina, and she didn't want a more formal salutation.

"I may be back in touch once you've returned to Thurene."

"I understand." I paused. "I have a question or two for you."

She waited.

"Were you aware that a civic patterner named Judeon Maraniss has been working for Legaar Eloi?"

"I really can't comment on that."

That meant she knew.

I grinned. "On another subject . . . do the names Stella Strong, Maureen Maud Gonne, or Astrid Forte mean anything to you?"

There was the faintest stiffening at the last name, but she shook her head. "Should I?"

"I've been asked to locate them—or her. I think they're all the same individual. This isn't connected to Time's End."

"I can't help you here, Seignior Donne." She gestured toward the small transport flitter. "The flitter is ready to lift off." We both knew that it could have lifted off long before.

I stood, then eased my way down the two steps off the porch and walked across the browning grass toward the flitter. She accompanied me. She didn't say anything, and I could sense that she was linked elsewhere.

As I was about to step into the transport flitter, she smiled abruptly and turned to me. "The investigatory team confirmed that you were pinned under the tree and that a rather large explosion shredded a significant area."

I almost shrugged. "Did they find anything else?"

She grinned. "Let's just say that there's nothing that concerns you, Seignior Donne. Not obviously, at the moment. Along with the bill for transport back to Thurene, we'll send you a waiver."

That did puzzle me. "A waiver?"

"We release you from responsibility for damage to the trees and watershed, and you agree that RT has no responsibility for your injuries. You also agree to testify in the unlikely event that our investigation uncovers proof of who was behind the attack on your flitter and the subsequent destruction. That's only if RT takes justiciary action against those responsible."

In short, RT was going to be investigating other means of dealing with Legaar Eloi. "That seems fair."

"I thought you'd see it that way." She smiled again, warmly. "Take care of that arm, Seignior."

"I'll do my best."

After she stepped back, I climbed into the flitter. The hatch closed, and I sat alone in the rear passenger compartment as the craft lifted off. The couch was the most comfortable position I'd been in all day, and I could almost forget the muted throbbing in my forearm. The RT information specialist reminded me of someone, and yet she didn't. Her matter-of-fact manner was similar to . . .

Siendra—that was it! I frowned. For all that I couldn't have explained why, I had the feeling that Siendra was more genuine. To be Krij's business partner, she would have had to be. Krij didn't go in for false warmth.

Would RT do anything in handling Legaar Eloi? If they did, would I ever know? Somehow, I doubted it.

What I didn't doubt was that whatever the Elois and Maraniss were doing, it was important enough and possibly dangerous enough that Legaar had no compunction about sending a commando team out, then cutting them off when matters went bad.

It had to be Elysium. The only problem I had was that I still didn't have the faintest idea of what Elysium was and how it connected to either Maraniss or Legaar Eloi. And for whom was Seigniora Reynarda fronting? She certainly couldn't be a cover for the original Fox. It was amusing in a fashion that we all referred to the unknown fox as the original, when the unknown had actually taken the name of a former marshal. But then, so far as I knew, no one had ever uncovered the unknown Fox's true identity, while even the histories mentioned Marshal Reynardo.

32

Deities are invented by fallible and finite beings in the hope and desire to create immortal perfection; unfortunately, such deities only reflect their creators and inspire their followers to similar imperfections.

The bulky cast placed on my forearm by the RT forester had hardly been a medical miracle, but it had reduced the pain to manageable agony. As soon as I'd gotten back to the villa, I'd had my systems take over. After an antiinflammatory treatment, and an initial regrowth session that lasted almost a stan, the villa's med-system replaced my field splint cast with a nanospun flexicast that fit under a shirt. The nerve blocks were set to maintain an intermittent low-grade dull ache. Otherwise, the system told me, "You will be tempted to act as if the bone were not broken."

Were people that stupid?

Probably. At times, pain serves a most useful purpose, even for me.

By that time, the sun had set, and I was exhausted. I gratefully had climbed into bed and collapsed into an exhausted sleep. That state had lasted only a few stans before the nightmares began.

The first was predictable—a repeat of the events on Pournelle II—except that I was watching and telling my former self that it was more than an ambush. Even in the nightmare, I didn't listen to myself.

The second was a modified replay of what had just happened at Time's End. This time I got potted with a bracketed missile launch that destroyed the nightflitter, and started a raging fire that turned thousands of hectares of RT forests into ashes. Somehow I escaped and was standing stark naked before the planetary justiciary trying to explain why I wasn't guilty of inciting the events that led to eco-cide. The justicers weren't listening, but I jerked awake before the verdict was read.

I got up soaked in sweat and walked around my bed-chamber to cool off.

It was just past midnight. Should I try sleeping again?

A leaden feeling and several yawns convinced me that I should at least make an attempt.

I woke well after dawn, convinced that I'd had more nightmares. I was unable to remember them. For that I was thankful.

As I began breakfast—an orange from one of the trees in the courtyard garden, a single poached egg topped with cheese, and a small butter croissant, accompanied by a large mug of earlgrey—I set Max to scanning the news. By the time I started on the second mug of earlgrey, he reported that there was nothing about what had happened at Time's End. Not a thing.

After breakfast, I sat in my study and reflected. I tried to, anyway.

Fiorina Carle had known about Maraniss, but either hadn't connected me to the link between Maraniss and Legaar Eloi or hadn't wanted to call attention to it. I got a definite feeling of insignificance. Not only that, but I was feeling less than competent in the whole business. I *knew* something enormous was about to happen. I also knew it was called Elysium, and it involved a modified jumpship generator and infringement on Lemel Jerome's patents, and would take a lot of power. Part of what it was *might* involve the transport device, because Lemmy's patents had dealt with transport.

I frowned. Had Maraniss or Legaar found a technology that allowed instant on-planet transport? That would be worth billions, and would certainly explain why Legaar didn't want to let Lemmy know, and why the inventor had been silenced. Could it be that Elysium was the code name for the project?

Again . . . I just didn't know. That was another possibility. I did have a good idea that Tony diVeau had allowed himself to be suborned by the Elois just in order to keep Banque de L'Ouest solvent—and his own position. And somehow Sephaniah's daughter had been involved in the creation of the Sephaniah impersonator. Why that had been done, I couldn't say. It didn't fit.

I also knew that a number of the top Classic personnel had been transferred away from Devanta, and that Eloi Enterprises had moved funds and capital—as much as possible, I judged—out-system. Yet both Maraniss and Legaar Eloi appeared to be still on Devanta. Didn't they?

Max, interrogative physical presence and location of Legaar Eloi and Judeon Maraniss?

Probability exceeds ninety-three percent that both are currently situated at Time's End or at Pier One.

I would have preferred a probability of absolute unity. *Based on what?*

Legaar Eloi appeared as a witness in a preliminary hearing on the EsClox proceeding late yesterday, and he is scheduled to testify in two stans at the justiciary building in Thurene. Neither he nor Maraniss is manifested on any out-system transports . . . Max went on until I cut him off.

Let me know if Eloi doesn't show for his testimony, or when he does. I stopped. *Calculate the probabilities that the body testifying as Legaar Eloi is actually Eloi.*

Probability approaches unity. Civitas Sorores require physio-genetico-somatic identity verification.

That didn't preclude an absolutely identical clone—not if Legaar wanted to risk being destroyed by himself—but it was close enough to totally unlikely that I could bet on Legaar still being on Devanta. For now, anyway.

I wasn't going to get anywhere obsessing about what I didn't know. So I tried to recall the "new" angles I'd considered on my aborted recon before Legaar's commando goons had arrived. First, I reviewed the recording of the original request by "Nancy." I'd never followed up on either the names Vola Paulsky or Relian Cru, not beyond a quick data search. I set Max to work on a complete direct and indirect search. It didn't take long for the direct information to appear—after he informed me that Legaar Eloi had indeed appeared and was now testifying in objection to the amendment before the justiciary.

Incoming from Seldara Tozzi.

The last thing I wanted to do was explain my report to a doubtless angry Seigniora Tozzi. But the need to make the explanation wasn't going away. *Accept.*

Seldara Tozzi wore a silver jacket over a brilliant white pleated blouse, and dark gray trousers. She was seated behind a wide and simple dark wooden table desk. I forced myself to smile and wait for her to speak. For a moment, neither of us did.

She smiled. I would rather have faced battle laser focused in my direction. Not really, but that was partly how I felt.

"Seignior Donne, I have read your report on the presentation to the Humanitas Foundation. I studied it, in fact. It is a remarkable piece of work. In fact, it is excellent. Upon reflection, I asked my great-granddaughter for her opinion about it. She agreed. Your work was precise, accurate, and concise. Your analysis was trenchant." The smile turned fainter. "There is one small problem with it, however. It doesn't bear upon your commission." Her voice remained cool.

"Principessa Tozzi, I disagree. Politely. It has a great deal to do with your commission."

"I would be *most* interested to know how that might be."

"If you would bear with me, I would like to ask you a question before I give you a fuller reply. Exactly how did your great-granddaughter respond to the report, and what did she say?"

There was no hesitation in her reply. "At first, she was disturbed that I had dispatched an observer to analyze Dr. Dyorr's presentation. After she read it, she said that it was succinct and accurate. She said she'd seen few analyses so impartial and accurate. She asked for a copy. I provided it."

"Did she say anything about Dr. Dyorr personally?"

"She did not. She did say that he would be pleased to know that at least some observers actually understood the import and impact of his research."

I nodded. "Good. I have done a great deal of searching behind the scenes. Both before and after the presentation. I have contacted, under accurate but misleading introductions, a number of professionals who would have every desire to reveal anything untoward about the doctor. Not a one did, even given every opportunity. There is absolutely not even a whiff of anything unethical or concealed by the doctor." I held up my right hand to forestall an objection. "That does not necessarily mean it does not exist. What it does mean is that if there is something not right, it is most likely something else. I had wondered about this from early on, but I wanted to see Dr. Dyorr in person, especially with your granddaughter watching him. There's no substitute for personal contacts."

"Doubtless you are suggesting the expenditure of more credits."

"No. I have not utilized all that you provided." Close, but not quite. "As you may recall, I also agreed to an absolute limit on your exposure. I would like you to consider a possibility for discovering more and possibly resolving this. You had said that your granddaughter had appreciated my report. Would you consider inviting me to a lunch with her and with Dr. Dyorr to discuss his difficulties in obtaining accurate and fair representation of his research?"

Seldara Tozzi offered only a momentary frown. "I don't know why you think this would resolve matters, but it could be done."

"How soon could this be arranged?"

"I suppose we should resolve matters as soon as possible. I doubt that we could arrange anything before Lunen, although . . ." She paused. "I might be able to work out something for Domen afternoon. Marie Annette was going to meet me for lunch. I will let you know shortly, Seignior Donne. Why do you think this would help?"

"I'm going to ask you to trust me on this, Seigniora. I will say that Dr. Dyorr would never let anything interfere with his medicine, his reputation, and his research. I think that will prove the key."

She nodded slowly. "I can see that might prove . . . useful." The slight hint of a predatory smile appeared at the corners of her mouth. "Very well. I will contact you with a proposed date."

"Thank you."

Once the holo vanished, I took a deep breath. I believed what I'd said. The only difficulty was that I had no idea of how I'd be able to resolve the problem. There was no doubt in my mind that Guillaume Richard Dyorr was not a samer. Not even a closet samer. What he was exactly was another question.

I decided to let my subconscious stew over that while I returned to the Maureen Gonne commission. I also hoped it wouldn't be too long before I heard from Myndanori.

The dossier on Vola Paulsky was slim—private citizen, born in Seveignon, Devanta, [date not given], degrees from Hyhail College and L' Université de Vannes, advocate in nonpublic practice, Carcassonne. A code followed the office link, along with the notation that all other personal information was restricted. Seveignon was a small town less than fifty klicks west from Vannes, and Carcassonne was about sixty northeast. Nonpublic advocacy meant she worked for a corpentity or a nonprofit . . . or possibly as a counsel for a government body. Previous occupations included a brief time as a literary instructor at Hyhail, followed by work for hire as an author of elaborate wish fulfillment scenarios for White Hyppogrif, Limited, an entertainment combine outside of Vannes.

There was even less on Relian Cru, except for an old story about a summer racquets competition, where "Lucky" Cru had won the youth division. The only other notation was that he was currently listed as in service to the Assembly of Worlds. No public information was available on what his service was or where. That was standard. It didn't help me.

Max had also come up with close to fifty passing and indirect references. I began to read. When I finished sorting through them more than a stan later, I knew just a little more. Vola had contributed to the Vannes Opera Civique and the Carcassonne Literary Society for the past twelve years. She had been listed as the pro bono advocate of record on behalf of a number of legally disadvantaged individuals in the Carcassonne subdistrict. There was no record of her appearing in any other proceedings. That suggested she was an in-house advocate who did not appear in justiciary proceedings for her employer, but I was only guessing at that.

At that moment, I got an incoming text document from an in-house advocate at Rothschild Thierry. As Fiorina Carle had promised, it included both a waiver and an invoice for special transportation services—two thousand credits.

That reminded me to put in an indemnity claim for the nightflitter. Gallian Re was not going to be happy even though I'd only been able to indemnify a third of the cost—and that had cost more than thirty thousand credits a year, my single largest expense. I wouldn't have bothered, except that much coverage had been required by the sisters, mainly to assure that I had liability coverage to protect others.

I had twenty days to pay RT, but I sent off the two thousand credits immediately. I hated owing anyone anything.

Then I linked to the code given for Vola Paulsky.

A slender, almost scrawny, and thin-faced woman appeared. The talking head was virtie, but based, I suspected, on Vola herself. "You have reached the Performing Arts Society. Please leave a message."

That was all.

I didn't leave a message. What would I have said? What performing arts society?

I eased back in the chair. I still hadn't any better ideas, and I was running out of time.

I must have sat in the study and stewed for half a stan.

Then I had an early lunch, and a long one. I didn't eat much, and my subconscious didn't come up with anything novel. So I finally went back to the study and began to reread what I'd had compiled.

Incoming from Siendra Albryt.

The message startled me. I jumped slightly, and the flexicast bumped the edge of the table desk. A wave of pain flashed up my arm. I managed not to shudder and bang the arm again. "Accept."

For once, Siendra wasn't wearing earth tones but a warm green shirt and a dark gray vest. I thought I liked her better in earth tones. Her pleasant expression changed to one of concern as soon as her eyes focused on me. "Blaine . . . are you all right?"

"I've been better. I lost the flitter and suffered a broken radius."

"It wasn't an accident, was it? It had to do with the Elois."

"I couldn't prove that, but I ended up getting treated by an RT forester and grilled by a top-level RT info specialist."

"How is your arm?"

"It's in a nanocast, with limited pain blocks. I can't really use my fingers." Not without a fair amount of discomfort, I'd discovered. I didn't want to talk about me. That could have been because Siendra seemed concerned. "What do you have?"

"I've talked this over with Krij. We have some information, but you can't disclose it to anyone." Unlike Krij, Siendra didn't press about the arm and flitter. Krij would have grilled me. She still would, when she found out.

"I won't." If Krij said not to disclose, she meant it. So did Siendra, I was certain.

"There are solid indications that the initial capitalization that backed Legaar Eloi came from Frankan sources."

Frankan sources? Why did the really lousy things in my life always seem to go back to the Frankans? "Why would they do that? How did you discover that?"

"I didn't. Krij did. She analyzed sector and system funds flows and applied some advanced probability analysis. A justiciary won't accept it as evidence, but she's never been wrong before."

"But . . . why?"

"It's a tactic for affecting a society's priorities. Various forms of vice generate large credit flows. Once they're large enough, they take on a life of their own. Social analysis shows that, over time, they turn a society inward. They make it more self-indulgent, more isolationist, less likely to attack or expand, or even to defend marginal territory or commercial activity that doesn't seem to bear on the society's immediate needs. Those needs veer toward present self-gratification." She paused. "That's my analysis. It won't stand up before a justiciary, either, but the probabilities compute that way and track with history and current trends."

"So our boy Legaar is tied up with the Frankans, and they're using him to soften us up. Those of us in the Gallian sector, anyway."

"It's cheaper than war."

"It's just another form," I countered. "And Legaar figures that he's been successful enough that it's time to shift most of his ops elsewhere, doubtless with more Frankan funds." Even as I said it, that didn't feel right, but I couldn't have explained why.

"That's the most likely possibility."

"You don't think so, either, but you don't have a better answer."

Her response was a shrug, followed after a moment by a sheepish smile.

"We'll have to think about that," I said.

She nodded.

"Before you break, Siendra . . . could I ask what you have on two other names? Vola Paulsky and Relian Cru?"

Her eyes glazed slightly, but her face was still alive. For all that, I was relieved when she smiled, if faintly. "There's not much. I'll send you the dossier on Paulsky." Her lips tightened. "You can't tell anyone the next, either."

"I won't."

"Relian Cru was junior engineering officer aboard the *Lafayette*. It's—it was—an older corvette. It was suffered an undetermined accident last month. Neither the crew nor the vessel survived. Relatives have been notified of the deaths, but not of the circumstances."

I didn't like that, either.

"More bad news?"

"Disturbing," I admitted. "He was one of the possible heirs in the inheritance commission I've been working on."

"That's unfortunate. Poor fellow."

"They called him 'Lucky,'" I added, thinking that the luck of Relian Cru had indeed run out.

"Not this time."

"No." I frowned. "The timing is suspicious, though."

"You're hardly suggesting that someone destroyed an Assembly warship for an inheritance, are you?" Siendra's tone was not-quite-bantering.

"No. But I have to wonder if someone got very interested when they learned one of the possible beneficiaries was dead."

"There has to be more than that," she pointed out. "Otherwise, they'd just wait and collect in the course of events."

Siendra was right about that, but what else could there be?

"Is there anything else I can do?"

"Not at the moment, thank you."

After her image vanished, I studied what she'd sent. Her dossier on Vola Paulsky was almost the same as mine, except hers listed Paulsky's employer—the Carcassonne Performing Arts Society. That answered which performing arts society. From the link, I'd have bet Vola was the only paid employee.

I leaned back in the chair, very carefully, and closed my eyes, thinking. Sometimes, it helped.

Relian Cru . . . dead. Vola Paulsky and Stella/Maureen/Astrid(?) the remaining heirs of Clinton Jefferson Wayles. What exactly had Angelique deGritz said about heirs—those that weren't able to inherit? Legally ineligible? She'd said there were definitions in the Codex.

Max . . . bring up the sections of the Codex dealing with

heirs and inheritances, especially the parts that indicate who isn't eligible to inherit.

Text appeared on the recessed screen in the table desk, but before I could even read one line, Max interrupted me.

Incoming. A Scipio Barca.

The name alone suggested a man at war with himself. Still . . . *Accept.*

The holo showed a man—or an alter-projection—who appeared angular and taller than I was. His face wore an apologetic expression, slightly haggard, in the way that was unlikely to have been reformulated to Barca's advantage.

"Seignior Donne, I'm Skip Barca. Jay Smith suggested that I might be able to retain your services."

If he used a contraction of his name, properly it should have been "Sip." I could see why he hadn't. "It's possible. Why did he refer you to me?"

"I'm a logo designer. I'm freelance now, but I was with A&R—that's really Anshoots and Reed—I was with them for almost twenty years. They've pretty much got the corner on the fundie market, the faith and pray crew, if you know what I mean. Now I don't know how much you know about the business, but successful logos generate royalty payments, and my agreement entitled me to a small share of the payments for life. That was whether I stayed with A&R or not. Most logos only last a few years, and you don't get the royalties unless they use the logo longer than the standard design life. That's two years . . ."

Already, I was learning more about logos than I'd ever wanted to know.

"Almost ten years ago, I did the logo for FM Pubs— that's Fair-meadow Maharishi Publications, very big in the transgalactic meditation field. They're still using it, my logo, I mean, but for the past three years, I haven't gotten a demi-cred. I went to Jay. That's because my cousin's husband knew him. He said that I had a good case but that it would cost me more in fees than I could recover. He thought you might be able to negotiate something." His big dumb blue eyes were almost pleading. "Oh . . . I'm sending his referral and my contract and closure agreements with A&R."

The text from Jay was simple enough.

Blaine—

Skip's getting stiffed by this Anshoots character. We could take it to the justiciary and win—in about two years and with ten K in costs, easy. It's also a reg compliance thing. I figure that if you go to Anshoots and ask him if he wants to pay poor Skip his three K in back royalties and keep paying or if he wants a reg compliance audit, he'll pay. I can't threaten an audit. With your sister's rep, you can. You can't lose. Neither can she. Let me know.

I checked the agreement and noted the authentication. I ran the codes through Max, and got back an affirmative. It was on register with the Civitas Sorores.

In short, Jay was suggesting a very legal shakedown. I liked it. I didn't know much about A&R, but I'd never liked the faith and power boys and girls. I even liked Skip for leaving them.

"Will you take the commission? I can't offer much."

"How about a third of the back royalties, and none of those from here forward?"

"A third?" His voice quavered.

"You'd lose credits if you went through the justiciary. This way you keep two-thirds of whatever I recover for you, and nothing from here on. And you don't have to come up with any credits up front."

Once he thought about it, he finally agreed.

After he broke the link, I checked on the physical location of A&R. I also looked at FM Pubs catalogue. That was clear enough. The logo design was credited to A&R. FM wasn't about to grant credit and not pay. That would have the sisters all over them. That meant that Anshoots was screwing the help and former help and pocketing the credits. I just loved how so many of the ostensibly faithful types did that. They weren't any different from anyone else; they just liked to think so.

Incoming from Krij.

Accept. What did she want? Or did she have more information.

Her green eyes lasered in on me, even from a holo projection. "Blaine." Her voice held the big-sister tone. "You broke your arm, and you didn't even think to tell me?"

"I told Siendra. I knew she'd tell you. What could you do?"

"What could I do?" That was an accusation, not a question. I couldn't have provided an answer she'd accept. I didn't try.

"We're coming over for dinner. You need company, and we need to talk."

"We?"

"You're stubborn enough that I need reinforcements. I'm bringing Siendra. We'll be there at five hour. Don't go anywhere."

"Where would I go? And how?"

"Sometimes, you're too resourceful, brother dear."

That hadn't been true lately, and if I'd been any less resourceful, I'd have probably been broke—or dead.

"Till five." She was gone.

As if I didn't have enough to worry about, now Krij would be nagging me.

Part of my thoughts suggested it would be a very good idea to enlist her aid and Siendra's to an even greater extent than I had so far. I wasn't doing all that well by myself.

I didn't like admitting it.

So I went back to the text about heirs and inheritances. There was more than a little there, and reading through it took time, more time than I wanted to spend.

I also needed to set up an appointment with A&R.

33

Those who merely ask why are cynics and skeptics; those who wonder beyond the "why" are the creators.

Before Krij and Siendra arrived, I had managed to set up an appointment for Lunen morning with Fillype Anshoots of A&R. I hated to wait over both Sabaten and the end-days, but Anshoots was supposedly in Vannes until Senen.

I checked vid-messages. One was from Myndanori, reminding me that she was expecting me on Sabaten evening—with or without a companion—and that she had some information for me that she preferred not to leave on the system. With what had happened over the last few days, I'd almost forgotten about the gathering. I certainly wouldn't be bringing a companion.

I immediately vidlinked back, but got no response, except for her talking head. I left a quick message.

After running through the rest of the messages, I'd also waded through the legalese defining classes of bequest beneficiaries and heirs. The Codex language on beneficiaries was anything but simple. What it meant wasn't that complicated—if I understood terms of law stated by the words. In effect, the first class of beneficiaries consisted of spouses and blood-heirs of the first level, siblings or offspring. The second class consisted of legal-heirs, those related to the bequester through legal action, such as adoption, legal partnership of some sort, and samer civil unions. The third class could have been loosely defined as remainder heirs of various types, such as more distant relatives, lien holders.

The wording defining ineligible heirs was even more precisely convoluted. Deceased heirs were ineligible, as were their offspring, unless the bequest specifically noted otherwise. Anyone involved in the felonious death of the bequester was also ineligible. Then there were the conditional and categorical levels of ineligibility. No planetary or continental-level individual could receive a bequest except from a blood parent, offspring, or spouse. The same limits applied to their offspring during the period in which they served. No justicer could rule on any bequest involving any heir who was related to the justicer by blood or law. And last, curiously, were two prohibitions. No bequest could be settled on any of the Civitas Sorores, or certain designees of the Sorores, while they served in that capacity, even to a blood-heir. Nor could a lien holder, even one related by blood, receive a bequest until the lien was discharged. No bequest could discharge a lien owed to the bequester's estate.

I wasn't quite certain I understood the rationale for the last conditions, but the language was clear enough. Did any of it apply to Stella/Maureen, who might also be Astrid? At that point, I didn't know.

In the midst of all that, I got another vidlink.

Incoming from Seldara Tozzi.

Accept.

This time she was in silver trimmed with black. She immediately began. "Luncheon is set for one hour on Domen. I do trust that you will be able to resolve matters satisfactorily at that time."

So did I. "I can only promise the beginning of that resolution, Principessa."

"I would appreciate a solid beginning, Seignior Donne."

"We aim to please." I bowed slightly.

"Good. Until Domen." She broke the vidlink.

Now I was in even more trouble. Yet . . . commissions like Seldara Tozzi's were what ensured the future. In my business, I could never tell, not for certain, what might end up being more important—and equally important—lucrative.

The next stan I spent on listening to sections of the dramas attributed to Terrie McGerrie, Carey Douglass, and Marley Louis. One aspect of her writing did stand out. Whoever she was, her language was always elegant in a subdued and balanced fashion. There was also something else about it . . .

Krij and Siendra have arrived, Max announced.

I was glad to get up and leave the study. I crossed the entry foyer. I made it to the front doors just before they reached the top of the steps.

Each carried a small sack as they stepped into the foyer.

"How's the arm?" Krij asked. She also flashcoded me the moment Siendra turned. *You have a lot to explain.*

"About the same as a few stans back." I didn't bother with a flashcode reply.

"You're going to tell me the details."

Beside her, Siendra smiled. She definitely understood that I wouldn't be all that happy explaining to my big sister.

"Siendra will cook. I'll help, as necessary. You will watch and explain how you got into this particular mess," Krij announced.

I didn't have to wonder why Siendra was there. One of the open secrets Krij and I shared was that while she was an excellent cook, she generally disliked cooking, especially on a day-to-day basis. She occasionally cooked for events like the brunch the week before, but only because she hated paying for cooks or caterers who were less accomplished than she was. But then, she was even more of a perfectionist in business.

Krij led the way to the kitchen. There she stopped and gestured at the double commercial stoves, the kind that had been in use in the best restaurants for centuries. Mine had only been there for fifty-odd years. They'd be just as solid and effective in another fifty. "He's got enough here to support a culinary staff of ten, and he's never used it, Siendra. Two burners on one of the stoves. That's all he's ever used."

"You're exaggerating," I protested.

"Oh . . . and the small oven. I forgot." Krij laughed.

"Would you ladies like some wine? I can offer—"

"The Rothschild sauvignon blanc for me," Krij completed the sentence.

I looked to Siendra, who had unloaded both sacks and neatly laid out the contents on the leftmost prep table. "Siendra?"

"A merlot, thank you." She had turned on the left oven before moving back to the prep table.

I opened a bottle of the 1347 Aubenade and poured Siendra's glass before I dug out the Rothschild for Krij.

Siendra was already slicing something—ginger anise, I thought—into thin strips by the time I settled onto a corner stool with my own goblet of merlot. I would have started with white, but since I'd opened the Aubenade, I decided to try it. I'd never cared for the slight edge to the Rothschild vintages, and opening a third bottle seemed . . . wasteful.

Siendra was deboning three Chymalk game hens. Her fingers were deft.

"You were good with weapons training, weren't you?"

"Blaine . . ." Krij mock-complained. "She's not one of your targets."

"That was an observation."

"I held my own." Siendra didn't looked up from the wooden expanse of the prep table.

"How did you break your arm?" Krij asked. "I'd like a few more details than offhand remarks about losing a six-million-credit aircraft and breaking your radius, and, by the way, the Elois were probably involved. You're sure the arm will be all right?"

"There was nothing crushed. The med-systems say it will heal fine, and before too long. Two weeks is the prognosis. If I were still SpecOps, it would be one, but that medtech is beyond my modest means." I took refuge behind my glass of merlot and watched Siendra finish deboning the game hens.

"And the flitter?"

"I'm sorry about that. The indemnity will only cover a third. It may be a while before I can replace it."

"Blaine . . ." Krij's voice bore an edge of exasperation. I'd heard it often growing up.

"It's simple," I began.

"It never is when you say it is."

"It's not simple, then. I'm trying to find a link between Legaar Eloi, Judeon Maraniss, and something called Elysium. You know that. The client has already paid ten thousand credits. I've confirmed that Classic Research has a facility on Legaar's estate. There's a dedicated fusactor power plant there. A large power plant. I've also confirmed that Maraniss is there, and that he's been working long stans. There's also some very high-end equipment there that's infringing on Lemmy Jerome's patents. Jerome found that out, and a good chunk of his dwelling got destroyed. He was in it. Jerome hired me to help find that out. He hadn't paid me."

"You had two different clients on the same commission?"

"I didn't know it was the same commission at the beginning. Anyway, I'd done some emissions surveillance a week or so back. I used the night-flitter. That confirmed that lots of power was being used. I got chased by three military RPFs, but they all had malfunctions and crashed on RT lands. After that, I got nothing. So I went out to do passive surveillance from a hilltop on RT lands."

"That's trespassing," Krij pointed out. "A minor matter for you, but not necessarily for RT—or the sisters."

I didn't mention the trespassing conviction for swimming in the reservoir. "Until Legaar sent a four-operative commando team after me I wasn't doing any harm to anyone. Or the RT lands. The commandos didn't even ask questions. They just opened up."

"And?"

"I made it to the trees and waited until they got close enough before I triggered the flitter's self-destruct."

"You couldn't have found a less wasteful alternative?"

"I don't do cost analysis well when I'm under attack." Before she could get in another question, I went on. "I was only using passive surveillance. No emissions except for a few seconds when I came from behind the hill and set down. It was dark. I was on full-stealth. I shut down and waited more than a whole stan. I was a good klick from his perimeter."

"That kind of response seems excessive."

"It's all excessive. Lemmy was tracking patent infringement. The royalties that he would have collected wouldn't have been noticed with Legaar's credit flow. Legaar wouldn't even have had to explain the use."

"What is the use?"

"I don't know, except that the patent has to do with improving energy effectiveness for jumpship generators, something to do with measuring the deformation of space in certain circumstances. It allows greater precision for jumpship transit choices. Legaar might have a jumpship at Time's End."

Siendra frowned. "There's no point in that. They're deep-space vessels. Operate a jumpship generator in-system, especially in a gravity well . . . it wouldn't work."

I paused. "It might also have applications for limited on-planet instant travel. That might prove a commercial success, and Legaar might have wanted to remove Lemmy from the profit stream."

"I don't see how it could work," added Siendra. "Have they found a way around the gravity well problems?"

"I don't know. I can't help thinking that there's another possibility. Using the power of a Hawking system."

Siendra looked straight at me. "Do you think he wants to do that?"

"I've been keeping track of both Maraniss and Eloi. They're both still here on Devanta. Legaar is still fighting the Sorores on the EsClox planetary defense leasing rule. I can't see him risking something that could threaten him personally. Or destroying the planet while he's on it. That's assuming that he and Maraniss could even get a Hawking system up and operating at full power before the space service or Special Ops shut it down."

Siendra nodded. "It would take days even for Legaar Eloi to get from planetside to far enough out-system where he wouldn't be in danger." After a pause, she went on. "I checked on Maraniss's background. He's got a grounding in some advanced and esoteric physics. It doesn't look like he knows enough to be an expert, but he might be using someone else's work."

"That might be why he went to Legaar," suggested Krij. "He stole the application and needs someone who won't ask questions."

"I—we still don't know what it is and whether it's even connected with whatever Elysium is."

"What else could it be?" That was Krij.

"I have that feeling," I admitted. "But I don't have anything that could really qualify as proof. Just a lot of suggestive events. Legaar has always relied on circumventing the law. Now, he's actually breaking it to keep whatever's happening at Time's End secret. He's funding a research facility when there's nothing in Eloi Enterprises that needs that kind of research. I can't help but wonder if he's onto some sort of commercial use of Lemmy's patents. It's something that wouldn't be obvious to anyone but Lemmy, and it represents potentially millions, if not billions, of credits. Otherwise, none of what happened makes sense."

"So they kill Lemmy to make sure no one discovers the link," said Krij.

"What about the commando team?" asked Siendra. "Was there anything about them? Anything about their weapons, their transport, even their uniforms?" She began to chop parsley and other herbs. Somehow, everything stayed in neat little piles.

"They didn't wear uniforms, not with insignia or emblems." I stopped. At the time, something about what the four had worn had nagged at me. "They were wearing what amounted to Frankan camos without insignia. I couldn't place what it was then, only that there was something."

"Either being attacked or breaking an arm does tend to concentrate one away from clothing." Siendra's words were direct, but not cutting. I had the feeling warmth lay underneath them.

"So we have Legaar Eloi originally bankrolled by the Frankans and being supported by a Frankan commando team," Krij said.

"With Eloi Enterprises' most valuable personnel all assigned to other systems." Siendra was creaming cheese in a bowl and folding in the herbs.

"Legaar's acting as if something terrible is going to happen here. But he and Maraniss are still planetside. That suggests something more like an invasion," Krij mused.

"No."

"It won't work."

Siendra and I had spoken almost simultaneously. Krij looked at me. I looked to Siendra. She was filling each of the deboned hens with the herb-and-cheese mixture. Then she used cooking nanosinew to seal each hen and truss each into a cylinder. Each went into the same baking dish, and Siendra slid the dish into the oven. "I'll have to make the glaze before long. If you'd slice the beans, Krij, at an angle?"

"I can do that," replied my sister. "You both were certain about no invasion." She picked up a knife and moved to the other prep table.

I decided to let Siendra explain. I had to nod to her before she spoke.

"The Assembly space service would love an attempted attack on an Assembly world—even in the Gallian sector. That would give them every excuse possible to try all sorts of new toys on the Frankans. Also, the Frankans don't have the troops to invade and hold a world."

"You're both saying that the Frankans are backing Legaar's efforts to make a large mess here on Devanta, but you have no idea what it is."

"That's right," I replied.

"But you're also suggesting that there's something commercially valuable involved. So why would they want to make a mess of Devanta?" asked Krij.

"I don't know." I certainly didn't. That was all too clear.

"So who engaged you?" asked Krij.

"I don't know. Not really. The hidden IDs checked, but

the contact was a corpentity shell. It could be any one of a number of corpentities who can't afford to oppose the Elois openly."

"What about Special Ops or the Sorores Civitas?"

"Special Ops doesn't ever use private contractors for investigations or arms sales. No colonel or marshal wants to face a court-martial. After the Oliver Affair, where—"

"The Sorores don't have any such prohibitions." Siendra looked to Krij. "Are you finished with the beans?"

"Oh . . . yes." Krij crossed the three meters between the two prep tables and set the bowl of beans on the side.

I hadn't even seen Krij slice them. She was like that. I'd been thinking about Elisabetta Reynarda. She could certainly have been a tool of the sisters. But I didn't see why they needed me to look into matters. "Why would the sisters approach me? They have far more in the way of resources than I could ever develop."

"You don't crack nuts with a sledge," Siendra said. "Nor with involuted legal regs and taxation policies. The sisters have a problem. Their power is either pervasively indirect or brutally direct. If they use much of the latter, the Elois and all their ilk would be petitioning the Assembly for a planetary reformation."

"One of two things would happen then," added Krij. "Either an Assembly observation team would arrive, and that would freeze everything, and nothing would get done, except whatever problem that was being addressed wouldn't be, and matters would just get worse. Or . . . a full-reformation team would arrive."

That possibility was remote. It was also terrifying. My second assignment with SpecOps had been the cleanup after the reformation of Aksarben. Truly, the entire planet had seemed to be galloping around, as if it had gone to the dogs. And the foxes, coyotes, and wolves. "There is that new Assembly definition of a repressive planetary government . . ."

Krij and Siendra exchanged glances.

"What is it?"

"We don't know how that fits. Not yet."

"But?" I pressed.

Krij shrugged. Siendra offered a faint smile.

I waited.

"TABS has been pushing for that change for almost thirty years," Siendra finally said.

I'd never heard of TABS. It showed on my face.

"Trans-Assembly Banking Services," Krij explained. "One of the subsections notes that regulations that restrict financial operations based on political factors and considerations, particularly market entry, are part of the integral definition of a repressive planetary government."

"Is Devanta that closed to outside financiers?"

Siendra laughed softly. "Not a single financial institution on the planet has ties to or is a subsidiary of an out-system entity."

"How did the sisters manage that?"

"The local citizenship rulings." Siendra sliced the mushrooms into paper-thin sections, then laid them across the top of the beans, setting them aside. Her knife flashed over the fularans, turning the long nuts into small rough cubes. They went on top of the mushrooms. "I can't do much more for a few minutes, not until the hens cook. It's a simple dinner."

That was fine with me. I stood and crossed the kitchen with the bottle of Aubenade. Siendra hadn't drunk that much, but I added a little to her glass.

"Thank you."

"What about the citizenship rulings?"

"You have to be a declared citizen of Devanta to own any real property or a security interest in any corpentity or the equivalent. Personal dwellings and the property on which they are situated and personal transportation are the only exclusions. Institutions must be incorporated in Devanta under Devantan law."

I still didn't get it.

"A declared citizen or Devantan corpentity must pay taxes on all income and all real property from all sources, and the rate is twice as high for income received from out-system sources." Siendra pulled up one of the high stools next to the prep table, then seated herself.

That made it very clear. "Outside entities would have to pay a high premium."

"They'd also be at a competitive disadvantage in other markets outside the Devantan system," Siendra pointed out.

"Doesn't that work the other way?" I was thinking of Eloi Enterprises.

"No. Not exactly." Siendra smiled. "You're thinking about Legaar Eloi?"

I nodded.

"The Elois have to be making a higher rate of return than their competitors in their out-system ventures because Devantan taxes are higher, and the sisters don't allow an off-setting credit for taxes paid in other systems."

"Or they're underreporting their income from those ventures?"

"Both," suggested Krij dryly.

"What will happen?"

"The Assembly is clearly sending a signal to the sisters," replied Siendra. "The next move will be theirs. In the meantime, they'll have to be careful in not being heavy-handed. And either they offer a concession to the Assembly, or they'll suffer consequences."

I definitely was getting the feeling that my coded message to Special Operations had been unwise. Once more, I'd probably been too impatient.

Krij frowned, then asked, "Have you gotten any new clients? Ones that are . . . more routine?"

The routine ones didn't pay as well. Krij knew that. "Just one. This afternoon, from Jay Smith." I grinned. "A logo designer's being shafted on royalties by a former employer. Jay suggested that all I had to do was threaten a reg audit by you."

"He sounds as sleazy as ever," Krij replied. "You have to deal with the lesser of two sleazes."

"Either the ethical sleaze or the unethical one," added Siendra.

Krij sighed. "If you're going to do it, tell him you'll file a section three gamma on him."

Siendra stifled a grin.

"I'll look it up, but what is it?"

"It's the religious extortion section of the Codex. Rather, it's the section of the Civil Code that notes that no use of religion, faith, or belief may be used as a justification for failure to pay lawfully incurred obligations or to abrogate any other civil rights and obligations. An audit under three gamma usually results in a felony conviction."

I noted that to the system. "I hate it when the ends seem to justify the means."

"You'd rather they didn't? You'd prefer ethical means leading to an unethical result?" riposted Krij.

"That wasn't quite what I meant, and you know it."

Siendra's lips curled ever so slightly, but she said nothing.

"Recalling the service or corpentities?" I asked her.

"The corpentities are worse." Siendra's words were matter-of-fact, but she didn't say more.

Krij took another small sip of the Rothschild. At gatherings, she always had a glass in her hand, yet I never saw her refill it. "That's why the financial institutions need government regulations and us. The corpentities define ethics in terms of self-preservation and law. Anything that isn't specifically illegal and increases profitability is considered ethical. That hasn't changed in the centuries since technological complexity necessitated a form of limited legal liability. What's most nauseating is that so many corpentity directors glory in ways to circumvent the law."

"Like Antonio diVeau? How's that going?"

"The bank's advocate sent a message saying that she was looking into it." Krij smiled. "That means that she's worried. Otherwise, she'd have said that it was a routine notification and well within the purview of the institution's policies and obligations. They'll most likely remove the notice and claim that it was a system error. That's the usual excuse."

Everyone had a "usual" excuse. That hadn't changed much over the centuries, either. "I used to think Legaar Eloi was a good example of going around things legally, with those kinds of excuses and lots of advocates. Lately, I think he's gone beyond that. I'm pretty sure he's ordered at least one murder, and his commando team wanted to take me out."

"That hasn't changed, either," Siendra replied. "Governments generally only care about appearances. So long as they seem to follow the laws and regulations and pay their taxes, so long as they don't vanish government officials and Garda personnel, and so long as nothing can be traced to them . . . then government doesn't care."

"Even the most honorable Civitas Sorores?" My irony was heavy.

"Especially the sisters." Siendra's voice was flat.

"Can we talk about something more cheerful?" asked Krij. "At least about one of your other commissions?"

"Which do you prefer? The honorable doctoral fortune seeker who isn't seeking a fortune, the strangely reticent heiress, or the mysterious and reclusive dramaturge?"

"How about the heiress?" Siendra grinned.

I liked her smiles and grins. I wondered why I hadn't noticed them before. "Her name is, variously, Stella Strong, Maureen Maude Gonne and perhaps Astrid Forte. She might be heir to something like ten million credits from a father who never married her mother, and yet she's never come forward. I was engaged to find her by someone who wants to remain anonymous. I'm supposed to certify her to the First Commerce Bank. All I've been able to discover is that she spent four years with the Thurenean Fashion Alliance and left suddenly." I nodded to Siendra. "You discovered that, if she is Astrid Forte, she has a registered legal identity, but that is clearly separate from whatever identity she is currently using."

"That's all you know?" asked Krij.

"She was extremely good at media relations when she was with TFA, and they were surprised when she left."

"I wonder what else was happening at TFA at the time,"

mused Siendra. "People usually don't leave positions where they're doing well unless there are other circumstances."

I wished I'd looked into that more closely.

"We'll have to continue at the table." Siendra left the stool with a swiftness so graceful that it appeared she had been sitting one moment and standing the next. "I'm going to be very busy for a few moments."

So I carried the wine into the small private dining room. Krij quickly set the table, since I was effectively one-handed.

In less than ten minutes I was seated at one end of the table, Krij to my right and Siendra to my left. The Iskling crystal chandelier provided a certain ambiance, as did two attractive women. Even if one happened to be my sister.

Siendra had set a platter before each of us. She had carved each game hen into thin circular slices, laid out next to the other, and garnished with poached spiced apples, accompanied with the beans and mushrooms almondine. I'd filled fresh goblets with a Sauvignon Thierry, vintage 1341.

I raised my goblet. "To you, ladies, for a meal and company far better than I expected or deserved this evening."

Krij laughed gently. "At times, you can be gracious." She did take a sip of the wine. "This is good."

I didn't tell her that I wouldn't have dared to serve her anything less.

"Sisters can be hard on their siblings," murmured Siendra. Her fingers brushed the back of my left hand, so lightly that it was clear she knew it hurt.

"Do you have any to be hard on?" I replied, in an equally low voice.

"No. I was an only child."

I smiled. I didn't quite know what to say. So I took refuge in the game hen. The meat was so tender I could cut it with a fork. That was good because I could barely use my left hand. The filling was tangy without being cloying.

"Delicious," I finally said. "I've never had this before."

"Siendra's a better cook than I am," Krij said. "She doesn't like to let anyone know it."

"Gender-typing?"

Siendra nodded.

I smiled. My expression was wry. Centuries before, so-called experts had predicted the demise of behaviors like gender-typing, direct person-to-person instruction, the demise of the family structure, and even the end of warfare. They'd been wrong on all counts, but then so vague is man's sight of himself, even from the heights.

"You have that expression," Krij said.

"What expression?" I offered innocence.

Siendra laughed. The sound conveyed warm amusement.

"The one you get when you're thinking about the human capacity for rationalization," Krij replied.

"Ah, yes—the delusion of rationality, the human belief that reason underlies our better actions, when in fact genetics, emotion, and somatic bias do—and reason merely is used to rationalize what we feel."

"If that were true, would there have been any human progress?" asked Siendra.

"Has there been?" My words were delivered archly, but I immediately laughed. "No . . . you're right, but the progress comes earlier. When you teach small children kindness, expose them to all sorts of stimuli, give them a sense of rightness and wonder, teach them to love words and books and ideas . . . that's what develops their emotional balance. That's where progress comes from, the child in each of us. As we get older, we just use reason to justify that child's decisions."

"You're an idealistic cynic, Blaine." Siendra shook her head, but the expression didn't seem like a condemnation.

I started to reply, but ended up yawning.

Krij gave me a sharp look.

"I'm fine."

"What about the reclusive dramaturge, then?" asked Krij.

"I haven't had much success, except in determining that she's a professional in the Thurene area and clearly successful under three pseudonyms. Her language is elegant, yet not in a flamboyant way . . ."

"It sounds as though you're intrigued, brother dear."

"In some ways. Her earlier work was rather depressing, though. There's more hope in the later dramas. I have to admit that I like that."

"Always the hopeful cynic," Krij replied.

"Cynicism is the last refuge of the idealist," suggested Siendra.

I had to agree with that. In fact, I might even have said that myself at one time or another. Much as I agreed, though, I had to stifle another yawn. My eyes were heavy, too.

"And the fortune hunter who isn't?"

"Ah, yes. The good doctor Dyorr. One of his possibly soon relations insists he's a hidden samer keeping a lover so that he can marry the heiress. Some of my contacts who know every samer rumor before it's been uttered claim there's no sign of anything like that."

"What do you think?" asked Siendra.

"I don't know. I've tracked down everything I can find on him, and I've observed him give a proposal to obtain research funding while his fiancée was watching. I don't think he's a samer, but . . ." I shrugged. I wasn't ready to mention my hunch.

"Maybe he's a straight-neuter," suggested Siendra. "Friendly to all, and gets along better with women."

"That wouldn't be a bar to his marrying the heiress, though." I had to stop halfway through and yawn.

"That's the third or fourth time you've yawned. You need some more sleep," Krij declared, rising from her chair.

"It's early. It's not even eight."

"We have to work tomorrow."

"On what?" I couldn't quite stifle another yawn as I stood.

"A client's compliance audit," Siendra replied dryly. "We're getting to that season." Again, she'd somehow gotten to her feet without my noticing. "We'll take care of the dishes."

They did, and quickly.

After that, I walked them to the front foyer, then to the door. I watched as they went down the stone steps and entered the small gray limousine.

Despite the dull pain in my forearm, I'd enjoyed dinner. More than I had in a long time, and, surprisingly, even more than the evening with Odilia. I wasn't quite sure why. Perhaps because I hadn't felt the need to be on guard, to watch and weigh every word.

34

If anything, my arm felt worse on Sabaten morning. That was before the sessions in the villa medcenter. Afterward, it didn't feel much better, although the diagnostics told me that it was already healing "nicely."

I didn't feel much like going anywhere, and I had nowhere to go. Not that I would discover anything by mere traveling. I thought about vidlinking to Siendra and Krij, just to thank them for the night before. Krij had mentioned an early client reg compliance audit, and I didn't want to intrude or leave a message. I decided to try later.

As for Myndanori, it was clear she wanted to let me know what she had discovered in person. Or that she'd found nothing. I didn't like the idea of dealing with the Tozzis only on the basis of my intuition, but . . . I might have to. I wasn't looking forward to that.

In the meantime, I needed to review and analyze the implications of what I'd discovered in my other commissions in a more considered light. So I settled down behind the table desk in the study and tried to approach things logically.

First, Seigniora Reynarda. Krij had effectively told me that she was probably an agent of the sisters. That meant that the sisters really needed hard evidence. Why? Because the Assembly was looking at Devanta closely? And if the Civitas Sorores acted against Eloi Enterprises without evidence, that would be another example of repression on top of what TABS was pressing? Or for some other reason? If Legaar

Eloi were an actual Frankan agent, then Special Ops could move against Eloi without violating the Assembly prohibitions on actions against planetary governments and citizens. But that raised another question. What if the Assembly and Special Operations *wanted* Eloi disclosed as a Frankan agent so that they had an excuse to meddle in Devanta affairs without requiring overall Assembly approval for a planetary reformation?

On the other hand, if Special Ops had to wait until the Frankans' involvement became irrevocably clear . . .

Either way, someone needed hard evidence. The sisters couldn't just walk into Time's End without it because they would risk losing their power and subjecting all Devanta to the horrors of reformulation. Without it, Special Ops couldn't act, even after the message I wished I hadn't sent, not without a series of courts-martial and a major Assembly scandal that would weaken the Assembly at a time when the Frankans were trying to build up their own power.

That still left a couple of large questions. What was Elysium, and why was it so much of a threat? And if the sisters knew that it was, why couldn't they do anything? If they didn't, why couldn't they find out more?

Or was it all some sort of hidden commercial struggle, with Legaar trying to make whatever it was workable on a large scale before others found out? Did he have a deal to sell it to the Frankans?

But what was "it"?

It was as though there wasn't anything to discover. But how could that be?

I might also be facing a hard question myself. If . . . if I did discover hard evidence, then what? If the evidence got in the wrong hands, all Devanta could suffer. But whose hands were the wrong ones?

I shook my head. I was speculating on who would get what I hadn't found and never might. And I still had four other unresolved commissions, and some of those might end up paying more as well. The sisters didn't exactly spend credits freely—not unless a lot was at stake. That thought didn't help my frame of mind, either.

Siendra's comment the night before had gotten me to thinking about the missing heiress. Why had Maureen left TFA when she had? Especially if she'd been doing well? But had she? Or had something else been going on?

Max . . . all info on TFA—Thurenean Fashion Alliance from eight years ago until the present. Check correlations with Maureen Gonne. Order chronologically, oldest first.

Within minutes, information piled up in the pending section of the system.

I began to sift through it. There was nothing of interest for the first six and a half years, just media presentations, fashion commentary, economic projections. Of course, there were spreads on the new fashions and lots of in-depth holos trying to sell clothing. The first intriguing article appeared in *Devantan Banker*—the netsys industry journal—close to two years ago in what amounted to the rumors column. It was called "Spare Change." I read the tidbit carefully.

. . . Melaryn Daavidou is recovering from a near-fatal drowning accident incurred in a Pays du Sud cataract-rafting tour. Daavidou is the assistant comptroller of TFA, but he will take medical retirement to complete rehab . . .

If I read that correctly, Daavidou had suffered severe brain damage and would never be the same. I wondered if he'd been invited by Tony. I tried a search on Daavidou, but found nothing else about the accident or about his efforts at TFA.

I kept searching through the slag, searching for more that had been overlooked.

In Duem of 1350, a little less than two years ago, after Maureen had departed, a civil complaint had been filed against TFA, alleging unspecified "civil abuses." The complaint had been settled. Then in Quintem of 1350 the Civitas

Sorores had frozen all records at TFA and begun a criminal investigation of the deputy director of TFA and her immediate subordinates and staff. The deputy director—a Magdalena Portius—had vanished, and her assistant had been found wandering in the River Crescent, his intellect reduced and his memories vanished. TFA had been placed under compliance monitoring.

But none of the stories or information revealed the nature of TFA's offenses. I tried the public regulatory record as well. The criminal and civil orders against TFA were on file, and still in effect, but there were no details except the notation that TFA was operating under a "personal civil rights" compliance plan.

"Civil abuses" suggested some form of sexual predation, but that was only a guess. The "accident" that befell the assistant comptroller and the vanishment of the deputy director suggested links through Tony diVeau to Legaar Eloi. Again . . . all guesses.

But . . . all that might well explain why Stella Strong/ Maureen Gonne did not want to claim her inheritance. If she knew more about the TFA scandal . . . and if Legaar Eloi were indeed involved, she might feel that no inheritance was worth that kind of risk.

Yet, once more, I really had no proof. I wasn't up to chasing people. Not physically. Not yet. I did make a hard copy of the names of the TFA top personnel and their staff assistants. Then I had Max run dossiers and seek personal images. If I had to chase people, it would have to wait until Lunen.

I wondered what sort of search I could run on Terrie McGerrie. I couldn't think of one.

So I went down and did a modified workout, one that took into account the sad state of my arm.

After cleaning up and dressing for the gathering at Myndanori's, I returned to the study.

I vidlinked to Krij. She wasn't there.

I tried Siendra. Neither was she, but I left a brief message.

"Thank you for last night. I appreciated the cooking and the company more than I can say." I did, too. That might have been because those kinds of words came hard, except in a professional sense. I didn't want to be professional with Krij and Siendra.

I turned and perused the shelves. I settled on a classic—*Culture Crash*. The Exton Land book ranked up there with *The Prince* and *The Republic*, although it had been written half a millennium after Machiavelli's masterpiece. Land had gotten more than a few things right in foreshadowing the fall of Old Earth and the Diaspora. But then, the truths of history are always there for those who will look. Most people can't bear to.

No one vidlinked. No one that I wanted to talk to or had to, and I enjoyed rereading the book.

At a little after seven, I set *Culture Crash* aside and headed down to the garage. From there I drove myself.

Myndanori lived in the Heights, the district just to the north of the Narrows. I had to use the communal visiting carpark and walk a good two hundred meters. Her dwelling was a narrow glass-fronted structure that rose three stories above the faux cobblestones. It towered above the brick bungalows on each side. That was somehow fitting.

Even more fitting was the red-smoky half-disk of Berg-erac almost directly above the dwelling as I walked up the rusty brick steps.

Before I reached the door, it opened. An angular man with eyes far older than the youthful figure he inhabited stood there. "You must be the mysterious Blaine Donne." He stepped back.

"I'm hardly mysterious." I entered the foyer. Loud voices reverberated from the sitting room beyond.

"Any straight-straight that Myndanori invites is mysterious. I'm Tyresias."

"Throbbing between two lives, no doubt?"

"For that, you ought to be the hanged man." Tyresias laughed good-naturedly. "Not the shadow knight."

"They don't hang people in Thurene. They just vanish."

"Blaine!" Myndanori emerged from the square arch into the sitting room on the far side of the foyer. She hurried across the room and flung her arms around me. "We must get you a drink. Tell me what naughty things you've been up to."

Her arm entwined with mine. My left. The gesture was possessive only in proclaiming me as a trophy of sorts. Her grasp was gentle enough to preclude any additional pain.

"Your arm is stiff."

"There's a nanocast on it. I had an accident."

"That sounds naughty enough. How did it happen? Did you hurt anyone else?"

"Let's just say that they paid for it," I replied as I accompanied her back to the small study. There an array of wines was set out.

"Besides the good doctor that you know about, I'm chasing an elusive heiress and a reclusive dramaturge. Neither seems to want to be found. There are millions of credits involved with the heiress." I studied the vintages and picked the Sauvignon Thierry. I poured half a glass. That would be more than enough.

"Tell me about the heiress. She couldn't be me, could she?"

"You're better-looking and doubtless more personable. Her name is Maureen Gonne or Stella Strong. She used to be a media linkster at Thurenean Fashion Alliance until several years ago. Then she vanished."

"TFA? There was a nasty little scandal there several years back. I don't remember all of it, but a sister of one of the models charged that she—the model, that is—had been conditioned to perform unspeakable acts and to enjoy it. The model vanished, and the sister fled to someplace like Moraviana. The Civitas Sorores did something, and I never heard another word."

"I think Legaar Eloi was involved. A deputy director also vanished."

"The Elois . . ." Myndanori shuddered.

"Do you know them?"

"Most thankfully, I do not. Those I know who have met

them insist that both are sadistic straights—puritanically conventional and privately hedonistic, without a single quark of compassion."

That sounded about right. I took a small sip of wine. "The heiress case is bizarre. You'd think someone would want to collect millions."

"I would." Myndanori laughed, tossing her head and flipping the short carrot red locks. They immediately settled back into faultless place. "Then I could really enjoy life."

"You already do."

"You could have, too, Blaine. Rokujo would have made an honest man out of you in a moment, taken you right out of the shadows."

"I need the shadows."

"Maybe this heiress does, too. Why does your client want her found? Usually, other potential heirs *don't* want people to come forward."

"I probably should have asked that question directly, but the client implied that she preferred the heiress get her share rather than having it go to the other potential heirs."

"And you believed her? You're getting soft, Blaine."

I'd told myself that earlier. "You may be right." I took another small sip of the Sauvignon Thierry. It didn't taste as good as it had the night before. "I've returned your vidlink . . ."

"This way . . ." She led me through the next door and closed it. We stood in an even smaller room—an actual library. "Everyone will think the worst."

"What—"

She gave me a passionate and very intimate hug before disengaging herself. "That, dear man, is part of my payment."

If that had been part, I wasn't sure I was ready for the remainder.

"There's not much there, and no one wants to say much."

"I'd figured that."

"But . . . one former lover of Darlya Rettek did let something slip. Oh, you were right about Darlya, but you have good instincts about women."

That was news to me.

"She is a samer, and . . . until recently, she had been having a very quiet . . . shall we say closeness . . . with Dr. Tozzi."

I couldn't help but nod.

"There's no proof other than what a few people have said," Myndanori went on, "but knowing you . . ."

"Your confidence in me is boundless."

"You'll manage. Now . . . back to the party . . . and you can't sneak off for a while."

I inclined my head. "I wouldn't think of it."

She led the way back to the sitting room.

She didn't introduce me. Tyresias had already spread the word. That was the way it worked. Two or three of the samer males looked in my direction, then away, more to confirm that I was straight-straight than to check me out.

Myndanori stopped next to a petite brunette whose long hair was swirled up into an elaborately coiled French braid. It emphasized her long, elegant neck. "Shanyta, you'd said you wanted to meet Blaine." Myndanori inclined her head in a gesture I couldn't interpret. Her eyes went back to me. "Let me know if you need anything."

I had to admit that Myndanori cut a fine figure. I knew that she meant what she said. I also knew that anything beyond continuing our past client-professional relationship would be trouble. The moment in the private library had emphasized that.

"Blaine Donne . . ." Shanyta's voice was warm and husky. I had the feeling she was a samer. "How long do you think the Garda will keep letting you walk the shadows?"

I wasn't about to answer that. Besides, I didn't precisely walk them. Occasionally, I used them to assist someone.

"Myndanori said that you were a straight-straight who talked like a straight-samer and acted like a hidden samer."

Whatever that meant. I shrugged. "We all do what we must. Sometimes, we even do what's right."

"What is right?" Shanyta's voice was huskily direct, without the game-playing of earlier words.

"If we knew that before we acted, life would be a lot

easier. And a lot messier." The most deadly people were those who *knew* what was right. Especially for everyone else.

My words got a laugh. "I see what Myndanori meant."

I wasn't about to pursue that. "What are your interests?"

"A polite way of asking whether I work or lounge. I work. I'm a talent coordinator for RealNet."

"That makes for a long week. Most people believe they have more talent than they do."

Shanyta nodded.

"You meet a few people." I paused. "Have you ever run across Terrie McGerrie or Carey Douglass?"

"The dramaturges?" Shanyta shook her head. "I like McGerrie more than Douglass." She offered a languid smile that was also predatory. "If what she writes is any reflection, I can see why you'd be interested."

I couldn't help frowning. "Oh?"

"Cool and reserved on the outside, white-hot within. Straight-straight female, I'd guess, too."

I laughed, ruefully. "I hadn't thought that. I'm trying to locate her for a client." I was clearly missing something about Terrie McGerrie, because Shanyta was a samer and could see something I hadn't. But then, I'd always had trouble reading beyond people's reserves, despite what Myndanori had said. Fortunately, as I'd discovered in my line of work, very few people were really reserved. They only thought they were.

"Best of fortune." With a polite smile, Shanyta slipped away.

I wandered from group to group. There were only four. No one had heard of either Stella Strong/Maureen Gonne or knew Terrie McGerrie/Carey Douglass as more than names. I got nothing new on Dyorr, either. That in itself tended to confirm my feelings.

A good two stans had passed, and I'd nursed half a glass of the Sauvignon Thierry through the whole time. There was only about one sip left. That suggested it was time to leave.

A loud voice caught my attention.

"Patrice thinks that the libertarian losswits would be happy to go through reformulation to get rid of the sisters." That statement was delivered by a pseudo-Apollo who had apparently just arrived. I hadn't seen him before, anyway.

"They may be losswits," replied Alorcan, a thin man, handsome in a reptilian way that proclaimed his mixed gender, "but they do have a point."

The distaste and disgust must have shown on my face.

"You disagree, Seignior Donne?" Alorcan delivered the "seignior" in a tone close to derogatory.

"No. I believe that people can be that stupid. Especially people who haven't experienced a reformulation. They haven't seen families disrupted and parents whose reconditioning has stripped them of all memory of family or children. They haven't seen the sudden poverty and the hunger created when political instability translates into profiteering and when food costs more than the poorest can afford. They haven't seen the riots and the bodies."

"And I suppose you have?"

"I'm a former special operative. I've seen it twice. I don't want to see it again. Especially not here."

Alorcan edged back.

The pseudo-Apollo beamed. "Surely, you won't argue that the sisters aren't repressive."

I laughed. Harshly. "All functional governments are repressive. By nature, government has to be repressive. It's only a question of who's repressed. If a government represses the anarchists, the criminal element, and would-be looters, we believe it's a good government. Unless we're among the repressed. If it represses the ability of people to express their verbal opinions, if it represses open economic competition and grants favors to those with ties to government, we claim it's bad government. Repression isn't the question. Whom government represses is."

"Any repression is bad . . ."

I just inclined my head in dismissal and walked back to the study, where I placed the empty glass on the sideboard.

Myndanori appeared. "You do have a way of getting the last word, dear man."

"It's only the last because I couldn't think of any more."

"You were most eloquent, Blaine," offered Myndanori with a cheerful laugh, tossing her head. "It's a pity you're not transgender-attracted."

"I'm not geneticized or conditioned that way, but if I were, you'd be the first person I'd look up."

"You're always gallant. It's too bad the straight-straight females don't appreciate it."

"I probably don't look in the right places." I smiled. "I apologize for my last remarks. You were kind to invite me, and I do appreciate your thoughtfulness. I especially appreciate the information."

"Oh . . . you'll have Apollon and Alorcan arguing for stans. They love to argue. It will be great fun."

She escorted me to the door and kissed me on the cheek before I left. It wasn't quite a sisterly kiss.

I stepped out into a cold damp wind. Ragged streamers of clouds obscured Bergerac. The red moon was low in the western sky, barely visible above the roofs of the houses of the Heights. Would that I could stand in the moon and call it good, sleep by night, and forget by day, but that would not be things as they are.

The drive back to the villa seemed longer than the drive out. Longer and lonelier.

35

Total direct honesty will destroy any human civilization as surely as will unspeakable vileness. It will also destroy all too many personal relationships.

After returning from Myndanori's gathering on Sabaten evening, I ended up working late because I had to develop two items for the luncheon the next day with the Tozzis and Dr. Dyorr. One was my approach to the principessa, and the other was the more formal media/development plan for Dr. Dyorr's research.

Then I slept late on Domen, almost to midmorning, when I woke with a start. I hadn't realized how tired I was until I let down a bit. Just a bit. I still went through a light workout before getting cleaned up, rehearsing my approach to the principessa the whole time.

I had engaged a fully armored private limousine for the trip to the palacio of Seldara Tozzi. This seemed wise, given my less-than-optimal physical condition. The trip to her palacio was uneventful, except we did pass what looked to be a kite festival in the Parc du Roi. I'd always wondered why it wasn't the Parc de la Reine. The archives had no answers to that question, but then, names are often a sop to the masculine ego.

Unlike Odilia, the Tozzis had no guardhouse at the gates to their palacio, only a virtie guard—and ornate permasteel grillwork that could have stopped the largest ground combat vehicle ever used. My implants also registered some rather large energy concentrations. The rotunda was neomodern, with smooth limestone columns. The capitals and bases were hexagonal and unadorned.

I'd arrived a quarter hour early, and I was met by a real doorman in a navy blue uniform at least a millennium old in style, with silver piping on his sleeves and trousers.

"Seignior Donne?"

I nodded.

"Katrinka will escort you. She's waiting inside."

"Thank you." I stepped through a stone archway that could have accommodated a shire stallion bearing an antique knight. Twin golden oak doors opened, and I was in a modest circular entry hall. Modest for Seigniora Tozzi. It was a good fifteen meters across and rose that much into a vaulted dome of amber intelligent glass that cascaded warm sunlight down upon me and the mosaic tile floor.

With the name Katrinka, I'd pictured a tall muscular blonde. The reality was a tiny black woman with deep-set brown eyes and short silver hair, fashion-silvered, not age-silvered. "This way, Seignior Donne. Principessa Tozzi will receive you in her private study."

The private study was just that, surprisingly, a space no more than six meters square, with bookshelves on two walls, a sitting area around a low table, and a table desk with a single comfortable chair in one corner. The carpet was a Sacrestan, patterned in deep blue and gold geometrics that made the one I'd given Krij seem exceedingly inexpensive.

Seldara Tozzi stood in front of the table desk. She wore a simple dress, but the material was anything but simple, casting not light but shadows from the fiber lines in it. Her scarf was silver, and she wore no jewelry.

"I thought you might appreciate the shadow-dress."

"As always, you are most elegantly tasteful." I inclined my head.

"Luncheon will be served shortly, Seignior Donne. How do you plan to proceed? I must inform you that I detest surprises."

"So do I, Principessa. So do I. That's why I'd like to ask you a question or two before we join your great-granddaughter and her fiancé." I managed a smile. "First, do you object to

Dr. Dyorr as an individual or more to the possibility that he might be using Marie Annette?"

"He's well regarded, extremely talented, and pleasant. I have no objections to that aspect of matters."

"Do you object to a marriage that is, shall we say, as much a partnership as a marriage, provided there is an heir who is well loved and cared for?"

"Are you telling me that he is a samer, Seignior?"

"No. In fact, after seeing him and following him and talking with a number of individuals, I'm quite convinced that he has never had a lover, much less kept one on the side."

"Then why didn't you just say so?" Her question was not quite snapped at me.

"Because I feel there's more at stake here, Principessa. I am going to ask that you merely begin the discussion about his work. I will ask some questions. I ask that you not show any anger or emotion until after luncheon, when we will meet briefly again." Before she could say anything else, I added, "I've already resolved the question for which you engaged me, but that isn't the question at hand. After our meeting, if you believe I have acted against your interests, I will return all fees and expenses."

That gave her pause. Then she laughed. "When a man bets his own money to prove his devotion to his client, I suppose I should at least reserve judgment."

"That's all I'm asking." For the moment. I hoped I'd read the principessa right. I could have just offered a report affirming what I'd just said, but that wouldn't have been right.

"Then we might as well join Marie Annette and the doctor in the family dining room."

I forbore to mention that they were both doctors and walked beside her down a smaller interior hallway floored with a golden creamy polished stone.

In the center of the family dining room was a single cherry table capable of seating twelve people. One end was set for four, with Caveline silver and Iskling crystal. The china I didn't recognize, except that it could have graced any human table in the universe. Shimmering white, with a thin black rim and a silver line in the middle of the black. Standing between the table and the sideboard were the doctors.

"I believe you have met Seigniore Donne, Marie Annette," offered Seldara. "Dr. Guillaume Richard Dyorr, Seignior Blaine Donne."

"After reading your report, I'm most pleased to meet you," offered Guillaume Richard.

"After hearing your presentation," I replied, "it's good to see you in a less . . . official setting."

"Shall we?" suggested the principessa.

Like the perfect gentleman he was, Guillaume Richard seated Seldara.

I made the effort with Marie Annette. She hesitated, as if almost to refuse, but then accepted the antique courtesy.

A servingman appeared instantly, and filled both water glasses and wine goblets. Clearly, the principessa had decided the wine and the meal. Then came a simple salad of mixed greens—nothing special except that every leaf in the salad was perfect and without blemish.

Seldara raised her goblet. "To a useful and productive luncheon."

We all sipped. The wine was a primitiva grigio, I thought, and not bad, although it wouldn't have been my choice.

"I thought that Seigniore Donne offered a most insightful report on your work, Dr. Dyorr." That was how the principessa began. "It struck me that his expertise might prove helpful in assuring that you receive the funding necessary for your work. That was one of the reasons for my inviting all of you here."

"And what might be some of the other reasons?" inquired Marie Annette. "You always have those . . ."

"I'm sure you'll let me reveal those in due time," replied the principessa. "You've always said that I've done things in my own sweet time." A knowing and cruel smile crossed Seigniora Tozzi's lips. "Not that you've ever said that directly to my face."

I could tell matters could get nastier, indirectly, and that was something no one needed. So I spoke up. "At a gathering of distinguished individuals as distinguished as this, there will always be secrets and reasons. I respect all those, but the point of this gathering is to present a strategy to assure a wider and deeper funding base for Dr. Dyorr's consciousness research."

"You have such a strategy?" Marie Annette's tone was dubious, to say the least.

"Actually, I do. As you all know, I attended the presentation to the Humanitas Foundation. You all know how I found the presentation. But, in reflecting over it later, I realized that it lacked one basic element. Not in the research or in the factual accuracy," I added. "Not from what I could tell."

Both Marie Annette and Guillaume Richard frowned.

I let them do so while I had a bite of the salad. Several bites, in fact, before I spoke again.

"I'm going to approach this in a roundabout way. Please bear with me." I turned to Marie Annette. "What do you think of the Masculist Forum?"

"What does this—"

"Please," I said soothingly. "I'm not judging. I just want your opinion."

She squared her shoulders. "I think that they make troglodytes look tolerant."

"So do you disagree with their position on genetic manipulation of the sex and gender tendencies of an unborn child or with the way in which they express that view?"

"Both."

"As a doctor, you look at the medical and societal impacts of such a technology, as well as the personal impacts, and you find their arbitrary and inflexible position less than tolerable?" I had another sip of the primitiva grigio.

"Exactly."

"So . . . if you were faced with a couple whose genetic makeup would most likely result in a child with either crossgendered or other sexual confusions, your view would be to take steps to preclude such confusion before the child was even born."

"Absolutely! Most ethical physicians would."

"Would it make a difference if the child were your child? Or the child of a relative?"

"Not at all." Marie Annette's voice was firm.

Guillaume Richard glanced from her to me, then said, with a touch of acidity, "Would it be possible to be a bit less roundabout?" His hand moved to touch Marie Annette's forearm. He squeezed it gently but did not release it.

I nodded. "I'll get there. I promise." I turned directly to Marie Annette. "Yet a large number of people on Devanta are passionately—and I use that word advisedly—supportive of the Masculist Forum. They clearly would rather have a child be confused, unhappy, and unsure of his or her gender and sexual identity than meddle, as they put it, with the unborn child. Why do you suppose that so many people support a position that is certainly not in the child's interest and is against what you would call good medical practice?"

The two doctors exchanged glances.

"Prejudice," suggested Guillaume Richard. His hand remained protectively on Marie Annette's.

"Ignorance."

"What fires that prejudice or ignorance?" I asked, quickly answering the question. "Emotion . . . passion if you will." I paused for just a moment. "You are both trained to look at matters logically. Dr. Dyorr presented an extraordinarily logical argument for supporting his research on consciousness. But . . . the one thing it lacked was a visceral emotional appeal."

"And you have such an appeal?" Marie Annette's voice remained critical.

"I have thought of several, but that raised another question. Why didn't the PR and media linksters at the Institute at least provide that sort of input?" I turned to Marie Annette. "I saw Daryla Rettek there at the briefing. I understand you know her, and she certainly knows of your relationship to Dr. Dyorr, and yet I would bet that she never raised the question of the need for an emotional appeal rather than just an intellectual one."

Marie Annette froze momentarily, just momentarily, at the mention of Rettek. Seldara Tozzi caught it as well, and I thought that would be enough. I'd still have to be careful, though.

"The problem is that, no matter what we think logically and superficially, emotion lies behind all decisions." I smiled. "It can support or hinder, inspire or inflame, but what one can never do is ignore its impact. People who have been close, often exceedingly close, can often deny their support or just refuse to offer their best judgment when their emotions are involved." Then I turned to Dyorr. "Even for those whose achievements and work are considered inspired and fueled by purely intellectual considerations, for whom mere physical pleasures are secondary, there is an emotional fire behind that intellect, wouldn't you say?"

Guillaume Richard smiled, faintly, but not coldly. "I would have to agree, and I apologize for my earlier comment. You do, indeed, know where you are going."

That meant the good doctor Dyorr also knew, and that might make matters easier.

Seldara Tozzi nodded, almost imperceptibly.

At that moment, the server appeared and removed the salads, replacing each plate with a larger one holding pasta prima regia, flanked by pears royeaux.

"I suggest we enjoy the meal for a moment." After saying that, I followed my own advice.

"I wish some in my profession would follow your example," offered Guillaume Richard, with a laugh.

"There are those like that in any field." Seeing him one-on-one, I couldn't help liking him, and I was getting the impression that he did care for Marie Annette.

I let everyone almost finish their entrées before I returned to the ostensible subject at hand.

"The key to getting greater support for your research, Dr. Dyorr, is linking the logical presentation of medical facts and potential gains to a deep human passion." I lifted the hard-copy bound report I had brought. "I have suggested several possibilities in this short report. One is the point that understanding consciousness will allow full restoration and maintenance of the minds of people who have suffered injuries, illnesses, or degeneration. We can look forward to remaining valued and contributing members of society so long as our bodies last. That would certainly provoke some kind of passion. Another emotional hook is the possibility of improving how we think." I laughed. "Of course, that would really upset people like the Masculists or the True Traditional Women. But then, the lower virtues are those most esteemed by the commons, and the lowest of those is blind reverence for rationalized prejudice."

"How would you go about implementing this strategy?" asked Marie Annette.

"Much in the same way as Dr. Dyorr already has, with the addition of the emotional keys I've laid out and the targeting of potential philanthropists whose emotional profiles are susceptible to such appeals." I smiled. "After you've read it and considered it, I'd be happy to answer any questions, but I doubt you'll need much in the way of further consulting. Now that I've pointed out the obvious, you both are doubtless quite able to manage matters from here on in." That was true on two levels.

Later, after tea and café, and after the doctors had departed, Seldara and I walked back to her private study.

Once the door was closed, she turned to me. She actually smiled.

"Marie Annette . . . I never would have guessed."

"You suspected," I pointed out. "That's why you came up with the samer idea for him."

"He's . . . what would you call him?"

"The slang term is straight-neuter."

She nodded slowly. "You're very effective, Seignior Donne. You wanted me to find out in a situation where I couldn't react immediately, didn't you?"

"I did. It's clear Marie Annette respects you, and she does want her own child. She wouldn't have proposed to Dr. Dyorr if she didn't. She had to have been the one who did."

"It turns everything around, doesn't it?"

"It does." After a moment, I added, "It's likely you'll have an heir or heiress, and he or she will be brilliant."

"You could be very dangerous," she said. "Not everyone wants or will accept what may be best for them."

"That's true," I admitted, "but that's also part of what I have to look for. Sometimes, I just have to provide what people ask for, knowing that it isn't what they really want or need."

She understood. She nodded.

As I rode back to my villa, the one I felt the most sympathy for was Dyorr.

36

A thought unexpressed is the beginning of a tale never to be told.

The rest of Domen, as well as Senen morning, were spent researching Legaar Eloi—indirectly, and after I recovered from the surprise of finding that Seldara Tozzi had transferred ten thousand credits to my account. She'd also sent a text message of exactly one line.

Even shadow knights must pay for their armor.

Her reaction was another reason why I'd found it unwise to "concentrate" on a single case. Sometimes, those that seemed minor were anything but that to those concerned. And sometimes, if infrequently, they paid better than the "important" cases.

Eventually—a half stan or so of marveling later—I got back to going through each and every outfit with which Eloi Enterprises had technology-sharing arrangements. All of them were in high-technology applications. Not military. At least, not directly. The reports on several suggested that they had some unique equipment. I bet it had military applications.

I certainly couldn't have been the only one looking into the matter. Clearly, the charter amendment being fought by EsClox was merely the tail of the comet. And if Eloi's silent partners were the Frankans, that and the technology-sharing agreements suggested he was using Classic Research as a front for repackaging technology and conveying it to them. I should have drawn that conclusion earlier, but who would have expected a sordid entertainment corpentity to have been funneling off high-level technology to rival systems?

On Senen afternoon, I girded myself up and did some research on Anshoots and Reed. The information was widespread and thin. Basically, A&R appeared to be just what Skip Barca had said—a design house that supplied graphics for any form of media from old-fashioned print to full-depth entertainment holo. They catered primarily to the fundie market and to media directors at smaller enterprises with fundie connections. They were located northeast of the Heights in a smaller commercial district that bordered the west end of the River Crescent. It wouldn't be hard to get there on Lunen.

Twenty years before, Fillype Anshoots had just been another freelance designer, trying to supply a range of graphics and design products cheaper than the next designer. He'd linked up with Rafel Reed. Reed had been a youth missionary for some obscure sect—one of the Saint offshoots. Anshoots and Reed discovered that they were indeed religious men who wanted to market to other like-minded small corpentities. It did seem more than slightly coincidental that they had both joined the largest fundie congregation in Thurene. Before long, A&R was the designated supplier to the Congregation of Infinite Mercy. Who was I to argue with success? Both were straights—how could they be otherwise? Still, to their credit, in more ways than one, each had married once and remained married to that woman. Besides a myriad of other seemingly irrelevant supporting details, there was little else on either Anshoots or Reed.

After that, I went to the Civic Codex and did a quick study on section three, and particularly subsection gamma. I was winding up that on Senen evening, and deciding exactly what to say to Fillype Anshoots, when Max announced, *Incoming from Siendra.*

Accept.

Siendra was sitting behind a narrow table desk. It wasn't

a virtie simulacrum. She had circles under her eyes. For the first time since I'd been introduced to her, she wasn't wearing anything green or cream or earth-toned. She wore a dark gray singlesuit, just loose enough not to be form-fitting. "Blaine, I'm sorry to have been so late in getting back to you. I was tied up until just a while ago. I'm glad that we could help a little."

"You helped more than that. I understand about the delay. Krij had said you two were working on a client project."

For the faintest moment, Siendra said nothing. Hadn't she been working with Krij?

"No . . . we finished that late on Sabaten. This was a professional commitment remaining from before Krij and I began to work together. It's a long-term contract that requires expertise from me periodically until the end of next year." She offered a wry smile. It didn't conceal her tiredness. "Neither glamorous nor especially remunerative, but, like many things, it seemed a good idea at the time."

I laughed. *That* I did understand all too well. "I think I understand that even better. I hope I do. I did appreciate the dinner. No matter what the so-called nanite experts say, real cuisine prepared by real people beats formulated food anytime. Especially at times like last Vieren."

"Thank you." She paused. "I didn't want you to think I'd forgotten manners."

There were stress lines running from her eyes, and her eyes were slightly bloodshot. What had she been doing?

"I would never have thought that. I'd like to talk, but you look ready to collapse. I wouldn't want to be the cause of overstressing my sister's partner."

"Nor would I want you to be charged with that, but it's my time right now." She smiled.

I liked the expression. "Then . . . you tell me when it's time to break off."

"You know that I would."

I couldn't help chuckling. "You're a dangerous woman."

"Mostly a tired one. Did you ever find your heiress? Or any traces?"

"No. Not really, but I think I know why I haven't had much success . . ." I went on to explain about the TFA scandal and the possible links to Legaar Eloi. I also watched the system indicators. The links were supposedly secure. Then, even Legaar would know I could prove nothing, and all I was telling Siendra was that I'd been unsuccessful. ". . . so if I were Maureen Gonne, unless I happened to have gotten very powerful and very wealthy, I'm not sure an inheritance would be worth the exposure."

Siendra nodded. "I can see that. But . . . most people are neither that restrained nor that perceptive."

"Not with millions of credits at stake. That's true. But she certainly vanished, and people don't do that without a reason."

"Could she be dead?"

"Not if she's also Astrid Forte—that's the registered legal identity . . ."

"The one I checked for you." Siendra moistened her lips. "I wonder who she really is."

"She can't be famous."

"No." Siendra frowned. "I wonder. She might be an operative for the sisters."

"Planetary intelligence types have registered identities?"

"There's a classification where the sisters can grant a registered identity for the needs of the planet."

"That would explain a lot." More than that, but explanation or not, I still had no proof. It was just another fact that *might* support an all-too-theoretical construct.

"How is your arm?"

"Better. The medcenter diagnostics report that I heal quickly. I can move my fingers without feeling it all over. I'll have full mobility and some strength in a few more days. Not full strength or healing, though."

"Good." She tried to stifle a yawn . . . and failed.

"You look like you need some sleep."

"I suppose so. But tomorrow will come too soon as it is."

"No rest for you wicked regulatory compliance auditors."

"Neither rest nor respite." Her laugh was shaky.

"No credits without grief and stress," I added.

"I should go." She smiled. "Thank you for linking."

"Thank you."

For a moment, after the holo projection vanished, I just sat behind the table desk. She'd vidlinked, but she'd thanked me. She'd meant it as more than an empty formality. I wasn't sure why, but I was happy that she had.

Then I forced myself into a more upright position. I was tired, but before I collapsed, I needed to conduct a quick review of my pending projects.

From the latest information available, Max calculated that Legaar Eloi was on Devanta. Most probably at his penthouse on top of Pier One in Thurene. The secondary hearing on the planetary charter amendment to require technology licensing to the government had been recessed until Jueven. I had nothing more than what Myndanori had led me to on Maureen Gonne and what Siendra had suggested. I had nothing at all new on Terrie McGerrie. I'd see Fillype Anshoots in less than half a day. At least Seldara Tozzi had seemed pleased.

With that, I headed for bed. I knew I shouldn't be attempting anything else until I got some sleep.

37

Human religions are based upon the twin assumptions that physical corporeality is a weakness and that an intelligent noncorporeal deity would provide superior guidance. Both assumptions are wrong.

At breakfast on Lunen morning, I was feeling more alert. Alert enough that I realized one thing that had escaped me the night before. What Siendra had been wearing the night before had been a shipsuit—or the equivalent. Was she still a reserve officer? Was that the commitment? She couldn't have been off-planet. She could have been doing sim training. I didn't know whether there was a space service reserve unit on Thurene, but no one was about to make that very public. Every system did have a reserve quota for the Assembly. Even Special Ops did. The SpecOps reserves trained either at the Vannes center or the one by the reservoir north of Thurene. Medically retired types weren't eligible for reserve status. I'd been glad about that.

The more I learned about Siendra, the more I realized how little I knew about her. She'd just always been Krij's business partner.

I was getting ready to leave for my appointment with Fillype Anshoots when Max linked.

Incoming from Seigniora Reynarda.

Accept.

She was entirely in black. I was certain the entire image was virtie, not that it mattered.

"I believe you will find it to your advantage for us to meet tomorrow, Seignior Donne."

"My advantage?"

"I should have said, 'less to your disadvantage.' I will see you at eleven hour at your villa." With that, she was gone.

If that had not been a veiled threat, I'd never received one. Just what I needed before heading off to meet with Fillype Anshoots.

Max, schedule Seigniora Elisabetta Reynarda for eleven hour tomorrow.

Scheduled, ser.

I checked to make sure I had my list and a secure link for what came after my appointment with Fillype Anshoots, then made my way down to the garage.

Getting to the public carpark close to A&R wasn't difficult. Time-consuming and comparatively expensive, because the streets there were older and narrower, and congested. Parking rates were higher. By law, they had to be. They had to reflect scarcity. Even so, I stepped through the second-floor archway of the Evangelical Association Co-op building at one minute before ten.

A timid-looking woman peered at me from the reception console. She was real, not virtie. The small space behind her was filled with racks. The racks held everything from print manuals and publications to dataflats. Some items displayed pop-up holos. Others were fronted with glossy print holograms meant to convey depth. They didn't. Most bore the cross or the crescent. I'd have bet he was also a member of the Masculist Forum.

"Blaine Donne to see Fillype Anshoots."

"Oh, yes, ser. Elder Anshoots will see you momentarily."

There was no space between her console and the racks. There was little enough behind the racks and the rows of doored cubicles against the wall. I didn't see anywhere to sit.

The door of the center cubicle opened, and a dark-haired man walked out through one of the openings in the racks.

"Seignior Donne." His voice was deep and warm. It didn't quite rumble. His eyes were a pale blue, his hair a black so deep that it shimmered. His smile was open and welcoming. He was a shade taller than I was. "Please come in."

I followed him into his cubicle. The table desk was narrow and bare. The console on the left side was small.

Anshoots settled into a worn chair suitable for a receptionist or a designer. "How might I help you? Your message was a bit unclear."

"I'm here representing Scipio Barca."

"I was under the impression that a Jay William Smith was his advocate." The warmth in his voice cooled but only a touch.

"Oh, Jay is. I'm in the regulatory business. We work together when it appears that a justiciary proceeding is likely to prove excessively burdensome and not in the interest of the parties."

Anshoots raised his eyebrows. "I don't see that there is any need for third parties here, Seignior Donne."

"Exactly. There's absolutely no need for advocates and their fees. As I understand the situation, a designer who was employed here for close to twenty years developed a logo for one of your clients. Fairmeadow Maharishi Publications, I believe. The agreement which I've confirmed as registered and authenticated names one Scipio Barca as the designer and A&R as the royalty recipient and disburser. I can't see how there can be any dispute about that."

"Oh, not in the slightest."

"Then I'm curious as to why you haven't paid him for the past three years."

"There must be some misunderstanding, Seignior Donne. Scipio Barca was one of our most valued designers. I would never have given him less than his due."

"I'm glad to hear that, Elder Anshoots. I'm certain that if you look into your accounting records, you'll find that there's been some oversight. I'm certain it's not your fault, but I know how these things can happen. Did I mention that I work with Albryt and Donne, the regulatory compliance auditing corpentity? They'd prefer not to institute a section three gamma complaint. Of course, they'd have no reason to if Skip Barca receives his back royalties of three thousand two hundred and twenty-one credits. Say within the next week. And by the tenth of the month thereafter."

Elder Anshoots's smile was strained. "We only want to do what's right."

"I know that, but sometimes the devil's in the details."

"You're Blaine Donne . . ." He offered a puzzled look.

I stood. "That's right. I'm the reasonable one in the family. My sister Krijillian is the managing director of Albryt and Donne."

"Ah . . . I see."

"Thank you very much, Elder Anshoots. I appreciate your taking care of this. I'd certainly hate to see it splashed all over the trade media that you'd been slapped with a three gamma civil charge."

"Please convey to Skip that I deeply regret the inconvenience."

"I will, and once he receives his royalties, I'm sure he'll understand that it was all an unfortunate clerical error." I inclined my head slightly before I left.

I walked back down the ramp and along Templeton toward the garage. Those relatively few minutes with Elder Anshoots had left me feeling like screaming a cry of literate despair. Except I was no poetic hero, and I certainly had no regalia that would have proclaimed me. Where was the mythic hound of heaven when we needed him? Except that hound was chasing to offer mercy, and mercy was in short supply among fundies, no matter what they claimed. Unless it was mercy for them. But that was just human nature.

I didn't like what I had to do next. Soliciting people in public places—even just for information—was technically illegal but not always prosecuted. If Javerr found out about it and wanted to make trouble, I could be back before the Garda. But I was running out of time and options.

I reclaimed my groundcar and drove southwest, paying yet another exorbitant fee at the carpark serving the lower end of the boutique area. In the cloudy grayness of a late midmorning, I stationed myself at a table by the café stop not that far from the ramps and lifts of Fashion Place, using my links with Max to compare the faces I saw with those on my target list. I had taken the precaution of loading several images of Maureen, including the one from TFA, into the personal display comm clipped to my belt.

A half stan before noon, I located my first target, an over-muscular man in black skintights, wearing a long jacket and designer shorts—brilliant blue. I made it almost to his shoulder before he turned.

"You're Gaston Gueran, aren't you? I'm Blaine Donne. I'm a finder's man, and I was hoping you could help me."

"What sort of racket—"

"No racket. I've been hired to find a woman named Maureen Gonne. She was a media linker at TFA until two years ago. There's no record of her after she left TFA."

"So?" Gaston had the kind of sneer I would have liked to remove. Permanently.

"I get paid if I find her. She gets paid, too. I imagine she'd be grateful."

"It sounds like a racket to me."

"If you don't believe me, go to the First Commerce Bank and ask about the bequest of Clinton Jefferson Wayles."

That actually turned the sneer into mere sullenness.

"I was hoping that you might know any little thing about her that might help me locate her."

"Straight-straight who hated men. Acted better than anyone else but good at charming the media linksters. Heard she came from a little place near Vannes." He frowned. "Gaullis . . . no, Degaulle, I think it was . . ."

That was all I got from Gaston.

All in all, I managed to talk to five TFA employees without learning more.

The sixth was Gretylia D'uryso. She was the admin coordinator for TFA in-house media.

"You're the shadow knight, aren't you? You're built like him. You move the same way."

"I do?" I hadn't been aware of anything like that. I shrugged apologetically. "Some people have said that. I'm just here trying to get some information so that I can locate someone who has an inheritance coming."

"That wouldn't be me."

"Maureen Gonne. She was a media linkster."

"She came from somewhere near Vannes, did her graduate work there, I think." Gretylia gave the smallest of shrugs. "She must have been good. No one ever complained, and at TFA everyone complains."

"Did she ever say where she was going?"

"I didn't even know she was leaving. One day she was gone. Like that. I put through the termination and contract work. No one ever said anything." With a smile she turned away. "That's all I know."

I could sense the Garda patroller before I even turned away from Gretylia.

It was Javerr.

I just stood and waited.

"You're getting very popular, Seignior Donne. I had a report that you might be out here soliciting. I hope that's not the case." His smile was even nastier than usual.

"Patroller Javerr, like you, I'm merely attempting to do my job. I have a commission to find a missing heiress. She worked in this area, and I've been asking people if they've seen her recently. I'm not asking for personal information. I'm not asking for credits, and I'm not asking for business."

He nodded slowly. "Just for the record, and so that I can tell the captain, who is this supposed heiress?"

I unclipped the display comm slowly and raised it, turning it so that Javerr would be able to see the small projection. I called up the TFA image. "Her name is Maureen Gonne. She worked around here."

Javerr actually studied the image for a moment. "Don't know her. Not the face, anyway. I don't suppose you would part with the name of your client?"

"Officer, you know I can't do that."

"You'd have to prove you have a client if I brought you in. You're really close to the edge on soliciting, Seignior Donne."

I offered a sigh. "I know, Officer. I haven't had much luck with standard methodologies."

"Knock it off, Donne. Stick to what you're supposed to."

"I will." I offered a crooked smile. "You can't blame me for trying."

"Go."

I departed.

Javerr's relatively cooperative attitude bothered me more than if he'd dragged me into Garda headquarters. Here was a Garda patroller who'd been trying to find anything to tag me with, hitting me with a light verbal slap on the wrist.

The business about the shadow knight bothered me as well. I knew some people understood my nocturnal roamings, but how and why would a junior admin type at TFA know?

The first thing I did when I got back to my study in the villa was check on that.

Max, interrogative netsys shows on me or the shadow knight.

What order?

Order? There were more than one or two? *Chronological, past to present. Project here.*

I watched for almost half a stan.

Every major Thurene news outlet had done a brief feature on the so-called shadow knight, either on the morning spread, the midday, or the early afternoon. So had some of the niche nets, including the male samer net—with the implied suggestion I might be one of them.

The cuts were brief, but there were plenty of vid-shots. Some were old. The most recent was along the South Bank where I'd kept the would-be lover from assaulting the woman who told him no. The later events in Deo Patre and the River Crescent hadn't been captured by the Garda monitors. For such small favors of fate I was grateful.

The commentary was similar.

"The shadow knight. Is he real or just an urban myth? Never-before-revealed monitor vids show that he is very real. Some say they know who he is. They won't tell. Others don't know and don't care."

"He saved my niece . . ."

"Without him . . ."

"Garda can't stop crimes. They can only catch people afterward. Sometimes that's too late."

"The shadow knight . . . an urban myth who's made Thurene a better place . . . at least for most of us."

I was sweating by the time it was all over.

Were the media clips why Javerr had been easy on me?

I didn't think so.

But who had pushed it? Why?

It had to have been the Civitas Sorores. While all of the views of my actions had come from the Garda public monitors, no one on the Garda would have wanted to make public the limitations of public surveillance in preventing violence. Not even Shannon.

Incoming from Krij.

Accept.

"Blaine! How could you?" Her black hair was actually disheveled.

"The vid-clips? I didn't. I didn't even find out until a few minutes ago. It's either the sisters, or someone has breached their security."

She looked at me for a long time. Then she sighed. "I knew you'd get into trouble with that."

So had I. But I'd felt I'd had to do *something*.

"I found out two more things about Maureen Gonne," I went on. "Did Siendra tell you about her?"

"She mentioned that she might be an agent."

"First, it's likely that she is also Astrid Forte. Second, the admin type had no advance notice. The same day Gonne left was the day the termination went in. How likely is that for someone doing an outstanding job?"

"Rather unlikely. It's all theory, though."

Krij didn't have to tell me that. I knew it all too well.

"What are you going to do?"

"Stay out of the shadows for a while. Try to find another angle on the Elysium business. Keep working. What else can I do?"

"Try not to dig any deeper holes."

I laughed.

After Krij broke off, I tried searching the civil directory for names that might be covers for Maureen or Astrid.

Incoming from Andres Hevaness.

I didn't know an Andres Hevaness. *Accept.*

The holo image was a saturnine figure, with a large head, almost triangular, with golden eyes and tight-curled short dark hair. His skin was bronze. His shoulders were twice as broad as mine. I thought there might be two golden horns on each side of his skull. There was no holo background. That suggested he was linking from someplace other than home or work.

"Seignior Donne?" The voice was so low it almost created subsonics.

"The same. What can I do for you?"

"Apollon Renzies said you solved problems."

Apollon Renzies? The Apollon who had been at Myndanori's? "It depends on the problem."

"I can tell you. Do I have to come to you?"

"No. If you're comfortable with it, we can start by vidlink."

"It's like this. I've had this conapt for years. It's in Creteor, you know, just below the back of the Heights. Ten years ago, well, Escamillo, he was . . . anyway, we partnered. It didn't last. He always wanted to fight first. He left a good five years ago. Then, this week, he starts vidlinking claiming that half the conapt is his because we were partnered. Besides the job at the Minoan Palace, it's all I really got."

"What kind of partnering?" I asked.

"Just as partners. I figured we could go full later if it worked out. It didn't. Now . . . he's claiming I owe him."

"If you didn't register as full-union samers, but only as partners, then the conapt isn't subject to community property."

"You're sure about that?"

"I'm not an advocate. I can't do legal work. And this isn't

something that ought to be muscled. But I can tell you whom to contact, what to tell him, and how much you should pay. He can file for damages for you if this Escamillo doesn't stop bothering you."

In the end, I referred Hevaness to Jay Smith, with detailed instructions. I declined any payment.

38

Expecting matters to worsen ensures that they will; expecting them to improve is merely foolishness.

I was awake and up early on Marten. Not by choice. I hadn't slept well. Another of Siendra's phrases had been going through my head. This time it was "neither rest nor respite." Was that the way I felt as well? Or was there some other reason her phrase echoed through my thoughts? I'd also been worrying about Elisabetta Reynarda and her not-so-veiled threat.

The only good news was that I could wiggle my fingers and move them without pain. Nanomeds did speed up healing—a lot. For that, I silently thanked the medcenter.

I'd gotten through dressing and breakfast and was sitting in my study wondering which commission offered the prospect of the quickest resolution.

Incoming from Krij.

Accept.

Krij was in green again, dark and light, with a black belt. "Blaine, I can't talk long. We're swamped here, but I have two things. First, Banque de L'Ouest backed off. They'll issue a correction and retraction, but they'll claim it was a system error. It's probably not worth pursuing further. Second, there's one more bit of information that I thought you might find useful."

"I'll accept the retraction on your advice, and I'd be happy to have anything useful. I'm not doing too well in finding much of use at the moment."

"Simeon Eloi and his entire family left on the *Etoile* this morning."

"For Firenza?"

"You already knew that?" Krij frowned.

"No. I knew that Princesse Odilia and her daughter were on the *Etoile* and going to Firenza. I didn't know anything about Simeon Eloi. Are there any Elois left on Devanta besides Legaar?"

"I don't have any way of finding that out."

"What about access to full-clone facilities? Does Legaar operate anything like that?"

Krij laughed. "That's totally illegal, and he's been doing it for years. Most of the nymphs he provides for his guests are clones. The others are back-gene modified at the same place."

"The facility must be at Time's End." That was the only way it made sense. If the clones never left Legaar's private property, there was no evidence of cloning, and the Civitas Sorores couldn't enter the estate without some form of real proof.

"Probably." After a brief silence, Krij cleared her throat. "Oh . . . there's one last thing. Siendra was worried that you might have been upset that she didn't get back to you until late on Senen."

"She doesn't need to worry." Siendra worry? The most reserved and composed lady I'd known in years? "If anyone understands the needs of dealing with commitments and what they can demand . . ."

"Blaine . . . in some ways. Siendra's not what she seems."

"None of us are."

"Blaine! Would you listen?"

"Yes, elder sister dear."

"She's the only surviving child of a samer triad lost in the Cloud Chaos. She can tell you, if she chooses, just how bad it was. Just don't ask her. Don't even hint at it. She got an education by going through the space service ranks, and then, just below the max age, going back to the Marist

Academy under the ranker option to get her degree and commission. She's extraordinarily competent, especially in reading most people. You're anything but most people. You act, then think."

The retort I'd had in mind died. Less than fifteen percent of the space service rankers who entered Marist graduated and got commissioned. Close to a third of those graduates died on hazardous duty on their first tour. Siendra had told me she'd been an Assembly space service officer. She just hadn't explained how she'd gotten her commission.

"I see I finally got your attention."

"You did."

"Siendra's very reserved. You've noted that. She made an effort in coming with me the other night. I just wanted you to understand. No . . . she's not samer. She's cautious."

I understood that as well. None of the space service academies were exactly bastions of sexual privacy or choice.

"Don't you dare say a word to her about what I've told you. She hates pity even more than condescension. I've looked for a good business partner for a long time, and I don't want to lose her because of your misplaced feelings."

"Then why—"

"Because you understand just enough to jump to the wrong conclusions. You'll protect anyone whom you think needs it without asking them."

I nodded. We'd had that conversation before. She was right. I didn't like it, but I wasn't a total idiot.

"I have to go. Until later."

I just sat behind my table desk for a time. Krij could be very protective. She'd been protective of me when I'd needed it, and certainly of her daughter Andrea. I just hadn't realized that Siendra was also in that ambit of concern. I should have.

The fact that all the Elois except Legaar were either out-system or headed there chilled me. Yet . . . short of liquidating my assets, which would be difficult, if not impossible on such short notice, and fleeing from an undefined "something" that I couldn't even pin down, exactly what could I do? I didn't even have a nightflitter left.

Then, as I'd proved on Pournelle II, and since, I did have a tendency to be impatient. At the very least, I could wait to hear what Seigniora Reynarda had to say.

Incoming from Myndanori, Max announced.

Accept.

Myndanori—or her image—wore shocking green. "Blaine, dear man. Was what I provided useful?"

"Most useful, and I think I've resolved matters quietly." Certainly profitably.

"Good!" There was a pause.

She was asking for details, but I couldn't provide them.

"Oh . . . Apollon says to say thank you for pointing Andres in the right direction. He's already been in touch with the advocate."

"I'm glad I could help. If I can ever be of assistance . . . you'll let me know?"

"That I will, dear man."

That left the Stella Strong commission and the reclusive author. I decided to concentrate on the author.

Marley Louis, Carey Douglass, or Terrie McGerrie wrote intricate works that showed a deep understanding of people. The fact that she had left Donacyr D'Azouza suggested that he should have been left. That also raised another question. Did I really want to find her for him?

Except . . . he hadn't asked that. He hadn't even been in touch, and that made little sense.

Nothing about that commission made any sense.

McGerrie's works were successful enough commercially that she was still writing, but none had cracked the top ratings. Was that because she understood too much? There was also a sense of history behind the well-chosen words.

Query. Find any historical links between the names Terrie McGerrie, Marley Louis, Carey Douglass.

In less than two minutes, Max had an answer.

All names are variations on the names of once-well-known but now obscure female writers of the pre-Diasporan period on Old Earth. They are all linked to the term speculative fiction.

What did that linkage mean? It certainly argued that the individual using the cover pseudonyms had a certain historical understanding as well. It also argued for brilliance, yet clearly the individual did not want her literary or dramatic abilities linked to whatever her true profession might be. But why speculative-fiction-based pseudonyms?

I didn't get too much farther in the time before Max announced, *Seigniora Reynarda is arriving, ser.*

Thank you, Max.

I stood beside the table desk and waited. Given her highhanded threat, I didn't feel that I needed to meet her at the study door.

She walked in. Her eyes fixed on me. She wore the same kind of clothes as she had the last two times—except that this time the short jacket was light gray trimmed in black, while the singlesuit was dark gray, with matching dark gray boots. She was still wearing the silver fox pin.

"Seignior Donne, have you been successful?" Her words were just short of mocking.

"You asked to see me. It wasn't even an inquiry, but a threat," I pointed out. "I agreed as a courtesy. You've already paid me and dismissed me."

"Seignior Donne, you have tracked me and invaded my privacy. That is not acceptable. For what reason was that necessary?" The black eyes were darker, somehow.

"Possibly for the same reason that you set me running as a lure for Eloi Enterprises. You already knew there was a link between Maraniss, Legaar Eloi, and Elysium."

"I never said there wasn't. Your commission was to find evidentiary proof."

"Why? Because TABS, the Elois, and the Assembly—"

Energy flared everywhere—and a wall of blackness slammed through my shields.

Seignior Donne . . . Seignior Donne . . .

Max was on the fringe of what I could pick up. I blinked. Overhead, I could see the pale ivory of the crown molding. I was still in my office, lying on my back beside the bookcases.

What happened?

The systems suffered a massive energy overload, ser. It was focused to a point three point four meters of front of you. It had the characteristics of a variable-geometric particle beam.

What happened to Seigniora Reynarda?

The system has no record. She vanished from all surveillance coincident with the focused energy attack. Analyzers detected no hydrocarbon or other organic residues.

She vanished, and you don't know how? I lurched to my feet. There wasn't even a hint of black or brown on the Sacrestan carpet before my desk. My face felt flushed from the heat.

That is correct, ser.

I felt a bit dizzy. I sat down in the chair behind the table desk, trying to gather my thoughts. Had Elisabetta Reynarda—or her body—been destroyed right before me? Or had she somehow vanished? How could either have penetrated the villa's defenses without leaving some sort of record? It was a warning of some sort, but for what? Not to follow the commission? Or not to follow the seigniora?

Was her disappearance/removal/focused explosion somehow connected to whatever had moved me from the limo after the opera? But . . . if that were the case, that suggested that Elisabetta Reynarda had to be a creature of Legaar Eloi and Maraniss. Why would they commission someone to track down and make obvious a connection that no one knew anything about?

I'd known the commission would be a problem, but it was clearly far larger and more deadly than I'd ever anticipated—and I still didn't even have the faintest idea what Elysium was beyond Maraniss's description of an ideal city. Were he and the Elois planning to wipe out Thurene and start over with an ideal city? That made no sense, because even Legaar Eloi didn't have the adequate resources for such an effort, and the Assembly of Worlds certainly wouldn't stand by and let that happen. Or did they have some technology that would change any city into an

Elysium? And would that change effectively force the Civitas Sorores from power?

There is a Garda flitter incoming, ser.

I didn't need that. But what I needed wasn't likely to be what I got.

Hold the defenses, Max. I stood and walked slowly to the study door, then across the entry foyer. I stood outside and watched as the flitter set down.

Surprisingly, the Garda patroller who walked up the steps was not Javerr, but Donahew.

"Officer Donahew." I inclined my head.

"Captain Shannon has requested that you come to Garda headquarters."

At least, Shannon was requesting. "Did he say why, Officer?"

"He only said that, if you were going to stick your neck out, Seignior Donne, that you should be fitted for armor."

That sounded all too much like the colonel I'd known. "I'll accept the invitation." Not that I had any choice.

We walked down to the Garda flitter. Just as a precaution, I ordered Max to put all the villa defenses on full alert and response until I returned.

Nothing happened on the flight to Garda headquarters. Donahew escorted me off the rooftop landing area and down the ramps. We kept going down. That did concern me.

The colonel was waiting in a small office at least two levels below ground. There was nothing on the gray walls. The only furnishings were a flat oblong table and two chairs, one on each side of the table. Shannon sat in the one facing the door. There was nothing on the table.

"Ser . . ." offered Donahew.

"Thank you, Donahew. I'll take it from here." He looked at me. "Sit down."

I sat. I didn't have that good a feeling about what might come next.

Shannon just looked at me until the door closed and we were alone. "You never learn, do you?"

"Probably not. What didn't I learn this time?"

"You'll find out." He stood.

Behind him, a section of wall split apart, revealing another ramp leading downward. He nodded toward the ramp. "This way."

"Am I being charged with anything?"

"What good would that do?" He started walking.

I debated whether to follow.

"Javerr will be returning shortly." Shannon did not look back over his shoulder. "You really don't want to see him."

I started after Shannon. "Why does the Garda allow him to remain on duty?"

"Call it an accommodation with reality," the Garda captain and former SpecOps colonel replied. "Those with extreme wealth will always buy influence. It helps to know who's influenced and by what means."

At the end of the ramp was a small private maglev car. The hatch was open.

"Get in."

I didn't have anything better to do. Besides, a private maglev capsule suggested matters might not be quite so bad as they could have been.

The maglev trip was short, possibly less than two klicks. When the hatch opened, I asked, "Where are we?"

"Exactly where? I couldn't say. This area belongs to the Soror Tertia."

That made sense. She was the sister who controlled the Garda and the Planetary Defense Force. "Why me?"

"Who else?" Shannon laughed. "I'll wait here for you. Just go through the door there and to the open door at the top of the ramp. When you're done, come back here."

With my implants, I could sense some energy flows, but they were beyond my tech or protocols. I wasn't going anywhere. Not until I got a better answer. "Why me?"

"Because there isn't anyone else. Not in time. Now, go talk to the sister. Even you don't want to piss her off, Donne."

He had another point there. I got out of the maglev car and went through the door and up the ramp. The walls were gray. So was the indestructible carpet that covered the ramp.

There were no decorations on the walls or carpet. Why was there always so much gray in the intelligence areas? Because the more you knew, the less obvious matters were?

No sooner than I had stepped through the open archway than the two sides of the door irised shut behind me. I stood in a narrow room, four meters wide, and close to six long. Energy shields divided the chamber, wavering and shifting enough that I could only make out the general image of a woman in black beyond the shields. She sat behind a small console desk, facing me. A black hood shadowed her face.

"Seignior Donne."

"Soror Tertia." I inclined my head slightly. "Apparently, I'm here at your invitation. Was Seigniora Reynarda your agent?"

A light laugh greeted my words. "After a fashion."

"What do you wish of me?"

"To tender an invitation."

"Oh? Like the one offered by Seigniora Reynarda?"

"That was an example of what that technology can do."

"You're making an offer I can't refuse, I see."

"We needed to get your attention in a fashion that indicated the severity of the situation. Legaar Eloi and Judeon Maraniss are about to activate a certain technology that will have adverse impacts on all Devanta. The example you witnessed was nothing."

"A Hawking field and a modified jumpship generator?" I suggested.

"A very modified field and generator. From what we can tell, they intend to wipe out Thurene and most life on Devanta. Obviously, we would prefer that they don't."

"Where do I fit in?" I had a very good idea where that was. But I could be wrong. I'd been wrong before.

"There are two ways in which Legaar can be handled. Locally, or by the Assembly of Worlds. If we call for Assembly assistance, that is a de facto admission of inadequacy."

"Reformulation and a loss of your power."

"Yes." The admission was without equivocation.

"Interstellar protection is the duty of the Assembly. Why

can't the Assembly space service stop the Frankan forces bringing the Hawking field?" That was a guess on my part, but it was the only thing that made sense.

"They are occupied elsewhere at the moment. They are likely to remain so."

"Oh . . . TABS and the Eloi connections have bought enough Assembly politicians so that it becomes a test of whether you can get out of the mess?"

"Essentially."

"So why don't you just send in a Garda team and take out Classic Research?"

"Whom would you suggest? Officer Javerr? Patroller Donahew? Do you think they could? Or that they would obey Captain Shannon?"

Sister Tertia had a point. I didn't like it. "So you want someone not in the Garda organization."

"A team not in the Garda organization."

"Where will you get the rest of the team, then? From the streets of Thurene?"

"Sarcasm doesn't become the shadow knight. We have the rest of the team."

"I still don't understand . . ."

"You will."

"If I might ask . . . why should I?"

"You mean . . . exactly what benefit accrues to you?" The light sardonic laugh followed. "Survival, for one. Second, if you become part of the effort, the authentication will be retroactive to your engagement by Seigniora Reynarda. That effectively means, if the effort is successful, you will be fully indemnified for the loss of your nightflitter, as well as the other damages incurred from the Eloi operation. Third, you will receive a paid consultancy of five thousand credits monthly, plus a five-hundred-credit-per-stan fee for all services in excess of ten stans per month. The minimum term of that consultancy would be ten years."

Matters were worse than I'd ever thought. "How soon before things heat up?"

"Five to seven days."

"I'm not exactly in the best shape."

"We know. That is secondary."

Both the Sister Tertia and I knew neither of us had much room to maneuver. "Who else is on the team?"

"Do you agree?"

"I agree." What real choice did I have?

"Colonel Shannon developed the plan. He and you, and a highly trained pilot with unique specialization, will execute it. You will all be briefed by the best intelligence specialist on Devanta. The timetable is very precise."

"What exactly am I supposed to do?"

"Enter a facility more secure than an Assembly operations center, disable or kill anyone there, and single-handedly operate a console and equipment you have never seen before to neutralize a system that could conceivably rip apart a section of our universe."

Her description made Pournelle II seem like a walk down the South Bank. It was also absurd and impossible.

"It is not quite so impossible as it sounds," the sister added.

"You don't want the Assembly to learn about the technology Eloi and Maraniss have developed, do you?" I couldn't resist asking.

"Would you?"

"What is it?"

"That will be covered in your briefing. Captain Shannon is waiting for you." With the last of her words, the screens cut off all light from her end of the chamber.

It was an effective dismissal.

I turned and walked back to the maglev.

The capsule hatch closed behind me, and Shannon nodded.

"Where to now?" I asked.

"A special medical facility. Where else? You need some remedial work."

I had the feeling I'd need a lot more than that, and I wasn't looking forward to any of it.

The maglev's next stop was farther away, and shielded. I

had no access to Max, the villa, or even to any commonnet. Shannon ushered me straight to a med-chamber whose energy and equipment made my villa medcenter look several centuries out of date.

A doctor was waiting.

"You're the remarkable Seignior Donne." Those were the first words out of the doctor's mouth. Her manner and tone made both Krij and Siendra seem maternal by comparison. Yet I doubted she was more than 150 centimeters tall and slender to match. Slender with the strength of a nanite-steel rod. "Off with your clothes above your waist. We need every minute. We're doing a full arm regression-rebuild, with reinforcement backup."

I didn't care for the "reinforcement backup." I pulled off my shirt and jacket.

Shannon vanished without a word or a glance, leaving me with the doctor.

"On the table there. This shouldn't be too bad. You've already got a week of nanite-boosted regrowth."

Not too bad? I could hardly wait.

39

Legaar paced around the penthouse study, with its hidden
and remote links to the Classic Research operations center
at Time's End. His movements were like that of a graceless
cougar, each of his tailored Drelaan shoes hitting the high-
impact carpet as hard as a sledge falling onto it.

"The schedule for delivery is almost a week. Why so
long? The sisters are nosing around, and somehow Shannon
or someone has gotten Special Operations interested. Only
TABS is keeping the Assembly at a distance." His words
were like awkward dark-voweled birds clattering down on a
slate roof. His eyes turned away from the single console.

"I told you the approach would be slow." I'd told him far
more than once, but he always wanted to believe that technical limitations were obstacles that could be removed as
abruptly and thoroughly as he'd removed people. "They'll
have to make a slow and shielded approach coming in-
system. The energy of a high-speed approach would alert
both the IS monitors, the PDF, and possibly even the Garda.
The Assembly couldn't overlook anything that blatant,
much as they might wish to."

"A polar approach?" His eyes flicked as though his attention were elsewhere, and that was less than optimal because
even when his attention was fully present, his concentration
focused all too often upon the trivial or upon the short-term
acquisition of greater power.

"High ecliptic. There's more debris there."

"It's taken forever to set this up." He rocked back and forth from one foot to the other, and the hideous and expensive shoes creaked under the stress. "Forever . . ."

"It's unique, and unique technology that conveys that kind of power takes time to assemble and coordinate. But it won't take that long once they're in position. We'll have roughly ten hours after the Hawking complex comes online before the first brane-flex break occurs. That should provide enough time for the last transfers."

"That's easy enough for you to say, Judeon. All you have to transfer is yourself and a few personal items. You haven't had an entire corpentity to consider."

"That's because I moved most of the heavy objects early on," I pointed out. "I might also observe that you have, upon more than one occasion, noted that there are few indeed in your various organizations that merit either rescue or restitution." Or anywhere in Thurene or on all of Devanta.

"I've had to relocate my family and my very best people."

"There is a cost to everything, especially for a new knowledge of reality, but when it's all over, you'll be able to dictate to the Assembly. In effect, you'll be running the Assembly. With the complex fully active, you can remove entire fleets. The space service will think you've destroyed them." Hurled hundreds of light-years and who knew how far forward or back in time, the warships would certainly be neutralized. Some would be destroyed, but none would be around to cause trouble.

But then, shortly after that, neither would Legaar.

40

Infinitely small needles of white-hot agony twisted through my arm and shoulder. From what I'd undergone in SpecOps regen, I was prepared for that. I wasn't ready for the nanoscale blue ice frozen hydrogen explosions that warred in the same area. I passed out.

When I woke, I was in another chamber. My entire left hand, arm, and shoulder were encased in a medunit. A second unit encased my right hand, arm, and shoulder. The only difference was that the right side throbbed slightly. I felt nothing on the left. My head ached as well, and my brain felt as though it had been squeezed. That had to have been a side effect of something else. Humans don't have the nerves for direct pain reception inside the skull.

My nose and cheek itched. I could turn my head enough to rub the cheek against the medunit. But not my nose. It was hard to ignore the itching.

I lay there, thinking. Trying not to envision the purplish gray mass that had engulfed my hands, wrists, arms, and shoulders. I could almost imagine the white-hot needles burning the length of my arms. The nerve blocks stopped the actual pain, but I knew that without them, I'd be convulsed in agony.

Why my right arm? Or had the doctor discovered something there as well?

I did my best to push that away and concentrate on what

little additional information I'd obtained from the Third Sister. Shannon had known about Eloi and Maraniss for a time, yet he'd let Javerr bully me. That made sense now. So did the sisters' indirect methods. I still didn't like either. The sisters also knew at least something about the technology Legaar Eloi was using. Yet they'd apparently done nothing. That was what I didn't understand.

"Seignior Donne." The doctor appeared. She was smiling.

I waited.

"You're in remarkable shape for an ex-operative. In fact, you're in better shape than most operatives on duty."

I hoped so. I'd worked at it. "What time is it?"

"It's only five hour."

"What day?"

"Marten, of course. The way your rebuilding and reinforcing is going, you'll be out of the right unit late tonight and the left one sometime around noon tomorrow."

"What are you doing to me?"

"Accelerated healing of the fractured radius, and some repair and strengthening of your arms, forearms, shoulders, and fingers. Oh . . . and upgrading your implants and comm faculties. You'll need those as well."

"Why the strengthening?"

The doctor smiled, faintly, almost sadly. "I don't know. I was only told that your mission profile required it."

"What about my head?"

"In addition to the implants? A little nanite clean-out, making sure there were no lesions in critical areas."

She was hedging on that.

"What else?"

"You'll have faster reactions in certain situations. We strengthened certain linkages."

"What will that cost me elsewhere?"

She laughed. "You're skeptical. The only thing it will cost you is patience. Over time, unless you're careful, you'll wonder why people take so long to react to situations."

I'd already had that feeling. I didn't say so.

"Your reactions in those areas are already well above normal. That's true of all special operatives. I was assured that you'll need to be faster for your mission."

The absolute certainty in her words chilled me.

"You're doing well. We're going to enhance your sleep—"

"No slumbereze!"

She shook her head. "You shouldn't ever use one. They're not designed for people with brains like yours. We'll be using something else . . ."

I took some consolation in the fact that my own feelings about the slumbereze had been right—before a gentle velvet darkness enfolded me.

41

To listen, even to hear, is not to know.

Barely after I'd eaten breakfast on Miercen, one-handed, Shannon appeared in my personal rehab room, carrying a black case and pushing a high, wheeled table. He set down the case and moved the table until it was a meter from the one medunit to which I remained attached. Then he walked out and returned with two chairs. He placed them next to the one already in the room.

"Are you 'Captain' or 'Colonel' today, ser?" I asked.

"From you, Donne, it doesn't matter. You can make any title sound like an expletive." He did grin. In fact, he was beaming. He opened the case and put a small device on the table. "You're not mobile yet, and we need to begin briefing you and the pilot. After the morning briefing, the doctor should be able to disengage the medunit, and you'll be able to get dressed. We'll have a pleasant lunch, and then everyone will go into separate afternoon simulation sessions."

"You're briefing us?"

He shook his head. "I'm just the ops designer. The intelligence head will do the briefing."

"Who's that?"

He gestured.

A tall woman in RT royal green entered the room. I'd met her before. Fiorina Carle. *That* definitely explained why it had taken so long for RT to send a flitter after me and why RT had made no fuss about my "crash" on the corpentity's lands.

"Captain Donne." Her words were clipped.

I should have felt that my former military rank was a good sign. I didn't. Especially not in my present situation. "Are you a former Assembly intel type?"

"Colonel, third sector, retired." She smiled politely.

"And RT is working with the sisters?"

"Not all of RT. Just those who count. We call it enlightened self-interest."

"Isn't all intelligent self-interest enlightened?"

"Donne . . . we need to get on with the briefing," interjected Shannon.

"I thought there was going to be a pilot here."

"Oh . . . there is." Shannon's words were dry.

"When am I going to meet this mysterious pilot?"

"In a moment." He grinned again. "I'm going to enjoy this."

"Don't tell me that our pilot is Officer Javerr." That would have been hard to accept.

"He's qualified. He's a one-term space service pilot, but he's far from the best. You know that he's not acceptable for other reasons. Besides, we have one far better qualified. Far better."

From Shannon's grin, I should have guessed. I should have. I didn't.

I couldn't say anything when Siendra walked into the room. She wore the same unmarked dark gray shipsuit she had worn on Senen evening when she'd vidlinked. I thought I saw the faintest hint of an embarrassed smile on her lips and face, but it vanished so quickly I wasn't sure. Again, I could have been wrong. "Colonel Carle, Colonel Shannon, Captain Donne." Her voice was pleasant but professional.

Shannon motioned to the empty chairs. Siendra took the one closest to me.

Colonel Carle had remained standing. A quick link flashed somewhere, then the chamber closed in on us. The walls remained in place, but a top-level security screen dropped around the space, and the door locked.

Carle began to speak. That allowed me to swallow and regain a bit of composure. "Major Albryt has extensive experience in high-speed space and atmospheric insertion maneuvers. She was rated as the top ship-handler in third sector the year before she completed her Assembly obligation." Fiorina Carle turned to Siendra. "Captain Donne was awarded the Assembly Star of Honor for neutralizing an entire planetary defense system as well as rescuing another SpecOps officer. He managed most of the recovery with one arm while paralyzed from the waist down."

From Siendra's reaction, muted and concealed as it was, I could tell that was news to her. It should have been. The service had never given out the details—for obvious reasons—and I'd never told anyone. I'd been stupid and fortunate enough to survive and redeem most of my mistakes, but I hadn't cared to have Krij or anyone else pointing out all the stupidity I'd exhibited dealing with the Frankans on Pournelle II.

"Now that everyone is here, I'd like Colonel Carle to begin," Shannon announced.

"The mission objective is simple," Carle stated. "To render the technology and equipment being assembled at Time's End permanently inoperable and incapable of being repaired or understood by anyone. The conditions under which the mission must be undertaken are what make its accomplishment difficult. First, there is already an Assembly politico-socio-monitoring team in place on Devanta with observers and snoops widely placed. While we think we have located most of them, we know we do not have all of them under observation. Second, an Assembly fleet is on standby should the monitoring team determine the political situation on Devanta requires prereformulation assistance."

None of us could have missed the cynical dryness of Carle's words there.

"Third, a Frankan combat-engineering team is maneuvering what appears to be a Hawking field generator insystem. Fourth, the Assembly space service knows this and is permitting it to occur. This is most probably being allowed so that the space service will have a documented and definitive reason to launch a full-scale attack on Pretoria. Successful deployment of the Hawking field will also neutralize Devanta's influence in the Assembly of Worlds for the foreseeable future."

"The space service views the situation as without a downside to them, regardless of outcomes," suggested Siendra.

"Exactly," replied Carle. "If the Civitas Sorores manage the situation so that nothing overt occurs, the Frankans lose a combat-engineering team and some costly equipment, and it costs the space service nothing. In addition, Eloi Enterprises will be neutralized, and the Assembly will quietly claim that the sisters acted in response to Assembly pressure. This will reduce perceived Devantan influence. If Legaar Eloi and Judeon Maraniss succeed in destroying Thurene and escaping, blame will fall on the sisters and the Frankans, and the space service and the Assembly will have the provocation to do what they've wanted to do for decades."

I had a question. I hesitated, but finally asked, "Don't the Frankans see that? Why would they risk an interstellar war just to meddle in one system?"

Carle's smile was cold. "We believe that they are nowhere as weak as the Assembly space service believes. Certain analysts have noted that a small but significant fraction of total Frankan energy usage for more than a decade cannot be accounted for. In addition, there are certain energy fields in the third sector. We believe, but cannot prove, that Devanta is a trap. It is likely that the Assembly sector fleet will be destroyed, as will the fleets being sent against Pretoria."

The more I heard, the less I liked what I'd learned. "And the Assembly cannot deduce what you have?"

"They do not wish to speculate upon what they cannot prove. That is always the weakness of those who control vast bureaucracies. Now . . ." Carle's voice turned brisk and cool. "The mission is simple in concept. Major Albryt will take a modified corvette, accelerate to the highest in-system velocity possible, and release an equally modified armed combat flitter. That will be piloted by Captain Donne and will be targeted at the Frankan Hawking Assembly. Captain Donne will have two special torps. Either should be sufficient to deal with the Frankans at the comparatively high velocity involved. Major Albryt will recover Captain Donne and proceed to Devanta. There she will accomplish a high-speed insertion that will release Captain Donne on target for Time's End."

I hadn't volunteered for a suicide mission. My face must have showed that because the intelligence colonel smiled. "We're not making you a suicide missile, Captain. One of the features of the technology being employed by the Elois is that there is a temporal component associated with transport, especially transport attempted within a planetary gravity well—or a relational relativity field, if you prefer. We also possess this obsolete technology, and it will be used to project your flitter temporally behind the Frankan defenses. You will be required to hit two checkpoints, Captain. One to get behind the defenses, and one to escape the ensuing catastrophic explosion. In a capsule, that is Phase I of the operation."

Obsolete technology? Was Phase II, presumably Time's End, even worse?

"You're suggesting that this . . . Elysium technology isn't particularly new," I said.

"It's not." Carle's voice was somewhere between clipped and resigned. "The technology that Classic Research has rediscovered dates back half a millennium. It was abandoned for several reasons. It's highly unstable. The backlash when it's confronted with powerful shields will wipe out the entire operating system. The damage to the spacetime fabric in the surrounding area will often create swirling singularities of an unpredictable nature for centuries, if not longer. Residual singularities in sections of the former Naquyl Confederacy still claim ships that ignore the warnings."

I was supposed to transit that madness of space, knowing its less-than-jocular procreations?

"The Assembly's IS high command knew Eloi and Maraniss were planning this, then?" asked Siendra. "It's a power play to remove the Civitas Sorores?"

"We're not privy to their motivations," replied Carle, "but that is the most likely probability. Devanta has the greatest degree of local autonomy of any system in the Gallian sector."

"Particularly economic independence and autonomy?" I asked.

Carle nodded. "We need to get on with what you need to know about the mission." She cleared her throat. "Even without a link to the Hawking field, the Elois have enough power at Time's End to use the projection field to level all of Thurene. Phase II is more complicated, unfortunately, and will require a greater use of Captain Donne's and Major Albryt's considerable skills." She nodded to Shannon.

"Phase II requires a targeted attack on the master controls to the technology. These are located at Time's End," Shannon began. "In the Classic Research laboratory there . . ."

The first holo projection was a satellite view of Time's End. Colonel Carle zoomed it in, not on the Classic Research laboratory, but on the low hill less than half a klick to the northwest of the lab.

"There is a class-one fusactor under this hill. Rather, the hill was built around it. Classic Research obtained the permits for an old-style class-three fusactor. That was actually built and is currently operating. What was not known at the time was that Legaar Eloi had already built a shielded class-one facility beneath the class-three facility. It was not brought up to operating levels until the legally permitted power facility was already operating. The existence of the class-one facility was not determined definitively until Captain Donne accomplished an instrumental sweep of the area several weeks ago." Carle nodded at me.

I'd never had instruments for that. How had the sisters . . . ? "You added detectors to Lemel Jerome's detector, didn't you?"

"That was Colonel Shannon's idea."

"So you caused his death."

"No. We didn't change anything," Carle replied. "We just added a few items. Legaar Eloi would have traced the tap back to Jerome even if we had done nothing. Like you, Captain, we didn't anticipate Legaar's immediate and violent reaction. He's generally used credits to obtain his ends, indirectly and without tracks."

"There were tracks in Lemmy's death?" I raised my eyebrows.

No one said anything.

"Can you explain why I got a disrupted signal on Domen, but Lemmy died on Senen?"

"Why don't you just let the colonel brief us, Donne?" suggested Shannon. "You might get your answers more quickly, and the rest of us could learn something as well."

Shannon was probably right, but I was feeling even more manipulated than ever, and I hadn't thought that possible. I should have. I nodded.

"The time differential is a result of the temporal backlash channeling associated with the technology." Carle waited until the second holo projection appeared. It was a schematic floor plan. "This is the floor plan for the operations area of the Classic Research laboratory. The ramp from the maglev enters here . . ." After that came a whole series of interior views of the facility, ending with one that displayed the operations center main controls. "These are controls you'll have to operate, Captain Donne. We've built a complete duplicate of this board." Carle looked at me. "Some functions we know; others are probabilities; still others are unknown."

I didn't doubt her. What I didn't understand was how they could have information in such detail and yet not know how some controls and systems worked or even need me to charge in and muck with things.

"You might wonder how we can provide these views and know so little," the intelligence colonel went on. "That has to do with the projection technology itself. It creates a two-way, space-time conduit—if you happen to have the equipment to monitor it. We've been careful not to alert the Elois to our possession of this mirror-equipment. We've only used it when they've powered up. Their power usage and field projections overshadow our passive observation. Also, we can't draw the kind of power they have. Even the Civitas Sorores can't divert the power output of two full fusactors on demand. You will notice that the controls are far more manual than at most installations. That is not deliberate lower tech, but a necessity. Wireless and broadcast signals or inflected power controls have a tendency to create unplanned and unpredictable variations in the projection field. Virtually every control device in these boards is insulated and served by insulated conduits and leads. It is designed to be impervious to implant controls or other energy fields."

At least that explained one reason why they needed a physical presence in the operations center.

After the overview came two solid stans of detailed holos and information on the corvette's projected flight path toward the Hawking complex, the entry and exit points, the timing, and the recovery. Then came the same level of details for the attack on Time's End. I had my doubts about the entire mission. It was far too complex. If anyone made a single mistake, nothing would work. At the same time, I didn't have any better ideas. Not ones that would give either Siendra or me a chance to get through it all in one piece.

I had the feeling that had been planned, too.

Still, at the end of the morning briefing, I had to ask, "What if this doesn't work?"

"Then the Devantan PDF will be forced to use far more direct and messy methods, and several million people will die. That's the minimum extrapolation."

I hadn't expected anything different, but I'd had to ask. The question I didn't raise was how the sisters had let such a sorry situation arise. There wasn't any point in that.

"That's it for now." Shannon stood. "Donne, join us in the private dining room as soon as you can. It's three doors down."

Siendra let the colonels depart before her. "We need to talk before you draw any conclusions."

We certainly did.

42

Faith is but a poor substitute for understanding.

As Shannon had indicated, almost before the security screen had lifted, the doctor was standing in the doorway. She did wait until Siendra and the other two had left before walking toward me.

"You're ahead of schedule on the healing." She linked to the medunit. It fell away, leaving a light nanite-spun cast on my forearm. It was almost invisible. "I'd still be a bit careful there, Captain."

"I'll try, Doctor."

"There's a uniform in the fresher if you want to change. You need to come back here for another check after your afternoon activities. Before your evening meal."

"Yes, Doctor." I smiled as I spoke.

She did return the smile before she turned and left.

After showering in the adjoining bath-fresher, I donned the shipsuit that had been provided. It was a match to the one Siendra wore. Like hers, it bore no insignia, but it was tailored to me. The integrated nanite protection and link system were better than what I'd had on the Pournelle II mission— and that had been the best available to SpecOps at the time.

Shannon, Carle, and Siendra were seated around the single circular table in the small private dining room. The tablecloth was cream linen, and the cutlery was silver. The goblets and glasses were crystal. There was no wine. The remaining chair was between Colonel Carle and Siendra. I eased into it.

"We didn't think you'd be long, Captain." Shannon offered a pleasant smile.

"Thank you." I turned to the intelligence colonel.

Before I could say anything, she said, "The installation here is considered secure, but the servers are not cleared for this mission."

In short, don't talk about it except behind the full security screens. I hated taking anything on faith alone, but I wasn't being given enough information to do otherwise. At that point, a server appeared with a tray bearing four salads. Each held thinly sliced apples and pears over red leaf lettuce, sprinkled with chopped toasted almonds.

"Do you follow the work of Devantan dramaturges and writers?" I asked.

"Not really," replied Shannon. "I've seen enough of what passes for drama."

"You mean," interjected Siendra, "if it's real, it's either too upsetting or too boring, and if it's neither, it's not real?"

"Something like that." Shannon took a bite of the salad.

I looked to Carle.

"I like a good drama, if it's exciting. It's a break from the fine detail of what I do most of the time."

I could see that.

"What about you?" countered the intelligence type.

"I like a little of everything, if it's good. Even opera."

"It's often less exciting than what follows," suggested Carle, her voice pleasant. "That can be chilling, especially comparatively."

I got the hint. I couldn't help but wonder how much she'd observed, particularly during the opera.

That was about as interesting as the conversation got during the remainder of the meal. The main course was clearly less than exciting—competently prepared veal scaloppini with slightly overcooked pasta.

As I was taking a last sip of iced tea, Shannon rose. So did Fiorina Carle.

"Colonel Carle and I need to work out a few details. I'll meet you both at the maglev platform in half a stan."

"Yes, ser."

Siendra just nodded.

Once the door closed behind the departing colonels, she turned to me. "Blaine . . . there's something you should know. I didn't suggest, volunteer, or even hint that you should be the operative. I was told your name ten minutes before I walked into the briefing."

I believed her. "Shannon's a sadist. He didn't tell me. He just said he'd enjoy my finding out."

"I thought he hadn't said."

"Was it that obvious?" I laughed.

"It probably wouldn't have been to anyone else. I've been watching you for a while. Since I've been working with Krij."

"Carle doesn't miss much."

"No, she doesn't." Siendra smiled mischievously. "She doesn't like opera, either."

"How much do you know about that?"

"About opera? Very little. That you occasionally attend it for professional reasons with attractive women who have information. That you ended up swimming in a reservoir after your last opera."

"You're an attractive woman with information," I pointed out.

"I can't take you to a private box at the opera on opening night. Carle told me that," she added quickly. "She's very thorough."

"Have you worked with her before?"

"Professionally. She's briefed me on several recon missions."

"Recon? You've been watching the Frankans for years, then?"

"And the Argenti and a few others. We can't afford to rely on the Assembly space service. That's been apparent for years."

"We? The covert intelligence service of the Civitas Sorores?"

"Who else?"

"Is it all women?"

"No. Shannon isn't female. Neither are you. It's whoever they think will best handle the tasks they need done."

"You *and* Krij, then." It all made sense. They'd had information I couldn't get anywhere else. "Another part of the reg compliance business."

"Exactly. If we seem to know more than the average corpentity type would, then, who else would? We see everyone's ops plans and finances."

"So . . . is Astrid Forte another intel type?"

"Blaine . . . I can't tell you any more than I have."

That meant yes. There was something about it that nagged me. I couldn't place it. Then it hit me, even though I certainly couldn't do anything about it at the moment. "Intelligence types for the sisters have the same legal standing as the sisters, don't they, both the restrictions and the benefits?"

"They'd have to, wouldn't they?"

That was another answer that wasn't technically an answer, but it explained a great deal. I thought I had my answers as to who my client in the Wayles inheritance really was— and why, even if I couldn't do anything about it at the moment.

For a moment, I just looked at Siendra. The dark gray shipsuit tended to wash her out. Even so, she was good to look at. I realized something else. She was the kind of woman who never quite looked the same from any different angle or in any light. She met my eyes, not challenging, but not flinching, just accepting.

"We should start for the maglev," I finally said. Then I stood.

"How is your arm?" Siendra rose with that quick and fluid grace that made it seem as though she were sitting one moment and standing the next.

"It aches a little at times, but it's much better. The doctor told me not to overdo it for a while. Say . . . one day." I laughed.

So did she, softly, but warmly.

I wondered why I hadn't seen the warmth behind the professionalism. Had it always been there? Had I failed to see it? Or had she become less guarded? If so, why? Just because she'd have to work with me?

Shannon was waiting on the maglev platform. He gestured toward the open hatch of the maglev capsule.

I let Siendra go first, then followed her. With only four couch-seats, the capsule felt crowded. The trip took almost a quarter stan. With Shannon there, I wasn't in the mood for talking to Siendra. Maybe I'd missed something, but there had been the slightest hardening of Siendra's voice when she'd mentioned Odilia. She'd referred to the princesse as an attractive woman who had information. The phrasing about not being able to take me to a private box on opening night was as close to a catlike remark as I'd ever heard from Siendra. Yet she'd wanted me to understand that she had not been the one to drag me into the mission.

When the capsule door opened, I let Shannon and Siendra get out first. She started toward the left-hand archway. Then Shannon did. I followed them both down the gray-walled and gray-carpeted corridor. Again, all my implants and access to anything beyond the facility were blocked.

The third arch opened into a cavernous space. Once inside, I could see full-cockpit simulators for several classes of spacecraft.

"Is this where you've been training?" I asked in a low voice as I caught up with Siendra.

She nodded.

"Donne! Over here," called Shannon.

"Here" was the cockpit of a high-speed in-system scout. Beside it was a complete set of space armor, without any ID. My size.

"You've got fifteen minutes to get into the armor and check out things and run through the checklist before we start the first sim run. The Phase I profile's in the system."

I eased into the armor. Even with the assists, it was heavy in standard grav. But then, it was designed primarily for null gee. Once into the cockpit, I linked to the systems. The sim-links were solid. They felt "real." I began the scout check-list.

Seals and locks—tight.

Power—standby.

Habitability—green . . .

I finished the checklist and began to run over the mission profile. In theory, it was simple enough. Siendra would ac-celerate the *Aquitaine* to max in-system velocity and re-lease my scout, short of the Frankan defense fields and the point where the projection field lens would appear. I would continue to accelerate. Once through the projection field lens, I would fire two torps. The properties of the field and lens would energy-invert the torps, and I'd have to avoid the lens and its peripheral effects and angle toward the pickup point and the second field lens. That was if every-thing went right. It might, but we had to be prepared for other eventualities as well.

Coyote one, this is Coyote lead. Even through the links, I could hear and feel Siendra's "voice." *Comm check.*

Coyote lead, comm is clear and strong.

Max acceleration will commence in two minutes.

Stet. Understand two minutes . . .

The first run was smooth. That was just to make sure Siendra and I both had the profile down. After that, it got worse. Much worse.

Carle—or Shannon or both—made sure everything went wrong. Siendra lost a converter, then a thruster. One of my torps refused to launch. The target projection field was lo-cated off course line . . .

I was damp with sweat when I finally left the cockpit simulator and extricated myself from the armor. I was more than ready to walk in the cool of a mortal garden.

Shannon had other ideas. "You've got a half stan break to get a bite to eat. There are rations over there and some wa-ter and iced tea. Then we need to get you onto the boards."

I didn't want to admit how tired I felt. I might have been

in good physical shape, but operational shape was something else. Besides, Shannon was sweating, too. "Now?"

"You'll be about that tired by the time you reach the ops center at Time's End."

There wasn't any point in arguing. I didn't. I walked toward the corner of the artificial cavern that held two tables with chairs.

Siendra was seated at one table. Her shipsuit was damp in places as well. She motioned to me. After taking a ration pack and a large beaker of iced tea, I joined her.

"How did you think it went?" I took a long swallow of tea.

That brought a wry smile. "Not bad for the first time we've worked together. Not smooth enough or seamless enough to rest on our nonexistent laurels."

"Have you flown the *Aquitaine* before?"

"Yes, but not since her latest modifications."

"She wasn't originally designed to carry a scout." That was a safe assumption. No corvette was built that way.

"No. They reduced crew space to two tiny staterooms to accommodate the larger drives and the oversized converters. It was a rush conversion."

"Why us?"

Siendra shrugged. "Who else do they have?"

"I haven't the faintest idea who the sisters have. Nothing on Devanta is ever what it seems."

"As things are, they're transformed upon the blue guitar."

"Blue guitar?"

"It's a paraphrase from pre-Diasporan poetry. In a way, the Civitas Sorores are that kind of instrument. That's why neither the Frankans nor the Assembly care for Devanta, if for different reasons. The sisters don't foster the illusion that what one sees is reality. In even a moderately high-tech society, the excess of information ensures that what we see is not reality. We're allowed, even encouraged, to select our own personally compatible vision of what we wish reality to be. That's why Thurene needs a shadow knight. Or a

Fox. There have to be those who see behind the illusion of reality."

I wasn't sure about how effective the shadow knight was or had been. The Fox had been a legend who had vanished when he or she had become too publicized. I also realized that I'd just heard the longest statement Siendra had ever made in my presence.

"For something necessary . . ." I broke off what I'd been about to say. I'd almost said that the sisters had discouraged the shadow knight. But, in support of what Siendra had said, I realized that such apparent opposition was an illusion. They'd only created the illusion of opposition. Likewise, I'd have bet that the media stories, ostensibly in support of the shadow knight, had probably come from Legaar Eloi, setting up the shadow knight to be discredited for failing to live up to the media image. Only in the shadows of obscurity could the knight of shadows or the Fox of the past flourish. I shook my head. "Excessive familiarity killed the Fox." I took a bite of the ration cube. "It may destroy the shadow knight."

Siendra nodded. "Despite what people say and wish to believe, reality lies in the shadows. Too much light blinds, and too little engenders nightmares and fantasies."

"You're almost as cynical as Krij."

"More so in some ways. Less in others." The hint of a faint smile crossed her lips.

"What are you doing next?"

"Nav work. Standard positioning won't work the same way once we near the projection fields."

I had the feeling nothing would work the same way.

"Donne! You ready for the Phase II intro?" Shannon's voice echoed through the artificial cavern. But then, what was real in a high-tech society?

"Coming, Colonel." I stood and smiled at Siendra. "Till later."

I got a warm smile in return. It was better than words.

Shannon led me to the far end of the simulation bay. The

mock-up of the Classic Research center took up that entire end, a space a good fifty yards wide. When I stepped into the "operations center," I found myself facing four operator stations. Those seats were vacant. The boards themselves were almost six yards wide, slanted panels filled with mechanical switches and gauges. Mechanical? Even after Carle's emphasis on the mechanical nature of the setup, the extent of those devices brought me up short.

I took a position roughly in the middle of the board.

The main projection field power controls to twenty percent.

The boards had actual rheostats. I reached out and turned the oversized dial.

Fifty-one percent.

I readjusted the power.

Set the beam focus at ten yards, coordinates to follow . . .

Where were the focus controls?

I had to search for the information, then move to the second station. The focus controls were calibrated levers. The coordinates were established by three flat matrices above the focus controls.

Wrong sector.

Frig! Sectoral controls had to be entered semimanually.

From there, Colonel Carle's familiarization techniques got inexorably more demanding.

I was so tired that my entire body was shaking by the time I finished the session with the mocked-up control boards.

I just wanted to sit down. Instead, I had to trudge to the med-chamber for a short session with the doctor, then back to the small and elegant dining chamber with the less than elegant food.

This time, we were served second-rate tournedos with oversautéed white mushrooms, and brown rice that was too crunchy. The servers left, and the doors locked. The security screen shielded the chamber.

"The Frankan team has been detected," Fiorina Carle began. "We can run you through two more days of sim training here. On Sabaten, you'll be shuttled to the *Aquitaine*. Late on Sabaten, once all systems check, we'll begin to shift you to the attack point. We estimate three shifts."

Shifts? I raised my eyebrows.

"We'll be using the projection field equipment to move the ship. That way, the Frankans and the Eloi team won't see any energy emissions moving toward their field local point, not until the very last phase of the attack. Their EDI screens might show momentary leakage flashes . . . if they're watching, but those will be far below the levels for even a scout. The main emissions will appear in back-time and presumably forward-time loci. You'll just have to sit tight until everything lines up."

"How long before they're in position?" asked Siendra.

"Anytime from early on Sabaten to sometime late on Domen. It will take a minimum of ten stans to power up."

"What about Legaar?" I asked.

"The justiciary hearings will end tomorrow. We expect he'll return to Time's End."

"The Assembly fleet?" asked Siendra.

"It's out of range," Carle admitted, "if it's there at all."

"Convenient. Close enough to mop up, but not interfere."

"Why do you think you're here, Donne?" growled Shannon.

"Because you can't get anyone better without involving SpecOps and making matters worse, and because I still have a few shreds of idealism remaining. Those are in danger of vanishing as it is."

I caught the hint of . . . something . . . from Siendra.

"Enough. We can only use the tools we have." Carle's professional smile at Shannon was cold enough to freeze a warm-water lake solid.

It also chilled the conversation.

I'd barely finished eating when Shannon announced. "Major . . . you have another nav session. Captain, the doctor and the therapists are waiting for you."

In the end, after mechanically swallowing the last of some sort of flan that was really a pudding, I walked back to the med-chamber. There the doctor ran brief diagnostics, then replaced the nanite cast on my still-recovering arm with a light nanite med-sleeve.

A massage followed.

Eventually, I collapsed onto the bed.

I *had* left SpecOps, hadn't I?

43

*Beyond, our city beckons bright; this world
falls to endless night.*

Three long days of hearings had frayed Legaar even beyond his normal impatience. For the last day, every word out of earshot of the Devantan Justiciary had been growled or barked at those around him. I'd hoped that he would calm down once he returned to Time's End, but that had not occurred. He'd sent me back by flitter, then showed up later. If anything, his level of irritation had increased, and his attention span had decreased. Yet he clearly had gone to one of his spas. His skin was softer, and he reeked of oils, of midnight nothings with near-mindless cloned nymphs, not that clones ever had to be mindless. That was just one of his precautions, and doubtless necessary for them to stand him.

For all that, he kept pacing back and forth behind the operators of the control boards.

"They're beginning their approach, ser,"

"It's about time," Legaar growled. "We wait here. We're exposed, and they scuttle through the darkness. How long before they can bring the field online?"

"Online with minimal power would be two stans after arrival at the focal point," I said. I'd told him that before, at least once. "Four hours for low-level full power. They're roughly two days out. We'll know more later."

"You're sure that the PDF and the Assembly can't detect them?"

"They're stealth to all EDI and standard detectors. We're using projection-type tags that only register on our screens.

You can tell that because there's no PDF or Assembly reaction. Don't you think that there would be a reaction to a Frankan craft otherwise?"

"The sisters are devious. So is the frigging PDF."

"That could be, but until we activate the full fields, there's no link to us. It's just a hostile Frankan force with which we had nothing to do," I pointed out. "Even after that, it would be difficult to prove anything even if the sisters could take this facility, and they can't."

"Assembly Special Operations could," Legaar snapped.

"They have to have proof. They invade Devantan private installations without solid evidence, and half the Assembly would secede." I refrained from checking the backlinks.

Legaar whirled. "This had better work, Maraniss."

It was more than a little late for that kind of irrational reproach, more like the mythical Lucifer asking if he should revolt after he'd already raised his standard, but Legaar was far less intelligent than Lucifer, and appearing less so than before the hearings, not that his intelligence had ever been excessive.

"Oh, it will work." Indeed it would. It just wouldn't work quite the way Legaar thought it would or that the Frankans thought.

44

Practice does not make perfect; it only reduces the possibility of error. Even so, humans can find ways to circumvent both practice and wisdom.

For the next two days, I moved from one training setup to the other and back again. By the end of Jueven, Shannon was also adding warm-up and refresher exercises from SpecOps. There wasn't time for more than that, but I'd kept in shape.

"You haven't lost much," Shannon had admitted grudgingly.

Working in the shadows had provided some benefit, it appeared.

Early on Sabaten, Siendra and I were strapped into a military hilifter—a fast high-gee courier. Except for helmets, we were in space armor. I had the feeling it was the first time we'd been together without an overriding imperative in three days—or without the feeling of someone eavesdropping.

"How are you feeling?" she asked.

"Rushed, but good. How about you?" I shifted my weight slightly in the acceleration couch and checked the restraints again.

"I'd rather not be a passenger."

I laughed. "Pilot's syndrome. We'd all rather be at the controls. That's because we know everything that could go wrong. That's even when the probabilities are low."

Final check on restraints. Two minutes to liftoff. That was the pilot. I didn't recognize her from the link, and we'd never seen her.

Restraints checked, I pulsed back, a moment after Siendra had.

Neither one of us spoke, just waited.

Commencing liftoff.

Unlike the old-style torches, the hilifter started with a moderate two-gee acceleration that increased to six plus before dropping to about a half gee. The last ten minutes brought a one-gee decel. The hilifter rendezvoused directly with the *Aquitaine*. The corvette was tethered to the PDF geostationary orbital station. Tethered, not locked, and without a life-support umbilical. The only connection to the station was the tether and a power/comm cable.

Locked to target. You're cleared to proceed. Good luck.

Proceeding, replied Siendra. *Thank you.* "Helmets."

I put on my helmet and checked it. *Helmet on. Armor security checks.*

Armor secure, Siendra reported. *Proceeding to lock.*

The ship-to-ship seal wasn't perfect. That showed in the low lock pressure that dropped once the hilifter's outer hatch opened. The *Aquitaine*'s lock opened to Siendra's codes. We didn't waste time in squeezing into the courier's small lock—and cycling it and getting out of it into the corvette. There's nothing romantic about two sets of space armor in that tight a space.

Once inside the *Aquitaine*, Siendra ran through a habitability check, then linked, *You're clear to enter and inspect the scout, Captain.*

Yes, ser. Proceeding this time. I did take a moment to put my small gear bag in the net in the copilot's minute compartment—essentially a sleeping space padded on all sides.

Unlike battle cruisers, corvettes weren't designed to carry other ships, even those as small as single-person scouts. Some of the modifications were invisible, such as the beefed-up screens and the detectors that were almost as powerful as those on a battle cruiser. Others were clunky, such as the access to the scout that was attached "below" the corvette.

I had to unfasten a hatch in the passageway aft of the

cockpit manually, then refasten and seal it behind me while floating standing in a tubular space that barely allowed me to squirm around to unfasten a second hatch in the outer hull of the corvette. Below that hatch was the outer lock of the scout. It had been reconfigured with an iris lock so that the scout could be entered while still attached to the underside of the corvette.

I pulsed the access codes. The lock did iris open, and I pushed and squirmed "downward" through the lock. Then, with one boot under a hold, floating roughly "upright" in the scout lock, I had to shut the lower corvette hatch manually, ensuring the seals were tight. From there, matters were more routine.

Scouts had no cabins or spaces, just a cockpit that could barely hold a single pilot in space armor. I wedged myself into the couch and tried to link to the ship. That took a moment because I'd almost forgotten I needed to turn a manual lever to connect to the corvette's power. Or rather the power from the station currently powering the corvette.

Then I ran through the diagnostics and the prelaunch checklist. Other than the lock modifications and the power linkage, the scout controls were standard. It could have been any of those I'd used over the years in Special Ops. It wasn't, not with the beefed-up drives, but it looked that way from the checklist.

When I was done, I reported. *Scout is green and ready for prelaunch checkoff, Major. Request permission to return to courier this time.*

Granted.

I left the power link in the connected position but powered down everything except minimal habitability. Then I had to go through the lock and two hatches in reverse to return to the corvette and its cockpit. There I took off my helmet and racked it, then levered myself into the copilot's couch.

Siendra was already there, ready to begin the departure checklist.

"Did the hilifter pilot know our mission?" I finished checking my restraints.

"No. She only knows it has to be secret and dangerous. We were delivered to the ship without going through the station, nor was she ever told who we are. She might guess at me. She'd be hard-pressed to come close to you."

"Do you know her?"

"It felt like Captain Delacroix, but that's a guess. Stand by for departure checklist."

"Yes, ser."

"Restraints."

"Set and locked."

"Drives."

"Off-line."

"Screens and shields."

"Off-line."

"Habitability."

"Minimum . . ."

The checklist showed no problems, and she brought the fusactors online smoothly, then the rest of the ship's systems up to full.

"Tether and station power."

"Disengaged."

Siendra looked at me, then nodded before link-transmitting, *Delta OpsCon, Coyote Alpha, ready for departure.*

Coyote lead, cleared to depart. Traffic at your two six five, orange, inbound.

OpsCon, commencing departure this time. Inbound traffic noted.

Stet, Coyote lead.

I didn't say anything for a good half stan, not until we were clear of traffic and well established on an outbound vector.

"There's no sign of the Frankans on the EDI."

"There won't be, Captain. Neither of them nor of any Assembly vessels. The Frankans are shielded, and any Assembly warships will be beyond EDI range."

"What's the trade-off between shielding and power . . . weapons?"

"Almost half of the available power for drives, Captain."

Siendra was sending a clear message. I heeded it. "Thank you, ser."

She was a good pilot. Even with automatics and the ship's system vector analysis, most pilots still have to make several course corrections on the shortest of in-system hops. That's with a defined physical body as a destination. Three stans later, with only minimal words between us and one minor course correction, we came to rest in a relatively dust-free area well out-system of Devanta and its moons. "Rest" was a relative term as well. Our position was close to stationary with regard to the system bodies.

"Now what, ser?" I knew very well. But what else could I say?

"We wait. It could take as much as a stan for them to check all the vectors before they can use the projection field to move us."

"I think Eloi or his people used something like that to move me, but it didn't take a stan."

"They moved you from a predetermined position at a close to predetermined time to another predetermined location. Even so, you're fortunate you survived."

"I did have a nanite bodyshield."

"You triggered it before you knew what was happening, didn't you?"

"Yes. If you wait until you know what's happening, it's too late."

"That's true of the best in any high-intensity occupation. It's why you survived your tours in Special Operations and why Colonel Shannon pushed for you."

At least, she wasn't calling me "Captain." "Do you know if Colonel Carle wanted someone else?"

"She never indicated that to me, one way or the other."

I didn't know what exactly else I could say. The dichotomy in Siendra between the person I'd glimpsed at times in recent weeks and the dispassionate consultant and professional officer left me disconcerted. I understood the need, yet I felt that, in her, those two individual aspects of her being were far more separate than in anyone else I'd ever known. I also felt that the width of the gap between the two "selves" was anything but good for her.

Yet . . . who was I to make any judgment of her, even silently? I had my own dichotomies. Was that because I felt each man must become the hero of his world? Or that I struggled to escape a permanent dream, one interrupted neither by day nor night?

Neither by day nor night? That sounded like a phrase of Siendra's . . . and someone else's as well. But whose?

Words and phrases swirled through my thoughts. I didn't need the distractions, and I pushed them away and accessed the shipnet, carefully, checking indicators and screens. Our detectors could barely make out Devanta, Bergerac, and Voltaire. I still didn't pretend to understand why a field that would eventually focus on Time's End required or used a Hawking field so far away, but Carle had just said to think of it in terms of a lever and a fulcrum, with Voltaire as the fulcrum, and the distance from the field multiplying the impact in both time and space.

The space around me seemed to contract.

"Ser . . . they're locking in."

At that moment, a brilliant light, intensely white and intensely blue, both and neither, blotted out everything. Then, as suddenly as it had flared through the corvette, it was gone. We were back in normspace. Somewhere else.

Even as I tried to locate us, Siendra was faster.

"We're within half an emkay of target point two."

That was good. Any distance of less than one point five emkay was acceptable.

"Frig . . ." Siendra murmured.

"Ser?" I could tell she was focused on the comparator. I didn't understand the physics behind it, but it used the stellar field of the local sun to determine absolute system time. Or whatever it was that we perceived as such. There was no such thing as absolute universal time. More than a few of the deists had been appalled when early interstellar travel had proved that. Most, like humans throughout history, still denied what technology and science had verified. Often time after time, century after century.

"The field displaced us foretime almost two stans."

That had been presented as a possibility, if remote. It also meant I had less than a stan to get into the scout and ensure all systems were green and ready for launch. "I'd better get moving."

"Go."

I was already out of the copilot's restraints. I made sure that they were retracted before I donned my helmet and left the cockpit to wrestle with the two hatches.

A quarter stan later, I'd finished the checklist and had the scout's fusactor on line. I was sweating inside the armor, and that would leave me clammy later.

Coyote lead, Coyote one, ready for launch. Interrogative estimated time.

Estimate one eight minutes before projection transfer.

Understand one eight minutes. Standing by. What else could I do?

I checked the EDI, but there were no major energy sources within range of the scout's detectors. Several beacons appeared, basically locators on dark bodies in the Trojan group, the kind of space junk that screens and detectors didn't always pick up.

As I waited, I found my thoughts drifting back to Siendra. Just who was she? The quietly humorous and witty woman who saw far more than she let on? The brilliant reg compliance consultant? The extraordinary pilot? Of course, she was all three, but . . . behind the different facades which attribute was paramount? Or was the gestalt something beyond the attributes?

Was I being fair or accurate? Could anyone be described in terms of perceived attributes? Could I? Why was I trying so hard to define a woman I'd ignored for years? And why had I ignored someone so quietly attractive and intelligent? Merely because she was my sister's business partner?

The second field transfer swooped in on me even more quickly than the first and with the same bicolored brilliant light. That I hadn't sensed anything jolted me as much as the sudden shift in position. My personal questions about Siendra had to wait.

In the instants after we were hurled back into normspace at an impossibly high velocity relative to system bodies, I ran through the system diagnostics. All indicators remained in the green.

Coyote lead, Coyote one in the green. Ready for launch.

Stet. Coyote one, commencing acceleration this time.

Ready for acceleration. I was pressed back into the scout's couch even before I finished my link to Siendra. Gee forces continued to build before leveling out at close to six, jamming me into the back half of my armor. That was the way it felt, anyway.

Except for the comparatively large-mass system bodies, my detectors showed nothing. I would have liked to link into those of the corvette, but that link didn't exist. All I could do was watch and wait. The theory behind the attack approach was simple—seemingly impossibly high in-system velocities, coming in-system from out-system, at such high speeds that no standard defense could adapt, and so suddenly that the defenders had no time to react by spraying all sorts of matter into the scout's flight path.

The gee forces remained stable.

Time to release. Fifteen on my mark. MARK!

Stet. Fifteen from mark.

The magcouplers let go exactly on time, and the gasjets separated us. I hit full accel as soon as I had enough separation, and my attitude didn't leave the drives angled at the corvette. The scout's gee load was actually lower than the corvette's had been, but the cumulative velocity continued to build. I had to push away the thoughts about where I'd end up if anything went wrong.

My concentration—and calculations—had the scout directed on a course-line vector fed into the scout from the corvette just before separation. I knew my detectors wouldn't pick up the target for the first quarter stan after separation. That knowledge didn't help my state of mind as the scout accelerated in-system, on a direct line for Voltaire, thousands of emkays ahead, yet with that distance shrinking prodigiously. Somewhere behind and above me, Siendra was piloting the *Aquitaine* on a curved arc that was supposed to bring us together for a rendezvous just short of Voltaire. If I hit my targets correctly . . . if the interaction of the projection field and the scout and my modified torps worked as designed . . . ◼

If they all didn't, the odds were still that the Frankans wouldn't survive, because they'd be slashed to shreds by the energy and debris that would result from imperfect harmonies, but some of that debris would be me and the scout. I was working for harmony, because that was the only way I'd survive.

Suddenly . . . I could pick out the energy distortion pattern that marked my target entry point. All I had to do was make the center of that faint sphere of energy distortion. Even with the EDI focused and on full sensitivity, that target area winked in and out of existence. Although the briefings hadn't mentioned it, I had the feeling that I wouldn't be doing myself or the scout ship or the mission much good if I hit the target area at a time when there was no energy distortion.

Then indeed, I would be headed downward to darkness on extended wings. Even if scout ships were only lifting bodies without wings.

The energy target field flicked in and out of existence. There was some sort of pattern, but the analyzer couldn't determine it. Not only that, but there was no way to determine distance and closure because the energy wasn't in the "now" long enough for the EDI to lock in the range. I kept the acceleration constant.

I was almost on the pattern when it vanished.

My gut reaction was to cut the drives. I didn't. I boosted the acceleration slightly, all that I could, and the energy field swelled around me. This time, the white and blue merged into a coruscating intensity that burned through my closed eyelids.

I opened my eyes and focused on the shipnet. Ahead, swelling rapidly, was a roughly spherical shape that looked like a solid nickel-iron asteroid. The EDI emissions indicated that it was neither solid nor an asteroid.

Torp one . . . arm . . . launch.

Torp two . . . arm . . . launch.

As soon as the second torp was away, I used the steering jets to angle the scout, so that the continuing acceleration would carry me wide of the target.

I was supposed to be well clear before the torps struck, but I had no way to tell if the separation was adequate. It must have been, because the EDI registered a violent surge of energy, and the minimal shields of the scout shuddered. That was it . . . no sound of explosions in space, because nothing carries sound. No lighting up of things because there's no atmosphere to diffuse the light. Just a flare of energy on the EDI.

Then . . . there was another brilliant blue-white flash that filled the scout, if instantly and timelessly. Had that been a backlash from the collapse of the Frankans' Hawking field . . . or from the sisters' far weaker field?

Before I could speculate more, I lurched forward against the restraints as the scout hit the second energy pattern, and red-violet light flared around me. On the far side of that, I was farther in-system.

Behind me the EDI indicated a faint haze where the pseudoasteroid had been. That haze showed that it was still there. Yet, before I had entered the projection field, it had been destroyed, with only residual dispersing energy and no haze.

I hoped that meant that I'd dropped backtime some—but not too little, I hoped. More would be better than less, within limits. The chronological uncertainties could be more than an inconvenience, it was clear.

I steadied the scout on the course line aimed at Voltaire's north pole, immediately cut the acceleration to nil, and began checking the EDI and detectors for signs of the *Aquitaine* and Siendra.

Five and a half minutes later, the energy haze that represented the Frankan installation flared, then vanished. I couldn't help but take a deep breath.

I was still worried. From what I could tell, my in-system velocity was more than thirty percent higher than calculated. The time-drop-delay had been calculated, theoretically, to let the *Aquitaine* get farther in-system so that with my higher velocity I would make the rendezvous from out-system, but the delay had been less than projected, and that could mean more than a little trouble.

Another three minutes passed before I could detect the *Aquitaine*.

Coyote lead, approaching from your one seven three.

Coyote one, Coyote lead standing by for link. Couplers ready. Suggest decel.

I almost laughed at the dryness of her tone, even over the link. I immediately hit full decel for three minutes. I was still on decel as I checked closure. Still too fast.

Request thirty percent acceleration. Decel beyond my parameters.

Stet. Accelerating this time. Forty percent.

Siendra was right. Absolute velocity didn't matter where we were, just so long as we were on course and linked. Relative closure rates were everything . . . if we had enough power reserves.

Even with full decel, I was still closing too fast. I cut power to the shields and fed it into the drives. The scout shuddered, and the converter temperature began to rise toward redline. The *Aquitaine* continued to accelerate, and the closure rate dropped into the amber. High amber, but amber.

The converter temp flirted with redline but remained just below.

Sweat oozed down the back of my neck, leaving my shoulders cold in the armor.

Coyote lead, estimate CPA in one plus twenty. I finished fine-tuning the scout's shields so that they matched the hull profile.

Coyote one, couplers ready.

Shields flat, retainers charged. Standing by.

The docking was hard, so hard that I rattled around in my armor and my forehead hit the armaglass. Somehow Siendra used the gasjets to lift the *Aquitaine*'s aft section, then contracted her shields to the corvette's hull.

Linked and secure, Coyote one.

Well done! Very well done, Coyote lead. After a moment, I added, *Thank you.*

You did your part just as well, Coyote one. Thank you.

What else could I say at the moment?

Altering course this time, Coyote one.

Stet. Interrogative time to transition.

Estimate one six standard minutes.

Stet.

I went back over the scout's diagnostics. The shield generators were barely in the green, occasionally flickering into the amber. Power reserves were down, barely enough for the last phase of the mission, but the drain for habitability until my next separation from the *Aquitaine* would be minimal, comparatively. All I had to do was watch and wait.

I did that, noting as Voltaire—and Devanta beyond—grew larger and larger in the detector screens.

Coyote one, two plus to transition.

Stet. Coyote one green. Standing by.

The diffuse energy focus was barely discernible on the scout's detectors.

We twisted **back** through time and forward in distance, so that we were barely above the level of a geostationary orbit around Devanta.

Backtime estimated at twenty-one minutes.

That wasn't that long in the grand scheme of things, but it should have been enough to leave Maraniss and Eloi without enough time to react.

Coyote one, commencing reentry this time.

The *Acquitaine* didn't have low-level atmospheric landing capabilities. The only spacecraft that did were shuttles like the hilifter and scouts. Siendra's job was to get me down into the high stratosphere on the proper course line because scouts didn't carry sensitive enough nav gear for long-range planetary orientation. If I wanted to surprise Eloi and Maraniss, I needed to be on target at high speed.

Stet. Interrogative power.

Power parameters will be tight, Coyote one.

If Siendra said they'd be tight, they'd be tight.

How tight?

Tight.

The scout couldn't calculate those vectors and power requirements, but my guts told me she wouldn't make it under those conditions, and she'd be too high for a safe capsule drop and too low for orbital recovery. The proverbial dead pilot's curve.

Interrogative power with a release at minus two.

Negative early release.

If you don't release Coyote one at minus two to release, Coyote one will sever links and accelerate at that time.

There was the slightest hesitation.

Will release at minus one point five.

Stet. Coyote one will go full power at one point six minus. I wouldn't, because that was just outside my limits, but I *had* to tell her that I wouldn't let her stretch it out.

Stet. Even over the links she didn't sound happy. I didn't care. I wanted her to have a chance to get out of it all alive.

Three plus twenty to release at minus one point five.

Understand three plus twenty—now ten—to release at minus one point five. Standing by.

Even with the scout's shields at max, the outside temps were rising. That always happened with high-speed reentry. Nestled beneath the corvette, with fluxes and high-temp oscillations swirling around the scout, I was effectively blind. I would be until I was well clear of the corvette and lower in the stratosphere.

Centered on reentry course line this time. Two to release. Standing by for release.

The corvette bucked, then steadied. I checked all the readouts. Still blind.

Releasing now! Good luck!

There was no point in replying, not with the instant inference upon separation.

The scout tried to buck upward as we separated, but I held the nose down, making sure that I wasn't overridden by the emergencies. I didn't want the *Aquitaine* suffering any last-moment damage.

For the next minute plus, all I could do was hold the scout in the right heading and attitude. Then the instruments began to register. I was only five degrees off heading, but coming in high and hot. I made both corrections quickly. At my velocity, waiting could be fatal.

Once more, after I was on target, the fallback position was even greater destruction. If I failed on the final approach, there would be little enough left of Time's End. If I made the approach and failed to nullify the console, both the PDF and the Garda were standing by to attack in force if necessary. I didn't want to give them that option. Call it a matter of pride. Also a matter of survival. With their weapons, neither the scout nor I would survive.

Once the outside temps dropped, I raised the nose to kill off more speed and increase my rate of descent to get closer to the planned descent angle.

After a few moments more, the screens registered the western coastline near Nordhavre, if well below me. Beyond to the east lay the Malmonts and the Nordmonts.

By now my screaming descent had registered on every planetary tracking system, but no one would have the time to react, not since my final approach had been planned away from any cities or PDF defense facilities, and any hastily fired missile would likely harm far too many innocents.

I was at thirty thousand meters at the coastline, and fifteen thousand as I passed north of Vannes. From there I had to steepen the descent and angle slightly north, but I had Time's End locked in. The Classic Research facility's defense screens sparkled in the display, but against a scout at my speed, there wouldn't be much they could do, not with the mission profile and not until I was almost on top of them.

By then, if they did hit the scout, the debris would shred the facility as thoroughly as an ultra-ex cluster.

At fifteen klicks out, I began to spread the shields, piling up a shock wave before me. Then, at less than five klicks, beyond the effective accurate range of the hidden weapons and RPFs, I flared, hard, letting the atmospheric shock wave blast toward the Classic facility.

Then I armed the remaining torp and fired.

The reduced-yield warhead blew open a corridor strewn with debris, one that pointed toward the operations control center.

My power reserves were almost gone when I dropped the scout the last two meters onto the plaza on the west side of the crumbled walls of the Classic Research facility. I scrambled out of the restraints, and, wearing space armor, headed for the lock. If I moved quickly, I might actually reach the center before anyone realized I was headed there.

Then matters would get interesting.

45

In Elysium will all die living still an eternal lie.

By Sabaten afternoon, we had the first indications that the Frankan installation was in place. By then, Legaar's pacing had become incessant, and his demands to know what was happening, the barking of a caged mastiff.

"When will they be ready for us to act?"

"How long?"

"How long now?"

"Not long." I'd kept saying that often and with less and less patience, if through the rotating shells of purpose and anticipation. Before long, all would be well, and I would be with Magdalena in Elysium, while Legaar Eloi would have to deal with his own fate, ending with a headstone as white as the skeleton of the Garden of Eden.

"Projection field sweep," I ordered.

Only with a field sweep could we provide the energy to get an accurate screen view of the Frankan pseudoasteroid holding the equipment soon to generate the Hawking field. Once the field reached full power, I could ensure that the Elysian universe would continue to inflate and supersede the poor remnant of the anthropic mess that had spawned it.

"We're beginning to get the power lead, ser," called the first tech.

"How soon before we can turn the beam on Thurene and leave?" asked Legaar. "Don't we need to leave?" His eyes twitched. "Don't look at me like that!"

"Not that long, after all we've waited." I turned and kept

my eyes on the screens and indicators. The one drawback of the technology was its need for hard conduits, physical energy manipulation, and the avoidance of broadcast power and signal interference. "Two stans after we have full steady power."

"Two stans? That's too long. We need to leave."

That was unlike Legaar, but I supposed anyone could bend under strain, especially a bullyboy like the concupiscence king. "I can't change that. That's a tech requirement." I managed a long, slow breath, trying not to choke on the stench of metal and oil and the excessive scent in which Legaar had apparently been bathing himself since his return from Thurene.

"It's too long."

"Hawking field flow at ten percent," reported the lead tech, the one in the center seat. Almost a stan passed before he added, "eleven percent."

"Come on," growled Legaar. "We need to go."

Was he drooling from the corners of his mouth? Legaar Eloi? I hadn't seen that before. His fingers dropped to the weapon at his belt, a sprayer-gun, the kind that destroyed everything within fifty yards with a fan pattern of expanding fléchettes. He caressed the weapon before glaring at me once more.

"Turn the projection field on Thurene as soon as you can."

"I will. We don't have enough power yet, and the two fields aren't linked."

Legaar was clearly becoming more unstable, and I just wanted to be rid of him, but I had to get to the projector controls to do that, and I needed an excuse to do so, because the techs were his. So were the security systems. In this, as in everything, timing was paramount. Even sleep navigates the tides of time.

"Power's dropping off, sers! It's gone."

Something was wrong, terribly wrong, not that I wanted to blurt it out, but the power indicators from the Hawking field, the field that had been building so predictably and steadily, had vanished. They had not dropped or declined or surged. It was as if the field had not been there at all.

Something attacked the Frankans. Yet there had been no sign of it. It was gone. The entire installation was gone, including the concealed ship, the pseudoasteroid, all as if they had never been. The sweep field revealed nothing, nothing at all.

"Let me have the controls." I stepped forward. The lead tech moved, more than happy to let me take over when matters were going wrong.

"Fix it now!" ordered Legaar. "Whatever it is."

"I'm looking into it." What I was really looking into was getting rid of him.

"Ser! There's an inbound. Aimed directly at us, ser, from an orbital drop."

Special Operations or the frigging Assembly space service! Legaar would have to wait. "Full screens!"

"They won't stop something at that speed, ser!"

"They'll slow it." I began to shift the field toward the incoming.

"What is it? You failed me!" Legaar lurched forward, grabbing the tech who had reported the incoming. Legaar was shuddering, almost in convulsions.

Even before I could finish trying to refocus the projection field, I had the feeling that it was too late. The entire facility shuddered. Sections of the facade crumpled under the shock wave. Dust billowed from everywhere. With a rumble, the west end of the building peeled away, and sunlight mixed with more dust. The lights flickered and dimmed, then went out for a moment. I was glad the facility was hard conduit inside and out.

Legaar was gibbering. "Take out Thurene! Take it out!" He held the sprayergun, pointed directly at me.

Things added up. It wasn't Legaar but a clone, and there was no help for it now.

"Yes, ser. Here we go." The Legaar clone watched as I eased an edge of the field to where he stood. Then I twisted the field and flung the clone *somewhere.* Into the past, deep space, the future, it didn't matter, so long as it was gone.

The techs had vanished. Much good it would do them.

I rechecked the power. The Hawking field was gone, but I had full power remaining from both Time's End fusactors, and that would have to do.

I would not have my loves lie wrecked, steered by the falling stars. Not now, not ever. Thurene and the real Legaar could scrabble on in their anthropic muddled mess of a universe.

Sitting at the field controls, I twisted the main rheostats to divert full power from both fusactors, wrenching it through the helices to create a here-now bridge to Elysium. To my right, the gateway shone as it shimmered into shape, a golden silver arch back to Magdalena.

Thud. A figure in gold marched from out of the swirling dust, that line of demarcation where the corridor had been ended by the explosion that had ripped away the west end of the building. The shining figure looked like the ancient concept of a robot, for all that it was but an operative in space armor. Still, the operative's steps were far swifter than any automaton and I could not swing the field to remove him and hold the gateway. All I could do was set the timer to cut power to everything in twenty seconds. Once the gateway collapsed, they would never locate me, for the coordinates had always been in my head. That I had ensured.

I set the time, then rose and dashed through the gate, just ahead of the operative in space armor.

Magdalena would be waiting . . .

46

Following another to his or her heaven is a journey to hell.

Even with the powerboosts of the space armor, it took me more than a few minutes to get out of the scout and up the ramps to the operations center from the rubble-strewn west end of the facility. Once there, I recognized the operations screens and boards immediately—even from the end of the corridor into which my last torp had provided an entry. Climbing over chunks of stone and brick and composite had me sweating heavily inside the armor. I wasn't about to take off the nanite-coated protection it provided.

A single figure remained at the console. It was Maraniss. I saw no sign of Legaar Eloi or of anyone else. Maraniss's hands moved deftly across the dials, levers, and rheostats.

Almost directly between us appeared a shimmering arch, nearly three meters high and two in width. Golden white light poured from it. Maraniss turned in my direction, but I kept moving toward him. For an instant, he stared at me. Abruptly, his hands went back to the console, where he twisted a dial. Then he jumped from the seat and took three quick steps. He vanished through the archway.

I ran toward it, then stopped. Ahead of me, veiled in a misty golden white light, stretched a city of white towers. Not a single concentric circle of shadows, but, instead, a whiteness as soft and as bright as new snow under a golden rising sun. I thought I saw a deep green sea to the right of one of the towers, but before I could be certain, the arch vanished, and I was looking at a greenish wall, splotched with dust and dirt.

Had that city been Elysium? Had he used the projection field to reach it? How? Where was it?

I shook my head. Those questions would have to wait. I turned back to the boards. At the very least I had to make sure that the projection fields were inoperative. Quickly, I dropped into the center seat, looking at the board. From what I could tell, the dial that Maraniss had turned had been a timer of some sort. I twisted it back on. Nothing happened. I reset it to zero, then noted the toggle beneath it. I flipped the toggle. The boards came alive.

Power was still available, then.

I began the diagnostics that Carle and Shannon had effectively programmed into me. After close to ten minutes, I had managed to manipulate the main projection field controls enough to create a small field just outside the damaged research facility. Moving it was clumsy, given the armor, and the delay between what I was doing and what appeared on the screens above the console boards. For all that, I wasn't about to remove the armor. It was the only protection I had. While I didn't sense anyone near, that could change any moment.

Supposedly, I was to use the field to disable the power links, but that didn't seem like a good idea with the roughness of my control. I could just as easily end up doing something that would blow up the fusactors or divert the power where it shouldn't be.

The best idea I had was to use the field to destroy the boards themselves. That would be delicate as well, especially since I was still in armor and sitting at the boards. I spent a few more minutes practicing, then took a deep breath.

I stopped. The external sensors were relaying a sound I knew all too well, the unique vibrations of a Garda flitter. There weren't supposed to be any that close.

The first rocket exploded near the west end of the building. The second was on the east end. My guts told me it had to be Javerr, either in person or by remote. I didn't have time to verify that, and no comm link. My chances of getting out against a concerted rocket attack were slim and none.

I had no idea how long the attack might continue or when other flitters might arrive and what they might do. My only practical option was to get rid of the flitter. I just hoped it was on remote rather than personally piloted, but, in a way, I didn't care. Frigging Garda idiots—or they had orders to get rid of me.

I concentrated on the projection field, just sweeping it through the sky where I thought the flitter would be. The vibrations stopped.

Reddish light flared everywhere, Then beams and masonry began to rain down around me, and the entire board before me went dead. The lights went out as well.

Before I could move from the console, something large and dark and heavy slammed into my armor.

47

When I finally could see and think again, I was in a med-crib. Someone stood and looked at me. The blurry vision wore an earth-toned jacket. She stood out in the dimness.

"Siendra?"

"Yes. I'm here."

"Good." I concentrated on looking up at her. After a moment, my vision cleared. Siendra wore a cream blouse and a warm brown jacket. Her scarf was multicolored, with a hint of brilliant greens and blues. She had circles under her eyes.

"How long?"

"You've been in the medcrib for almost a week. It's evening on Jueven."

I didn't want to deal with that. I was alive, and so was she. "You made it back." I fumbled and found the controls that elevated me into a half-sitting position. At that point, I realized that only monitors were connected to me. That was a good sign. I kept looking at her, taking in the line of her chin, the hazel eyes, the honest brown hair.

"I'm not a shadow."

"I wanted to make sure." How could I explain? "You were so set on taking me down too far. I couldn't let you do that."

"You were incredibly arrogant, Captain. You threatened to rip holes in the corvette."

"No captains, no majors." I couldn't help smiling. Just seeing her face exhilarated me beyond anything I'd felt in years. "You're stubborn. You wouldn't have listened otherwise.

Success would have been nothing without you." My throat
was so dry. I looked for water, or something.

Siendra handed me a beaker.

"Thank you." The water tasted so good, but I didn't take
my eyes off her.

"You would have risked Thurene?" Her voice held a mixture of something. Anger and amusement?

"I never risked Thurene." I hadn't. On the vector I'd
taken, if I hadn't made it, the scout would have obliterated
the Classic Research facility and a goodly chunk of real estate around it, but that wouldn't have risked Thurene. The
risks had come after I'd set down. "You know that."

"You risked Thurene and yourself."

Had I? Really? Probably. What could I say to that?
"Better me than you." I tried to keep the tone light.

"Oh?"

"Not a thousand ships, but a few topless towers did come
down."

"You'd risk yourself but not allow me that choice?"

"I was selfish." I was. I would have found it hard to live if
I'd survived and she hadn't. Now . . . I could admit that was
why I'd had to rescue Brooke. Except my feelings for Siendra were far stronger.

"You'd better never call me Helena . . . or even Mar-
guerite."

"Never."

"The scout was absolutely drained of power. You cut
matters close."

"Not as close as you would have." I couldn't help smiling
as I looked at her.

Her face remained pleasantly noncommittal.

"Did it work? I mean, to keep the Assembly and the
Frankans out of the system?"

"There were complaints about all the power blackouts,
but both the space service and the Frankans are treading
gently. The space service discovered just how large the
massed Frankan fleets were and decided against attacking.
The Frankans withdrew quietly. No one's saying why, but

I imagine it has to do with the removal of a certain installation without a trace."

Her smile turned sardonic. I even liked that.

"The official explanation is that a large section of a private estate was destroyed by an asteroid fragment in an untracked orbit that intersected the ecliptic almost vertically. The publicly available satellite tracking scans aren't precise enough for anyone to dispute that, and since Legaar Eloi isn't exactly popular, the destruction of his estate didn't exactly raise public outrage."

"Was he there?"

"No." The enigmatic smile returned. "He and his brother Simeon were on Firenza. Both of them died of a virulent form of food poisoning. Either that or a Frankan assassination for default on a significant commercial loan. Such occurrences are less than unusual on Firenza. No one is terribly upset."

I couldn't help but wonder if Odilia had played a role in that. I doubted I'd ever know and wasn't sure I wanted to.

"What about Maraniss?" she asked. "Do you know what happened to him? The Garda couldn't find any trace of him. Or of Officer Javerr. He was the one who led the follow-up."

"Javerr was the one who put all the rockets into the ops center while I was inside. He got caught in the backlash of the projection field." That was as good a way to put it as any and better than Javerr deserved. "Maraniss fled through the field. Somehow, he'd found or created a city with white towers. I think that was his Elysium. When I reached the ops center, he was alone at the boards. There was an archway . . . and golden white light was coming from it. He ran through the archway. I started to follow. Something told me to stop. I could see the city and a deep green sea. Then the archway vanished."

Siendra nodded. She didn't even look skeptical.

"What was it?" I asked.

"Colonel Carle thinks he created a pocket universe. He would have used the Hawking field to inflate it to a full parallel universe."

"And now?"

"Without that kind of power, it will slowly deflate. No one knows how long that would take. Years, decades . . . centuries." She shrugged.

"They can't locate it?"

"The rockets destroyed enough of the center that the power links were severed. There were no coordinates stored anywhere. Besides, if the Hawking link had been completed, there was a good chance it might have started a deflation of our universe. No one wants to risk that by searching for it."

"Universe savers . . . that's us."

"I'd rather we skipped the delusions of grandeur. Too many people have them as it is."

She was right about that as well.

"The rest of us are better off with them dead or gone."

"Neither you nor I was the one who made those decisions; nor would it have been for the best had we done so."

Neither you nor I. Neither you nor I. The words reverberated in my thoughts, the elegant words that were so hers. Finally, I understood what my subconscious had been trying to tell me for weeks. Either . . . or . . . Neither . . . nor. The same constructions in all three writers. I smiled even more broadly. "Do you prefer Terrie, Carey, Marley, or Siendra?"

"From you . . . Siendra."

"I looked everywhere except where I should have."

"I hid beside Krij."

"She was the one who created Donacyr D'Azouza, wasn't she?"

"I was furious when I found that out." For the first time, she actually looked angry. "I almost broke the partnership up over that. I told her I would if she did anything more. Regardless of *any* consequences. That was why you never heard from him again." Siendra shook her head.

"Krij . . . she wanted the best for both of us. Will you keep on with the partnership . . . now?"

"That depends."

"On what?"

"On you."

"Me? You're suggesting that I become part of . . . everything?"

She nodded again. She was trying to keep from smiling.

"What will the Soror Tertia say?"

"You already know. Who better to add?"

"Blackmail . . . on two levels." But I understood. Krij was Krij, and Siendra was Siendra, and both had to have everything personal in the open. So did I. Anything other than a three-way professional partnership would leave someone out. "Do we all get registered legal identities?"

"We don't need them." Siendra smiled. "Who would dare to steal yours?"

She waited.

"Sign me up . . . should have done it years ago." I stifled a yawn and grinned. "Except I wouldn't have found you." Or Krij wouldn't have. Or Fiorina Carle . . . or whoever.

"I found you. I just didn't do anything about it until you noticed me."

I wasn't about to admit that I'd been so stupid and stubborn that it wouldn't have worked out any other way—or that my big sister had been wise enough to get me to look.

Despite my best intentions, I was yawning again.

"You're still tired."

"All I've done is sleep."

"You had to heal. You had massive bruises all over your body." She reached out and covered my right hand with hers.

Heal? I'd had to heal in more ways than one.

I could feel my eyes closing, but it didn't matter. She'd be there.

Epilogue

History is the rationalization of the
irrational by those who should
know better.

Siendra looked at me across the breakfast table.

"I finally figured out who my actual client is."

Her brow furrowed. "Your client? Which one? We were talking about changes to the master suite."

"Oh . . . the Wayles inheritance. I mostly had it figured out while we were training. When you said that intelligence types had the same rights and restrictions as sisters. You'd already as much as admitted that Astrid Forte was an intelligence type. She had to be the one who stopped Legaar Eloi from infiltrating the TFA for access to body types and clone source tissue, or whatever. According to the inheritance code, she cannot inherit while she is an operative, but the bequest stays open for a minimum of 301 years if she can't be located. There were three heirs. Her half brother died in Assembly service, and if Vola Paulsky—"

"Vola Paulsky?"

"The other half sister named in the bequest. If she can get Stella/Astrid declared as a beneficiary while she's still an operative—"

"Vola gets it all," Siendra pointed out. "So she commissioned you because it's a crime knowingly to name an intelligence operative, and she had to know. What will you do?"

"I'll just send a polite note to Vola saying that I'd been engaged in a search for her half sister before I discovered the true circumstances. When I did, I realized that pursuing the commission would be committing a felony, as would be any effort to bring her half sister's name into any legal proceeding designed to disenfranchise her, even by siblings with the best intent. And I thought she'd like to know that so that she wouldn't inadvertently run afoul of the law."

"She'll disclaim it all."

"I'm sure she will. I'm also certain that she won't pursue it, and that Astrid will have the option of claiming the inheritance if she ever leaves the service of the Soror Tertia."

"You have a luncheon today?"

"Tomorrow. A new client . . . I think. A reference from the great-granddaughter of La Principessa Tozzi."

"I'm glad I won't be there."

"It will be fine." And it would be, as it had been with the Tozzis, in the end, although that commission, as with everything in Thurene, had proved that nothing was ever quite what it seemed.

Incoming from Krij.

I looked to Siendra. She nodded. She could have accepted, because she was now linked to Max and the vidlink had been to either of us.

Accept.

The holo projection appeared to one side of the breakfast table. Krij's cool green eyes went to Siendra, then to me. "I see you're both decent. That's almost a disappointment. You've only been married two weeks."

"Don't push it, sister dear." I managed not to laugh.

Siendra smiled, choking back laughter.

"I'd like to come over this afternoon, around four, to discuss a possible new client."

"Who might that be?" asked Siendra.

"Banque de L'Ouest. Apparently . . ." Krij drew out the word ironically. ". . . the former vice director of entertainment and leisure created a number of irregularities . . ."

As Krij talked, I linked to Max. *Find out what happened to Antonio diVeau, vice director of entertainment and leisure at Banque de L'Ouest.*

Max came back immediately, and I scanned the short

obituary. About the time Siendra and I had begun our simulator training, Tony's ground-car had suffered a nanite shield malfunction that had crushed him to death when he'd been working late. His body hadn't been discovered until long after any resuscitation would have been possible.

". . . The managing director is interested in how we might be able to get them back into compliance with a minimum of publicity and public notice . . ."

This time, I nodded to Siendra.

"Four would be fine," Siendra confirmed.

"Good." With that, Krij was gone.

"I thought you knew about that," Siendra said.

"Tony? No. I must have missed it. Who did it, do you think?"

"It could have been ordered by either Eloi. When the Frankan shell corpentity pulled their funds after the death of both Elois, all their affiliated businesses collapsed. Matrix picked up some of the subsidiaries, but no one has touched the escort service."

"What about the escorts?"

"They're all gone."

Somehow, that was also like Thurene. Maybe all high-tech cultures were like that.

"And what about Maraniss?" asked Siendra, gently.

"He's locked away in Elysium. Forever."

"That doesn't sound like such a terrible fate. Ruler of Elysium—wasn't that what he wanted?"

"Do you remember what the original Elysium was? A resting place for the heroes, a place where all had been done, and nothing more could be done, where every soul was a ghost of his or her previous self."

Siendra waited, knowing I had more to say.

"Elysium is a miniature universe, birthed in a way from the dark energy of ours. So long as Maraniss and Classic Research held the portals open, Elysium was vital, perhaps even growing. With the links severed . . ." I shrugged.

"It's a living death."

"Before that long, the brane will begin to reshape that part of itself—and there won't be any Elysium."

"But can't Maraniss create another portal?"

"With what? He has power sources there, and he knows the theory and the equipment needed, but he doesn't have the technical infrastructure to build what he'd need—not in a lifetime, let alone in five or ten, or even twenty years. Before that, he'll be lost in the white shadows he's created."

"How long, do you think?" Siendra mused.

"Who knows?"

Siendra reached out and squeezed my hand. I wrapped my fingers in hers for a moment. "Let's go down below."

"You were down there last night and early this morning."

I grinned again. "I know. Humor me."

We walked from the breakfast room to the study and down the hidden circular staircase. I let Siendra go first.

Filling the underground hangar was the darkness and the angled stealth curves of the latest Special Operations–style nightflitter. I'd been surprised at the delivery late yesterday. A ferry pilot from Thurenan Arms had flown in and requested clearance to land. He'd handed me all the dataflats and manuals, saluted, and left as quickly as he could by the regular flitter that had trailed him. He had barely looked at me.

The new model was slightly over twenty-five meters in length, with more than a few features that I could never have afforded or obtained on my own—such as rockets and a gun that fired nanite-composite shells.

"It's larger," I mused, hiding a grin.

"It has to be," Siendra replied. "It's configured for two pilots."

"Was that your contribution?"

"You didn't think I was about to let you go off alone, did you? Not in an armed nightflitter."

After admiring the gift—or reparations—of Soror Tertia and the Civitas Sorores, we turned and walked back toward the hidden staircase and up to the study. It now had two table desks and chairs in opposite corners. They matched.

Siendra turned and put her arm around my waist. We looked toward the east, where the sun stood above the courtyard walls, casting shadows across the stones, shadows that changed with the light. As Siendra and I had.